fallen
SPARROW

fallen
SPARROW

A PEYTON COTE NOVEL

D.A. KEELEY

MIDNIGHT INK
WOODBURY, MINNESOTA

FIRST EDITION
First Printing, 2015

Book format by Bob Gaul
Cover design by Kevin R. Brown
Cover art: iStockphoto.com/17105661/©AndrewSoundarajan
           iStockphoto.com/16684700/©EricVega
Editing by Nicole Nugent

Midnight Ink, an imprint of Llewellyn Worldwide Ltd.

This is a work of fiction. Names, characters, places, and incidents are either the product of the author's imagination or are used fictitiously, and any resemblance to actual persons, living or dead, business establishments, events, or locales is entirely coincidental.

Library of Congress Cataloging-in-Publication Data
Keeley, D. A., 1970–
  Fallen sparrow: a Peyton Cote novel/D.A. Keeley.—First edition.
    pages; cm
  ISBN 978-0-7387-4221-2 (softcover)
1. Border patrol agents—Fiction. 2. Criminal investigation—Fiction. 3. Domestic fiction. I. Title.
  PS3603.O773F35 2015
  813'.6—dc23
                        2014050153

Midnight Ink
Llewellyn Worldwide Ltd.
2143 Wooddale Drive
Woodbury, MN 55125-2989
www.midnightinkbooks.com

Printed in the United States of America

For Lisa

ACKNOWLEDGMENTS

As always, I offer a heart-felt thank-you to Kevin Stevens, former deputy chief of the US Border Patrol. Kevin, thank you for taking time from your busy life to field my questions. Your insights and feedback are invaluable and certainly made this book more authentic and much better.

Thanks to the people at Midnight Ink: To Terri Bischoff, for believing in Peyton Cote; to Beth Hanson, for all you do to promote my work; and to my editor Nicole Nugent, who is simply the best in the business. Period.

To Julia Lord and Ginger Curwen, my agents: Thanks for having my back and for your unwavering belief in me. Thanks to Kim Sprankle, for reading my drafts.

And to the home team, Lisa, Delaney, Audrey, and Keeley: This, and everything, is for you.

There's a special providence
in the fall of a sparrow.
—Shakespeare, *Hamlet*
Act V, scene ii

What if man is not really a scoundrel…
then all the rest is prejudice…
—Fyodor Dostoyevsky, *Crime and Punishment*

ONE

THE CHARRED REMAINS OF the cabin were black and smelled like the dying embers from campfires of her youth. A two-by-four tore away from the remnants of the ceiling and fell, hitting the soft ash floor like a branch landing in new-fallen snow, causing the cinders to dance and spark, and spawning a small flame.

US Customs and Border Protection Agent Peyton Cote stood outside the cabin and pocketed her radio. The volunteer firemen could take their time; there was nothing left to do but douse the ashes.

She moved around the perimeter, not risking entry because the walls were gone. Three scorched two-by-fours supported the entire roof. She recognized a metal bed frame, twisted and blackened. Above the cabin, past the lingering smoke clouds, lay a stark juxtaposition to what she viewed: a rolling canary-yellow canola field, the warm summer breeze swaying it back and forth in the distance.

It was nearly 2 p.m. on a fine Tuesday in June in tiny Garrett, Maine, along the Canadian border. At 8:20 a.m., Marie St. Pierre had called the station saying she'd seen two men, in the light of the

1

full moon, cross her husband's potato field around midnight the previous night. The field spanned 450 acres and ran east to Canada.

Behind Peyton, glass and wood lay near the tree line, forty-three paces away, by her count. She'd seen gasoline explosions. The flames here were long gone, but the lingering heat—even standing thirty feet away—told her this fire had burned extraordinarily hot.

What had exploded and when? Marie never mentioned hearing a loud sound.

The broken beaker on the ground stopped her.

Peyton inhaled slowly, her mind turning cartwheels and transporting her back to the West Texas desert, to a shotgun shack she'd once stumbled upon. The long-held memory triggered a realization—and a fit of terror.

She turned and sprinted back to the line of blue spruce trees, stopping finally to exhale like a swimmer bursting through the water's surface.

For a split second, her mind ran only to ten-year-old Tommy. At that moment, she wasn't an agent, only a single mother. She breathed in the fresh air, gathering herself, hand shaking as she unclipped her cell phone from her service belt.

"Jesus Christ," she said aloud, then: "Bring DEA, and tell them they're going to need HAZMAT suits. We might have a crystal meth lab in Aroostook County."

———

"The land is owned by Fred St. Pierre," Peyton said an hour later, glancing warily through the pine forest at the four men in HAZMAT suits.

She'd been joined by State Trooper Leo Miller and Garrett Station Patrol Agent in Charge, or PAIC, Mike Hewitt. The three stood, sipping coffee a safe distance away, watching the fire marshal and three DEA agents sift through the remnants of the charred cabin.

"Fred owns all of this land?" Miller asked. Peyton nodded. "Hell of a tax bill," he said.

"This morning," Peyton said, "around eight, Marie St. Pierre, who was my second-grade teacher about a hundred years ago, called the station to report two men had crossed her husband's potato field last night around midnight."

"That's Canada to the east," Hewitt said.

She knew what he was insinuating: a potential unmanned border crossing.

The day hadn't begun with fires and long-distance hikes. Peyton arrived at the station after using a half-day of vacation time for a field trip with Tommy's fifth-grade class to a classmate's lakefront home for an end-of-the-school-year swimming party.

In northern Maine, Border Patrol served as backup for local and state law-enforcement agencies, so her shift began with a call to a domestic dispute. Next was the trip to Marie St. Pierre's farm. Peyton had grown up in Garrett and had requested the transfer home nearly four years earlier. She knew the people and culture well. In this region, where farming was a way of life, the federal government was viewed with hostility. And she knew why, had seen it firsthand: many local farmers struggled to compete when the Canadian government subsidized its potato farmers. So she'd brought Mr. and Mrs. St. Pierre cookies, a thank-you for the tip, and started what she hoped would be a routine follow-up hike across Marie St. Pierre's property.

"You don't think this was a fertilizer explosion?" Hewitt asked her.

3

"Not on a potato farm," she said. "And no one should go near the place until we know what was in there. The fumes could be toxic."

"Fred isn't going to like having fire trucks cross his fields," Miller said.

"I'm sure they'll try to avoid the crops," Hewitt said.

The annual potato harvest dominated the region. Schools commenced in August and closed for three weeks so teens could help bring in the crop. Peyton, the daughter of a potato farmer, had grown up before machinery ruled the labor force. She'd worked the fields each fall, side by side with laborers, lifting rocks from the potato rows to spare the mechanical picker from ingesting the stones.

Now, for the most part, Aroostook County schools closed to honor tradition, though some farms still used teens. When stopping to check migrant workers' documents, she loved talking to the kids. They might listen to Shakira on their iPhones as they work now, but they still wore jeans and flannel shirts, still felt the same cold hard potatoes in their palms that she'd felt nearly twenty years earlier.

"Last time I was at one of these fires," she said, "I was with six other agents."

Hewitt, wearing a nylon field jacket, poured Peyton and Miller coffee from his thermos.

"In El Paso?" Miller asked.

"Just west of El Paso, along the Rio Grande. There were seven of us there, but as luck would have it—"

"The place still burned to the ground?" Miller interrupted.

Afternoon sun slanted through the dense pine canopy.

"No. I was the one to find the body—or part of it."

"Lucky you," Hewitt said.

"Part of it?" Miller asked.

"Explosion," Peyton explained. "I found a hand that looked like a slab of blackened tuna. At least this time I only found shards of glass. I spotted the first ones near the tree line."

Miller had been scribbling on his pad and looked up. "So we're talking an initial explosion? Not a fire that *led* to an explosion?"

"That's my guess," Peyton said. "Happens all the time at these places. That's why the cooks are in such high demand. They find a body in there, chances are it won't be a local."

"You sure this is Fred St. Pierre's cabin?" Hewitt said.

"He owns all this land," she said. "About five hundred acres back here. When I was a little girl, I used to play in these woods with his daughter, Sherry. In high school, after my father lost our farm, I worked the harvest for Fred, picking rocks one year."

"You stay in touch with the daughter?" Miller asked.

"I hear she's downstate," Peyton said, "a professor at the University of Southern Maine."

A quarter mile away, in the potato field, a deer moved quietly over the dirt. It was something Peyton loved about her job, about this region. Maine's northernmost county, Aroostook, was a land mass the size of Rhode Island and Connecticut combined, but home to fewer than seventy-two thousand residents. She loved conducting a border sweep on foot and seeing deer, moose, and bald eagles. Even stumbling across a black bear, which always led her to draw her service weapon, was a treat she knew few people outside this remote region experienced.

But this rustic environment also meant 137 miles of international border for agents to prevent contraband from entering the US. It was easy to see why 9/11 terrorists had crossed the border here—a relentless cause of shame for agents assigned to this post.

Up here, the memorial catch phrase *Never Forget* was replaced with *Never Again*.

"After we hear what Mitch says"—Hewitt pointed toward the fire marshal—"I'd like you to go talk with Mr. St. Pierre."

She nodded and drank more coffee.

Miller said, "I've got to call in my location." He walked away, cell phone held out, searching for reception.

They watched Miller talk on the phone for several seconds.

When he returned, he said, "My boss wants confirmation of what we think it is."

"We haven't verified anything yet," Hewitt said, "so I'd appreciate you not spreading this all over."

"I've seen these before," Peyton said.

"So you're sure?" Miller asked.

"It's not verified, Leo," Hewitt said.

Peyton turned to him. "There are a few ways to find out."

Hewitt nodded. "Yes, there are."

Then they heard the shouts and turned to see one of the young DEA agents vomit in his mask.

TWO

"MOM," TOMMY SAID, "I can't do it. I just can't."

Tuesday evening, Peyton looked across the kitchen table at her ten-year-old son, his blue eyes turning away.

"What am I going to say to you, Tommy?"

Peyton's sister, Elise, was at the stove, adding green peppers to her spaghetti sauce. Tuesday nights had become what the sisters referred to as "sacred sister nights." Younger sister Elise and her four-year-old Max and adopted daughter Autumn, three, ate with Peyton and Tommy every week, the sisters alternating houses. Elise had lost her husband, figuratively at first, then literally, three years earlier. He left her for a former student, with whom he'd fathered Autumn. When he passed, Elise adopted the baby. Now she was raising her as her own, while taking classes year-round in hopes of becoming a high school teacher.

"I know," Tommy said, "I know. If I put my brain to it—"

"Your mind to it, yes. So why do you say you can't do it?"

"Because it's the truth." He was crying now and looked at his aunt, embarrassed. "Mom, you don't understand."

Elise poured a glass of red wine and set it before Peyton. "Things don't always come easily to people," Elise said to her sister.

"I know that," Peyton said.

"Do you?" Elise asked and went back to the stove.

Peyton watched her, but Elise said nothing else. Their mother, Lois—who Peyton thought incapable of going a single day without mentioning her daughter's divorce ("It's against the Church"), her career ("Why aren't you a stay-at-home mom?"), and her gun ("What kind of lady did I raise?")—had gone home after watching Tommy all afternoon.

Autumn, playing with Polly Pocket dolls on the floor, reminded Peyton that not everyone started out life with advantages. She was the product of Elise's late husband's affair, and Peyton had found her as an infant, abandoned, on a cold fall night near the border.

Peyton exhaled, turning from Autumn to Tommy. "Tell me what I don't understand, Tommy. Tell me again."

Peyton looked past him out the window over the sink. The Aroostook County skyline was vastly different than the one she'd viewed in El Paso for seven years, and this was never more evident than at sunset. In the distance, a canola field, like a yellow river, rose to meet the setting summer sun. She'd never forgotten the Aroostook vistas—not when she'd left for the University of Maine and lived in Orono and not when she'd served her mandatory seven years on the Southern border.

Elise tossed a salad. "You'd think this was my house," she said, "the way I'm working tonight. How about you take a break and help your tired aunt, Tommy?"

Tommy looked at her as if considering the lesser of two evils: math homework or dinner help? He stood and went to help his aunt.

Peyton picked up Autumn and held her. She looked around the kitchen. She loved the new granite countertop. The contractor had finished it only the week before. An agent's salary went further here than it might in other sectors throughout the country. After living with her mother for close to a year, she'd purchased a three-bedroom, two-bath cape two years earlier. But the house had been built in the seventies, and she felt as if she lived in a continuous cycle of saving to update another room every few months.

"Every time I do a math problem," Tommy said—Elise was showing him how to slice a cucumber—"it feels like I'm climbing a wall, and someone keeps knocking me off, and I have to start again."

"Math was never my strong suit either," Elise said.

"Where, sweetie?" Peyton said. "Show me where it happens. I taught you how to carry the one yesterday."

"And my teacher showed me how to carry the one again today," Tommy said. "It's always someplace different. Every time. I told you that yesterday, Mom."

Max pushed a green-and-white John Deere tractor across the floor.

Tommy had, indeed, told her that. And he'd said it the day before, too. His story never changed. So what was she doing? Interrogating her son? Hoping he'd say something different, as if long division would suddenly click? Fifth grade had proved more difficult than she'd anticipated for this little boy in a New England Patriots jersey. And his failing math quizzes had piled up. Tommy had now been referred to a learning disabilities specialist.

Her cell phone vibrated. She saw the office number but didn't answer. Right now, the office could wait.

"What's your math teacher's name again?" she said.

"Why?" He looked at her, and she could see his wheels turning.

"Relax, sweetie."

"Don't call her, Mom. She'll think I'm stupid. It's bad enough meeting with Dr. Thompson."

"Who's Dr. Thompson?" Elise asked.

"An educational consultant the district hired," Peyton said; then to Tommy: "No one will think you're stupid. How many times have you met with Dr. Thompson?" Thompson was evaluating Tommy.

"Three. Don't call my teacher. Please."

"Why?"

"It's bad enough at school. Please don't."

She looked at him, saw the fear in his eyes. What was "bad enough" at school?

Elise, standing behind Tommy, shook her head, as if to say, *Let it go, Sis.*

"Okay," Peyton said.

After dinner, and after Elise and Max had left, Tommy read her a chapter from a Percy Jackson book. She didn't call Tommy's teacher afterwards. She, of course, emailed her instead.

———

"Why didn't you pick up when I called the first time?" Patrol Agent in Charge Mike Hewitt said.

"I was with my family," she said. "When my son was in bed, I checked for messages. There weren't any. Figured it was a question about my shift and someone else answered it."

She was in gray sweatpants and an oversized T-shirt and was curled up on the living room sofa with a Lisa Scottoline novel, sipping a glass of wine.

10

"I called your work phone," he said, "not your personal phone."

She knew what he meant. She dog-eared the page and closed the book, took a sip of wine, and set the glass on the coffee table.

"And if you'd have left a voicemail or called a second time I'd have known something was up and would've picked up, Mike. But you didn't, and I was with Tommy. I like to compartmentalize my life as well as I can, which usually isn't that well, but I'm trying."

"You're saying that when you're home, you're home?"

"I'm saying that I try to be a mom when I'm home."

"Look, I was calling because your theory just got more interesting."

"What does that mean?"

"The guy they pulled from the burned-out cabin wasn't killed by the fire," he said. "He had a bullet hole in his forehead."

"Have they done an autopsy? The hole wasn't caused by flying debris during the explosion?"

"No. They found a twenty-two slug in the guy's skull, Peyton. Can you meet me tomorrow morning at eight?"

"I was going to email you tonight. Tommy's teacher wants to meet me at eight."

"I have a meeting with Wally Rowe at eight thirty. Can you come by after that?"

Rowe had begun life as an FBI agent. Now he was Secret Service, stationed in Boston, and responsible for coordinating trips to the region by any top government officials or diplomats. The last time Rowe made the eight-hour drive from Boston, the president had taken a fishing trip to an Aroostook County sporting camp. Rowe had visited Garrett Station to be briefed on border activity, and since Hewitt was the top-ranking federal official in the region, he'd had been included in several security details, and he'd brought some agents with him. Peyton remembered sitting in her truck at the end of a dirt road while the president (and what seemed like a small village of Secret Service agents) scoured a brook for rainbow trout. (If memory served correctly, the only one to catch a fish that afternoon had been the president's seven-year-old grandson.)

"I can come by around nine," Peyton said.

"Don't cut your meeting short to do it," Hewitt said. "Tommy having a hard time in school?"

"Yeah."

"Anything I can do? Maybe take him out for ice cream, talk to him."

"That's a kind offer, Mike. Pete took him to the batting cages last week."

"Same guy you brought to the Christmas party?"

"Yeah," she said, "Peter Dye."

"I remember," Hewitt said. "I talked to him for a while at that party. Nice guy. A teacher, right?"

"Yeah," she said. "We're sort of dating."

Sort of dating. What the hell did that even mean? Even she didn't know what—exactly—she and Pete Dye had been doing for the past six months.

"That was nice of him," Hewitt said. "I'm sure he's a good role model for Tommy."

"Tommy's failing math, and the special ed teacher is having him tested. I really need to be at this meeting."

"Yeah," Hewitt said, "you do. We can catch up when you get to the office."

"Thanks for understanding," she said.

THREE

PEYTON WAS AT GARRETT Station Wednesday morning at 7:15, seated at her desk in the "bullpen," as agents called it—an open area in the center of the stationhouse where agents' desks were aligned nose to nose, not only allowing them to share desktop computers (Washington skimped on computers for agents on the Northern border) but to talk face to face about cases. Or about the Red Sox. Or a hundred other topics she'd heard over the years.

According to the open file on her desk, Fire Marshal Mitch Lincoln wasn't finished processing the scene. But, given what she read, the cabin was being used as a lab of some sort.

A crystal meth lab?

Lois arrived at the house before seven and made Tommy breakfast, so Peyton had cut out early and now sipped bitter black coffee. Regardless of the taste, she needed it. She'd lain awake staring at her bedroom ceiling, thinking of Tommy and of the meeting in forty-five minutes. Now she was in her comfort zone, lost in the reprieve of work.

"Peyton, you've got a visitor," Linda Cyr, the silver-haired receptionist who resembled Aunt Bee from *The Andy Griffith Show*, called from her desk near the front door.

Peyton knew who it was. And she knew she wore a smile as she crossed the bullpen.

"You beat everyone to work again today," Pete Dye said to Linda.

"He's flirting with me again," Linda said to Peyton when she reached the desk. "See?" She pointed to a Tim Hortons paper coffee cup.

"You bring all the girls coffee?" Peyton asked him.

"No, just Linda," Pete said.

"Oh," Peyton said, "I guess I'll go back to my desk."

"I might have an extra cup for you," he said and extended a cup to her.

He'd gotten into the habit of dropping off Tim Hortons coffee for her on his way to school when she was working midnight to 9 a.m.

"You're here early," he said. "I swung by your house. Your mother told me you'd already left. She also made another pass at me."

"How embarrassing," she said. "I'll talk to her."

"No, don't. I think she's a pistol."

"She's something alright."

"Busy tonight?"

"No busier than usual. Soccer practice. Then homework."

"A late dinner? Keddy's?"

She looked at him. Those jade eyes. Was the five-o'clock shadow intentional?

"Sure," she said, "but I can't meet you at Keddy's. Come over around seven."

"Your house?"

"Yeah."

14

"Great," he said, and glanced at his watch. "I have a kid coming for extra help this morning. And they don't call it Keddy's anymore, not since it was sold, and that was years ago."

"Anyone who grew up here still does," she said.

Keddy's was now the Reeds Inn and Convention Center. It was a ten-minute drive down Route 1A from Garrett, and it had changed hands and been renovated but still housed her late-father's favorite Italian restaurant. Given that Reeds, Maine, had a population under ten thousand, the place was a monstrosity. It had 120 rooms, a pool and fitness center, and a bar with live music on weekends. Winter— when snowmobilers descended upon the region from all over the East Coast to take advantage of Aroostook County's Interconnected Trail System, spanning 2,300 miles—was the Inn's busy season.

"There's a low-fat blueberry muffin here," he said and set the paper bag on her desk.

"You saying I need to diet?" she asked.

"No, I was … That's what you ordered the last time we went … "

She was grinning. "It's too easy."

"Very funny," he said and smiled. "My student's going to be waiting. Have to run."

She thought he might kiss her, thought he was leaning forward to do so, but then he turned and went out the door.

Linda and Peyton watched him go.

"Does he shake your hand after a date?" Linda said.

"We're taking things slowly," Peyton said.

But she knew the glacial pace of their romance was her decision, and, although he said all the right things, she wondered if her reluctance to allow him into her bedroom was bothering him.

———

15

Finished reading the fire marshal's update, Peyton took her coffee and knocked on Hewitt's office door.

"Got a sec?" she asked, peeking in.

He waved her in.

"I'm not interrupting, am I? I saw the Ford Taurus with government plates."

"Wally Rowe will be here for two weeks," Hewitt said. "It's fishing season."

"Doesn't sound like a stationary-surveillance detail," she said.

"Correct. You won't be ordering pizza. And there will be a lot of prep work, too. We'll work with the Secret Service to give the all-clear to every goddamned brook the president wants to fish."

She sat down across from him, wondering how the "all-clear" would work. Would the Customs and Border Protection agents and the Secret Service review an area the day before the president planned to fish it?

"Got a list of places he's fishing?" she said.

"They're keeping that confidential."

"From you?"

He shrugged. "You know how it is," Hewitt said. "It's the president. Everything is need-to-know. Besides, idiosyncratic crimes are on the rise."

"Which is just a fancy way of saying individual nut-jobs go rogue. People who don't like that their politicians can't agree on anything, or who don't like tax hikes or the government's new health-care plan, or that someone burnt their toast that morning, flip out."

"Pretty much," he said. "Like the nut-job who shot Gabrielle Giffords, the Arizona congresswoman."

"Any word on the cause of the explosion yet?" she asked.

"No. They're still processing the scene."

16

Hewitt leaned back in his seat. His running shoes were next to his desk. She knew he ran to work, showered, and changed into his uniform before 6 a.m. He'd been a Navy SEAL and still looked the part. His desk was immaculate, but he moved a yellow legal pad an eighth of an inch, centering it on his desk blotter.

"The fire marshal agrees that it was some kind of lab," he said, "but there's nothing conclusive that points to crystal meth. It does smell terrible out there still."

"Think the lab blew up accidentally?" she said.

"You know what you need to make crystal meth?"

She nodded. "Pseudoephedrine, red phosphorus, iodine crystals, methanol, acetone, toluene, sodium hydroxide, and muriatic acid. It's dangerous stuff."

"You sound like a science major," he said.

"We dealt with those labs a lot in El Paso." The pepper-spray canister on her belt was digging into her lower back, and she shifted in her seat.

"And these labs do blow up a lot," he said.

"If the crank cook survives, they're usually disfigured, and the burns are horrific. It's why good crank cooks are in high demand."

"Maine DEA is coming, but that cabin was about fifty yards from the border."

"You're saying we'll be in on it?" she said.

He pointed at her.

She smiled. "*I'll* be in on it?"

"Yeah. You found it, and you know the family."

"Think about the crystal meth angle, Mike. Red phosphorus is impossible to get in most places without the purchase being a red flag. But it's also used to make fertilizer. So if you live among potato farmers, you can buy the stuff, and no one would think twice about it. This place is made-to-order for that operation."

Ironically, a reason for her return to the area also made the place appealing to drug traffickers: a declining and sparse population, just ten individuals per square mile. The expression "more moose than people" meant tranquility to her. But it meant a down economy to traffickers. What she saw as a culture unto itself—an unspoken us-against-the-world mentality spawned from winter temps running to fifty below; a population that hunted for reasons other than sport: here, freezers were packed with venison, moose, bear, and partridge because the cost of a hunting license could save thousands at the grocery store—also led to some have-nots looking for a way to make a quick buck. Poverty led to vulnerability, and vulnerability led to corruption.

"Maybe the place is made-to-order for a crystal meth lab," Hewitt said, "but, according to Maine DEA, we don't have a crystal meth problem."

"But maybe they do across the border," she said.

"In Youngsville?"

"Or somewhere in New Brunswick. I'm saying we're two hours from Fredericton, New Brunswick, a little more than that from Bangor, five from Portland, and eight from Boston."

"Hub of the universe," he said and smiled. "You think it's being transported?"

"Maybe." She finished her coffee and tossed the cup into the wastebasket. "The question is: where was it being sold?"

FOUR

NANCY LAWRENCE LOOKED ALL of twenty-four and had a Carrie Underwood poster on one of the classroom walls near a verb-tense illustration.

"I saw her in the Portland Civic Center," she explained. "She was great."

"I bet," Peyton said.

Nancy Lawrence had blond hair and was slim, and the length of her dress seemed more appropriate for a cocktail party than classroom instruction. Then again, what did Peyton know about fashion? She counted wrist ties and a Taser among her accessories and attended her last youth soccer game wearing a .40 pistol.

"Thank you for coming in, Mrs. Cote."

"Please, call me Peyton."

"Oh, sorry. It's a habit my parents drilled into me."

"Call your elders mister or missus?"

"Um, would you like to take a seat?" Nancy Lawrence pointed at the chair across from her.

It was a classroom chair designed for fifth-graders. Perfect. Now Peyton felt huge *and* old.

"Anyway," she said squeezing into the seat, "thanks for taking time to see me. I'm worried about my son."

"He's being evaluated."

"Yes, and I'm awaiting the results. But I wanted to see how he's doing in your class?"

"Students change classes in fifth grade," Nancy said. "Not all districts do it like that. But, here, fifth grade is middle school. I only have Tommy for math."

"And how is he doing?"

"To be truthful," Nancy said, "he needs to work harder. He's failing."

"He finds the material very difficult, but he's working hard—two, three hours each night."

"Really?"

A buzzer sounded. Nancy Lawrence drank some coffee. It smelled like hazelnut. Peyton wished she'd been offered a cup.

"Yes, really. Ms. Lawrence—"

"Call me Nancy."

"Nancy, his scores are not indicative of his effort."

"I'm glad to hear that."

Peyton watched as Nancy Lawrence crossed her legs and bobbed her ankle. She wore an ankle bracelet and had a tiny heart-shaped tattoo near her right ankle.

"Where do we go from here?" Peyton asked.

"What do you mean?"

"Can he get extra help?"

"Are you offering to pay for a tutor?"

"I guess," Peyton said. "There's no free time during the day when he could meet with you?"

"No."

Peyton wouldn't have been surprised if Nancy Lawrence snapped her gum and twirled her hair around an index finger.

Garbed in her uniform greens, Peyton crossed her legs, her military-style boot dangling three inches off the floor, and felt her iPhone vibrate in a cargo pocket of her forest-green work pants.

"Is there a plan to help Tommy?" Peyton asked.

"We don't have an IEP, if that's what you mean. Once the testing is completed, Tommy's teachers will meet to put together a plan, if the testing dictates one is needed."

"IEP?"

"An individual educational plan," Nancy said. "LD kids get them. They're district-mandated, maybe even state-mandated. The district makes us create them." She reached for her coffee cup.

"You say that like you don't think much of them. Do they work?"

"Sometimes they work," Nancy said. "I like them just fine. They're not easy to create or to execute. And, truth be told, I think a lot of the consultants who run these tests overdo it. Not every kid who struggles has a learning disability. Some kids just need more time or need to work harder."

Peyton cleared her throat.

Before she could speak, Nancy Lawrence said, "Tommy's teachers are meeting later today. I think the testing has been completed, but I'm not sure. We all want Tommy to get what he needs."

Peyton stood. She felt flushed.

"Are you okay, Ms. Cote? I'm sorry if I upset you. I'm sure this is disappointing for you."

"It's not my child who I'm disappointed in, Ms. Lawrence. Please be clear on that."

"I feel like you're upset."

"I'm sorry if my child is an inconvenience for you," Peyton said and walked out of the room.

She started down the hallway, rounded the corner, and saw Tommy at his locker. His back was to his mother. But Peyton saw a boy much taller than Tommy standing near him, speaking. The tall boy grinned, but his expression wasn't joyful—he wore a sly, cruel smirk. Peyton had seen the adult version of that smirk—on coyotes who promised Mexicans an escape into the US only to take the life savings from the desperate and leave families in the treacherous conditions of the West Texas desert.

Her palms felt damp, and she stopped walking. The tall boy was pointing at Tommy now, laughing. He pushed Tommy's shoulder. Tommy rocked backward. Another buzzer sounded, and the taller boy turned and walked away.

Tommy leaned forward, his shoulders sagging in relief. He stared into his locker for several moments before gathering his books.

She stepped back so he wouldn't see her.

But when he turned around, books in hand, she saw that he was crying.

———

Peyton needed coffee and time to clear her head. She left Garrett and drove ten minutes south to Tim Hortons in Reeds, parked, and went inside.

It was a pleasant June morning, but she didn't get iced coffee. She took hers black and went to a booth near the window.

It had been bad enough when Tommy came home upset (embarrassed) three times after being pulled from class to be tested. But now it was apparent that Tommy was just a number to his teacher, who, Peyton thought, didn't believe in the concept of learning disabilities. Nancy Lawrence assumed that if Tommy was failing he simply wasn't working hard enough.

But something else about the conversation bothered Peyton, something she'd inferred: Nancy Lawrence viewed some kids as simply "slow." And that enraged Peyton.

Her son was struggling. And what if Tommy was in fact diagnosed with a learning disability? She'd known agents whose children—usually boys, in fact—were deemed to have Attention Deficit Disorder. The stigma was of behavioral issues. She didn't want that for Tommy. Didn't want him pigeonholed at age ten. Yet there was no denying that Tommy needed help. He was struggling academically, and it was spilling over into other areas; his confidence was taking hits, and now it looked like he was being bullied.

She, too, needed help. Needed to talk to someone who knew about the educational system, about learning disabilities, about what she could and should do for her son.

She was glad she would see Pete Dye that night. Dye taught US History at the high school, coached girls' basketball, and tended bar some nights to help make his mortgage payment. He could offer an overview of the district and maybe tell her if having Tommy tested for a learning disability made sense. They'd grown up together, but hadn't started dating until six months ago.

She thought about Tommy's ten-year-old life and compared it—as she often did—to her own at that age. Her parents hadn't had much, but they'd had each other. And her life hadn't been nearly as complicated as Tommy's. No crushing academic failures. No bullies. No fathers who took little interest in her.

From her vantage point, she could see the Aroostook Centre Mall. The mall might have been a far cry from what had been available in Texas, but it did have a JC Penney, a Staples, a Kmart, and several smaller retailers. And not wanting to rely solely on the Internet, the Aroostook Centre Mall was more than sufficient for her shopping needs. Given her career choice and ensuing daily uniform, fashion had long given way to practicality. Besides, the last time she wore heels, when she'd gone to dinner with Pete, she'd slipped and nearly fallen.

FIVE

Mid-morning Wednesday, Peyton climbed the steps, crossed the wraparound porch, and met Fred St. Pierre at the door of his 1928 farmhouse.

"The farm looks great, Mr. St. Pierre," she said.

And it did. It could've been just a week ago when she and his daughter Sherry played in the barn. Had it really been more than twenty years?

"Looks like you just painted the barn."

"I did. Like the new color, eh?" he said, his French accent as thick as ever. He was lithe with a weathered face that had seen too much sun and wind, and he had leatherlike hands. He wore a green John Deere cap with oil smeared on the bill; blue jeans; worn engineer boots, the steel toe showing; and a red flannel shirt over a long johns undershirt.

"The barn used to be red," she said, "didn't it?"

He nodded.

"I like it white. Looks great."

"Peyton, eh, Christ, what the hell happened to my cabin? Marie told me she called you. If that weren't bad enough, eh, I've got fire trucks and the fire marshal driving across my rows. And I couldn't spray this morning."

"I was hoping you might be able to help me learn what happened to your cabin, Mr. St. Pierre. Did you hear an explosion?"

"Call me Fred, Peyton." He looked her up and down. "You've really grown up, eh?"

She cleared her throat, caught off guard by the remark—and by his eyes studying her figure. As a little girl, she'd spent many nights in Sherry's room, in sleeping bags.

"I just want answers. Couldn't afford to pay someone to build the cabin, so Freddy and me poured the slab and framed that one and another on the other side of the property. Then I finished the insides of both myself. Eh, Christ, it took me six months. I'm not so young anymore."

She noticed he walked with a limp now.

"Invite the girl in, Fred," a voice called from behind. This one, too, had a French accent. "Where are your manners?"

"Sorry," Fred said. "I just don't know how I'm going to replace that there cabin. 'Bout killed me to build the first one. Arthritis in my leg, eh."

He held the door, and she entered the house, feeling Fred St. Pierre's eyes on her the whole time. He might have changed, morphing into a dirty old man, but the inside of the farmhouse remained the same, which spoke volumes about Marie.

As Peyton had as a little girl, the first items she noticed were the fireplaces—four in all, and she could see two from the kitchen. But it still felt like there were more, seemingly one in every room. She'd never forget eating crepes at the huge dining room table, a

26

tiny eight-year-old among the hulking men working the potato harvest. Now the kitchen fireplace housed a wood-stove insert. She sat down at the kitchen table. The candle in the centerpiece smelled of cinnamon.

"Jesus Christ," Fred said, "eh, Marie, that candle, well, it smells awful." The insult, although harsh, was delivered in that sing-song cadence Peyton heard only among French-Canadian English speakers—*JEEzus CAARist*, eh, Marie, that *CANdle*, well, it smells *AWful*—which gave the slur a nursery-rhyme quality.

"Just trying to cheer the place up," Marie said to the floor and moved to the counter, where she wiped a spot of water with a paper towel.

While Fred was a farmer in his late fifties and dressed the part, Marie wore her hair in a short blond bob and wore floral capri pants with a white silk blouse, open at the throat, exposing a thin gold chain. Her stylish appearance made her look much younger than her husband. Peyton looked at Marie's flashy capris. Hard to picture this woman belonging to the same bridge club as her mother, Lois, who was a farmer's wife through and through and whose wardrobe ran to ankle-length conservative-colored dresses.

Watching Marie pour coffee into a thick ceramic mug, Peyton thought the woman might well have been a suburban Boston housewife.

"Sugar, sweetie?" Marie went to the fridge and put a small container of half-and-half on the table.

"No thanks," Peyton said. "Black is fine."

Fred St. Pierre shifted in his seat. "So what the Christ happened to my cabin, eh? Marie says she called you about someone on our property. I could've handled that myself."

"I appreciated her calling. She did the right thing."

"Have you caught him?" Fred said.

"It was two men," Marie corrected, "not one. I just saw shadows and flashlights, but there were two."

Fred said, "Marie, pour me coffee."

Marie nodded once, went to the cupboard, took down a cup, and brought her husband coffee after carefully adding cream.

"Have you caught anyone yet?" Fred said.

"Are you saying you think the fire was arson, Mr. St. Pierre?"

"I wired the place myself. Wasn't no electrical fire."

"We're just beginning our investigation."

"Well, I can't have fire trucks and people driving across my rows. We planted last month. There's a lot of work to do. Farming is hard enough, you know?"

"I know," Peyton said. "Believe me."

He nodded, and she knew he was remembering her father and his lost farm.

"We do, though, have an ID on the man who died in the fire."

"Who was it?" he asked.

Peyton took her iPhone from her cargo-pant pocket and slid it across the table.

"This is a passport photo," Peyton said. "He's Canadian. Came to Montreal about ten years ago and was living in—"

"Youngsville," Fred interrupted. "You sure it's him?"

She nodded. "They found his wallet at the scene, and Canadian Immigration confirmed his identity. You know him?"

"Of course." Fred held the photo out to Marie, who looked at it and immediately covered her mouth and turned away.

"That's why," she whispered.

Fred looked at her. "That's why what?"

Marie went back to the counter. "More coffee, anyone?"

"No thanks," Peyton said.

"His name was Simon," Fred said, pronouncing it *See-moan*. "I told him he was the only person I knew from Montreal with a Russian accent."

"Russian?" Peyton said.

Fred nodded. "Get me some sugar, Marie. This coffee, eh, it's too strong."

"Then why don't you make it yourself, old man?" Marie said. "I'll tell you why. Because you don't even know how."

He shot her a look but met Peyton's eyes and then refocused on his boots. "I could figure it out."

Peyton cleared her throat. "His full name was Simon Pink. Listed his occupation as an oil-truck driver. What can you tell me about him?"

"I needed someone to deliver potatoes, eh? He drove several loads to upstate New York for me. I don't like to drive anymore, and my truck, well, she's old. Simon, he told me he went back to school at Northern Maine Community College to get a degree in diesel hydraulics technology, so he said he could fix the engine if she broke down. That put me at ease, so I gave him a job. After last year's harvest, well, there, he said he needed work, so I had him shingle the cabin roof."

"Last fall?"

Fred drank some coffee and made a face.

"Woman, can't you make decent coffee?" he said.

Peyton nearly jumped to Marie's defense, but she needed Fred on her side. "Did Simon Pink roof the cabin last fall?"

"Yeah. Him, me, and Freddy Jr."

"Tell me about his Russian accent."

"I liked the guy," Fred said. "Don't get me wrong. But, well, there, I never really believed him either. I grew up in Quebec. He said he lived there, but he didn't know nothing about the place. I don't think he actually lived there. I let him stay in the cabin last fall, until it got too cold and he got his own place in town."

"So there was no heat in the cabin?" Peyton said.

"No," Fred said.

Something had led to the explosion, and it hadn't been the heating system. Peyton was feeling better about her theory.

"So Simon Pink wasn't working for you in the winter?"

"No. He was done before Thanksgiving. Freddy Jr. and me, we do the work in the winter. We work on the equipment ourselves. I don't pay anyone in the winter."

"He was such a sweet man," Marie said. Her voice seemed to trail off as she said, "So gentle." She moved back to the counter, always on her feet, Peyton noticed. "I can't believe he's dead," Marie said and carried the coffeepot to Peyton. "Did he die trying to put the fire out?"

"I don't think so."

"What happened?" Marie asked.

"Did you hear anything last night, Marie?"

Marie was looking at Peyton. She said, "No. Why?"

Peyton said, "Who used the cabin on a regular basis?"

"No one this summer," Fred said. "I slept out there occasionally last spring"—his eyes ran to Marie—"but not recently."

"Why?" Peyton asked.

"Not your business."

Peyton looked at him. Should she threaten him with a formal interview? Remind him of a potential subpoena? Not here. Not yet.

"Who had access to the cabin?" she asked.

"No one," Fred said.

"You can't see it from here, correct?"

"So what? I'd know if someone was out there."

"What was inside it?"

"Nothing much."

"Fred, the fire marshal believes the cabin was being used as a laboratory of some sort. Do you have any knowledge of that?"

"No," he said. "What does that mean?"

"They found some metal that didn't burn. It looks like the cabin was used to make something."

"Like what?"

"You have any theories?" she said.

"No," he said. "What is this? What's going on?"

"Just routine questions."

"Eh, well, they don't feel routine. Was the fire set? Did the fire marshal say that?"

"He thinks there was an explosion of some kind."

"What does that mean?"

"That's about all the information I have," she said.

"Peyton."

Peyton turned to Marie.

"Did Simon die in the explosion?" Marie asked. "Or was he trying to put the fire out?"

"That's really all I know, ma'am."

"I always know when women are lying to me," Fred said, his eyes running from Peyton to Marie and back to Peyton. "You know more. What do you think happened out there, eh?"

"I wouldn't want to speculate, sir."

"I'm asking you to."

"When was the last time either of you saw Simon Pink?"

Fred thought a moment. "Last week. Might have run into him at the store."

"And when was the last time you saw Simon Pink?" she asked Marie.

"Same."

Peyton smiled at the couple. "I've taken up enough of your time. Would it be alright if I dropped by again sometime?"

"Of course," Marie said and walked Peyton to the door.

"Thanks for your time, Marie." Peyton started down the steps. It was another beautiful mid-June morning, nearing seventy degrees. She remembered what it had been like to wear the uniform, including the Kevlar vest, in the hundred-plus temps of El Paso.

She heard the front door close and was surprised to hear Marie's voice: "Peyton, I hope you won't tell your mother about Fred. He's just gotten old, and, well, he's changed."

Peyton stopped on the steps and turned back. "Does he always treat you like that?"

"He loves me. Please don't tell your mother. I see her often."

"Bridge club," Peyton said.

Marie nodded.

"I won't say a thing," Peyton said and took a business card from her pocket. "You called the office to reach me about the two men on your property. Here's my cell number, if you ever need to talk."

"Thank you."

"Marie, one final question: What oil company did Simon Pink drive for?"

SIX

DURING THE DAY SHIFT, three field agents conducted routine border sweeps—driving to various locations, observing wooded areas, or walking trails and sign-cutting—leaving Peyton and two other agents on duty to follow up on open cases. The corpse of murder victim Simon Pink made the fire on the St. Pierre property high-priority.

Aroostook Oil and Heating was located at the north end of Academy Street in Reeds, a ten-minute drive from the station-house. It was the site of a renovated farm. Peyton didn't need to ask why the venue had leapt from farm to private business. One of two things had occurred: the farmer had worked the land until old age then sold the place off, or the farmer hadn't been able to keep up with the Canadians' government-subsidized potato prices and was driven to selling or, like her father, had lost the farm.

She pulled her white-and-green Ford Expedition to the side of the barn and climbed out, recalling the day when she'd been thirteen and watched the bank's men and her father around the kitchen table, hearing the words "small, maybe a trailer, on one acre." Charlie Cote hadn't taken the trailer the bank men offered. Instead, he'd built his own house—the 1,200-square-foot home in which her mother still resided. Usually Peyton smiled when she thought of her late father. Now, though, she remembered his slouched shoulders at the kitchen table as he signed the bankers' papers, recalled his first day as janitor at Garrett High School and the look on his face when they'd seen each other in the hallway, and finally the day his heart gave out. It taught her that when you take a man's way of life, you take his dignity, and when you take his dignity, you take his life.

She entered Aroostook Oil and Heating glad to push those thoughts aside and think of the bullet hole in Simon Pink's torched skull.

She crossed what had once been a parlor complete with a stone fireplace and leather furniture. A young receptionist sat, head buried in a textbook. In her early twenties, the raven-haired woman wore jeans, a blouse with three buttons undone, and stylish short boots with two-inch heels. She closed *The Principles of Accounting* and centered her keyboard, ready to type, but looked up instead.

"May I help you?" Her words were spoken in a default tone, but there was an oh-shit quality in her voice Peyton had come to anticipate when entering someplace in uniform unannounced.

"I need to speak to whoever might be in charge."

"That would be Gary. Everything okay?"

Peyton smiled, moved to the stone fireplace, and stood near the hearth.

"Gary owns the company."

"If he's in charge of personnel," Peyton said, "then he's the guy I need to see."

"Is everything okay?" the receptionist asked again.

"Of course," Peyton said, reading the girl's name plate: Samantha Buckley. She took her iPhone out and made a note of the jumpy receptionist.

———

"Sammy told me you have some questions about our employees," Gary Buckley said.

It was a leap, albeit a subtle one, from *If he's in charge of personnel, then he's the guy I need to see* to *questions about our employees.*

"Not exactly," she said. "Is Simon Pink still employed here?"

He shook his head. "No way."

The crow's feet around Buckley's eyes said he was older than he looked. Or maybe life had thrown a lot at him, and stress had caused the wrinkles. Peyton had interviewed enough people to have seen both scenarios many times.

Buckley wore a Maine Winter Sports Center golf shirt and looked like a guy who used the winter months to Nordic ski. Peyton hadn't done much Nordic skiing, preferring snowshoeing, but she knew of the Nordic Heritage Center, located between Reeds and Garret, a place where Olympic Nordic skiers and biathlon athletes came to train year-round. She'd been inside the 6,500-square-foot lodge once and took Tommy hiking along the mountain-biking trails in the summer.

"Not a fan of Mr. Pink?" she said.

"Care to see his application and résumé? Sonofabitch lied to me. Said he was an out-of-work chemist."

She said, "I'd like to see his file."

"I'll go get it. Guy should've listed 'creative writing' on the damned résumé."

Buckley got up and left the room. He returned with two paper coffee cups and a manila folder under his arm. He set a coffee in front of Peyton and handed her the folder. She read Simon Pink's résumé. It was suitable for the work Buckley hired him to do.

"You said he told you he was a chemist," she said. "The top qualification he lists here is a commercial driver's license."

"Maybe he was full of shit about being a chemist." He shrugged. "He said he took his driving classes at Northern Maine Community College. We needed a driver, so I hired him."

"And?"

"And it didn't work out," Buckley said.

"Tell me about it."

"He worked for me a year ago. The guy was weird. I could tell that about a week into his employment. He was in this office for something, and he starts talking about the World Junior Biathlon."

"At the Nordic Heritage Center?"

"Yeah. I'm on the board of directors out there. At the time, the Junior Biathlon was six months away. But I told him we were planning, looking for volunteers. Then the guy offended me."

"How?"

"He called the place a liberal outpost where yuppies hang out and talk about liberal politics."

"The only people I've ever seen out there," she said, "are the athletes training for the Olympics."

"A handful of them live there and practice, yeah. The whole conversation was bizarre. Then he got an OUI, so I cut him loose. I hear Fred St. Pierre hired him. Fred sure as hell didn't check references. Pink in trouble again?"

"He's dead," she said.

"Drunk driving?"

She shook her head.

"Well, I never wished the guy any harm. But I admit I didn't want him around here. I never felt like he was really stable."

The coffee was no better than that which they brewed at Garrett Station. On the wall behind Buckley hung a photo of him and a boy kneeling next to a slain deer. Buckley held what looked like a .30-06; the boy held a shotgun. Both barrels pointed skyward, away from the deer and each other—they were hunters who knew what they were doing, not victims of "buck fever." With his free hand, Buckley was lifting the deer's head by the antlers, smiling broadly at his conquest; the boy's expression was different, sullen. She imagined the boy had either vomited or turned away when Buckley had undertaken the gruesome work of field dressing the deer.

Buckely turned to the photo. "Know any hunters?" he asked.

She nodded. "I hunt," she said. "My father introduced me to it. Now I take my son. Field dressing a deer isn't for the faint of heart."

"No. My boy didn't do well on that day," he said, eyes still on the photo.

"My father used to send me out to the road after we shot one, so I wouldn't have to watch."

"Ever shoot one yourself?"

She held up two fingers.

"Two?" He shook his head and whistled quietly. "Don't take this the wrong way, but you don't look like a hunter."

"I'm tougher than I look," she said.

"I bet you are. You single?"

"What made you think Simon Pink was unstable?"

He chuckled and drank some coffee. "All business, huh?"

She waited.

"I just always felt like the guy was full of shit," he said. "I don't know if that makes sense. Just something about him. Never seemed like he was leveling with me. I can't really describe it."

He didn't need to. She'd questioned thousands of people at the international border crossing between El Paso and Juarez, had been lied to hundreds of times, and had relied on gut instinct and a well-earned grasp of human nature and the signs people unwittingly offered—a blink, a sudden urge to wipe a damp palm, an unwillingness to look her in the eye—to know when she was being bullshitted.

"Funny thing was," he continued, "that I could never see a reason to lie."

She said, "What did he lie about?"

"I don't know. It wasn't like that, not like I caught him in a lie. I just never thought he was telling me the whole truth. Just little stuff that didn't add up. Like he said he was from Youngsville, but he didn't have a French accent."

"Did he have any accent?"

"He sounded like Drago from *Rocky IV*."

That went with Fred St. Pierre's "Russian" accent claim.

"Anyway," he said, "the guy smoked like a Canadian—two, three packs a day. That's really all I can tell you. I have another meeting in five minutes."

She stood and said she'd show herself out.

"Come by anytime," he said.

She thanked him—and wondered why he hadn't asked exactly how Simon Pink died.

SEVEN

THE ROAD WAS DOTTED with Norway pines and black spruces. She hated the Expedition's air conditioner, but in the summer, riding with the windows down meant an onslaught of Aroostook County's official bird, the mosquito. She considered it a trade-off: Moving from El Paso meant no more 120-degree desert hikes. ("But it's a dry heat"—bullshit!) Instead, she'd traded the heat for the perils of mosquito season, which lasted two-thirds of the summer. At least this far north (one actually drove *south* to get to Montreal), summer meant daylight for eighteen hours.

Her window was partly open, but she still heard the CB radio crackle and a smattering of voices over the rush of wind. The frequency was used by all law-enforcement agencies in Aroostook County, and she knew many residents among this aging population owned scanners and followed the police and Border Patrol calls throughout the day. In fact, the scanner in the Garrett Barber Shop had provided never-ending fodder for conversation since her late father had sat in those chairs.

All of it made radio transmissions about as private as a Web page—and made her cherish her iPhone. The radio was typically used only for mundane calls or requests for backup. But since the region had only three state police detectives and many municipal forces had fewer than five officers, Border Patrol served as backup on nearly every police assignment. And since Aroostook was the largest county east of the Mississippi, totaling seven thousand square miles, it also meant a lot of driving.

But this call wasn't far away, and Peyton had been there once already this day.

She nearly leapt to grab the radio and offer her services as backup. She wanted to be at the scene.

After all, she knew her interview had caused this domestic dispute.

———

Marie St. Pierre was sitting on a rocking chair on the wraparound porch, crying quietly, when Peyton pulled the Expedition next to the state police cruiser just after noon, got out, and bounded up the stairs.

"Mrs. St. Pierre, what happened?"

"Nothing," Marie said and stopped crying as if on cue—and, Peyton thought, like someone who'd practiced doing so.

Marie sat as if frozen in the rocking chair, staring at the farmland like she was itemizing every inch of the five hundred-plus acres.

A tractor, its tires as tall as a man, sat motionless in the field. Two long arms extended from the tractor's sides like skeletal wings resembling something from a science-fiction movie. Peyton knew the arms sprayed insecticide, and she knew the cabin was likely air-conditioned and had a Bose stereo—whoever used the tractor, in fact, would be more comfortable in it than she was in her Ford Expedition. But no one was in it now; the cab was empty.

Peyton had been at domestic dispute scenes offering obvious victims: black eyes, bruises, missing teeth. This scene offered evidence, too.

"Did Mr. St. Pierre hit you?"

"God no." Marie was looking straight at Peyton now. "Hit me? Good God, Fred would never do that."

"Tell me what happened." Peyton took the chair next to her, looking at the woman's cheek.

Marie began to rock. The chair creaked as it arced forward and rolled back. Peyton remained silent. She could see the gray roots in Marie's hair. Stress? Or a bad dye job? She wouldn't press her. Not yet. The best interviews, she learned long ago, occurred when the witness steered the discussion.

The sun was high overhead, offering golden shafts that traversed the canopy of the yard's lone maple and splashed onto the hood of the Expedition. Peyton felt the impulse to put on her sunglasses, but didn't. Sometimes an interview relied on non-verbal language. And Marie had a palm-size bruise on her face. A slap? Or a punch? No sunglasses. Eye contact could make the difference in getting her to talk about it.

"Who called the police, Marie?"

"I did."

"What did you say when you called?"

"I don't want to talk about it."

"There's an officer inside with your husband," Peyton said, "right?"

"Yes."

"Then he can't come out here, Marie."

Marie's right hand absently bunched the fabric of her dress as if drying her damp palm.

Peyton's hands were folded calmly in her lap. "What was the argument about?"

Marie turned to face her, narrowed her eyes, and opened her mouth. But the would-be protest passed, and she went on rocking, staring at the field.

"It's going to come out, Marie, one way or the other."

Marie shook her head, but she said, "Fred asked me about Simon Pink. None of this is your business, Peyton." She looked down at her left hand and twirled her wedding band. "I knew you when you were a little girl. Now, here you are. I can't believe you're here."

"It's been a long time," Peyton said.

"You haven't been here since Fred made Sherry call you and say she couldn't spend time with you."

"Why did Fred hit you, Marie? Tell me what happened."

Marie looked at the tractor. "The crop wasn't great the last couple of years. Not for anyone. Can't control the weather, you know? Makes it so hard on these farmers."

Peyton waited. She'd interviewed enough people to see the pattern. The tension between them had passed. Now Marie was chatting. Eventually, she'd get to it.

"Fred asked me why I was upset when you told us what happened to Simon. We started to argue."

"Where was your son?"

"I don't know where he is today. I was afraid, so I called the police. I overreacted. Fred didn't hit me. I told the police woman as much when she arrived, but she won't leave."

There was only one female police officer in Aroostook County. Peyton knew Maine State Police Detective Karen Smythe well.

Both females worked in militaristic, male-dominated settings; they had much to talk about over coffee or dinner once a month.

"There's a bruise on your cheek, Marie. Detective Smythe won't leave without finding out how that happened. And neither will I."

"Fred didn't do that. I fell."

"This morning, when I showed you the photo of Simon Pink," Peyton went on, "you said 'that's why.' What did you mean?"

"I don't know what you're talking about."

"You were upset when I told you Simon Pink was dead, Marie. Did you know him well?"

"Not really. But the man was killed. That just upset me."

"I see. It didn't seem to affect Fred the same way."

"He's a man."

"Simple as that?" Peyton said.

"I guess so. Peyton, I'm really not comfortable talking about this with you."

"Why did Fred sleep in the cabin, Marie?"

"He didn't."

"When I was here this morning, he said sometimes he did."

"Really, Peyton, I don't have anything else to say. I mean, I'm on the school board and the Potato Blossom Civic Council." She looked away. "I just fell. That's all."

"Marie, you called the police."

Peyton knew damned well Fred had smacked Marie. But Marie, like so many battered women, now denied it.

"Like I said," Marie continued, "that was a mistake, an over-reaction."

"What upset Fred?"

Marie was staring at the steps, shuffling her feet. The reaction made Peyton think of Tommy, the way he looked when she asked about his school struggles. Human nature, people's most base and instinctive reactions, never deviated much.

"I'm pretty sure I know," Peyton said, "and I can get the tape of your 911 call to hear exactly what you said."

That got her attention. What had she told the 911 dispatcher that she wanted kept private?

"I don't have anything more to say, Peyton."

———

Fred St. Pierre was seated silently near the coffee table in the den, across from Karen Smythe, a petite, raven-haired, former University of Maine cheerleader who had very little tolerance for bullshit.

Peyton could see them as she crossed the kitchen. A pot of stew was on the stove, its lid bouncing gently, the kitchen smelling of seasoned meat.

"Fred, this is going to boil over. Should I turn it down?"

Fred was staring at the coffee table. He turned to look at her over his shoulder. His face was pale now and his eyes red. He was no longer the arrogant man who'd evaluated every inch of her only a few hours earlier. If he'd been five-ten when she'd been there that morning, he was five-six now.

He looked at the stove. "I don't know, eh. Marie started that before ... She does the cooking. I don't know."

Peyton turned down the heat. "Were you going to say 'before we started fighting'?"

"No."

"What, then?"

He shook his head. "Before I hit her. I already admitted I did it."

Peyton said, "Why did you hit her?"

"Because I wanted her to leave. Now it's too late."

The officers looked at him, but he offered no clarification, only: "Arrest me, if you want. But I ain't saying another thing about it, eh. It's between me and Marie. Only us two. You get that? Ain't no one else involved. Get that?"

"Karen," Peyton said, "can I see you out here?"

Karen nodded and came to the kitchen.

"Mr. St. Pierre," Peyton said, "we'll be right here, if you need us."

He shrugged.

Peyton pulled the door to the den closed.

———

"Something isn't right," Peyton whispered.

She and Karen Smythe stood near the kitchen sink, ten feet from the den door.

"He's said no one else was involved several times," Karen said. "Do you know the couple?"

"Yes," Peyton said.

"Well, I plan to arrest him."

Through the window over the sink, they could see Marie rocking slowly on the front porch, staring out at the fields. Maybe a half-mile beyond lay the burned-out cabin, a small black shell against a windswept yellow canola field in the distance.

"The guy confessed," Karen said. "He slapped his wife. That can get him up to a year in the pen and a two-thousand-dollar fine, and I told him as much."

"We both know that's only if he's got a previous record," Peyton said, "and he doesn't."

"You ran him through the system?"

45

"I was here this morning," Peyton said.

"About the stiff in the cabin?"

"Yeah. They both knew Simon Pink. I'd like to talk to the two of them together. There's something more to this."

"Fred! Oh, my God! What are you … ?!"

It was Marie's voice.

Peyton turned to see Marie, on the other side of the kitchen window, sliding lower in her rocking chair, desperate to get away from whatever was to her right.

"I'm so sorry, Marie." It was Fred's voice, and it seemed quiet in the aftermath of Marie's shout. "There ain't no other way for us."

"Don't!" Marie shouted. "We can talk to her. She'll forgive us."

"I hope she can forgive me."

Peyton unclipped the safety strap on her holstered .40, and in one fluid motion yanked the pistol from its holster and ran onto the porch.

EIGHT

PEYTON AND KAREN SMYTHE were ten feet behind Fred, who stood facing Marie.

"Drop it!" Peyton yelled.

The blast from the .357 knocked Marie backward, toppling her rocking chair.

Peyton watched Marie go over backward and screamed again for Fred to drop the gun. Out of the corner of her eye, Peyton saw Karen crouch behind a wicker love seat, her 9mm sited on Fred's back.

"Drop it, Fred!" Peyton shouted again.

"I'm sorry," Fred said again; then, in a whisper, "but I have to go."

"Put the gun down, Fred," Karen said. "This is over."

Still with his back to the officers, Fred nodded, bent, and reached toward the ground. But instead of laying the gun down, he dropped to his knees, quickly placed the barrel before him, and squeezed the trigger.

Karen shouted something inaudible.

And Peyton's scream—"Don't do it!"—was lost amid the large pistol's blast and its echoed report, which seemed to go on and on, ringing in Peyton's ears—ceasing only when she realized what the red and white mucus was that covered the toe of her left boot.

———

"Requesting two ambulances." It was Karen Smythe who called it in; after all, it was a murder-suicide, and homicides belonged to the state police. "No need for sirens and lights," she said, looking down.

The scene had been cleared—the .357 kicked to the side (and later bagged as evidence), the search for pulses completed (which, given the state of each body, was futile)—and now Karen began to formally process the scene. She was stringing yellow crime-scene tape and awaiting the ME. The crime-scene technicians, depending on where they were coming from, could take longer than an hour to arrive.

"Fred climbed out the den window," Peyton said, "and came around the porch. The .357 must have been in the den the whole time."

"Is Hewitt in the office?" Karen asked.

Peyton nodded. "I'm sure he'll be here."

Mike Hewitt had fallen into something of a dual role: PAIC at Garrett Station and, given his experience and this young group of state troopers, a crime-scene consultant for the state police.

Wearing latex gloves, Peyton stood over the corpse of Marie St. Pierre and looked down. The flesh of the woman's torn face resembled a bludgeoned watermelon.

The trajectory of the second bullet had ripped part of Fred St. Pierre's skull away, leaving bone fragments, blood, and tissue, like Play-Doh, pasted to the porch ceiling.

"There's a bullet hole in the roof," Karen said.

"Judging from the back of his head"—Peyton motioned to the body—"Fred got the barrel into his mouth."

The corpse of Fred St. Pierre had fallen near his wife's feet. His eyes were open, locked in a never-ending stare; his head turned toward Marie, as if he'd focused on his final earthly act as he departed this world for whatever lay ahead.

"You said you thought your interview this morning led to the fight," Karen said. "I assume I'll be the lead officer on this one. Can you fill me in?"

"It was my idea to leave him in there alone," Peyton said. "This is on me, not you. And I'll make sure it goes down like that."

"Peyton, he'd have shot her whether we left him alone or not. Even if we'd have cuffed and stuffed him, he'd have posted bail, gone home, and done it then. You heard what he said to her. He thought they both needed to go."

Peyton was squinting at a huge maple tree to the west, where a single robin perched.

"That conversation was bizarre," Karen continued. "You were right. There is more to this than meets the eye. She was talking about someone forgiving them. And he said he had no choice about them both having to die."

———

They re-entered the kitchen, and Peyton realized the scent of cordite was still present and wafting in from outside.

"Think the cabin has something to do with this?" Karen Smythe said.

"No idea," Peyton said, finally turning off the stove. Marie's stew, like a lot of things now, would never be finished. "But I do think Simon Pink had something to do with it. I think there was something there."

"Love triangle?"

"Possibly," Peyton said. "I'll be looking into it as well."

"Because of the cabin?"

"Yeah. That scene is still being processed by the fire marshal. But my guess is it was a lab of some sort, very close to the border."

"I heard about that," Karen said. "If it's crystal meth, I'll be surprised. I haven't heard of that being a problem around here."

They had returned to the den. Karen lifted several magazines off the coffee table, saw nothing of interest, and examined several desk drawers.

"Red phosphorus is hard to get in most places," Peyton explained, "but it's used to make fertilizer. Fred was a potato farmer. No one would think twice about him having it."

"I can't see Fred St. Pierre as a meth cook," Karen said.

"Someone else might have been doing the cooking."

"And he was the landlord?"

Peyton shrugged. "This farm covers five hundred acres. Pretty good place to hide a lab. And Fred St. Pierre would be about the last person anyone would suspect."

"What would his motive be?"

"Money," Peyton said. "He's a farmer. A lot of them take out huge operating loans. There's a lot of pressure each year to pay those back. I've seen it firsthand."

"Your family?"

"Yeah," Peyton said. "My father lost our farm when I was in middle school."

"Sorry," Karen said.

"It's the past," Peyton said, but of course, it never would be.

"You hear Fred say something like, 'I hope she can forgive me'?"

"Yeah."

"Think he was talking about you?" Karen asked.

"Why would he need forgiveness from me?" Peyton said.

"I don't know. Maybe he felt guilty, thought this put you in a bad spot."

"Because I knew them? My mother does play bridge with Marie—or did. But that scenario doesn't feel right. She wasn't close to my mother."

"I don't know," Karen said.

"I'm going to the second floor." Peyton started for the stairs.

"Okay. I'll go through the living room. Don't move anything, or the crime-scene techs will flip."

"They'll never even know I was there," Peyton said.

———

Peyton knew the state police would own the domestic-dispute-turned-homicide crime scene, which meant Karen Smythe was affording her a professional courtesy: an informal crime-scene walk-through.

A brown leather purse lay on a table in the upstairs hallway. According to Marie's driver's license, which Peyton found in the purse, she'd been only fifty-eight. Judging from the school photos in Marie's wallet and framed pictures scattered around the house, Sherry had a son, maybe Tommy's age, and a daughter a little younger. The young girl looked just like Sherry. The boy, though, had his own look, distinctive from either parent. Marie would never see her grandchildren grow up.

In a side pocket of Marie's purse, Peyton found a passport and nine crisp hundred-dollar bills. Had Marie been planning a trip?

Peyton returned the items to the purse. She hadn't been in the house regularly in close to twenty years, but Sherry's room hadn't changed much: basketball trophies, a University of Maine banner, yearbooks, even a stuffed bear Peyton could remember them playing with in elementary school. Except now there were photos of Marie and Fred with two grandchildren—the little girl, a dead ringer for her mother, and her raven-haired brother—in the hayloft with Marie, on the tractor with Fred, and one picture Peyton found particularly sad: the two kids side by side at the dining room table for a holiday dinner.

The third bedroom, to Peyton's surprise, looked lived in. A man's shaving kit lay atop the dresser. Did Freddy Jr., Sherry's younger brother who worked the farm with Fred, still live at home?

Would he return to find crime-scene investigators and the ME?

She wouldn't wish that sight on anyone—Marie, nearly decapitated, lying near an overturned chair; Fred, the top of his skull missing, eyes open, lying facing his victim—let alone the couple's younger child.

She moved to the dresser and found a small-caliber handgun and $500 in Freddy's sock drawer.

She crossed the hall. Familiarity with the region gave her many professional advantages—she knew the roads, the land, and many residents—but having spent her childhood among these people also posed challenges. As she rifled through Marie's underwear drawer, she felt as though she was violating the woman who'd welcomed her into this house so often when she'd been a young child and whose eyes always met hers with sympathy after Fred made sure she no longer received invitations to visit.

The lingerie in Marie's drawer was more exotic than she'd anticipated. Had she ordered Victoria's Secret panties and a red teddy for Fred?

Peyton was closing the drawer when she spotted a manila envelope.

The downstairs was empty when Peyton returned to the den.

Nothing seemed out of the ordinary. *The Journal of Northeast Agriculture* lay open on the coffee table next to a now-cold cup of coffee. Apparently, Fred had been reading an article about fertilization. Next to the journal was a book titled *Politics of Eastern Bloc Countries* written by Dr. Sherry St. Pierre-Duvall. Peyton had lost touch with Sherry during high school—Fred had seen to that—and she knew Sherry had overcome a lot to earn her Ph.D.

Peyton looked around the room and tried to imagine what happened. Marie called 911 for help. That much she knew. And Peyton had witnessed the argument's conclusion. But how had it begun? Had Fred seen Marie's reaction upon hearing of Simon Pink's death—hand suddenly covering her mouth, the odd whispered statement: "That's why"—as something more than the sympathy one would normally feel at the loss of an acquaintance?

The envelope she'd found upstairs made that theory credible.

Peyton had been struck by Marie's reaction. But she was paid to note deviations in expected behavioral patterns. Fred wasn't. Had he been suspicious to start with and found Marie's reaction equivalent to a confession? If so, a confrontation was the logical progression.

And what of the couple's final conversation? Pleading for her life, Marie said, "We can talk to her." Talk to whom? And from whom did Fred need forgiveness?

On the porch, she found Karen, wearing footies and latex gloves, standing on a chair and holding a flashlight to a hole in the roof. She was looking for the .357 slug.

"I was going to send out for coffee," Karen said. "Want a cup?"

Peyton thought it was a good idea. Karen would be here a while: a murder-suicide was unusual in Maine, unheard of in tranquil Aroostook County.

Peyton nodded. "They have a son, Fred Jr., who works the farm with his father. The room upstairs looks like he still lives at home."

"How old is he?"

"Maybe thirty," Peyton said. "I found five hundred dollars cash and a handgun in the sock drawer in the room I assume is his."

"Where is he now?" Karen said.

Peyton shrugged. "And Marie had nine hundred dollars in cash in her purse and two passports."

"Two?"

"Yeah. Only one was hers."

Karen looked off into the distance. "This is turning into a shit storm."

"Yeah," Peyton said. "We're going to need that coffee."

———

"Any idea where the son of the St. Pierre couple is?" Mike Hewitt asked.

"No," Peyton said. Her iPad in hand, she was reviewing her notes.

They were near Karen Smythe's dark Interceptor. Karen was there, but Hewitt was looking at Peyton.

"I'd like to have someone meet him," Hewitt said, "before the poor bastard shows up at this scene." He looked at the porch, where yellow crime-scene tape had been spread and two sheets covered the corpses, and shook his head.

"You both realize the report isn't going to make either of you look very good," he said. "You left him alone. He got a .357 and ... " He pointed at the porch.

"That's on me," Peyton said. "I asked Karen to step out so I could ask her what Fred said to her. Then I wanted a few minutes alone with the couple before Karen arrested him."

All of five-two, Karen had to look up at Mike Hewitt, but she stared him in the eye nonetheless. "The guy was passive as hell, Mike. Neither of us had any idea he'd hidden a gun in there. I think it didn't matter. He'd have posted bail, which certainly would've been low, given that he has no record and a good reputation, and then done it when they were home. He said as much."

"What did he say?"

They started at the beginning—with Peyton's first interview—and alternated speaking, as each woman recalled details, finishing with how they'd searched the house.

"I don't know what your boss will require, Karen," Hewitt said and turned to Peyton, "but you need to write this up, Peyton. A copy will go in your file."

"I know."

"I don't think that's right, Mike," Karen said. "You weren't here. You don't know what took place. You didn't see him. *You'd* have done the same thing."

He looked at her, started to speak, then closed his mouth and looked out over to the trees at the far end of the property. The sun was shining.

"Peyton, tell me about the son," he said.

"I've seen him in the Tip of the Hat a couple times in recent years, so I'd recognize him. But I don't know if he has another job or where he hangs out."

"Between the mother and son," Hewitt said, "they had a lot of cash in this house."

Peyton felt beads of perspiration on her brow. She wore a T-shirt beneath her Kevlar vest, which only trapped the sweat against her body.

"Maybe I'm getting old," Hewitt said, looking at her iPad.

Peyton didn't respond. Wasn't in the mood for small talk. She was thinking about her personnel file, about what was in it already. Three years earlier, she'd been suspended for crawling into an overturned van, a decision that forced her to shoot and kill a man for the first time in her career. He was a man she'd known growing up. She was a single mother, and her ex-husband's alimony would never put food on the table or clothe their son. She couldn't afford a personnel file weighed down by a trail of mistakes.

"Tell me more about Fred St. Pierre Jr.," Hewitt said.

"I don't know him very well. Growing up, I spent a lot of time here with his sister. Then, during our first year of high school, his sister, Sherry, simply cut me and everyone else out of her life. No more boyfriends. No friends. Quit varsity basketball. But she did get straight As and graduate valedictorian."

"Wish I'd had those priorities in high school," Hewitt said. "I wouldn't be scraping brains off a ceiling into evidence containers. I'd be a financial wizard with a thirty-foot boat."

If he was still angry and thinking of writing a formal reprimand for her personnel file, he wasn't showing it.

"We'll have someone else make the call to the daughter," he said. "When she gets here, though, you can interview her."

There were three Border Patrol vehicles at the house now. A second state police cruiser pulled in belonging to Leo Miller, who'd been at the original investigation of the burned-out cabin.

"I was busting a kid for shoplifting," Miller said, getting out of his car, "when the DD call came across the radio. Look what I missed. This will be big for six months."

"You missed a family tragedy," Peyton said. "That's what you missed. I knew the couple."

"Oh. I didn't mean it like that."

"Right," she said.

Miller swatted at the black flies. "Jesus Christ, the flies are bad today." He slapped the back of his neck then spotted Karen Smythe crossing the front porch with two Border Patrol agents and hustled toward her.

Peyton and Hewitt watched as Karen stopped Miller and pointed at his hands. He quickly retrieved gloves from his duty belt, snapped them on, and proceeded into the house.

"Don't touch a thing, Leo," Karen called after him.

"Got so excited he forgot latex," Peyton said. "He needs to get out of the area for a while."

"Location has nothing to do with it," Hewitt said. "Guy needs to grow up." He looked out at the idle tractor in the field. "This is going to be a big operation for a young guy to run by himself."

"True."

"Fred said he was sorry," Hewitt said, "then blew her brains out?"

"Mike, I knew them."

"I know. And I'm sorry to put it like that, Peyton, but that's what happened. I can't get my head around it. The guy is reading a magazine one minute, smacking his wife the next, and shooting her and himself after that?"

"Sad to say, but abuse happens in this country a lot, Mike."

"She had close to a grand in her purse and a passport," he said. "Where was she going?"

"Maybe as far away from Fred as she could get," Peyton said.

"Think she was cheating?"

"Likely."

"So," he said, "the husband shoots her because he's jealous?"

"I don't think so," she said. "That doesn't make sense to me."

"Guys who murder their spouses aren't usually the most rational people in the world. Maybe he didn't think he'd hit her hard enough."

She shook her head. "Just doesn't feel right. Not this case. Not here. I'm telling you, Mike, she was surprised when he walked onto the porch with a gun. We were *all* surprised. Fred went from zero to a hundred in five seconds. I was talking to Karen, but I heard the surprise in Marie's voice. And she said something strange to him."

Hewitt's gaze could be laserlike, and his blue eyes were intense now. She'd felt his stare several times in his office, the last time being when he suspended her. She thought she'd done the right thing by entering the overturned van, but he'd said she'd gone "Lone Ranger." She could still feel the pain in her chest where her Kevlar vest had saved her life that night.

"He was apologizing for what he was about to do," she said, "and she was saying they could ask for forgiveness."

"From who?"

"Not sure," Peyton said. "He said, 'I hope she can forgive me.'"

"No one knows who he's talking about?" he said.

"I know the family, and Marie plays cards with my mother every week…"

"So it could be you?"

"I guess," Peyton said. "But I doubt it."

Hewitt took his phone from his pocket and checked for messages.

"None of it makes sense," Peyton said. "Marie knew Fred had guns in the house, yet when he stepped onto the porch with one and pointed it at her, she asked what he was doing. I think she expected this fight to blow over."

"Sounds like this wasn't their first fight."

"True, which makes me think Marie accepted her husband's physical abuse, but never thought he was capable of murder."

"But if that's right," Hewitt said, "why call the cops? She must have known it was different this time."

Peyton couldn't think of how it would be different. But if his theory was correct—and it very well could be—it meant Marie was scared.

Of what?

And why?

"*I* think the asshole knew this common occurrence was going public," Hewitt said, "so he killed them both."

"Too drastic," she said. "It's got to be something else. When I asked why he hit her, Fred said, 'Because I wanted her to leave. Now it's too late.'"

"Too late for what?" Hewitt asked.

She shrugged. "Killing her doesn't make sense. I keep replaying it in my mind. It just doesn't fit. Why say he's sorry right before shooting her? That's like saying he didn't want to kill her but had to. That doesn't jive with a domestic dispute that turns into a murder. It's as if the two were unrelated."

"Seems to me like the violence escalated and he killed her," Hewitt said. "Simple as that."

She looked away. She and Sherry had played in the woods surrounding the farm one winter day and returned for Marie's homemade hot chocolate. That afternoon Fred St. Pierre had come to seven-year-old Sherry's room and scolded his daughter in front of Peyton. Sherry had forgotten to water the living room plants, and Fred pointed a thick finger at her, his face red, and told her, "How dare you, eh? You appreciate nothing." Then he called Peyton's mother and said it was time for her to go home. Sherry had stood at the front door with tears in her eyes that day as she waved goodbye. Peyton, for her part, had never forgotten the humiliation on Sherry's face.

"Look into the passports and nine hundred dollars," he said. "We've got more than a grand in cash, two passports, a lab on the border with a murder victim inside, and now a murder-suicide."

"There isn't a lot coming together on Simon Pink. But one former employer mentioned a chemistry background."

"That might play well with your crank-cook theory."

"It might. I'm going to chase that down. He seemed to have been conservative and outspoken."

"A conservative crank cook?" he said.

"Takes all kinds. Any word from the fire marshal?"

"Gasoline and matches."

"That'll do it," she said. "So arson led to the explosion?"

"That's now the working theory. Could have torched the cabin for the insurance money."

"They built that cabin themselves. And these were simple farm people, Mike. Marie was on local boards, something of a community leader."

"That's what I hear."

"Can we have someone look at their financials?"

"I already put Mitchell Cosgrove on it."

Cosgrove had been a CPA before becoming an agent.

"To be clear," Hewitt said, "I don't want you going off on your own if ICE or HSI shows up and trumps you."

When she'd begun her career, there had been a total of ten thousand Border Patrol agents and the US Border Patrol had its own investigative arm, the Anti-Smuggling Unit (ASU). Now, within the Department of Homeland Security (DHS), there were subsidiaries—among them Immigration and Customs Enforcement (ICE) and their Homeland Security Investigations (HSI) unit. ICE had been created in 2003 and absorbed all of the investigative duties of what had been US Immigration Investigations, US Customs Investigations, and US Border Patrol's Anti-Smuggling units, making ICE the investigations arm of the Department of Homeland Security. And within ICE, which now totaled twenty thousand agents, there was an international offshoot, Homeland Security Investigations (HSI), featuring 6,700 special agents working 200 US cities and 47 countries, using undercover and plainclothes agents to focus on human and goods trafficking into and out of the US. Peyton mostly approved of the increased awareness, but she hated getting caught up in the alphabet soup.

"Think ICE and HSI will be here?"

"That cabin is near the border," he said. "If someone's smuggling meth into Canada, HSI might very well want to be involved. You may be asked to desist."

"No problem," she said.

He looked at her, his brows rising.

"Are you saying I'm stubborn, Mike?"

"Meeting adjourned," he said.

NINE

PEYTON WAS HOME, WORKING on dinner at the kitchen counter Wednesday at 5:45 p.m. If she'd been stationed in a California sector, her salary might have meant a two-bedroom apartment on the sixth floor with a view of a brick wall; in Aroostook County, though, her government salary made renting a thing of the past. Even as a single mother, she could buy a home for her son.

And now she was in her favorite room: The kitchen had finalized her decision to purchase the home, though it had taken a few updates to fully fulfill her vision. The cupboards were now framed in glass, the appliances were stainless steel, and a large granite island dominated the space.

Tommy, wearing a Boston Red Sox shirt with David Ortiz's number 34 on the back, was at the island, math sheet before him, and, based on the independence with which he worked this night, making progress.

Had she overreacted about his academic growth? Had the meeting with Nancy Lawrence been premature? She'd notice a slight decline last year, but maybe that was to be expected. Maybe the work was just getting harder. Maybe Tommy didn't need additional academic support, after all.

Or maybe she was trying to reassure herself that her kid was just like every other kid.

The ten-year-old looked up. "I can feel you looking at me, Mom."

"Just getting dinner ready." She knew she couldn't hover, had to allow him to do it on his own, and turned back to her dinner preparations.

"Is Mr. Dye coming for dinner?"

"I already told you he was," she said.

"Why can't Dad ever come for dinner?"

"He can come for dinner anytime, sweetie."

"Tonight?"

She turned from the counter to find her son staring at her. And she was reminded instantly that for someone who made a living in part by knowing when others were lying, she herself wasn't very good at doing it. Jeff McComb, her ex-husband, a local realtor, wasn't welcome in her house. She knew it. Jeff knew it. And, apparently, their son had picked up on it, too.

"Dad says you don't like him."

She set her knife down—her grip on the handle having grown tighter at the mention of her ex-husband—and walked to her son.

"Tommy, your dad and I like each other just fine. And we have one very important common interest: you." She kissed his cheek.

"Can Dad come for dinner tonight?"

"Mr. Dye has already made plans to come tonight."

"How come I never get to decide if he should come over?" He started doodling, unwilling to meet her eyes.

"Because he's my friend," she said. "I can invite him here, Tommy."

"But you get to decide if my friends are allowed over."

"Yes, Tommy. I'm the parent."

"You always say that."

"I always say it because it doesn't change. Someday you'll be the parent, and you can decide."

He frowned. "You always say that, too."

She leaned to kiss his forehead, but he pulled back.

"He's not going to be my dad," Tommy said.

"That's true. And no one wants him to be. You already have a dad."

"Can Dad come for dinner tomorrow?"

"Tomorrow?" she said.

"Uh huh."

"Sure. I'll call and invite him."

"Okay," Tommy said.

And damned if he didn't point to her phone and wait for her to do it.

———

Thirty minutes later, the TV hanging beneath the cupboard played the *CBS Evening News*. She stood at the granite counter and cubed steak on a wooden chopping block.

"Where's Tommy?" Pete Dye said.

He'd replaced her son—who'd retreated to his bedroom as soon as Pete arrived—at the island and now sat drinking Shock Top Pumpkin Wheat beer from a frosted glass she took from the freezer.

"Upstairs," Peyton said. "I met with Nancy Lawrence this morning."

"And how did that go?"

She turned from the chopping block to face him. "You ask that like you know the answer," she said.

"I don't know the answer, but I do know Nancy. I can't imagine she did well with your direct approach."

She smiled. "I'm not that direct."

"You're not exactly passive."

"I don't think she gives a shit about my son. And I have a major problem with that."

"I think she likes summers off," he said.

She moved to the stove, picked up a wooden spoon, and pushed the steak cubes into a frying pan. The news reported that the president was planning a "short vacation to northern Maine." The room smelled of soy sauce and onions. The steak, when browned, would find a home in her stir-fry.

"Meaning she's not in it for the kids?" she said.

"She's not the only teacher I know who got into it for summers off, Peyton."

"I don't care why she got into it. I care about my son. I don't want him pigeonholed, but I want him helped." She pushed the meat around with a wooden spoon.

"Having him tested?"

"Yes. The teachers are going to meet when the results are back."

"Push it," he said. "The test costs a lot—the district usually pays—and Michael Thompson, the consultant, is very good. Some teachers don't like him because he sees that kids get what they need."

"And I'll advocate for my son," she said.

"Good," he said. "I've seen what happens when parents don't. The cracks are huge, and too many kids fall through."

"I'll stay on top of it," she said. "Will the other kids know if Tommy gets services?"

"Does it matter?"

"It might," she said. "I think he's having a hard time right now."

Pete looked at her, waiting. Condensation ran down the beer glass and pooled on the table. He wiped it with his bare hand. She brought him a paper towel.

"I think he's being picked on," she said.

"He told you so?"

"No. I was at school and saw something."

"Boys are different, Peyton. They push each other, punch each other in the arm. That stuff."

"That's not what I saw. He was being humiliated. I saw it on his face. He slumped away when the others laughed."

"What can we do about it?"

"*We?*"

"I want to help," he said.

She put down the spoon, crossed the room, and kissed him on the cheek.

"Thanks," he said when they broke, "but it's no big deal. It's what I do. It would be like you helping me ..." He looked for the words.

She started to laugh. "What, bust a drug smuggler?"

"The analogy doesn't exactly work, but ..."

"Sure," she said. "You're a good guy, Pete Dye." She smiled at the rhyme.

"I keep telling people that," he said.

"Where were you ten years ago?"

"Watching you marry Jeff. I was at your wedding, remember?"

"How could I forget? At least you never said I told you so."

"Is Tommy avoiding me?" Pete said.

She moved back to the stove, picked up the wooden spoon, and moved the hissing steak tips around the frying pan.

"Probably," she said. "It's complicated."

He nodded. He wore khaki pants, a white button-down shirt, and brown loafers. She liked his five-o'clock shadow.

"When we went for ice cream after his last soccer game," he said, "you went to the counter to order, and Tommy and I stayed in the booth. I asked about his dad. He said he never sees him. I could tell he was upset."

"The fact of the matter is that you taking him to the batting cages last week was the first fatherly thing anyone has done for him in six months," she said. "I moved here, in part, so he could see Jeff, but now Jeff's dating a woman with two kids."

"And Tommy's the odd man out?"

"Yeah," she said. "Makes me tear up just saying it."

"I'll take him out again," he said and stood. Didn't move closer, simply rose to his feet, as if paying the situation the attention it deserved.

"Jeff has to do it," she said.

Pete moved to the window and stood looking out, his back to her. "When I was a kid, my old man walked out. You remember that?"

"I do," she said.

"I was the man of the house at age ten."

"I know."

"So you also remember what a punk I was for a while there."

"Not too long."

"But for a while," he said. "Got into fights at school. Did everything but get arrested."

"You were always a nice person, just confused."

"I know what it's like to feel alone when you're a kid. I'd like to help Tommy."

"That's the sweetest thing anyone has said to me since I moved back. But I think Tommy needs space for a while."

He was looking at her now. "When you want me to try to engage him, let me know."

"You can get him for dinner," she said and smiled.

———

She could hear Pete's footsteps overhead and Tommy's padded movements, courtesy of his white athletic socks. She set the stir-fry on the dining room table, still thinking of Tommy's testing and of what a formal learning-disability diagnosis might mean for him.

Would it help him?

Or would it leave him forever labeled?

She knew where Pete Dye stood, and she trusted him. But she also remembered kids leaving her classes in elementary and middle school to attend the "resource room," the dumping ground for the "dumb kids." She remembered, too, their faces as they paused at the door, the shame in their eyes. She didn't want that for Tommy, didn't want him singled out.

"He said he wasn't hungry," Pete said, when he and Tommy entered the room, "but I convinced him to eat."

The smile on Pete's face was forced. Tommy was staring at the hardwood floor.

"My dad's coming for dinner tomorrow night," Tommy said.

Pete Dye looked at Peyton, who frowned.

"That's great," Pete said. "You and your dad will have a good time."

"I know we will," Tommy said. "We always do. He's just really busy or he'd be over here a lot."

"I know that, too," Pete said.

The meal was awkward, the conversation stilted and disjointed.

How's soccer, Tommy?

Fine.

Boy, the stir-fry is great, Peyton.

How's soccer, Tommy?

Didn't you just ask me that?

Pete Dye said he had to go as soon as the dishes were cleared from the table. And she couldn't blame him.

She walked him to his truck. He opened the door and turned to kiss her goodnight. She smiled, but he offered only a cursory peck on the mouth and abruptly pulled away.

"I wish he didn't think I was trying to replace Jeff," he said. "I have no intention of doing that." His broad shoulders blotted out the light from inside his pickup.

"The sad thing is," she said, trying to shrug off the sting of the stifled kiss, "a replacement for his absent father is exactly what he needs."

"He's coming for dinner tomorrow?"

"Yes," she said. "I hope that doesn't bother you."

He shook his head, but his eyes left hers. The official start of summer was still a week or so away, but the evening air was warm, and the sun was still above the horizon.

He started to get into his rusting Toyota pickup but turned back.

"Peyton, where does everything with Tommy and Jeff leave you and me?"

"You and me?" She looked up at him, head tilted. She'd spent years cognizant of her facial expressions amidst tough conversations and tried to hide her emotions here. "It won't have any impact on what's between you and me," she said.

"Is that realistic?"

"Why do you ask?" she said.

"I guess I'm trying to figure out what exactly is 'between you and me,'" he said. "What we have, where we're headed."

"You sound unhappy."

"Just confused. We've been dating for months."

"This is about sex," she said. "I told you I need to take things slowly."

"That's not it."

"Bullshit."

"No," he said. "That isn't it, although that would be nice." He grinned, but saw that she wasn't smiling. "Bad joke," he said. "I just need to know where I stand in your life."

"Pete, maybe it's my job, maybe it's everything going on with Tommy, or maybe it's just me. But I take things a day at a time."

"You never look to the future?"

She hesitated. Did she look to the future?

"Because I do," he said.

"Don't put me in a position where I have to choose between you and everything else in my life."

"I'd never do that, Peyton. But I need to know some things." Again, he looked like he might kiss her but didn't. "You mean a ton to me," he said. "I'll call you tomorrow."

Then he climbed in his truck and drove away.

She stood alone in the driveway for several minutes after he was gone.

TEN

PEYTON WAS AT HER desk by 8:15 Thursday, reviewing a file from the FBI's counter-terrorism office in Washington.

She was reading about Simon Pink.

Next she scanned her email and spotted a message from Secret Service Agent Wally Rowe that Hewitt had forwarded to Garrett agents. The message was cryptic, as expected: the Secret Service would be "in the region in the coming days" and agents "might be called upon" to serve in "various activities." (Even the *CBS Evening News* had guessed that much.) And people said government officials spoke in vagaries.

"Here you go." It was Hewitt, setting a second file on her desk. "Come to my office when you've read it." He turned and was gone before she could tell him what she'd learned about Simon Pink.

It took her twenty minutes to read Hewitt's new delivery and learn that the cause of the fire was officially arson. But she was more concerned with what the fire marshal had found at the site.

"What do you make of page four?" she asked, taking a seat across the desk from Hewitt.

Hewitt shook his head. "I have a call in to Mitch Lincoln, the fire marshal, about that. Looks like they were building bombs."

"IEDs?" she said.

The light reflected off the gold leaf pinned to his lapel. The leaf was a designation of his status as Patrol Agent in Charge.

"Sure looks like it," he said. "They found detonators."

"Why torch a place with bomb-making materials? You know it'll blow up."

"It makes no sense," he agreed.

"I got background on Simon Pink," Peyton said. She glanced down at her iPad, checking her notes. "He immigrated to Montreal at age eighteen. According to a contact I have with the Mounties, Pink never got so much as a parking ticket in North America."

"That's your background info?"

"There's more," she said.

"From the Feds?"

"FBI," she said.

"If the FBI has background on him, there has to be something in his file."

"Of course." She smiled. "Simon Pink wasn't Russian, like everyone thought. He was Czech."

"Just never bothered to correct anyone?" Hewitt said.

"It appears so. He had a few scrapes with Czech officials in Prague when he was a kid there. Fights at an anti-government protest."

"And Canadian Immigration welcomed him?"

"You know how that goes," she said. "A couple fights as a kid on his record. That's all. He was coming to study chemistry."

"And he ends up shot in a torched cabin with bomb-making materials," Hewitt said. "Was the FBI watching him?"

"If he was on any of their lists, obviously he was way down at the bottom."

"I want to talk to Mitch Lincoln about the cabin again," Hewitt said.

Peyton heard the stationhouse door open and saw Hewitt look past her.

"You having breakfast with Karen Smythe?" he asked.

"No."

"Uh oh," Hewitt said. "Then she's here on business."

Peyton turned to see Maine State Police Detective Karen Smythe cross the bullpen with receptionist Linda Cyr. Peyton knew Karen had done a triathlon the previous year. She also knew she was single. By choice.

Miguel Jimenez, the station's youngest agent, who was also (very) single, looked up at Karen and absently fixed his hair after his night shift.

"Got a minute?" Karen said when she reached Hewitt's office. "I need to speak to you both."

"Peyton," Linda said, "is Pete Dye bringing coffee this morning, or should I put the pot on?"

"Make a pot."

"Everything okay, sweetie?"

"Make a pot," Peyton repeated.

"You're here on business," Hewitt said to Karen.

"And I come bearing gifts," Karen said.

———

"Marie St. Pierre purchased two plane tickets to Prague for next month," Karen said. She pulled a second metal folding chair from the wall and sat next to Peyton. "Did either of you know that?"

"No," Hewitt said. "No one here knows that. That's your gift?"

"I'm always thinking of you guys."

Hewitt scribbled notes on a yellow legal pad. Peyton shared her new information regarding Simon Pink with Karen.

"And Simon Pink is the other name on the two tickets we found under a pot in a cupboard over the stove," Karen said. "Marie hid them, apparently, where she knew Fred would never find them."

"Because he never cooked," Peyton said.

"You're smiling," Hewitt said.

"I appreciate little victories," Peyton said.

"Meaning she pulled one over on her husband?"

"Kind of. He treated her terribly."

"She should've left the sonofabitch," Karen said. "That would've been the real victory."

"True. But she's not like you or me, Karen. She's more like my mother—not that my parents' relationship was like theirs. But that's the kind of woman she was. She'd stay with him no matter what."

"Submissive?" Karen said.

Peyton made a face. "That's not it, exactly. More like dedicated. That's the word. She'd stay with him because she believed you have to lie in the bed you make. People up here see things through to the end. It goes with the territory. You grow up in a farming community, you understand there are many things you can't control, and the way through it all is riding it out."

The phone on Hewitt's desk rang.

Hewitt lifted the receiver, introduced himself, then said, "Leo, settle down." He listened, then said, "Slow down and tell me." As he listened for nearly a minute, his eyes moved from Peyton to Karen. "Got it. Thanks."

He hung up, then scribbled more on his legal pad, set the pencil down, and blew out a long breath, eyes returning to Peyton.

"How well do you know Fred St. Pierre Jr.?"

"Not very. Like I said, I knew him a long time ago, when we were kids."

"Well, we have a ballistics match on the .22 slug in Pink's head. It came from Fred Jr.'s pistol. Leo Miller has him in lockup, wants to move him to Houlton. He's salivating at the idea of interviewing a real live murder suspect."

"He has jurisdiction, right?" Peyton said.

"Yes, we do," Karen said, "but even I don't think Leo's the best candidate to interview a murder suspect."

"I'll play the Homeland Security card," Hewitt said.

"State cops hate hearing about that card," Karen said and smiled.

"I know," Hewitt said, "but it's a really useful card. We have a lab that was destroyed close to an international border. It can buy us a little time. Peyton, can you talk with Fred Jr. when I get him here?"

"You can get him here?" Peyton said.

"I think so. There's one other thing you should know. His sister is coming up here. She was handling the funeral arrangements. But now she's bringing a Portland attorney, too. You said you knew her."

"In middle school," she said.

"The attorney makes me think she's going on the offensive."

"Probably looking out for her brother," Peyton said.

"Maybe you could happen to run into her, feel her out, get an idea of what she thinks, see where she falls on her parents' death and her brother's arrest."

"Sounds like you want me to interview her."

"I'm sure her attorney wouldn't allow that. I just think it would be convenient if you happened to bump into her and have a talk."

"I was planning to offer my condolences if and when she came to town. Let me know when Freddy arrives here. I'll interview him."

"Great," Hewitt said, and reached for the phone. "Now you two will have to excuse me. I have an ace in the hole to play."

"Before we go," Karen said.

"Yes?" Hewitt waited.

"Have you typed up the reprimand yet?" Karen said.

"For Peyton?" Hewitt said. "We talking about the St. Pierre shooting?"

"Yeah," Karen said.

"Let it go, Karen," Peyton said.

"Karen," Hewitt said, "you're way out of line getting involved in that."

"I've lost a lot of sleep over that, Mike. Peyton shouldn't be punished for what happened. Anyone would've made that call. I'm asking you to think about it."

"You're out of line," Hewitt repeated and looked at the door.

"And you're wrong, Mike. I don't work for you. I can say that."

She stood, and Peyton followed her out.

ELEVEN

PEYTON ENTERED THE INTERVIEW room Thursday at 9:45 a.m. with two Styrofoam cups of coffee. She set the coffees down, removed a recorder from her pocket, started it, and recited the date, stated who she was, and said the suspect's name. Then she asked Fred St. Pierre Jr. if he'd been read his rights.

"Yeah, sure," he said. "Whatever."

She handed him a coffee, and he took it without thanking her.

"Place ain't exactly cozy, eh?" he said, the French accent reminding Peyton of his now-late father's. He smelled like fertilizer, an earthy, pungent scent.

"It's an interview room, Freddy, not a Marriott."

"One metal desk, one chair? Feel like I'm on *NCIS*. You know me, eh, Peyton. You know I didn't shoot Simon Pink, right?"

"The slug is from your .22."

"That don't mean nothing. Don't prove I did it."

She sipped her coffee. Tim Hortons wasn't Starbucks, but it was popular in the region, and until Aroostook County got a Starbucks (or pigs flew), it was as good as it got.

"Any theories," she said, "as to how a slug from your pistol ended up in Simon Pink's head?"

"I got no idea. Last I knew, my .22 was on top of my closet."

The state troopers had found it in his sock drawer. Following the shooting, they'd gone through the St. Pierre house. Aside from the .357 Fred Sr. had used to kill Marie, it was the only other gun discovered.

"You know what the last two days been like for me?" He was staring at the Formica tabletop.

"I should've said this earlier," she said. "I'm terribly sorry for your loss. I truly am."

"I mean, I get home, see the blood on the porch—"

That was a relief to Peyton: Fred Jr. hadn't seen the corpses.

"—then I get questioned by Leo Miller about my parents. He tries to tell me my father shot my mother then shot himself. I still don't believe him." He looked away. "Leo says you saw it happen."

"That's true, Freddy. Again, I'm terribly sorry."

"I can't believe it, eh. I mean, that couldn't happen, right? You know my parents."

"I hadn't seen them for a long time. But what Leo told you is true."

He leaned back in his chair, folded his arms across his chest, and cursed under his breath.

She didn't speak. He hadn't requested his attorney yet; he could curse all he wanted, so long as he kept answering questions.

"How long have you known Simon Pink?"

"*Known*? I didn't exactly know the guy, eh. Papa hired him. He worked the harvest a couple times."

"Doing what?"

"Driving, so I didn't see him often."

Potato trucks weren't cheap. Peyton remembered a day when she'd been a girl and was called in from the field to help load a truck. She'd stood beside the conveyor belt, tossing potatoes that had fallen off it back onto the belt. She remembered watching them tumble into the back of the truck before Claude, her father's most trusted employee, drove them to upstate New York. "Take it slow," her father had reminded Claude more than once. That truck, it had seemed to her back then, was worth as much as the farm itself to her father since the crop couldn't be delivered without it.

"You and your father ran the farm together, right?"

He looked at her, nodded, and she saw his face change.

"Jesus, he's gone. Really gone, eh?" And the tears came.

Fred Sr. had died nearly twenty-four hours ago. Maybe it had taken a day to sink in. She'd lost her own father, had spent a day traveling back from El Paso, had sat on one plane then the next, staring out the window, thinking about him, about the words *I'll never see him again*. Fred Jr. was doing that here.

"Who hired the truck drivers, Freddy?"

"Papa. I was in charge of the field, the kids, and the tractor drivers."

"Who hired Simon Pink?"

"What do you mean?" he said and shifted. "I told you already. Papa hired Simon," he said, pronouncing the dead man's name as his father had—*See-moan*.

"Was he the only truck driver?"

"Papa drove a load once in awhile, but we only have one truck. When it's on the road, if someone wants a load of potatoes, they send a truck to us, and we load it."

"What are your responsibilities during harvest?"

"I just told you, eh. I oversee the fields." The crying had subsided. He'd ridden the emotional wave, been distracted, and had gotten swept away. He'd catch the wave again and be exhausted in a few hours.

"Did your mother prepare a big midday meal during harvest?"

She remembered the noon meal her own mother cooked each day—meat, potatoes, dessert—the entire crew squeezing in on formal and folding chairs around the dining room table, her father leading the conversation. They'd covered local politics, sports, anything but the work at hand. The work was hard, and it would come later. The midday meal had been about welcoming these employees into her father's home. And he was respected for it. It was a tradition. She wondered if it still existed; hoped it did.

Fred Jr. shook his head.

"Hard to believe that after all the work you and your crew do in the field, you wouldn't want to know who, ultimately, is handling the potatoes, transporting them. I worked a bunch of harvests, Freddy, remember?"

"So what? I didn't shoot the guy, Peyton."

"Where were you Monday night?"

"I got an alibi," he said.

And with that statement, a red flag went up. Using the *A* word never made the suspect more credible.

"Let's hear it."

"I was with my girlfriend."

"All night?"

He smiled. "All night long."

"Lucky lady."

"Got that right."

"What's her name?" she asked.

"You going to call her?"

"You said she's your alibi," she said. "I bet you told her to anticipate a call."

"What's that supposed to mean?"

"Tell me her name."

"Nancy Lawrence. She teaches middle school," he said. "What
did I say?" he asked, eyes narrowing.

It had been an amateur mistake: she'd slipped, displayed her
disbelief that he and Nancy Lawrence were dating.

"Spend much time in the cabin behind your house?" she asked.

"No."

"When was the last time you were there?"

"Last fall."

"What's it used for?"

"What do you mean? It's just a cabin. What's it got to do with
the farm?" he said.

"I was hoping you could tell me, Fred. What was it built for?"

"Dad spent some nights out there."

"When?"

"Last year."

"Doing what?"

"Sleeping."

"Your mom go with him?"

Fred Jr. shifted, uncomfortable now. "No," he said. "Just Dad."

"There a reason for that?"

"It's private."

"Three people are dead," she told him. "We don't have time or a
reason now to keep things private."

"More reason to keep them private now than ever," he said.

"What do you mean, Freddy?"

He shook his head.

"Your mother throw your father out of the house?"

"I told you. It's private."

She leaned back in her chair. "Want more coffee?" she said. She wanted to know more about the cabin, but they had time. He wasn't going anywhere.

"I'll probably need it, the way this is going, eh."

"I'll get us some coffee," she said, "but one question before I go: Your dad told me you helped him roof the cabin. Is that right?"

"Yeah. So what?"

She stopped the recorder, pocketed it, and left the room.

———

She paused in the hall outside the interrogation room. The bullpen was at the end of the corridor, but she didn't walk to it. She stood, replaying bits of the conversation with Fred St. Pierre Jr. in her mind.

He'd announced that he had an alibi—a move that always looked suspicious—for the night Simon Pink was shot to death and his body torched. The details of the alibi would be checked, of course, but none of it felt right to Peyton.

Nancy Lawrence and Fred St. Pierre Jr.? An item?

Peyton knew Nancy Lawrence types. She'd gone to Garrett High School with plenty of them—teenage girls who acted (and often looked) much older than they were and who undeniably believed they were better than the local boys. Too-big-for-this-small-town types. She hadn't respected that mentality then, didn't now.

Or maybe her instant disbelief that Freddy was dating Nancy Lawrence said something else. Something about Peyton herself.

Maybe she'd grown cynical, her worldview soured after more than a decade as an agent. Had she jumped to a conclusion? Profiling could come in forms other than race and ethnicity. Maybe Nancy Lawrence *would* date a man like Fred Jr., a guy who wore Carhartt and had grease under his fingernails and smelled like fertilizer.

"Excuse me," a voice called from the bullpen, the tone slow and deliberate. "Where is my brother?"

———

Peyton turned around, looked down the hallway, and instantly recognized the former Sherry St. Pierre amid the desks in the area where Linda Cyr, the receptionist, sat.

"Where is my brother?" she repeated.

"Please, come sit down, ma'am," Bruce Steele, the station's lone K-9 handler, said, motioning to a chair near his desk.

"No thank you. I want to see Freddy. Now."

"Ma'am," young Miguel Jimenez said, "you really—"

"I said *now*!"

"Sherry," Peyton said, hustling toward her.

"Peyton?" Sherry said. "Peyton Cote?"

"Yeah, Sherry. I'm talking to your brother right now. He's cooperating fully."

Sherry shook her head. "The interview is over," she said.

"The interview is voluntary, Sherry," Peyton said. "Your brother is cooperating. I think he wants to know why it happened."

"My attorney—Freddy's attorney—will be here momentarily. The interview is over."

Gone were the faded Levi's and flannel shirts from high school. Wearing boot-cut DKNY jeans, high-heeled suede boots, and a cardigan over a white blouse, the sleeves of which were creased and cuffed neatly over the sweater, Sherry looked far more stylish than any professor Peyton remembered at the University of Maine. The only hint that she was an academic was her large-framed purple glasses. She figured Sherry had waved goodbye to Aroostook County on her way to Boston to attend the Harvard Kennedy School of International and Global Affairs and never looked back.

She also noticed the dark puffy rings around her one-time friend's eyes: the past two days had seen lots of tears.

Once the Portland-based lawyer arrived, Peyton knew the show was over. She wanted just a little more time with Freddy. To get it, she'd have to pacify Sherry.

"Bruce, can you take this coffee to Mr. St. Pierre?"

Steele stood and did so.

"Sherry, it's been a long time."

"Yes, it has."

"Too long," Peyton said and smiled.

Sherry paused, caught off guard, and, judging from her expression, momentarily forgot her brother, instead recalling a past the two women shared.

"More than fifteen years," Peyton said, thinking of when the girls were fourteen—and of the phone call during their freshman year that ended their friendship. She remembered, too, hearing Fred St. Pierre's deep murmuring voice in the background as Sherry had spoken that night.

"You're a professor now?"

"Yes," Sherry said.

Peyton had known people who achieved excellence to prove something to a parent and guessed Sherry was one of them. The woman's father had sure as hell given her motivation.

"Where's my brother, Peyton?"

"In that conference room." She pointed. "He's under no duress. He and I were just talking. Could you and I chat for a couple minutes?"

"What has he told you?"

Peyton thought about the question. Sherry would soon have access to every detail of the interview Fred could remember.

"Your brother told me he has an alibi for the night Simon Pink was killed."

"What is it?"

"Come with me," Peyton said and started walking before Sherry could argue.

———

"The past eighteen hours have been absolutely unfathomable," Sherry said. Peyton could smell Obsession perfume. "You have no idea what it's like. I mean, first my parents, then my brother. No one knows what this feels like."

"I'm sorry for your loss," Peyton said.

But Sherry wasn't listening. She muttered, "I didn't sign on for this."

They were in Mike Hewitt's office, Hewitt having offered to "step outside for a few minutes" when he saw Sherry following Peyton. Peyton was in Hewitt's high-backed leather chair; Sherry sat across the desk in the seat typically designated for visitors (or Peyton).

The situation wasn't new. Peyton had listened to someone who sat on the wrong side of the table make a statement or ask a question posed to evoke an emotional response hundreds of times: *Agent, you have kids? Know what it's like to not be able to care for them? You'd drive a car with birth certificates over the border, too, lady, if you couldn't feed your kids.* Once, a man had told her he'd smuggled drugs, simply driven a car through a border crossing, to earn money to get his wife cancer treatments. She'd caught him, and he'd gone to prison. That one was tough. Darrel Shaley. Peyton couldn't forget his name.

Each time someone posed a statement or question, she didn't respond. It did no good to do so because she knew emotional appeals didn't matter. Emotion had nothing to do with her job. She manned an international border and stopped contraband from entering or leaving. Period. But each time someone offered her the bait, she also remained silent for another reason: truth be told, she knew if life had dealt her a different hand, she couldn't say for certain she wouldn't be seated across the table, too.

Somehow this interview was different. Sherry's voice was matter-of-fact, not urging sympathy. And her eyes offered something else Peyton didn't expect. The woman she hadn't seen in close to two decades was reaching out to her; her eyes were desperate for someone to listen. So Peyton found herself returned to childhood, at the St. Pierre barn on a fall day, sunlight streaming through gaps between wall boards, slanting in, turning the hay golden, she and Sherry feeding horses apples. Then, years later in middle school, the horses gone, in Sherry's room, listening to music, talking about boys and basketball, and laughing. She remembered Sherry's laugh as if she'd heard it the day before. And, finally, the night during her freshman year, Peyton alone in the hallway outside the kitchen, Sherry's shaky voice over the phone cracking and finally breaking.

"I mean it," Sherry said. "Any idea what it's like to learn that your father did *that* to your mother? I mean, *how can that happen?*"

Sherry was crying now. Not sobbing. Not head in hands. Just staring straight ahead, tears in rivulets down her cheeks.

"I'm terribly sorry for your loss," Peyton said again. "I have fond memories of your parents."

"Not of my father," Sherry said. "I don't believe that for a second."

"I focus on the early years, Sherry. The times we had on that farm as kids. I have some wonderful memories of those days."

"Those days all ended after my freshman year. You know that better than anyone."

"Almost anyone," Peyton corrected.

"Yeah," Sherry said. "Not better than me."

"I remember the night you called," Peyton said. "I've thought about it for years."

Sherry tilted her head. "Really?"

"Sure. We'd been friends since first grade. Then, with one phone conversation, it was over."

"I couldn't see you anymore. Couldn't really see anyone. I had to call to tell you." Sherry turned away to look out the window at the Crystal View River.

Peyton followed her eyes. "From here, the river looks black. Water's cold."

"I owe you an apology, Peyton. I cut you out of my life."

"No."

"Yes, I did."

"Not you," Peyton said. "I knew it wasn't you. That's why I never stopped reaching out."

"You knew?"

Peyton nodded. "It took a while, but I figured it out. It wasn't you."

"You knew that?"

"Not immediately. But we all figured it out."

Sherry took a deep breath. "It's humiliating to hear that, even now. You all knew my father forced me to cut ties?"

"It's been twenty years, Sherry. Let it go."

But Sherry's eyes widened, then narrowed, and her bottom lip quivered momentarily. And Peyton realized the weight of what she'd just said.

"I shouldn't have said that, Sherry. It might not be easy to just 'let it go.' I don't know what it was like for you."

"To be alone, friendless, for four years of high school? Not too great. My father made me call you and say I couldn't see you anymore. He was behind me as I spoke. He just thought…" But she didn't finish.

Peyton leaned back in the leather chair, her hands folded calmly in her lap. "We all have to come to grips with our childhoods."

"You never stopped reaching out to me—sitting by me at lunch, in the library during free periods, picking me for teams in gym class. And I never told you what was really going on."

"It's over, Sherry."

"Four long years." Sherry's hand went absently to her earring.

Peyton noticed the large diamonds for the first time.

"My father had dreams for me. He thought I was wasting too much time. That was the farmer in him." Sherry spoke in a low, quiet tone, the way many did, Peyton realized, when recalling the deceased. "Farmers always think they can work harder. In my father's case, he passed that on to me. We call it *transference* in the social sciences. But it wasn't passed on—not genetically and not as a learned behavior. Instead, he forced me to call you that night, to tell you I wouldn't be—"

"Wasting time," Peyton finished her sentence for her.

"That's what I said that night, wasn't it?"

Peyton nodded.

"But not wasting time," Sherry said, "actually meant something else—coming home and studying four hours a night, having no weekends, no friends, no boyfriends."

"Looks like it all worked out for you. You went to Harvard, and now you're very successful."

Sherry looked at her. Peyton watched as Sherry's hands clasped the long sleeves of her cardigan, as if drying her palms.

"There are many definitions of *successful*," Sherry said.

"I made my peace with it long ago," Peyton said, "and I'm sure you did, too. Let's talk about your brother and—and I know this is difficult—about your parents a little. Your father said something I need to ask you about before he..." She didn't finish, but Sherry rubbed her palms on her thighs and nodded.

"He couldn't have killed her," she said. "It doesn't make sense."

"Sherry, I need to ask you something about your parents' final seconds."

"Oh God. When you say it like that," Sherry said, her hand flashing to her mouth.

Peyton thought the woman, who looked so confident, so self-directed, might wretch.

"I'm sorry," Peyton said, "but I need to ask you this."

"What is it? I can hear it. I probably need to."

"One of the last things your father said was, 'I hope she can forgive me.'" Peyton looked at Sherry, who pursed her lips, brows creased in deep contemplation. Then she shook her head abruptly.

"No idea," Sherry said. "*Who* will forgive him? My mother?"

"I don't think so," Peyton said.

"Was it you, Peyton? He wanted you to forgive them because he dragged you into their abusive relationship?"

"I don't know. But I don't think so. Do you have any other theories?"

"None," Sherry said, her voice suddenly serious. "Now, tell me what my brother is charged with."

TWELVE

"THIS WHOLE THING IS ludicrous," Sherry said almost three hours later, shaking her head. She shifted on her seat, opened her briefcase, and took out a collection of papers. She searched desperately for something.

They were in Garrett Station's only conference room: Hewitt, Stephanie, and a state police detective Peyton had never seen before were on one side the table. Sherry, attorney Len Landmark, Sherry's husband, Dr. Chip Duvall, and Fred Jr. sat across from them.

Peyton and Maine State Police Detective Karen Smythe sat on folding chairs along the far wall.

Fred had his hands before him, the metal cuffs clicking lightly against the tabletop. Landmark had an iPad propped before him and scrolled through his notes.

But it was Sherry who Peyton noticed. Peyton watched Sherry shuffle and reshuffle papers frantically, her eyes racing from the stack of uncooperative papers to Stephanie. Why was she focused so singularly on Stephanie? Because Stephanie was the opposing attorney, or because Stephanie sat as confidently as one preparing for a card trick they'd done a thousand times?

Sherry stared at Stephanie as if it were only the two of them in the room. Somehow, for some unknown reason, this wasn't about Freddy anymore. What was Sherry trying to prove to Stephanie? And why was it necessary?

Whatever was taking place between the two women was lost on Stephanie, who was ever organized and tougher than two scorpions. She looked at Sherry, puzzled.

Peyton wondered if this was the same Dr. Sherry St. Pierre-Duvall who lectured at a university, traveled extensively, and published books. This version of Sherry looked confused and kept turning to Chip for reassurance. He nodded, and she continued.

"My brother is guilty of nothing," Sherry suddenly demanded.

Peyton had never met Sherry's husband, but she didn't like the way Chip patted her thigh, as if calming a nervous Irish setter during a thunderstorm.

"Sherry," attorney Len Landmark said, "let me handle this. It's what you're paying me for."

Sherry turned to Chip once again. He nodded, and she gave way.

"I get so sick of wearing blue every day," Karen Smythe whispered, leaning close to Peyton. "At least with green, you guys can accessorize a little. Every winter hat I own has to be dark."

"The last winter hat I bought came from Marden's," Peyton said, mentioning the surplus and salvage chain store known statewide. "Not sure I'd call that accessorizing. And thanks again for taking on Hewitt for me."

"Stop saying that."

"No one else has gone to bat for me."

92

"No one else was there. It's why you don't need to thank me. I genuinely think Hewitt's going too far if you get a formal reprimand. I'm not getting one. You did nothing to warrant that."

Peyton checked her phone, making sure it was set to Silent. She motioned to the detective. "What happened to Leo Miller?"

"Out of his league. Pulled off the case."

"This new guy looks young," Peyton said.

"And cute as hell. Looks younger than he is, though. He's about thirty-five. Very competent. And single"—she eyed Peyton and smirked—"if that matters to you."

"A lot of media in town, huh?" Peyton said. "I got four calls at home about the murder-suicide."

"That a 'no comment' regarding the cute-as-hell new detective?"

"A lot of media, huh?" Peyton said again, but she was looking at the detective, while her mind lurched to Pete Dye and to how they'd left things between them.

"We'd like the First-Degree Murder charge dismissed," Landmark said.

"Good luck with that," Karen whispered.

Peyton had grown up with Sherry St. Pierre, but most of her childhood memories also involved Pete Dye. He'd been a neighbor. And, as he'd said, she'd invited him to her wedding. The thing Pete hadn't mentioned, though, was the night at Madawaska Lake: a May evening during their senior year at the University of Maine, when the bonfire had died, when Jeff had left the party early, and when she and Pete sat at the end of the dock, feet dangling in the sunfish-rippled water at three in the morning.

He'd leaned in to kiss her. And it was she who'd pulled back that night. How would her life be different now if she'd not honored her relationship with Jeff on that dock?

"We're not dropping any charges," Stephanie said.

"Look, you get very few murders up here," Landmark said, "so I just want you to know that I can—and will—prove that Mr. St. Pierre Jr. is nothing more than a hard-working, carefree soul, who loved and still lived with his parents. And I will show that he was a close friend of Simon Pink. Counselor, you're wasting the state's money. You need to rethink this."

"Don't you dare patronize me," Stephanie said. "I've got a degree from Harvard Law and worked on Beacon Street for Little and Little for ten years before coming back to northern Maine."

"You aren't the only professional woman here," Sherry said.

Stephanie had been about to say something more to Landmark, but turned to Sherry and stared, confused.

Chip patted Sherry's thigh again, and she settled back into her chair.

"I don't like that," Karen whispered. "He pats her like a damned dog."

Peyton was about to agree when Chip said, "Ms. DuBois, no one is questioning your credentials. We're worried about saving the taxpayers' money."

"Just exactly who are you?" Stephanie asked.

"I'm Sherry's husband, but that's not important—"

"Chip," Sherry said, "I can speak for myself."

"No," he said. "I'll handle this."

"Actually," Landmark said, "I'm your attorney. *I'll* do the talking, Chip."

"And Sherry's paying you," Chip said. "And from what I see so far, she's *over*paying you. So we'll do things my way."

"This is so typical," Sherry said, but there was no bite in her voice; she was pleading. "This is my brother—my family—can you let me have control?" She looked away and spoke to herself, but Peyton heard her: "For once, goddamnit, let me have control."

"Both of you," Len Landmark said, "it's time to be quiet. Stephanie and I will discuss this case."

"You're unbelievable," Sherry said with finality to Chip, who momentarily glared at her, then turned to stare out the window like a man searching for something.

"Here's the bottom line, counselor," Landmark continued. "Our client was at the Tip of the Hat bar at the time of the murder."

"What?" Karen whispered to Peyton. "He told you he was with Nancy Lawrence, right?"

"Yes."

Hewitt turned and glanced at Peyton. She replied by offering a quick shake of the head, which Landmark failed to register.

Hewitt leaned toward Stephanie and whispered.

"What is it?" Landmark said.

Stephanie ignored him.

"Well," Landmark went on, "the evidence is entirely circumstantial. And you have no witnesses."

Stephanie could be ruthlessly blunt. Peyton had always appreciated her lack of bullshit. But even she was surprised by Stephanie's next play.

"I have to be in court in twenty minutes, Len." She smiled politely, wiping a few gray dog hairs from her blazer. "We'll talk again later, I'm sure."

"So you're taking this forward?"

"We have a murder, an arson investigation, and a murder-suicide," she said. "I think it's a safe bet to assume we will take this forward, yes."

"They're separate cases, Stephanie."

Stephanie slid her yellow pad into her briefcase.

"And your evidence in the murder is entirely circumstantial," Landmark repeated.

"We have the .22 slug and, according to the ballistics report, the gun from which it was fired," she said.

"The killer took my brother's gun," Sherry insisted. "Can't you see that? What's wrong with you?"

Stephanie looked at her for a long moment. Peyton thought she saw pity in the DA's eyes.

Finally, Stephanie stood. "Like I said, I need to be in court in twenty. Good day."

THIRTEEN

AT 5:15 P.M., THE sheen of sweat covering her face was like a wel-comed visit from a long-lost friend.

Peyton was at the dojo. She'd earned her black belt before she'd earned her undergraduate degree. What she was doing couldn't be called simply "maintaining" her skills. And it wasn't practice. She was training—the runner who seeks continually to best her time.

Quiet. That was how she described her mind while at the dojo; bare feet stalking back and forth across the mat, hands slashing in charged movements. But her mind was quiet.

No work.

No ex-husbands.

No struggling sons.

No stalled relationships.

No complicated mother-daughter bonds.

No self-serving middle-school teachers.

No contradictory alibis.

Her mind played white noise as her hands and feet found a rhythm, punching and kicking—again and again—the leather mitts held by sparring partners.

The temperature had dipped to the upper sixties by the time she showered and headed to her Jeep Wrangler. The wind blew hard, carrying the unmistakably bitter odor of the nearby potato-processing plant.

This was her third Wrangler since college. The canvas top was an option her mother always scoffed at, given Aroostook County's climate, but Peyton loved the convertible in the summer and was willing to sacrifice (she kept leather mittens and a wool cap under the seat, November through March) in order to enjoy summer months with the top down.

Off duty, she had something in mind that required Mike Hewitt's approval: she wanted to arrive unannounced to interview one of the investigation's players. Hewitt likely wouldn't go for it for two reasons: it might require overtime pay, and, depending on how the conversation went, the after-hours home visit could be perceived as harassment.

But if she handled the situation well, Hewitt wouldn't have to know, and she might learn once and for all where Freddy St. Pierre was the night Simon Pink was murdered.

She exhaled and pulled onto Route 1, which she followed to State Route 164, knowing full well she'd be late for the dinner date she and Tommy made with her ex-husband, Jeff. She wouldn't have time to cook anything and would have to grab a pizza on the way home.

But that was all right.

It would force Jeff to spend a little time with his son.

———

Peyton parked her Jeep Wrangler next to a rusted Volkswagen Jetta, walked to the front door, and rang the bell.

Nancy Lawrence opened the door, and Peyton saw her eyes narrow in recognition—and saw the front door close slightly.

"May I help you?" Nancy said.

"I was in the area and had a couple questions," Peyton said. "Thought I'd swing by. I hope that's okay."

The house was a small Cape Cod a half-mile down a dirt road. There were no visible neighbors, no streetlights. Peyton looked for dogs but saw none. Maybe her years in El Paso left her leery, but she sure as hell would have a dog if she lived at the end of a rural dirt road.

"Questions about Tommy?" Nancy said. "Can't this wait until I'm at school? I mean, I don't have any new information for you."

Peyton glanced over Nancy's shoulder. Saw nothing conspicuous. "May I come in?" she said.

"I'm making dinner."

"This won't take long, Nancy. I promise."

"You're not even in uniform."

"But you know I'm not here to talk about Tommy."

Nancy admitted nothing, just stood staring at Peyton.

"This is pretty informal, Nancy. Just a couple quick questions."

Nancy Lawrence wore a skirt shorter than the one she'd had on at school, and her white blouse was tight with three buttons undone.

"That's a pretty blouse you're wearing. You must have plans."

Before she caught herself, Nancy nodded, but then said: "No. This is just what I wore to work today."

"Really? You wore that to work today?"

Nancy shuffled her feet. Would Peyton check to verify that statement?

"Actually," Nancy said, "I just threw it on tonight. Hey, I'm not doing anything. Sure, come right in." She held the door. "You can go to the living room."

But when Nancy went to the stove and stirred a pot of boiling pasta, Peyton followed her to the kitchen and took a seat at the table, which, interestingly, was set for two, complete with a bottle of red wine and a sliced loaf of Italian bread.

"Who's joining you?" Peyton asked.

"No one."

Peyton glanced at her watch. She couldn't play games all night. And Nancy Lawrence wasn't tough; she was used to dealing with school kids all day, so Peyton said simply, "Nancy, who's joining you."

"Why do you ask?"

"I'm curious. I haven't had a date in months," Peyton lied. "Actually, I'm envious."

Nancy looked at her, wondering. Was she on the level? Just two single women talking now?

"Just a friend," Nancy said and sat across from Peyton. She moved a fork an eighth of an inch, making sure it was perfectly positioned.

"You're not dressed to see 'just a friend.'" Peyton offered a discreet just-between-you-and-me smile. "Hoping he becomes something more?"

Nancy looked down shyly, suddenly a teenager who'd been asked to the dance by the star quarterback.

"Actually, it's a doctor from TAMC."

"Lucky girl. A doctor from The Aroostook Medical Center?" Peyton gushed. "My mother would be kicking me under the table, if she were here."

Nancy's proud smile widened.

"Been seeing him long?"

"On and off for a month."

Peyton nodded casually, looking around the kitchen. She didn't like lying, even when it led to necessary information. The appliances were stainless steel and didn't go with the room's decor. They looked new and, having just furnished a kitchen herself, they looked expensive.

"Nancy, tell me, how does Freddy St. Pierre feel about you dating someone else 'on and off for a month'?"

"Excuse me?"

Peyton smiled. "Where were you Monday night?"

Nancy looked at the plate before her and realigned the salad fork again. Then she stood and went to the stove to stir her pasta, her back conveniently to Peyton.

"Monday?" she said over her shoulder. "Why do you ask?"

Peyton heard Nancy's voice shake ever so slightly, indicating that Nancy realized two things: she'd been walked down the road, and the next question would force her to decide how badly she wanted to remain Freddy St. Pierre's alibi.

"Where were you Monday," Peyton repeated, "from seven p.m. until Tuesday at seven a.m.? And please know that I won't be the only one who'll ask you this."

Nancy gave the pasta one final whirl, then set the wooden spoon down, and took three strides toward the table. Standing before Peyton, she lifted her wineglass, poured some from the chilled bottle, and took two large drinks, her eyes never leaving Peyton's face. Nancy set the glass on the table and licked her lips slowly.

"I was . . . um, with Freddy."

"Fred St. Pierre Jr.?"

"Yes."

"All night?"

"Yes, that's correct. A one-time thing."

"A one-night stand?"

"You're making me uncomfortable," Nancy said, examining the toes of her black shoes. They were heels, a little too high for teaching fifth graders, but just right for a night out—or a very sexy night in. Peyton didn't own anything like them.

"I've got to say," Peyton said, "you don't seem like the type to have one-night stands. In fact, Freddy says you two are dating."

Nancy opened her mouth to speak, but then closed it and stood thinking, glaring at Peyton.

"Is Freddy wrong, Nancy?"

Nancy shifted her weight from one foot to the other.

"Were you at the Tip of the Hat Monday?" Peyton said.

"No, here. All night."

"He met you here?"

"Yes, that's right." But then Nancy's face reacted as she'd been pinched. "No, that's wrong."

"Which is it?" Peyton said. "I'm not asking tough questions. Just answer truthfully."

Nancy pursed her lips. Peyton hadn't realized how pale the middle-school teacher was.

"We met at the Tip of the Hat," Nancy said, "and came here after."

"You're sure?"

Nancy nodded.

"I mean," Peyton said, "I don't want you to say anything you didn't agree to say."

"What does that mean? I don't follow you."

Peyton smiled and offered silence. Nancy couldn't hold her stare. She looked down, and the toe of her right three-inch heel started tapping against the linoleum tile floor.

"Freddy doesn't seem like your type, Nancy."

"Why do you say that?"

"Well, for one thing, he's not a doctor."

"That's a judgmental statement. I could ask why you don't help your son more with his homework."

Peyton grinned. "Of course you could. Let's wrap this up. To review, on Monday, you met Fred St. Pierre Jr. at Tip of the Hat, came back here, and spent the entire night with him. Here. And neither you nor he left at any point during the night."

"Yes."

"And you're willing to testify to that?" Peyton said.

"Testify? I have to testify?"

"It's likely."

Nancy looked at her for a long time, then moved her eyes down. Peyton watched her blond bangs sway ever so slightly as she shook her head.

"Damn it," Nancy said, under her breath.

"I need an answer, Nancy."

"Yes. Fine. Then it's true."

The obviousness of the lie made Peyton smile. "Thank you," she said. "I'll show myself out."

And she did, pausing at the end of Nancy Lawrence's driveway. She swatted black flies and wondered why the woman agreed to lie for Freddy St. Pierre, even when faced with a court testimony.

———

It was 6:45 p.m. when she entered her kitchen, glanced at the counter, and sighed. Jeff had offered to "bring dessert." A box of eclairs and a two-liter of Coke were on the counter.

Which meant Thursday-night dinner consisted of pizza, eclairs, and Coca-Cola.

She put the pizza box next to the soda and wondered—for the millionth time—if she'd mistakenly put work ahead of her responsibilities as a mom. The detour to Nancy Lawrence's house yielded information: Nancy's version of her relationship with Fred St. Pierre Jr. (a one-night-stand) didn't jive with Freddy's version (she was his girlfriend). But at what cost had that information been gained? She was about to serve Tommy hamburger-and-green-pepper pizza (green pepper being the only vegetable he found palatable) and eclairs for dinner. (The Coca-Cola would go unopened and leave with Jeff, thank you very much.) If she'd come straight home, there would have been time to make spaghetti sauce, as planned. Now, though, the only one getting spaghetti (and who knew what else?) was Nancy Lawrence's doctor from TAMC.

Peyton heard the TV in the living room and went to see what Tommy and Jeff were watching.

Tommy was alone on the couch, holding his Nintendo DS, a fishing show on TV.

"Hey. Where's your dad?" she said.

He looked up. "Huh? I don't know. His phone rang. He said it was important."

She turned and crossed the kitchen, moved past the first-floor half-bath, and found Jeff in the office—her office—seated in her leather chair, talking on the phone. He'd taken the liberty of helping himself to her scratchpad. She saw he'd written *$147,500, 2BR, 1.5 BA. Fixer-upper. Resale value???*

He held up his index finger and smiled. "Almost done," he whispered.

"Take your time, Jeff. Your son, who hasn't seen you in three weeks, is only sitting alone in the living room."

She turned and walked out, closing the office door on him.

———

Self-doubt can be like an annoying itch.

And as she set three plates at the table and put the pizza in the oven to warm, she scratched that itch: Jeff had infuriated her by ignoring Tommy (once again) for business. But hadn't she done nearly the same thing by stopping at Nancy Lawrence's?

The Southern border had been a great place for an agent, but a late-night shootout told her it wasn't so great for a single mom. So, with her career on the rise, she'd left for the slower Northern border. For Tommy. Was she losing sight of that decision? Had she on this night?

"Tommy," she called into the living room, "come out here, please."

He shuffled across the kitchen and sat on a stool at the island.

"Tell me about your day."

"It was fine."

"Tell me about it."

"I hate school," he said.

"Why?"

The office door opened, and Jeff walked out. "Sorry, pal. You'll understand when you grow up," he said. "Got to stay ahead of the competition. You understand, right?"

Tommy was looking down. "Sure, Dad."

———

"I feel like nobody talks when we eat dinner with Dad."

Peyton was upstairs with him at nine o'clock. Tommy was in his PJs, under the covers, and she'd just finished helping him read a chapter from *Peter and the Starcatchers*.

Perceptive as hell, she thought.

"You and your dad talked at dinner," she reminded him.

"No. Not really, Mom. He asked what my favorite sport is. He already knows that."

Or should, she thought.

"You and Dad didn't talk," Tommy said.

"Sure we did."

"No. You only talk to Mr. Dye."

She leaned forward and kissed his cheek. "I talk to lots of people, sweetie, including your dad. Now get some rest." At the door, she clicked off the light, and said, "You know how much I love you?"

"Yes, Mom. You tell me every day."

And every day is never enough, she thought, for maybe the thousandth time.

FOURTEEN

WHAT IS IT ABOUT friendships that continuously draw us back?
Peyton wondered, as she climbed out of her service vehicle Friday
morning shortly after eight.

She was, in fact, realizing that some friendships, a select few,
never end; even when you thought they were dead, it turns out
they were just teetering on life-support for more than a decade.

Sherry St. Pierre, now Sherry St. Pierre-Duvall, Ph.D., had called,
sobbing, and asked to talk. So Peyton was answering the call.

The bell chimed as the door to Gary's Diner shut behind her.
Peyton went to a window booth and slid in across from Sherry.

"Sherry, you sounded really upset on the phone," she said.

Sherry nodded. "Thanks so much for coming. I hope I didn't
call too early. I couldn't sleep."

The call came at 7 a.m. sharp, but Peyton shook her head.

"We shared a room for a month," Peyton said, "so you know
I'm an early riser."

"When I lived with you?" Sherry said.

Peyton didn't comment on that, just said, "I was already awake, making Tommy's breakfast."

"That was a hard time for me," Sherry said.

Peyton knew it had been. Sherry's father had heard Freddy teasing his ninth-grade sister about kissing a boy at a dance. Fred had become enraged and grounded his daughter. When Sherry tried to rebel by experimenting with alcohol and sex (at least that was Peyton's armchair analysis, years later), her father had thrown her out of the house. With nowhere to turn, she'd lived with the Cotes for a month.

"I'll never forget your family," Sherry said. "Few people have been so kind to me. I'll never forget that."

Peyton tried not to notice the whoopie pies diner owner Francine Morgan was sliding into a glass case near the cash register. But whoopie pies were, after all, Maine's official dessert. And, judging from the aroma, this batch was fresh from the oven. *Focus on bran muffins*, she told herself.

Tina Smythe, Maine State Police Detective Karen Smythe's older sister, approached with a coffeepot. Her T-shirt, beneath the apron, was green with the acronym NMCC across the front. Tina was taking evening classes toward an associate's degree at Northern Maine Community College and waiting tables at Gary's by day.

"Regular coffee, Peyton?"

"Yup. Just black. Good memory, Tina. And"—her eyes, once again, ran to the whoopie pies—"can I get a damned bran muffin?"

Tina followed Peyton's eyes and chuckled. "You and my sister. So self-disciplined. I bet you already ran today."

"Not true," Peyton said.

Tina went to the counter to check on a man eating *ployes*, a thin pancake-like food made with buckwheat flour that people in the region had enjoyed for years. Peyton watched him carefully roll one, dip it into maple syrup, and eat it. Shepherd's pie and *ployes*—two foods her mother prepared better than anyone on the planet. Lois's shepherd's pie was loaded with salt and her *ployes* were carb-heavy, but nothing tasted better.

Gary's was the hub of the green-and-white John Deere-hat-wearing universe at this time of day. The parking lot was lined with pickups. In a landscape of flannel and jeans, a blond, narrow-waisted college professor dressed in a sleek pantsuit and suede boots sitting with an auburn-haired uniformed Border Patrol agent drew looks.

Sherry glanced around. "Sometimes I miss living up here. It really is a simpler life."

"What makes you say that?"

"You can trust people here."

"Can't trust people in southern Maine?"

"Can't trust people many places," Sherry said, "can you?"

Peyton just sipped her coffee.

"I shouldn't have bothered you," Sherry said. "Maybe I just get myself overwhelmed."

"You were crying pretty hard when you called," Peyton said. "I was worried about you. Where's your husband?"

"I've been thinking about things since yesterday. I feel like the world is coming at me a thousand miles an hour."

"Understandable," Peyton said. "The loss of your parents and the accusations against your brother—the past forty-eight hours must've felt like a whirlwind." Peyton glanced around. "Again, I'm sorry for your loss. Is your husband joining us?"

"No. I told him I needed to talk to you alone."

"Why, Sherry?"

"I don't want him to hear us talk." Sherry looked down at her coffee mug; it was nearly empty.

"You sound like you're trying to protect him from something. What do you need to talk to me about?"

"It's just that I haven't seen you in so long, but I never forgot you. There have been so many times, over the years, when things made me stop and think that maybe you were the only one who ever really understood me. And that's because you knew my father, knew what he was like."

"I've thought about you over the years, too," Peyton said, "and what I think is that it must have been hard to be in your house, with your father. He was one of the most domineering people I ever met."

"He just wanted the best for us," Sherry said.

Peyton said nothing. She didn't wish to speak ill of the dead.

"He knew I had academic potential. He was right. But in other ways he made my life so difficult."

"In what ways?" Peyton asked.

Sherry shook her head.

Tina returned with Peyton's muffin and freshened Sherry's coffee. Sherry stirred in cream.

Moving on autopilot, Peyton took out her iPhone and checked her emails. Nothing pressing. But she wasn't really interested in messages. She was buying time. And thinking.

What did Sherry have to say that her husband couldn't hear? And from what did he need protection?

"You come back to the area often?" Peyton asked, casually sliding her phone back into her cargo-pant pocket.

"Why do you ask? What reason would I have to visit this area?"

"I imagine your folks wanted to see their grandchildren," Peyton said, realizing she'd used the past tense. She wasn't sure Sherry picked up on it.

"Actually, Chip has taken them here more than I have in recent years. I've been traveling for work."

"Where?"

"Where what?"

"Where have you traveled?"

Sherry made a little flutter with her right hand. "It's not important."

"You're talking to a single mom who works fifty hours a week and hasn't traveled outside the country, beyond distances she can walk to from a Border Patrol vehicle, in ten years. Humor me."

"I spend a lot of time in Prague, actually. It's a focal point of my research."

"Prague?"

"Yes, why?"

"You go there alone?"

"Yes, why?"

Marie St. Pierre and Simon Pink had plane tickets for Prague. But Peyton said only, "I hear it's a romantic city."

"Yeah, it is. But when I go, I'm there to research."

"Have your parents ever been there?"

"My parents? Why would they go?"

Peyton shrugged. "I have no idea. Maybe on an anniversary."

"You knew my father, Peyton. Romance wasn't exactly high on his list of priorities."

Peyton sipped more coffee. "What are you researching?"

"Why?" Sherry ate some Cheerios.

"Sherry, I haven't seen you since high school." Peyton wrapped both hands around her porcelain mug. MPG, the Maine Potato Growers' initials, were painted green across the side. "And you called my home, sobbing, at seven a.m. And you're on your way, I assume, to visit your brother, who's sitting in a holding cell, facing First-Degree Murder charges. I'm trying to start a light-hearted conversation."

Sherry set her spoon down and looked away again. "You always were a good friend. Most of my research has to do with the political landscape in the Czech Republic." Her cell phone chirped then. She retrieved it from her purse, looked at the caller ID, and sent the call to voicemail.

"You don't want to take that?" Peyton said.

"No."

"But your phone said 'Chip.'"

Sherry shook her head.

To the left of their window, three cars away, a light-green Ford Escape idled in the parking lot. The raven-haired driver sat reading. Peyton watched him turn the page of his book.

"What are you looking at?" Sherry asked.

But Peyton realized that Sherry, too, was looking at the man.

"Same thing you are," Peyton said. "That man. Never seen anyone sit in this parking lot before. Usually people come in, sit at the counter or a booth."

"I'm not looking at him," Sherry said.

"Jesus, look at his hand."

"That's a terrible thing to say."

"Not really," Peyton said and thought of the destroyed cabin. "I'm genuinely curious about what happened to him."

She had reason to be: Sherry St. Pierre-Duvall's mother had seen two men walking toward the cabin before the fire and explosion.

112

Simon Pink may or may not have been one of them; that left at least one suspect at large. Peyton retrieved her phone and made a note of the green Escape's license plate.

From fifty feet away, she could tell the man was missing two fingers and saw smooth strawberry skin, the result of a traumatic injury. She guessed a burn. But his wounds didn't look recent: no bandages.

"Well, I don't think his hand looks that bad," Sherry said.

Peyton shifted in her seat. The butt of her .40 was digging into her back.

"Peyton," Sherry said, and she pushed her cereal away, "I need to talk about my brother."

"Don't you want your attorney to do that?"

"Peyton, Freddy didn't kill anyone. He's innocent. You've known Freddy since we were young. You can't honestly think he'd kill anyone."

Peyton sipped some coffee.

"You won't tell me what you think?" Sherry said.

"Did you know your brother was dating Nancy Lawrence?"

"Yeah, sure, of course," Sherry said, and quickly looked out the window, focusing on the man in the green Escape.

Peyton didn't for one second believe Nancy Lawrence was dating Freddy St. Pierre. And given Sherry's inability to hold her gaze, she doubted Sherry did either.

"If your brother is innocent, I'm sure the system will bear that out."

"You can't actually believe that," Sherry said. "You and I both know many innocent people are on death row in this country."

"Well, I believe in the criminal-justice system," Peyton said.

"But you know it's flawed."

"I have faith in it, Sherry."

"You have to, because it's your job. But you know Freddy."

"What is it, exactly, you want from me?"

"Can't you talk to the state police, tell them—"

"That's why you wanted to meet with me?"

"I wanted to meet with you because I need a friend right now."

Peyton looked at her. "Okay, but think about this, Sherry. What are you asking me to tell the state police?"

"It might sound crazy, but it isn't. You can vouch for Freddy's character."

"Sherry, you know the system doesn't work like that."

Sherry dropped her head into her hands. "I know. I know." Her voice was muffled. "I'm just in over my head."

"In what?"

"I'm just overwhelmed, Peyton."

When Sherry looked up, her eyes were pleading. Peyton had seen the look before: desperation. Sherry needed someone, just one person, to understand.

"I'm so tired of always relying on other people," Sherry said, "of always needing other people."

"Sherry, what was your mother's relationship with Simon Pink?"

"He worked on the farm for a time, I think."

Sherry was a worrier, and Peyton saw the little frown lines tighten at the corners of her eyes.

"You think?"

"Freddy would know, Peyton. I haven't been around a lot."

"Your mother was planning to fly to Prague with Simon Pink."

"Why?" Sherry said, looking at her coffee. She'd already added cream but spooned in more. "This coffee is weak," she said.

"In fact, locals bitch about how weak it is," Peyton said. "So why are you adding more cream, Sherry?"

"Huh? I'll be right back." Sherry stood and then was gone from the booth, heading to the ladies' room.

Peyton ate part of her bran muffin. She looked at the whoopie pies as she chewed. The muffin had all the flavor of a shoebox.

At quarter to nine, the morning crowd had thinned, and the chime of the bell on the front door drew her eyes. Peyton waved, and Dr. Chip Duvall approached the booth.

"I'm Peyton Cote. Sherry is in the ladies' room."

Chip introduced himself. "Sherry has talked about you from time to time over the years."

"Have a seat," Peyton said.

He did, and said, "You're exactly as she described you."

"How's that?"

"Confident. She notices that in other people," he said.

Tina was back to take his coffee order.

Sherry approached the booth, head down, hand in her purse. She looked up at Chip and was startled.

"Oh, hello, sweetie. I'm surprised to see you."

"I used the lost-phone app to find your phone and figure out where you were," he said.

"I see. Please don't be angry."

"Where were you last night?"

"Writing. The book is going well. My research is coming together. I had to make some overseas phone calls and didn't want to keep you up. So I went down to the other room."

"I'd like to know where you are, at least," he said.

Sherry stared at her coffee. "Coffee's very good here," she said in a voice that was nearly a whisper. Then she caught herself, "But it's a little weak. Or maybe I just added too much creamer. You know how I always screw things up."

When Peyton had pleaded with Sherry to argue with her father, to tell him that he couldn't choose her friends for her, Sherry had said no. She just couldn't bring herself to stand up to him, didn't have it in her. And now, despite her academic prowess and publications, she was still blaming herself—even for weak coffee.

"Where are you guys staying?" Peyton asked.

"The Hampton Inn in Reeds," Sherry said.

"Or at least one of us is," Chip said.

"I've been very busy writing. And now planning a funeral and even trying to help with my brother's defense," Sherry said. "I haven't spent as much time with you as I need to. That's my fault."

"Sherry," Chip said, "he drove away as soon as I pulled in."

Peyton felt like she had when she'd searched Marie St. Pierre's bedroom—like a peeping Tom, given access to the personal lives of people she once knew well. Sherry's relationship was rocky, and Peyton didn't need to know that.

"I need to get to work," Peyton said, trying to politely recuse herself from the conversation.

"Before you go, Peyton, tell me what my father said before he … before …"

Had Sherry asked her this already? Grief made people do strange things, including forgetting. It wasn't easy to replay the murder-suicide.

"Your father said he was sorry just before he shot your mother."

"Good God. Sorry for shooting her?"

"I don't know what he was apologizing for. I was hoping you might be able to fill in some blanks for me."

"Well, I cannot," Sherry said, her voice now formal and slow as if speaking to a stranger.

Sherry leaned her head against Chip's shoulder, a move that clearly caught him off-guard. He seemed to stiffen before awkwardly draping his arm around her, a gesture meant to comfort her, but one that, like Sherry's speech, was far too formal.

Peyton felt like she was watching a stage performance. What was going on with this couple? And where had Sherry spent the night?

"My parents didn't always get along," Sherry said. "You know that."

"Is that where Simon Pink comes in?"

"I don't know what you're talking about. But my parents are dead, Peyton. Respect their memory, please."

Peyton sipped some coffee. "Sherry, your father was ordering your mother around while I was interviewing them."

"He treated everyone that way, but mostly women."

"Your mother was a classy lady with a lot going for her. She shouldn't have stood for it."

"That's easier said than done, Peyton. She couldn't support herself. And not everyone is independent."

"He hit your mother. That's why I was there. When she called the police, I went as backup."

"Why would she call for help? She didn't need help."

"Did you hear me, Sherry? He hit her."

"That's nothing new."

"Did he ever hit you?"

"He wasn't a bad man. And that's all in the past. I don't want to get into it. The past is over."

"The past is never over, Sherry. That's probably why you called me."

No one spoke then, each of them thinking their own thoughts.

"He was getting worse," Chip finally said. "I wanted him to get a physical. I was concerned that he was getting clogged arteries. He smoked for years, ate terribly, and didn't exercise."

Tina returned and asked Chip if he wanted to order. He shook his head.

"My parents are gone," Sherry said. "I can't lose my brother, too. That would be too much." She took in a deep breath. "We'll handle it."

"So let me help," Chip said.

"Not you," Sherry said.

"Who, then?" Chip asked.

Sherry shook her head. Then she turned to Peyton. "This is about that little slut Nancy Lawrence," Sherry said, growing animated, reaching for her coffee, spilling some.

Peyton was surprised but ignored the slur. "She's your brother's alibi, Sherry."

"No. He was at Tip of the Hat when Simon was killed." Her hand bumped the coffee cup again. Some sloshed over the rim. She inhaled, calming herself, and wiped the coffee with a napkin.

"Did you know him?"

"Who?"

"Simon Pink," Peyton said. "You said that like you knew him."

"No. I read his name in the paper."

That, Peyton thought, *was a mistake: a blatant lie.* There was no way the name of the man her brother was charged with killing hadn't come up in conversations with her brother or his attorney, especially if she and Chip were funding the defense.

Peyton looked at Tina and raised her finger. Tina nodded and prepared her bill.

"I don't trust Nancy Lawrence," Sherry said.

"How do you know her?" Peyton said.

"She went to school with us."

"She has to be ten years younger than we are," Peyton said.

Sherry stared at Peyton, silently. Her eyes opened and closed slowly, as if she were trying to focus.

When Tina brought the bill, Sherry said, "We'll get this, Peyton."

But Peyton insisted on paying herself.

When she got outside, the green Ford Escape, driven by the man with the deformed hand, was gone.

Peyton sat in the early-morning sun with her truck idling and watched the Duvall couple through the window. Chip spoke and pointed his finger at Sherry, who sat with shoulders slumping. The image reminded Peyton of Sherry as a little girl, of a cold winter day in Sherry's bedroom when her father had burst in, pointed his finger, and scolded his daughter in front of Peyton.

Sherry St. Pierre was now Sherry St. Pierre-Duvall. She had a Ph.D., had authored books, and traveled the world. But men, it seemed, were still telling her what to do.

And she was still letting it happen.

FIFTEEN

A HALF-HOUR LATER, PEYTON entered the interrogation room
with two cups of coffee.

"Eh, Christ," Freddy St. Pierre said. "You have any idea what it's
like to sit in a cell staring at the wall all day?"

She shook her head. "So I bet you're glad to have company."

"Where's my attorney?" he said.

"Probably working on your defense. We can wait for him, if
you want. That's your right, and it's totally up to you, Freddy. But I
don't think it's necessary. I just want to chat for a few minutes."

She slid the paper cup of Tim Hortons coffee across the table
and smiled at him. "Take it with cream and sugar?"

His eyes narrowed. "I hear they want to move me to Houlton,"
he said.

She didn't reply, but a move to the county jail could only improve
his wardrobe: he still wore the jeans and flannel shirt he'd worn the
day before, and, judging from the scent—a rich odor like sweat
mixed with manure—it was time he donned the orange jumpsuit.

"Troop F Headquarters is in Houlton," she said, "and this is a murder investigation. So it makes sense that they'd want you near the state-police barracks."

He drank some coffee. "But I want to stay here."

"You're going to be in a cell either way, Freddy."

He turned and looked out the window lined with bars. In the distance, like a reminder of all that had been lost, lay a potato field. Weeks from now, it would be a aglow with white blossoms, a prelude to the late-summer harvest. And then Aroostook County would brace for its annual hundred inches of snow, which made winter, not summer, the tourist season in this part of Maine. Up here, when it came to drawing visitors, lobsters gave way to snowmobile trails.

"Unless I make bail," he said.

"At a hundred thousand dollars?"

"It's steep, I know. But it ain't just about me, eh."

"What are you talking about?" she said. "What isn't just about you?"

Dark rings encircled his eyes, and his head bobbed slightly like a man either about to cry or nod off. His hands rested silently atop the Formica tabletop, one atop the other, fingernails caked with dirt. Then he reached for his warm paper cup and gently wrapped his hands around it.

He stared at the cup with the intensity of a man lost at sea spotting a life preserver.

"What is it, Freddy? You're focused on that coffee cup like it's the Holy Grail. What's going on?"

"I just … I need something to stare at."

"Why?"

"It's crazy," he said. "You won't believe me."

"Try me."

"I don't want to leave the farmhouse, eh. Don't want to be that far away from it."

"Houlton's only forty-five minutes," she said. "I don't understand."

"It's the last place I saw her happy," he said.

"Your mother?"

He nodded and turned away like Tommy sometimes did when she brought up Jeff McComb, Tommy's father, the man they'd moved back for Tommy to be near. The one Tommy rarely saw.

Except Freddy St. Pierre was in his thirties. So he was right: it was a little crazy.

Then again, who was she to say? She didn't know what it felt like to learn your father, the man you spent every day of your life with, even as an adult, had murdered your mother and then killed himself. And now the life you'd known was gone, like a puff of smoke lost in the wind.

She looked across the table.

When Freddy looked away—because his eyes were watery— she knew the time was right.

"Tell me about Nancy Lawrence, Freddy."

"She's my girlfriend."

Peyton handed him a napkin. I wasn't just a sympathetic gesture; she wanted him to know she'd seen him cry. The show of emotion was a demonstrative weakness, one most men were reluctant to show a female who, given their opposite places at this conference table, held power over them.

It had to be the right type of man, but sometimes, she'd learned, you could use his chauvinistic instincts to your advantage.

Freddy wiped his eyes and blew his nose.

"So I imagine," Peyton said, "that Nancy has come to visit you here."

"She's my girlfriend," he repeated.

"She's, what, six, eight years younger than you?"

He shrugged. "So what?"

"How many times has she been here to see you, Freddy?"

He didn't say anything, staring at his coffee cup.

"How long have you been dating?"

"Not too long."

"And you were with her the night the cabin burned?"

He looked up. He liked this question. "Yup," he said, his voice growing confident, like a student who'd been given the test question beforehand.

"How'd you meet her?" Peyton asked.

"Meet her?"

"Yeah, how'd the two of you meet?"

"Same as how I met you," he said. "We all grew up together."

"But she's younger than you and I. I don't remember much about her. How'd you two start dating?" She sipped some coffee and leaned back in her seat, just two old friends chatting.

"At Keddy's one night," he said. "Just started dancing one night. You know how it goes."

"No. How does it go?"

"Just started dancing, and ..."

"... and you went home together?"

"Yeah."

"To her house or yours?"

"Hers," he said. "I live with my parents."

Or did, she thought.

"And now you two see each other often?"

He pushed away from the table but didn't stand. He looked down, eyes focused on the table leg. She knew he didn't want to get into specifics.

"Freddy, does that question bother you?"

"No."

"Do you spend a lot of nights at Nancy Lawrence's house," she said, "or was Monday an aberration?"

"A what?"

"Was Monday a one-time thing?" she said.

He drank some coffee, then set the cup down. "I'd like to see my attorney now."

"We both know this isn't adding up, Freddy. If you didn't shoot Simon Pink, why do you have a bullshit alibi for the night he died?"

"I want my lawyer."

She shrugged and stood. "One final question, Freddy: why did your father really let Simon Pink go?"

Freddy stared at her, his jawbones flexing like a man struggling to hold back an outburst.

"I think I know the answer to that question. And I think it has to do with an upcoming trip your mother had planned."

"You don't know nothing," he said, but his eyes wouldn't meet hers.

At the door, she said, "You know where I am, if you want to talk. And if you do talk honestly, I might be able to keep you from going to Houlton."

He opened his mouth, but then closed it.

"One more thing," she said. "Yesterday, you told me you 'didn't exactly know' Simon Pink but you also admitted you shingled the roof of the cabin last fall. Only three of you worked on that roof,

Freddy—you, your dad, and Simon. How well did you really know Simon Pink?"

"I want my lawyer, Peyton."

"That's a good idea, because your lawyer told the prosecuting attorney he intended to prove that you and Simon were friends to show that you'd never hurt him. You two might want to get on the same page, Freddy."

When he didn't take the bait, she walked out.

———

It was 10:30 a.m. when she paused at the stationhouse coffee maker, saw the no-named coffee tin on the counter, and weighed her options: How tired was she? How badly did she need coffee? Was the kick worth the bitter taste? And, finally, when the hell would someone open a Starbucks in Aroostook County?

She poured a cup, diluted it with a lot of milk, and went to Hewitt's office.

"Plates on your green Ford Escape," he said, "are registered to a rental agency."

She sat down across his desk from him. "One of the two rental places at the airport?"

Aroostook County had only the tiny Northern Maine Regional Airport in Presque Isle. A puddle jumper to Boston's Logan International was required to fly anywhere beyond New England.

"No," Hewitt said. "Hertz out of Boston. Your professor friend is the name on registration."

"Sherry St. Pierre-Duvall rented the Ford Escape?"

"Her name," he said, nodding. "Her Visa card. That mean something to you?"

"Not sure," she said.

It meant that Sherry St. Pierre-Duvall obviously knew the man with the disfigured hand. It explained why she'd jumped to his defense when Peyton mentioned how bad the hand looked. But she had offered no indication that she knew him. And why had he remained outside?

"Something isn't adding up," she said.

"Like what?" Hewitt said.

"Not sure," she said, "but I just talked to Freddy St. Pierre for about twenty minutes."

"Jesus, Peyton." He leaned back in his chair and shook his head. "What?"

"He's in state police custody."

"He's in our building."

"Peyton, you interviewed the guy with no attorney present. And without telling the state police you were doing so."

"He volunteered to talk, Mike."

Hewitt said something under his breath, then: "So you think something's there with the Nancy Lawrence alibi?"

"I know there is," she said. "She would no more date Freddy St. Pierre than you would."

"So where do we go from here?"

"I might have indicated that if he were to talk to me," she said, "we might be able to keep him here."

"*Might have* indicated that, huh? As opposed to him going to the state-police barracks?"

"Anyone ever tell you that you have a way of looking at the negative side of things?"

"My ex-wife," he said. "What the hell difference does it make? A jail cell is a jail cell."

She told him Freddy's rationale.

"So he's as crazy as his old man," Hewitt said.

Empathy wasn't Hewitt's strong suit, so she wasn't about to try to explain Freddy's reasoning.

"And do you plan to ask the state police—who, oh, by the way, are running this murder investigation—if Freddy can stay with us? You going to tell them he misses his mommy and he's happier here?"

She grinned. "Anyone ever say you have a tendency to make things sound worse than they are?"

"My ex-wife," he repeated, "all the time."

"I'm just trying to get him to talk, Mike. I've known him a long time. He'll open up to me before he opens up to the state cops. And I didn't break any laws. I told him we could wait for his lawyer before I asked questions."

"I know you want to figure this out. You know all the players involved. But rein it in, please."

"Yes, sir."

"I mean it," he said. "You're involved in this thing because the cabin is near the border, and you were there when the murder-suicide took place. State police is still running the show."

"Of course they are."

"Is that sarcasm?"

"From me?"

He leaned back in his seat, head tilted. "I know seeing the murder-suicide was tough," he said. "Has the counseling team contacted you?"

"There was a message on my phone. I'm fine."

"Sometimes it's good to talk to somebody."

"I'm fine, Mike. Really."

———

Peyton was at her desk, reading an email from Detective Karen Smythe. Karen wrote that with only four state troopers assigned to cover all of Aroostook County, the stateys were more than willing to utilize the feds. It meant Fred St. Pierre Jr. would continue being babysat at Garrett Station for a few more days. As it turned out, Freddy wasn't going anywhere after all.

Peyton looked toward Hewitt's open door; he'd been CCed on the email, and she knew he'd be cursing her "luck" under his breath.

She had sixty-five unread emails and was hitting the Delete key with the speed and fervor of a videogamer when a Tim Hortons coffee was placed next to her keyboard.

She looked up and smiled at Pete Dye.

"School year is almost over," she said.

"With all the snow days we had this year, I feel like we're going until the Fourth of July."

"Thanks for the coffee," she said. "Damned email has me chained to the desk."

Dye was wearing a white button-down with a tie and khaki pants. He shifted from one foot to the other as if he'd been standing there for an hour.

"I owe you for dinner the other night," he said.

She pushed away from her desk and swiveled to look him in the eye.

"That's why you brought coffee?"

"Sorry I haven't called or texted," he said. "I've been busy."

During their conversation in her driveway, he said he'd call the next day. She hadn't heard from him. So the coffee was an apology.

"I don't run a restaurant," she said.

"I don't follow you."

"There are no IOUs after I invite someone to dinner, Pete. I invited you because I wanted to spend time with you."

"I didn't mean it like that," he said, looking around.

Linda Cyr was the only other person in the bullpen and, once again, was acting like she wasn't listening to an agent's private conversation, eyes focused on her Sudoku. (Peyton often kidded her, saying, "We'd have found bin Laden in half the time, if we had Linda working Intel.") Hewitt's office door was now closed. Six other agents were on duty and already in the field.

"I'm trying to figure out where you and I go from here," he said.

"Let's keep it simple."

"I thought that's what we've been doing," he said. "I was hoping we could take a step forward." He looked at Linda, who was still trying to act engrossed in her puzzle.

"This about sex again?" Peyton said.

"Not sex," he said. "Commitment."

She heard chair wheels grind. Then Linda stood, crossed the room, and went to the breakroom, closing the door behind her.

"Well," Peyton said, "sex doesn't mean commitment for everyone."

"But I know it does for you," he said.

She looked at him then, head tilted. "Just for me?" she said. "Not for you, because you're a player?"

He shifted and plunged his hands into his khaki pockets. "I'm a history teacher in northern Maine," he said. "That's what I am."

And, she had to admit, a very cute one.

"All I'm saying," he went on, "is that I recognize that it's not the same for me. I'm not a single mom. I don't have as much to lose."

"So you understand why I hesitate."

"Completely."

"Tommy is always priority one," she said.

"I just want to be with you," he said. "I've waited a long time."

"I don't believe for one second that you've been crying into your pillow for the last decade," she said. "In fact, your bed has rarely been empty, and we both know it."

"I'm thirty-five years old," he said. "And my bed has been empty for the past year."

She shifted some papers on her desk. Was that true?

"How about dinner tonight?" he said.

"Keddy's?" she said.

"Someone told me they don't call it that anymore," he said.

"That's my line." She had to smile.

"I'll get you at seven," he said and smirked as he walked away.

When the front door closed behind him, Linda walked out of the breakroom.

"Peyton," she said, and shook her head, "with those blue eyes and that blond hair, if he was any cuter, and I was any younger, you'd have your hands full trying to keep him."

"My hands are already full with that," she said, turning back to her screen, "believe me."

"Want to tell me all about it?" Linda said, eagerly.

"No, I certainly do not."

"Damn," Linda said, and went back to her Sudoku.

A new email had entered Peyton's inbox. She opened the attachment from the state lab and read it. She did not delete this one. Instead, she immediately knocked on Hewitt's office door.

———

Hewitt was nodding when she re-entered.

"You read the state lab's report," he said.

She sat across from him again. Through the window, the sun was over the Crystal View River, the natural boundary between the US and Canada. She remembered the man they, along with two game wardens, had pulled from there—a bloated, blue corpse whose pockets had been stuffed with air-packed marijuana. Had he fallen from a boat or tried to swim from one side to the other? Thinking of the dead man reminded her that they'd never learned the answer.

"So they definitely weren't making crystal meth in that cabin," she said. "Hard to believe Fred St. Pierre Sr. didn't know about what was going on in his cabin."

"Maybe that explains why he killed his wife and himself," Hewitt said.

"To avoid being accused of making bombs?"

"Slow down," Hewitt said. "You took two steps and jumped to the crystal meth lab, and that was wrong. We have no idea for certain what they were doing. This is Fred St. Pierre, we're talking about here, by all accounts a simple farmer."

Something was tugging at her from her mind's periphery.

What was it?

What had she missed?

"They had urea nitrate, a fertilizer-based explosive, and hydrogen-gas cylinders," she said.

"Is it possible that the hydrogen was being used for something to do with the farm?"

"Come on, Mike."

"Peyton, I'm no farmer. I really don't know."

"If this were any other place in the US, *you'd* be telling *me* they were making bombs."

"Not necessarily true."

"They were making explosives," she said. "That's why I found a shingle fifty feet away."

Hewitt said, "See if the neighbors ever heard explosions."

"Already on my to-do list."

"What else is on your list?"

"You hate it when I show initiative," she said, "don't you?"

"I hate it when you go off on your own because I usually get a phone call from Sector Headquarters."

"That's only happened twice," she said.

He sighed. "Please talk to Freddy's sister again."

"Also on my to-do list," she said. "One guy I interviewed told me Simon Pink had a chemistry background."

Hewitt moved a legal pad to where he could see it and reviewed his notes. "Things don't look good for Freddy St. Pierre. The DA likes the murder charge."

"We can't place him at the crime scene."

"Stephanie thinks she can get a conviction without it. And she thinks that eventually we will place him at the scene. But even if we can't, she thinks Nancy Lawrence will be a disaster on the stand."

"I agree with her on that," Peyton said.

The station's front door opened and closed. Voices were heard in the bullpen. Then Linda shushed the agents. It made Hewitt smile.

"She reminds me of my mother," he said.

"She's stricter than mine." Peyton stood, tired of sitting. "Two men are seen by Marie St. Pierre walking toward the cabin at midnight. The cabin burns to the ground. Simon Pink is found inside it the next day, shot with the handgun from the younger Fred St. Pierre's closet."

"Those are the facts," Hewitt said.

"It strike you as odd that mine was the only call to the fire department?" she said. "And that must have been three, four hours *after* the fire started, *after* the explosion."

"What are you getting at?"

"The explosion happened *after* the fire started," she said. "And the fire marshal believes someone torched the cabin with gasoline and matches."

"And?"

"It means someone is walking around with all the answers," she said and left the office.

SIXTEEN

Rhonda Gibson was in her mid-to-late sixties, and she opened the door maybe thirty seconds after Peyton knocked at 11:30 Friday morning.

"Mrs. Gibson, I doubt you remember me, but I used to sell you Girl Scout cookies."

"I remember you. Lois Cote's girl. The one who changed the tire when your mother got a flat. You were all of twelve. You and Lois had driven here to sell cookies, but you hit a nail in the yard."

"Actually, I was thirteen, and I'd just helped my father change a tire on the farm truck the week before."

Rhonda Gibson had pale-blue watery eyes and wore navy-blue polyester pants, a white blouse, and a pearl necklace. Had she raided Lois's closet?

She held the door open for Peyton and motioned to the distant neighboring house, more than two hundred yards away. The St. Pierre home was dark, a pickup and a Honda Accord in the driveway. But the state police and Border Patrol vehicles were gone now. The ambulances were, too.

"I can't believe it," Rhonda said. "What happened there, I mean. I heard the gunshots. It brought me out of my seat. There's nothing but farmland between our houses, but I couldn't see that far—just some cars, nothing more—but I heard the bang. Sounded like Thomas's rifle when he and our son used to shoot targets before hunting season. Before Thomas left me. Did you know our son?"

"No," Peyton said. They were inside now, standing in the kitchen.

"He must be about your age."

"I'm in my thirties," was all Peyton would give her.

"He's thirty-six. He spent most of his youth downstate. Anyway, he recently got transferred and now lives in the area. Your mother wants you to meet him, actually."

"I'm sure she does," Peyton said.

"Aren't you lucky to have a mother who cares so much?"

"Oh, I sure am."

"It was sweet of her to call him about you this week."

"My mother called him?"

Rhonda Gibson nodded.

"About me?" Peyton said.

"Yes. And he's really looking forward to meeting you Saturday. He says, from what Lois told him, you two have a lot in common."

"Saturday?"

"At your mother's house, Saturday night. We're having dinner with you."

Peyton stood staring.

"Coffee, dear?"

"Love some," Peyton said, "unless you have something stronger."

"What?"

"Love some, ma'am."

———

"Mrs. Gibson, you said you heard the gunshot the afternoon Mr. and Mrs. St. Pierre were killed," Peyton said.

She was stirring creamer into her coffee. Rhonda Gibson had poured creamer from the refrigerated container into a china dispenser. Lois, the apparent matchmaker, did the same when company popped in. Both women were traditional farm wives. And based on her own mother's life, Peyton assumed neither had ever wanted for more, a notion that perplexed Peyton.

But there was something else about these women that she understood completely and greatly admired. Rhonda Gibson was dressed to go to lunch or to a meeting. She even wore a faux-pearl necklace. Did she have plans for the day? Somewhere to go? Probably not. It was how her mother dressed—Lois Cote rose at 5:30 a.m. each day and dressed as if the president were coming to lunch. And she'd spent six hours one day the previous week meticulously maintaining her flower garden. It was an aspect Peyton loved most about Aroostook County: pride in one's self and one's things. And the pride and the care people took of their possessions had little to do with material costs.

"I heard two shots, actually," Rhonda said, pouring cream into her cup. She stirred, the spoon tinkling lightly against the cup's edge.

Peyton motioned to the picture window in the adjacent living room. "What did you see?"

"Nothing. It's too far for my eyes, but I know what I heard."

"Is it the first time you've heard something from the St. Pierre house?"

"I don't follow you."

"Had you ever heard gunshots—or what sounded like gunshots—on the St. Pierre property before that day?"

"Not in months. Oh, no—" Rhonda stood and moved quickly around the table. "I forgot." She turned off the stove and, using a dishtowel, retrieved a tin of muffins.

"I wondered what you were baking," Peyton said. "I smelled them when I got here. My muffins never smell like that, and they certainly don't look like that."

"I'll have these ready for you once they cool. I'm so happy you came when you did. I was baking for my son, but now someone gets to eat them while they're warm."

"No need to go out of your way on my account. Can you describe the sounds you heard previously? And how long ago was that?"

"Oh, months. They were louder than the shots this week. A bigger gun, maybe? Maybe Freddy got a moose permit and was target shooting."

Peyton sipped her coffee. "Mrs. Gibson, does anyone live with you?"

"My daughter, Sara. She's two years younger than my son." Rhonda stirred in more creamer. "My husband used to take his coffee strong. I'm sorry. I never got out of the habit of making it that way."

"The coffee is wonderful. Was Sara here in the spring?"

"Oh, yes. She's a homebody."

Peyton did the math: Sara Gibson was 34, still living at home. "May I speak to her?"

"I'll see if she's awake."

It was almost noon.

"Does she work nights?"

"No."

Rhonda Gibson stood and left the kitchen.

Peyton retrieved her phone from her pocket and checked messages: One from Pete Dye. She heard footsteps overhead, then two sets on the stairs. She slid her phone back into her pocket; she would read his text later.

"Peyton, this is Sara. She says she remembers you."

Peyton looked up. She remembered Sara Gibson as well. It would've been hard not to—she was dressed exactly as she had in high school.

————

Sara Gibson's face was only vaguely familiar, not one Peyton would recall in passing. It was her outfit—the skirt a good five inches above her knees, the blouse with four buttons undone, exposing lace from a black bra, and the four-inch heels—that gave her away.

Sara crossed the kitchen as if the room were still spinning. Given her blood-shot eyes, it might have been.

She extended a hand. "Didn't I used to know you?"

Peyton stood and shook hands. "You were a few years behind me in school."

"You played basketball. I remember. You scored a lot of points. There was a ceremony."

"That was a long time ago. They gave me a ball when I scored my thousandth point."

"And they hung a banner," Sara said. "It's still there."

"Nice to see you again," Peyton said.

It was noon, but Sara's hair was disheveled. Her mascara had run, her lipstick was smeared. And judging from her breath, she'd had far too much beer far too recently. She didn't seem the least bit apologetic or embarrassed by her appearance and seemed in no hurry to get to work.

"Can I ask you a few questions?"

"Why?" Sara said. "About what?"

"Your neighbors."

"Oh, the shooting." She seemed relieved.

"Did you hear anything that afternoon?"

"Hear it?" Sara said. "I saw the whole thing. I don't know why the newspapers and TV never called me. I was looking out my bedroom window, saw Fred shoot Marie, then pressed the gun to his temple, squeezed his eyes shut, and pull the trigger. I can't imagine what Freddy Jr. is going through right now."

"Was it the first time you heard noises like that coming from there? Did you hear anything Monday night?"

Sara looked embarrassed. "I was away all night on Monday." Then to her mother: "Do we have coffee, Mom?"

"Sure, dear. Peyton, I woke up Monday night, but I'm not sure what I heard."

"Can you describe it?"

"No. I just remember waking. Maybe I didn't hear anything. But usually I sleep soundly." She shrugged and moved to the coffee maker. "I'll pour you a cup, Sara. Did you meet any nice boys last night?"

"Did you see anything, Mrs. Gibson?"

"No. I went back to sleep."

Sara went to the kitchen table and sat. Peyton remained standing.

"I've heard a few sounds from time to time," Sara said.

"Can you describe them?"

"Like gunshots."

"Like the gunshots you heard the other day?"

"They were faint, like they were far away. I never saw anything, just heard them."

The cabin was well beyond the house. Had Sara heard explosions?

"When and how often did you hear these sounds?"

"Just once or twice. In the spring. I'm not sure what it was. Maybe a car backfiring."

Peyton looked at Rhonda, who was staring at the floor in deep thought. Was she embarrassed by her daughter's appearance? Had she wanted more for her daughter than Sara was finding?

Peyton stood, knowing she'd gotten all there was to get during this interview.

At the door, she paused. "Sara, did you report the sounds you heard in the spring to anyone?"

"No. Like I said, I figured they were target shooting or it was a car backfiring."

"Makes sense. Thanks for your time."

Peyton left her card and made the obligatory call-me-if-you-remember-anything statement at the door.

SEVENTEEN

PEYTON DROVE BACK TO Garrett Station.

Aroostook County was flat relative to its sister border in northern Vermont. As she noted the red maples, green and black ashes, and sugar maples—producing dramatic reds, yellows, and oranges against the mid-day sun—she recalled her time on the Southern border. She'd loved the long, low, blue Texas sky (like an inverted ceramic bowl, she'd read somewhere), and she remembered how, standing on a vista, you could see forever. But nothing matched snowshoeing on winter afternoons, crisp air exhaled in smokey puffs, sun reflecting off the white landscape; or summertime night walks beneath the full moon.

Peyton shifted, retrieved her iPhone, and plugged its charger into the dashboard.

Sara Gibson claimed to have seen the murder-suicide that had taken place nearly forty-eight hours ago. She described it in vivid detail, claiming Fred St. Pierre had put the gun to his temple, squeezed his eyes shut, and taken his life.

That made her testimony problematic. Fred hadn't put the barrel to his temple; he'd put it in his mouth. And those images couldn't be confused. Peyton surely wouldn't forget the frame-by-frame sequence anytime soon.

So why was Sara's story off base? Had she been too far from the events to get a good look and therefore allowed her imagination to fill in details? And why had she wished the media contacted her, especially since she'd refrained from reporting similar sounds months earlier?

Her explanation made sense. Gunshots weren't uncommon; hunters shot targets year-round in Aroostook County. There was a rod-and-gun club in town that most agents visited monthly in preparation for requalification sessions.

But if Sara knew the difference between the sound of gunshots and the sound of what Peyton now believed to be explosions, why hadn't Sara called the authorities upon hearing the latter?

Sara wasn't exactly an impeccable witness. This was a thirty-something party girl, a woman who still lived at home and whose mother was desperate to see her meet a "nice boy."

Peyton thought about that as she opened the front door at Garrett Station and found a "nice boy" of her own waiting to see her.

———

"He's been here twenty minutes," Linda said when Peyton entered.

Peyton carried a backpack and wore her forest-green uniform and boots. Her short ponytail protruded through the back of her baseball cap. In her free hand, she carried her iPad sheathed in a protective OtterBox case.

Across the room, seated in a plastic chair next to her desk, Dr. Chip Duvall, the southern Maine dentist and Sherry's husband—who patted her thigh like she was a Labrador—sat reading the *New York Times.*

"Doesn't want to see anyone else," Linda said. "Doesn't want coffee. Doesn't want to chat. He's just been sitting there, chewing breath mints and smelling like expensive cologne."

"Don't make a pass at him. He's married," Peyton said, although she doubted that would stop the silver-haired widow. "He say what this is about?"

Linda shook her head.

Miguel Jimenez, the station's youngest agent, walked out of the breakroom with a plate of *poutine.*

"Hey," he called, "want some?" and pointed to his plate. "I'm bringing this recipe back to Texas." He grinned. "I'll open a diner and retire."

She smiled. "French fries, cheese, and gravy? That's your ticket to millions?"

"It's addictive," he said.

"If I ate that every day for lunch, like you do, I'd weigh three-hundred pounds and be on cholesterol meds."

Chip Duvall followed the exchange, folded the *Times,* and smiled when Peyton set the backpack near her chair and sat facing him.

"Doesn't look to me," he said, "like you have trouble staying fit."

"Thanks."

"Or like food is your temptation," he went on.

She noticed his eyes appraising her. "How can I help you?" She slid the iPad to the center of her desk. Was he staring at her chest or eyeing her badge?

"Sherry met with you this morning."

She nodded. "You were there."

"Not for the full conversation," he said. Then he paused and looked around. Jimenez was sitting maybe fifteen feet away, eating his *poutine* with a fork and looking at his computer. "Is there someplace," Chip said, "more, ah, private where we can talk?"

"No."

"This is important, Peyton."

"What is this about? It's been a long morning, and I have a lot of paperwork, which I hate and want to get done."

"I think Sherry is in trouble," he said.

Peyton stood without saying a word and walked to the back of the bullpen. She turned right and went down the hallway.

"Peyton?" Chip called after her. "Agent Cote?"

She didn't stop until she reached the coffee maker. Poured a cup of black coffee and stood sipping. And thinking.

What the hell was Chip Duvall doing here?

She'd begun the day listening to Sherry speak of her brother's woes. Now her husband was here, saying *Sherry* was in trouble.

Several of Peyton's pressing questions were, at least peripherally, related to Sherry: What was the relationship between Simon Pink and Marie St. Pierre? And why did the two plan to travel to Prague?

Could Chip answer those?

Peyton poured a second coffee and brought it to him.

———

"You wanted more privacy," she said. "You got it."

"It's filthy out here," Chip Duvall said.

"Were you expecting the Marriott?"

They were in the six-bay garage at the back of the stationhouse, standing among snowmobiles, four-wheelers, a dog crate, a boat, and a green-and-white Ford F250 service vehicle that now served as the plow truck, a Fisher snow plow mounted to its front.

"We could go back to my hotel room," he said.

The statement gave her pause: had he just made a pass at her?

"I thought you needed privacy," she said.

"Oh, Sherry?" he said. "She's writing."

The relationship had seemed strained that morning, and Peyton had no intention of getting involved in Chip Duvall's marital crisis.

"What is this about, Chip?"

"I told you. Sherry is in trouble. I think you can help her. I think she knew about Freddy."

"Knew what about him?"

"I think that's why she's fighting this so hard," he said. "I mean, you saw her in the meeting with the district attorney. I think she knew and now feels a little responsible."

She retrieved her iPhone from her pocket, turned on the voice-recording option, and said slowly, "I'm going to record the rest of this conversation, Dr. Chip Duvall. Are you okay with that?"

"No," he said. "I'm not getting involved."

"You're not under arrest, Chip. I just want to make sure there's no confusion later on."

"No. This is all off the record."

"She's your wife," Peyton said.

"It's got to be off the record," he said.

She turned off the phone and slid it back into her pocket. "What exactly are you telling me?" she said.

"I think Freddy planned to do it all along, Peyton. And I think Sherry knew about it."

"What makes you think either of those things?"

"I heard some phone conversations. There was some money exchanged."

She waited.

When he didn't elaborate, she asked him to do so.

"That's all I know," he said. "They spoke about money on the phone. I think she gave him upwards of twenty thousand dollars, but I monitor our accounts closely. It didn't come from us."

"What was the money for? What exactly did you hear, Chip?"

He sat down on the edge of the snowmobile seat. A leather cover was on the cement floor. The machine's hood was up. Someone had been working on the engine.

Chip leaned forward, clasped his hands before him, and his shoulders shook slightly. "What have I just done?" he said. He was crying, tears hitting the concrete floor.

"Chip," she said, "it's time that we make this a formal discussion. You need to come with me."

He looked up, wiped his nose on the back of his hand, and said, "No. A husband can't be asked to testify against his wife."

"I'm not asking you to testify. I'm asking you to make a formal statement. At this point, I believe it would be in your best interest to do so."

"Hold on. Hold on. This isn't what I came here for. I thought you could help her. That's all. This can't turn formal." He stood. "This was a mistake."

She watched him walk out of the garage. There was no point in trying to stop him. He had a high-powered attorney in the area, and he was no fool. If he'd just incriminated his wife, he would know there were only the two of them present during this conversation, and his attorney would tell him that DA Stephanie DuBois surely wouldn't use a he-said-she-said scenario in court.

So what was Peyton left with?

Cryptic but incriminating background information. And two new questions: If Sherry had given Freddy upwards of $20,000, where had it come from? And what was it for?

She walked back inside to find Mitchell Cosgrove, the CPA turned Customs and Border Protection officer.

———

"Mike wants to see you, Peyton," Linda said, when Peyton re-entered.

"Is Mitch around?"

"Not until tonight."

Peyton nodded. Cosgrove was "pulling mids," which was how agents referred to working the midnight shift.

She sat down and sent Cosgrove a brief email, asking him to look into the finances of Freddy St. Pierre Jr. in hopes of turning up a money trail.

Peyton hit Send and went to Hewitt's office.

"Let's debrief," he said. "Tell me where you are, and I'll tell you some new information we have."

She walked him through her day, starting with the power break-fast with Sherry, running through her meeting with Sara Gibson, and finishing with the recent discussion with Chip.

"The bizarre, the weird, and the just plain crazy, huh?" Hewitt said.

"Yeah," she said. "That about sums up my three conversations."

"She gave her brother twenty thousand dollars?"

"It was cryptic information. Chip overheard a conversation. That's all. He hasn't seen any money go missing from his accounts."

"Do they have separate accounts?"

"That's what I'm asking Mitch Cosgrove to find out," she said. "I have no idea."

"Well, Bruce Steele ran Poncho the pooch all over the St. Pierre farm. Your friend Sherry and her attorney didn't like it much, but we got a warrant. Anyway, Poncho likes the place," Hewitt said. "A lot."

"He found drugs? There?"

"Not drugs. Detonators."

"Poncho smells those?"

Hewitt spread his hands. "Not sure exactly what he smells, but he led Steele to detonators and some other stuff."

"How much stuff?" she said. "Are we talking massive quantities?"

"No. Just a few in the barn."

"So Len Landmark will say they were using it to blow up stumps," she said.

"Maybe. But the Duvalls seem to be willing to talk to you."

She leaned back in her seat.

He smiled, nodding.

"You're hoping I can turn someone," she said.

"A mind reader," he said. "That's what you are."

EIGHTEEN

PEYTON ENTERED GARRETT HIGH School Friday afternoon before last period. In uniform, she received the standard reaction: the center of the hallway suddenly emptied, leaving her feeling like Moses.

A couple students nudged each other, pointed, whispered back and forth, and laughed.

She stopped short. "There a problem, boys?"

"No, ma'am," a boy in a tan Carhartt jacket and a green John Deere cap said.

"Where's Mr. Dye's classroom?"

The boy pointed.

She walked to the room at the end of the hall, peered through the narrow, wire-meshed window of the steel door (apparently events like Newtown made wooden doors obsolete), and saw Pete Dye behind a stack of papers at his desk.

When she knocked, he stood and waved her in.

"We still on for seven?" he said.

She held out a Tim Hortons cup. He took it, waiting for her reply.

"I'm here on business, Pete."

"Really? I don't get many visitors who wear guns." He pulled a student desk closer to his so Peyton could sit facing him.

"I hope it stays that way," she said.

"Yeah. Me, too. Poor choice of words for a teacher to use these days." He reorganized the papers so they were out of the way. "People think we're removed from school shootings up here, but you never know."

"My father used to talk about bringing a rifle to school during hunting season," she said, "leaving it in his locker during classes, and hunting after school."

"Lots of kids did that not too long ago. Think gun control is the solution?"

"Probably not, but I do know no one needs a semi-automatic for home protection."

He pointed to his stack of papers. "I'm psyched you stopped by. It allows me to procrastinate."

"How long will it take you to grade those?" The stack was an inch thick.

"Three, four hours," he said.

"I think I'd rather hike six miles wearing a Kevlar vest."

"Me, too. Last time you came here on business," he said, "you were chasing down a pregnant runaway."

"That's all you remember from my visit? Teaching's made you cynical."

"Seen the parents I deal with?"

"Hey, I'm having my kid tested. I might be one of them."

"Case in point."

She smiled. He'd always been able to make her laugh—when they'd been kids pulling high-school pranks, when they'd been in

150

college and had nearly dated, and since she'd begun seeing him several months earlier.

"You know Sara Gibson?"

"I still work at Tip of the Hat," he said, "if that's what you're asking."

"You're saying she's a regular?"

"She's there more often than I am, and you know I work there four, five nights a week."

"What's she like?"

Pete reorganized the stack of papers. "How can I say this without sounding like a jerk?"

"You probably can't. Just say it."

"She's not exactly selective in who she leaves the bar with."

"She gets around?"

"Understatement," he said. "She's sort of nuts. Maybe *desperate* is a better word. She's needy, looking for something."

"More than a one-night stand?"

"Oh, definitely. If you leave with her, she calls and calls."

"You're speaking from experience."

"Oh, God," he said. "Look, I told you my bed's been empty for a year. Yes, I did take her home once—more than a year ago—and I'm not proud of it."

"She ever leave with Freddy St. Pierre?"

"Maybe. I try to avoid her now. She's moved on, and I like it that way."

"Why does she do it? Is she attention starved?"

"No. I think she gets attention every night she goes to Tip of the Hat."

"God, what an existence," Peyton said and considered it: living at home, her mother waiting for her to wake each morning to see

151

if she'd met any "nice boys"; what boys there were in town knowing her reputation and thus using her; and the vicious cycle repeating, night after night.

Existence *was the appropriate word*, Peyton thought. That was no life.

"Know anyone Nancy Lawrence dates?"

"Bartenders are supposed to be discreet."

"But they never are."

He smiled. "I hear there's a young doctor, a real nerd-type."

That would explain the dinner date Nancy had told Peyton about.

"Anyone else?"

"What are you after?" he said.

"She date anyone else you know of, even for a short period of time?"

"I saw Nancy leave the Tip with Freddy St. Pierre once," he said, "if that's what you're after."

Corroboration. But what did it mean?

"Can I ask you a question?" Pete said.

"Depends."

"What's going on with Freddy? I heard some agents talking about him when I brought you coffee."

"Get your deer license yet, Pete?"

"Changing the conversation, Peyton?"

She just smiled. "See you at seven."

———

She was crossing the parking lot when she heard running footsteps from behind and someone call, "Excuse me."

She turned to see a boy, not much taller than Tommy. He had terrible acne and unkempt greasy shoulder-length hair and patches he might have called a beard. Was he trying to grow one, or had the acne prevented him from shaving? He wore a light-blue work shirt, MATT stitched into the breast pocket, and jeans with dark spots (oil?) on them. He was so short, his beard was probably an attempt to remind everyone that he was a junior or senior.

"How can I help you?" she asked.

The late-afternoon sun was high in the summer sky. The temperature had risen to the mid-eighties. If she weren't working, it would be a nice time to take Tommy to kayak on the river.

"You're not a game warden, right? Someone said you're not."

She waved a blackfly away. "That's right. I'm with Customs and Border Protection."

He plunged his hands—they were dirty with grime under his fingernails, like he worked on car engines—deep into his pockets.

"Border Patrol," she clarified.

"Okay. I think I saw something I should tell you about," he said. "I wasn't going to … but I been thinking about it for a couple days, and I hear sometimes these things can get turned around on you … and then I saw you … so …" He shuffled his feet. The toe on his right boot was worn to the steel. He looked around nervously.

"I don't want to take much time," he said. "It was three guys. I was doing something I shouldn't have been doing, but I think they …" He looked over his shoulder, back toward the high school.

"No one's around," she said. "It's just you and me."

"It wasn't even my property. And, like, I had my rifle and my light, but I didn't jack anything that night."

That night. "You were poaching deer?"

153

He nodded. "But like I said, I didn't see any. My father is out of work. We can't afford many groceries. And, like, I didn't do nothing that night. But I was in the woods, behind a tree, when I heard three voices." He looked down and moved a pebble with the toe of his worn boot.

"It was Monday," he continued slowly, "the night of the fire at that cabin. I think somebody got shot."

———

"Matt Kingston is the boy's name," Pete Dye told Peyton and Hewitt.

At 5:10 Friday evening, Pete was back in the bullpen at Garrett Station, seated in a straight-backed chair near Peyton's desk, his legs stretched out before him, ankles crossed. Still wearing khaki pants with a shirt and tie. His GARRET HIGH SCHOOL VARSITY GIRLS' BASKETBALL team jacket was draped over the arm of his chair.

Peyton thought he looked relaxed. She also thought he looked good.

He hadn't come to deliver coffee this time. In fact, he hadn't come of his own volition. So it was Peyton who got the beverages and, given that she'd asked him here, even a piece of Linda Cyr's cherry pie.

"Matt Kingston is a good kid," Pete continued. "I'd take him at his word, Peyton. You bake this pie? It's very good."

"I couldn't bake that," she said. "Linda's gone, but I'll pass the compliment along."

The agents working 3-to-11 were already on patrol duty. Only Miguel Jimenez, chained to his desk with paperwork from a Houlton-to-Fredericton cigarette-smuggling ring he'd busted, was moving about the bullpen. He left the room, and Peyton heard the microwave door open with a pop and slam shut.

Peyton pulled her iPhone out and fired a quick text to Lois: MOM, WKING LATE. HOME BY 5:30, OK?

She felt Hewitt's disapproving eyes on her.

"I need to confirm childcare," she said.

"No problem," Hewitt said.

Did he mean it?

"Mr. Dye," Hewitt continued, "thanks for coming in." Hewitt sat beside him, both men facing Peyton.

"Call me Pete," Pete said and shrugged, finishing the last of the pie.

The microwave beeped, the door popped open, and the bullpen was filled with the smell of steak and spices. Jimenez reentered carrying a plate of fajitas.

Pete looked at them.

"Want one?" Hewitt offered.

"Boy, you guys eat well around here. No, thanks. We're supposed to be having dinner at seven." Pete motioned to Peyton. "The pie will tide me over."

"I forgot the two of you are dating," Hewitt said. "That complicates things slightly."

"Pete isn't here in a formal capacity," Peyton said. "This is background only. But he knows the boy. And he's lived here his whole life. I think he can offer some insights."

"Background only?" Hewitt said.

Peyton nodded, then to Pete: "Tell us more about the boy."

"Good kid. Hard working. Gets picked on because he's small."

"If teachers know a kid is being bullied," she said, "why don't they stop it? I'll never understand that."

He looked at her, surprised. "I ... I haven't witnessed it first-hand. If I had ..."

"Is that relevant?" Hewitt said.

"Sorry," she said.

"Everything alright, Peyton?" Hewitt asked.

"Fine," she said.

Hewitt was still looking at her. "What we need from you, Pete"—he turned back to Pete—"is confirmation of this kid's character."

"We think he witnessed a crime," Peyton said. "He may be asked to testify."

"Peyton," Hewitt said. "Let's play this closer to the vest, please."

"We can trust Pete," she said. "This conversation never leaves this room."

Pete nodded.

"Matt Kingston has no criminal record," Peyton said, "nothing that shows up anywhere. But we don't want to get blindsided by information about him that comes out down the line."

"You won't get blindsided," Pete said. "He's a good kid."

"Who just happens to poach deer. See the problem?"

"Peyton, he poaches so his family can eat."

"The attorneys won't care about his family's financial woes," she said.

"Is that true about the deer jacking?" Hewitt said. "If so, I don't know if we can use him."

"I'm not sure you realize how far your government salaries go up here," Pete said.

"I don't follow you," Hewitt said.

Peyton did—and she knew what was coming.

"I hear some agents get transferred here, sell their homes in other parts of the country, and buy beautiful, big places up here. You know what the local economy is like—hell, what it always has been like, Peyton. Not everyone has a government salary."

She nodded. She knew she lived better in this region—where she'd bought her three-bedroom, two-bath Cape on ten acres for under $200,000—than she could on just about any other assignment in the US.

"I've got news for you guys," Pete went on, "Matt Kingston isn't the only kid poaching. And a lot of these families can't afford not to."

Peyton looked at Hewitt. She knew Pete spoke the sentiment of many residents. It might have been the first Hewitt was hearing about it, though. Jimenez was at his desk and looked up from his plate of fajitas. He looked ready to protest, but chewed and said nothing. Peyton knew Jimenez had a right to protest. He'd grown up in California, the son of two migrant workers, and had seen a Customs and Border Protection career as a way out.

"Federal salaries aren't making anyone rich," Hewitt said, "but your point is well taken. Is Matt Kingston articulate?"

"I guess. He works most evenings at Tip of the Hat, bussing tables, stocking the kitchen, washing dishes—that stuff. And he's an honor-roll student. I saw him carrying an SAT-practice book into work the other night."

"So he wants to go to college?" Peyton said. Her legs were crossed, and the black laces of her boots slapped against the leather as she bobbed her foot. "And he's going to pay his own way."

Pete Dye nodded. "No doubt. He'll probably go to the Reeds branch of U-Maine, live at home, and work. You know the story."

"Yeah," she said. "And you trust this kid a lot."

"I do. What exactly did Matt see? Why would he have to take the stand?" Pete said, leaning to retrieve his Nalgene bottle off the floor. His coffee was gone.

"Thanks for stopping by." Hewitt handed him his business card. "May we call you if we have further questions?"

157

"Is this about the Freddy St. Pierre thing? Serving as a key witness in a murder trial is asking a lot of a seventeen-year-old. You don't have any other witnesses, do you?"

Hewitt smiled. "Peyton said you were smart."

"Pete," Peyton said, "obviously, this is a delicate matter that must be handled with great discretion."

"Of course. Mum's the word." He stood and looked at them.

Hewitt nodded. Then Pete Dye turned and left the building.

NINETEEN

"AM I CORRECT IN assuming Matt Kingston witnessed the guy—I think the newspaper said his name was Simon Pink—get shot?" Pete Dye lifted his glass of Bud Light and sipped.

The glass was chilled, and Peyton watched a bead of condensation drip to the table.

They were in Keddy's, as planned, at 7 p.m. Friday. Pete had just arrived, and unlike Peyton, apparently wasn't ready to compartmentalize. She had no problem leaving work at the office this day. In fact, the last thing she wanted to talk about with Pete was the Simon Pink murder. Mostly because she couldn't.

"My mother's staying with Tommy," Peyton said. "She's had a long day. Arrived at my house this morning at seven, and she'll sleep in the guest room tonight."

"Babysitting?"

"She calls it 'grandmothering,'" she said and smiled at him, relieved he was letting go of their previous discussion regarding Matt

Kingston. She smiled a lot when she looked at Pete Dye. That crooked smile. Too cute for his own good. Or maybe for *her* own good.

She sipped her beer and made sure her phone was set to vibrate. No calls or texts from Lois.

"You didn't answer my question," he said. "Did Matty see the guy get shot?"

The one question she hoped he wouldn't ask.

The one she couldn't answer.

They'd begun the day on a different (but equally-as-difficult) topic: sex and commitment. She was holding out, and she knew it was killing him, but she needed to be sure. Now she had to withhold something else, something that to one not employed in a criminal-justice field, might seem inconsequential.

"Pete, I can't talk about an ongoing investigation."

She waited and watched. Would he be insulted? He wanted to be part of her life, but she wasn't letting him in—not in her bed (yet) and not in this aspect of her professional life.

A live band played in the adjoining bar. A loud, low rumble, was punctuated occasionally by a voice that sounded like porcelain shattering.

"Besides," she went on, "if Matt Kingston witnessed a homicide, you're better off not knowing about it."

He set his beer down. "You can't tell me because I might be in danger if you do?"

"It's more than that."

She met lots of people who found her job interesting. *What's it like? Do you get scared chasing people at night all alone in the desert?* And the one only a handful have the guts to ask: *Have you ever shot anyone?*

"It's just that"—she tried to read his expression; was he angry or desperate?—"you need to understand I can't talk about an on-going investigation. That's protocol."

"When you were married, did you tell Jeff about your work?"

"No."

"That bother him?"

"At the start. Then he grew disinterested in things that he wasn't at the center of."

"I can understand that," he said and smiled, "on both fronts."

"Does it bother you?" she said.

"Yes."

The waitress appeared. He ordered a steak, rare, a salad, and a baked potato. She asked for the cobb salad.

"What are your plans for the weekend?" he said, when his salad arrived.

"Nothing much," she said. "Tommy's soccer season just ended, so we'll probably lay low."

"I've been wanting to have you to my place for dinner," he said. He set his salad fork down and looked thoughtfully at her, choosing his words carefully, suddenly a shy seventeen-year-old asking a girl to the prom. "You've cooked for me several times," he said, "and you'll probably find this hard to believe, but I'm actually an excellent cook. How's tomorrow sound?"

"Love to," she said, "and I'm not surprised that you can cook, Pete. But my mother committed me to dinner with her friends."

"I don't understand. She promised her friend you'd be there?"

"That's my mom." She tried to laugh it off, but the laugh was forced, and she knew he picked up on her tension immediately. For one who made her living with her poker face, she found social situations—especially those with men—different. It wasn't easy to be evasive to one she cared about.

"I'm confused." He pushed his salad away.

"My mother does a lot for me, Pete. I'm trying to appease her."

"She wants you to meet someone, is that it?"

"Her friend's son is coming to see his mother. My mother invited them for dinner. My mom watches Tommy every day after school and is sleeping in my guest room tonight so I can be here with you."

"So you're going on a blind date?"

"No. I'm not looking at it like that. A nice elderly woman offered to cook a meal with my mother. Her son is also in town. That's the long and the short of it, Pete."

But she knew it wasn't. Both her mother and Rhonda Gibson viewed the dinner exactly the way Pete Dye did.

"My mom likes you a lot. You know that, right?"

"Sure," he said.

"Look, I'm appeasing my mother because she helps me out so much. That's all."

He nodded. But when the main course arrived, he spoke little, ate quickly, and spent most of his time avoiding eye contact, staring, almost longingly, she thought, at the bead curtain behind which was the bar and the live music.

When the bill came, she offered to split it.

And he let her.

TWENTY

"You guys trying to keep me busy?" Stephanie DuBois said, entering Peyton's kitchen the way she entered every room—like her hair was on fire.

And it could have been. A flaming redhead, Stephanie had a personality to match. She wore bright colors, short skirts, and, much to Peyton's admiration, had been held in Contempt of Court twice recently.

She swung her briefcase onto the island like it were a rucksack.

"I mean, I like billable hours as much as the next lawyer, but it's almost nine o'clock."

Hewitt said, "Got to pay for that BMW somehow."

"No," Stephanie said, "that's my ex-husband's problem. I made sure of that."

"First or second ex?" Peyton said.

"Second. First covered my ski house at Sugarloaf."

"If I didn't know better," Hewitt said, "I'd think you represented my ex-wife."

"If I had"—Stephanie grinned—"you'd be living in a cardboard box, agent."

"You're a real princess," Hewitt said. "Want a beer?"

"Coffee. But don't brew a pot on my account."

"It's a Keurig," Peyton said. "Want Starbucks?"

"Why can't all law-enforcement officials be like you, Peyton?"

"I ask myself that every time I attend a boring meeting." She moved to the coffee maker.

"Excuse me," Hewitt said.

"Except, of course, *your* meetings, Mike. They're never boring." Stephanie laughed, and Peyton smiled.

"Hey," Hewitt said, "I thought you were having dinner with Pete Dye."

"Already did," she said.

Peyton put a coffee cup beneath the dispenser. She saw Hewitt look at the wall clock. Yes, the dinner had ended with the main course. Yes, Pete had declined dessert. And, yes, neither she nor Pete had wanted to chat over coffee.

"This must be important if you left your date early," Stephanie said.

"The date was over," Peyton said curtly.

"Ouch," Stephanie said. "Sorry."

Peyton shook her head. Coffee made, she added a splash of cream and set the Red Sox mug in front of Stephanie. All three sat at the kitchen island.

Briefcase open, Stephanie's iPad was before her. "Tommy in bed?" she asked.

"Yeah." Lois had departed since she got home early.

"Tell Stephanie what we have," Hewitt said. He had not asked where Tommy was.

Peyton explained her recent visit to Garrett High School.

When Peyton had finished, Stephanie looked up from her notes. "This kid, Matt Kingston, is seventeen?"

Peyton nodded.

"That's confirmed? He can't be tried as an adult?"

"We just met with a teacher," Hewitt said, "but we'll get his birth record."

Stephanie nodded. "So Matt Kingston goes out to jack deer on the St. Pierre property, but before he sees a deer, he hears voices and a gunshot. And all of this is on the night Simon Pink is murdered with Freddy St. Pierre's gun?"

"Yeah," Hewitt said, "and the timeline matches up."

Peyton sprayed the granite counter top with glass cleaner and wiped it down with a paper towel. She'd splurged on the granite, and her mother, God love her, left crumbs everywhere.

"Deer-jacking won't look very good," Peyton said and threw the paper towel away.

Stephanie leaned forward, elbows resting on the island, holding her coffee cup with both hands. An Alex and Ani bracelet dangled from her wrist. "If we go forward with the prosecution of St. Pierre," she said, "this kid will have to take the stand. And, no, confessing to attempted deer-jacking will not serve him well. And if I were cross-examining him, I'd make a big stink about him being at the murder scene with a weapon of his own."

"But Simon Pink was shot with a handgun," Hewitt said.

"That isn't the point. The kid was there. He had a gun. Half the time, criminal prosecution is about muddying the waters, and the deer rifle is a great distraction. If he can shoot a rifle, he could've fired a handgun. That might be enough to plant reasonable doubt."

"Jesus," Hewitt said, "you really did work for my wife, didn't you?"

"Something else," Stephanie said, "will certainly be brought up: Why didn't the kid call the cops that night? He waited almost a week, until he happened to see Peyton."

"He said all he knows is he heard a gunshot," Peyton said. "Then he saw the story of the murder on the TV news. Thought about it for several days. Then I was walking by…" She shrugged. "That's what he told me this afternoon. He's scared and confused."

"Sure. All of that's fine and good. But you see where I'm going with this. He hears what he hears, then just slips off? Went back to his truck and drove home? That isn't exactly helping his credibility."

"Said he read about the fire in the morning," Peyton said. "Mentioned it to some kids who, at first, told him not to say a thing since deer-jacking is illegal. But then, after news of the murder broke, he had second thoughts."

"And you were in the right place at the right time?"

"You don't believe it?" Peyton said. "This kid sat in my truck and told me all of this. He's sincere."

"I get paid to play devil's advocate," Stephanie said. "Here's the bottom line: I don't think this is enough to put Freddy St. Pierre away. Maybe we'd use Matt Kingston to corroborate witness testimony. But I think if we face a good defense team, this kid could eyewitness himself right into a juvenile center for at least a few months."

———

When Hewitt and Stephanie left, Peyton sat alone in her den with a sealed envelope Tommy brought from school.

The windows were blackened mirrors now. The light cast from her desk lamp turned her glass of merlot a shade of magenta. She rolled up the long sleeves of her University of Maine sweatshirt

166

and skimmed the report once, quickly. Then, slowly, she reread the results.

"Mom, what does it say?"

She looked up. Tommy was in the doorway.

"It's almost eleven o'clock, sweetie. You shouldn't still be awake."

"Does it say why it takes me longer than everyone else?"

There was a desperate, pleading look in his eyes that she'd not seen there before. He wanted—needed—an answer to this question.

The report was nearly twenty pages long, had been completed by Dr. Michael Thompson, an educational consultant, and deemed Tommy to have above-average intelligence. The final diagnosis explained a lot.

"Come here, sweetie."

He came closer, and she lifted her ten-year-old onto her lap like he was three again.

"Do you know what dyslexia is?"

TWENTY-ONE

SATURDAY AT 5:30 P.M., Peyton climbed out of her Jeep Wrangler and walked with Tommy toward her mother's home, toting a bottle of merlot.

The sun was still high overhead. Summer was a reprieve for those living in a region where winters began in October and ended in mid-April, and darkness during winter months often fell before 4 p.m. For those who loved the outdoors, Aroostook County summers—when the sun rose before 4 a.m. and temps rarely cracked eighty-five—made the winters worth it.

She paused at the front door and exhaled.

"What's wrong, Mom?" Tommy said. "Don't you want to see Gram?"

"Of course, sweetie." But her mind was elsewhere, and she wished she were as well: she hadn't heard from Pete Dye since the previous night's dinner date, she was tired from the events of the week, and a night at home would've been nice. But sometimes you do things for family.

She didn't knock. She turned the doorknob, and they entered.

Seated at the kitchen table, smiling at something Lois had just said, was the detective she'd seen for the first time in the conference room at Garrett Station during the meeting between Sherry St. Pierre-Duvall and Stephanie DuBois.

Peyton kissed her mother's cheek and handed her the bottle of wine.

"You didn't have to bring this," Lois said.

"I know," Peyton said.

Tommy hugged his grandmother. "Can I go to the playroom, Gram?"

"*May* I?"

"May I go to the playroom?"

"Certainly. There might even be a new soccer ball in there for you."

"You spoil him, Mom," Peyton said.

"A grandmother's prerogative." Lois took her daughter's thin L.L.Bean jacket and grandson's hat. "Come with me," she said, and Peyton followed her mother to the small office off the kitchen.

"Can you believe that woman?" Lois whispered, setting the jacket on the desk chair. "I mean, really. I told Rhonda not to bring anything, that *I* was preparing *everything*. Well, what did she do? She brought maple syrup pie. Is she trying to say my dessert— brownies—wasn't enough?"

"Mother, I'm sure she wasn't trying to insult you. Just trying to be nice."

"Well, go out there and throw the brownies away. I'm making pudding au chômeur."

"Mother, you don't have time. Besides, this isn't a contest."

"Who said anything about a contest? This is much more important than a silly game, Peyton. And, as a woman, you need to learn that. Don't you want to find a husband? Go throw the brownies away. We'll see whose dessert gets eaten."

Peyton shook her head and went back to the kitchen, her mother on her heels. Peyton looked at the brownies, uncut, still in the baking pan, and left them there.

"You must be Peyton," the detective said. "Your mother has been telling me all about you."

Her mother looked at the brownies, saw Peyton had done nothing with them, and shot her a look.

Peyton ignored her.

"Oh, no. The brownies are burnt," Lois said. "I'll make pudding au chômeur."

"They don't look burnt," the detective said. "I'm sure they're—"

"Leave it to a man to try to tell a woman how to run her kitchen," Lois said. "Just sit there, cutie."

The chair Peyton pulled from the kitchen table squealed against the linoleum floor when she sat across from him. "You'll have to excuse my mother," she whispered. "She's a bizarre cross between a 1940s housewife and a raging sexist."

"Was I just objectified?" he asked, grinning.

Peyton laughed. "Oh, yes. *Cutie* is code for something much worse. And don't believe a thing she says about me."

He had a nice smile. Maybe six-one, he wasn't thin, but whatever he weighed, he carried it well. He had dark eyes and was clean-shaven. His hair was neatly trimmed and the color of wet tar.

"I'll remember that," he said.

Lois was taking items from the fridge, lining them up on the counter, but paused to point at the detective behind his back, and mouthed, *What do you think?*

Rhonda Gibson entered the room.

"Your grandson just met me in the hallway, Lois. You're so lucky to have a grandchild. I wish one of my children would get married and have kids."

"Oh, boy," the detective said. "Let it go, Mom. I think I'll have that beer you offered me, Lois."

Everyone laughed.

He extended a hand to Peyton. "Stone Gibson. I understand you're a Border Patrol agent. I think we have something in common."

Peyton shook his hand. "The Simon Pink situation. Not so sure that's a good thing to share—a corpse."

He smiled. "I hadn't thought of it like that."

Rhonda and Lois were at the kitchen counter. Lois had set out her pudding au chômeur ingredients but was mashing potatoes and adding garlic; Rhonda was cutting her pie.

"I was at the discovery session," Peyton said, "or whatever they're calling that meeting between attorneys."

"I've been doing this for almost twenty years," he said. "I've never seen anything like that. Not even sure why we were all there." He leaned closer, whispering, "My mother and little sister tell me you interviewed them. Most excitement they've had in years."

Peyton smiled. She figured his sister, Sara Gibson, had more excitement than that perhaps nightly, but she said nothing.

"Did you grow up here?"

"Until I was eight or so. Then I moved with my father downstate." His eyes ran to his mother, checking to be sure she wouldn't hear. "My parents' divorce was a real mess. Long story." He wore jeans and a dark T-shirt under a pull-over fleece. He folded his arms across his chest.

She motioned to their mothers standing side by side at the kitchen counter. Now there were dinner rolls preparing to enter the oven and a salad being tossed. Lois had started her second dessert.

"If they keep trying to outdo one another," Peyton whispered, "we won't eat until midnight. You've got plenty of time."

————

"My father took off when I was six." Stone Gibson was seated across the living room from Peyton, who sat alone on the sofa. Lois and Rhonda were still in the kitchen.

"Did you grow up in the house next to the St. Pierre farm?"

They were both drinking beer from the bottle. Peyton had brought wine, but she liked Geary's Pale Ale, and Stone Gibson had brought a six-pack of Sam Adams Summer Ale.

"Yeah," he said. "Until I was eight. My father took off, went to Old Orchard Beach. When the divorce was final, I went to live with him. Ever been there?"

"Sure. It's like the Fort Lauderdale of New England."

He sipped some beer, nodded. "A party town, especially in the eighties. My father was a contractor. He was into some other stuff—prescription-drug dealing mostly—and went to Warren for a while when I was in my twenties. I'd made it through the Academy by then, but his record hasn't helped my cause."

"Professionally?"

He nodded. "Always a lot of questions to answer when you're the son of a convict and you want to be a state police detective."

"College?" she asked.

"Me? No way. No how. I joined the OOB Police part time when I was eighteen. I was working as a carpenter—the one good thing my old man taught me. I kept my nose clean, or"—he looked away, the way she'd often found people did when they had something to hide—"clean enough, and then I got on full time. Two years there, then at twenty, I went to the Portland Police Department, and by twenty-three, I was a statey."

"A lifer," she said. "I like that. You always knew? Never wanted anything else?"

"Like what? I'm not the smartest guy in the world. Wasn't going to be a brain surgeon. And I couldn't afford college. Besides, I like figuring things out and putting things together—probably why I like carpentry—and I understand people well enough to ask good questions and know when I'm being bullshitted."

It made her smile. She could've made the same statement about reading people.

"What?" he asked.

They had some things in common, but she didn't answer. Instead, she raised her beer bottle. "To the job."

He raised his beer. "The job."

Her cell phone chirped in the kitchen.

"Peyton," her mother called.

"I know," she said. "I know."

She left the room and grabbed her phone. "Peyton Cote here."

"Agent Peyton Cote?"

"Who is this?"

"Tom Dickinson, but that's not important. A young woman left your card on the bar at Tip of the Hat and told me something I think I need to pass on to you."

"What is this about?"

"I don't want to say over the phone."

Who had she given her business card to recently? She looked past the kitchen table at Stone Gibson, thinking of his sister.

She turned to face the cupboard. "Do you know the young woman's name?"

"Yeah, sure."

She'd given her card to Marie St. Pierre and Sara Gibson. Only one of them was still alive.

"Please tell me the name."

"I'm no rat. But this seems kind of big, if it's true. And I need to get out in front of this thing."

"I need to know what you're talking about," she said.

"I'll give you what I have, but then I go back to my life. I don't want to be involved. Can't be involved."

"I'll meet you at Gary's Diner for coffee in an hour."

"It's Saturday night. I have plans."

"So do I," she said. "I'm canceling mine. One hour." She hung up and turned to her mother.

"Don't you dare say it, Peyton."

"Mom," she said, "I need to be somewhere in an hour. Can Tommy stay here with you?"

"Good God. All you do is work."

"If this could wait," she said, "or if I could send someone else, I would. Believe me."

Stone Gibson had come from the living room. "Everything okay?"

"Yeah, fine," she said, not willing to put him in a conflict-of-interest position yet, not until she first heard what his sister had done and said.

"Peyton," Lois said, looking straight at Stone Gibson, "I forbid you to leave this house."

"Mother, please."

"Mrs. Cote," Stone said, "I've been in her position. Sometimes things come up that can't be helped. I'm not offended. I promise you."

Lois turned to her pudding au chômeur, muttering.

"I'll pick Tommy up by eight thirty," Peyton said.

"He like the Red Sox?" Stone asked.

"Does he ever," Lois said.

"I know Stan Roberts, the backup outfielder. I'll tell him about going into the clubhouse last summer."

"He'll love that," Peyton said, appreciating his help, no matter how ironic it was, given who she was leaving to talk about.

———

"Thanks for coming," she said when Tom Dickinson squeezed his large frame into the booth to sit across from her.

"Did I have a choice?"

"Everyone has choices."

"Not me," he said.

Up close, he looked vaguely familiar. He had raven hair worn like an eighties rocker and continually tucked it behind his ears. The dark hue went well with his brown eyes. A cross was tattooed on his right wrist, but that wasn't the tattoo she recognized. He also wore a diamond stud in his ear that was larger than her engagement ring and a Rolex that looked real. (She'd seen enough knock-offs in El Paso to know the difference.)

They ordered coffee, then she said, "I think I've seen you at Tip of the Hat."

"I don't live around here, but when I'm in the area I go there once in a while. And I like talking to Jerry, the bartender."

"Jerry Leon. He was my neighbor when I was a kid," she said.

"I thought he was ex-military."

She nodded. "He's in his seventies now, but he was stationed at Loring Air Force Base back when it was open during the Cold War. He came back to Aroostook County when he retired. That was twenty years ago."

"Always wondered how old that guy was," Dickinson muttered.

Their coffees arrived. She was in a hurry but wouldn't rush. He had something to say. He'd get to it.

"I made a phone call before I called you," he said. "You'll be hearing from someone in Boston."

"Boston?" She looked at him. "Why?"

"Look, lady"—his demeanor changed, and this was no longer a casual conversation; now he was the ex-con she knew him to be— "I'm not much of a do-gooder. But since that ditz told me stuff, and she was drunk and talking loud, and about ten people saw me talking to her, I need to get out in front of this thing before she winds up in court. I can't go to court."

"Sara Gibson?"

He nodded. He wore a leather New York Yankees jacket and snake-skin boots she'd seen in Texas for $500.

"You've got a New York accent," she said. "I saw that same neck tattoo on a federal inmate once."

"It was a bad idea to get the tattoo," he said. "I'm working on the accent."

"Trying to lose it?"

"Yeah. Trying to sound more Midwestern, more nondescript."

Something clicked into place. She leaned back in the booth, folded her arms, and said, "I'll be damned. That's how you got my unlisted number."

"So you know why Boston is calling you?" he said.

"I've heard about people in witness protection being up here."

"Keep your voice down," he said. "I don't live here, but I like to fish up here. So you know why I can't go to court, right?"

"I'll be damned," she said again. "You want to fit in, lose the Yankees jacket."

"I'm not wearing a goddamned Red Sox jacket."

That made her smile.

"It's not an easy life," he said.

"What did you do, Tom?"

"White-collar shit. I was an accountant, if you believe that. But it doesn't matter anymore. I'm paying for it, believe me. I had a life in New York, a daughter who's seven now. I move around a lot. Haven't seen her in two years. When I do, it's for fifteen minutes at an interstate rest area."

She didn't know what to say, because she didn't know how to feel—he could have done a lot or a little.

She was wondering about it all when her unlisted cell phone rang for the second time in an hour. This time the area code was 617: Boston, as promised.

TWENTY-TWO

"HAVE A NICE SUNDAY?" Mike Hewitt asked Monday morning when Peyton sat down in his office to discuss the information she'd given him over the phone Saturday night.

Was his question genuine?

Saturday night, she side-stepped his hint (he hadn't made it a directive, after all) that they meet Sunday morning to discuss Dickinson's claim and to debrief the case. Instead, she spent Sunday with Tommy hiking and fishing for brook trout.

"Tommy and I had a nice Sunday," she said. "Thanks for asking. I hope you did as well."

"I worked," he said.

A passive-aggressive remark? She tried to read his expression but couldn't. Was she being hypersensitive, reading into things because her career often ran counter to her home life?

She exhaled.

Had she done the right thing by spending the day with Tommy? Certainly. Should she have conferenced with Hewitt instead? No way. If she'd had a penis, she'd not be facing these self-doubts. She shook her head, annoyed.

"What is it?" he asked.

"Nothing," she said.

"Well, this certainly is turning into a mess. Tom Dickinson, or whoever the hell he really is, is in the federal witness protection program?"

"Dickinson is a government-provided alias," she said. "That's all the FBI would say. Details of his situation, I was told, are on a need-to-know basis."

"I called the FBI to follow up," Hewitt said. "They had never heard of that alias. Had no idea who I was talking about. You sure this guy is legit?"

"My phone call only lasted about five minutes, but I spoke to someone who said they were FBI."

"Well," Hewitt said, "speaking of federal assholes, you missed some fireworks here yesterday."

"Sunday?" she said. She shifted in her seat. *Let it go,* she told herself. *You weren't scheduled to work.*

"Bruce Steele came back to the station furious. He and the state police arson team were thrown off the St. Pierre cabin site. Sent home."

"By whom? CIA or FBI?" she said.

"FBI."

"What does the FBI want with the cabin?"

"No one has told me a thing. I have a conference call later today."

"Does Wally Rowe know?"

"He's Secret Service, Peyton."

"Well, this is our case, Mike. Don't let Washington—"

"Washington is going to do whatever the hell it wants. You've been doing this long enough to know that."

Both statements were true.

"More Secret Service is arriving today," he said, "because Michelle Prescott-MacMillan is coming to Aroostook County tomorrow."

Peyton had seen the president's daughter on TV. CNN had said Prescott-MacMillan was lecturing at her alma mater, Harvard Kennedy School of International and Global Affairs.

"When is the president arriving?"

"Now that's *really* need-to-know," Hewitt said.

"The dates were on the TV news, Mike. And they're in my email somewhere."

"Didn't think you read your email."

"I do, sparingly."

"Within seventy-two hours," he said. "Depending on when he can get away."

"Let's switch gears," she said. "Sara Gibson told Dickinson that Nancy Lawrence took money to leave the bar with Freddie St. Pierre and to let him sleep on her couch the night of the murder."

"How does Sara Gibson know that?"

"Dickinson says Sara told him she saw the exchange of money and heard the conversation in the ladies' room at Tip of the Hat."

"So, right now, according to third-hand information—provided, no less, by a federal felon in the witness protection program—Fred St. Pierre Jr. didn't shoot Simon Pink?"

"If I didn't know you better," she said, "I'd almost think you were cynical."

He grunted.

"The FBI says we can't use Dickinson, just his information," Peyton said, "because it would compromise his situation."

"So he can't testify," Hewitt said.

"But we can be creative."

Hewitt tilted his head. "What, exactly, do you have in mind?"

———

The Hampton Inn in Reeds was overkill for the area, Peyton thought. There were several locally owned hotels, and she hadn't thought the Hampton Inn would make it. She'd thought (maybe even hoped) local businesses would run it out. But, like the Wal-Mart in town, it had not only survived but thrived. Allegiances fade quickly in a down economy.

She parked her service vehicle, entered the lobby, and walked to the desk.

"I need the room number of Dr. Sherry St. Pierre-Duvall."

"I'll call the room and put you on the line."

The girl behind the counter was college-aged, wearing the standard-issue dark blazer. Her name tag read TANYA. Probably an intern, maybe a hotel-management or recreation major at the University of Maine branch at Reeds.

Peyton looked around. No one was nearby.

"Actually, this is official business," she said. *Official business.* Even to herself she sounded like a TV caricature.

"Really?" the young woman said, eyes widening. "I can lead you to the room."

"No, that's okay."

"No, really. I mean, I don't mind. I'm studying journalism. Maybe I can—"

"No. Just tell me the room number. And this is all off the record. Understand?" She knew she had no way of enforcing her request but thought the student-journalist might buy it.

"Nothing's off the record unless I agree to it. The Duvalls have rooms 210 and 418."

"Two rooms?"

"One is a suite," the girl said, nodding.

———

Peyton took the stairs, and Dr. Chip Duvall answered the door when she knocked.

"Oh, Peyton, hi. Is this a personal visit? I guess not. You're still in uniform."

The chain was still on the door.

"May I come in, Chip?"

"Of course."

He closed the door. She heard the chain rattle, and the door reopened.

The first thing she noticed was the room looked like he'd just checked in: both queen-sized beds made perfectly, TV remote next to the TV, desk materials organized.

"Where is Sherry?"

"Oh, she just stepped out." He wouldn't look at her.

"Will she be back soon?"

"Um … probably."

His cell phone vibrated on the circular table in the corner. He went over and read the text message.

"Will she be back soon?" Peyton asked again, moving to the center of the room.

Both closet doors were open. And a red flag went up.

Chip set the phone down, thinking.

"I'd like to talk to Sherry, Chip. Where is she?"

He looked out the window.

Across Route 1, peopled moved to and fro in the Wal-Mart parking lot. Framed against the late-morning sunlight, they all seemed caught up in separate lives.

"You came to see me because you thought Sherry might be in trouble," Peyton said. "Now I'm reaching out, and you're stalling."

"Not stalling," he said, turning to look at her. "I'm a dentist. That's all. It's what I am. It's what I know."

"What does that have to do with me coming to see Sherry?"

He took a step toward her, his face softening, a faint smile appearing on his face. "I've got a bottle of wine on ice in the bathroom sink. Have a drink with me."

"It's not even lunchtime," she said.

He sat on the corner of the bed. "It's funny, when Sherry described you to me, she never told me how lovely you were."

Lovely.

"The last time I was called *lovely* was by my grandfather," she said.

"Is *sexy* better? Sherry's not going to be back for a while."

He held both hands out, palms up—a *What do you say?* gesture—and looked at the bed, then back at Peyton.

She turned and walked out.

At the end of the hall, she didn't take the stairs. This time, she took the elevator. And this time, she went up to the fourth floor.

When the door of suite 418 opened, it wasn't the man's face that she recalled.

It was his hand.

TWENTY-THREE

ALL SHE SAID WAS: "I'm looking for Sherry."

Not even a last name. He would know who she meant. No *I'm Agent Cote with US Customs and Border Protection.* No *official business* this time. She was in uniform, and the look on his face said her arrival was an unexpected complication.

What had she complicated?

"Sherry and I have been friends since childhood," she said. "I was nearby and thought I'd take her for coffee."

"Who is that, Kvido?" It was Sherry's voice.

Kvido had opened the door of the suite but didn't ask her in. He was missing two fingers on his right hand, the skin at the edges of his palm smooth and strawberry-colored. He stepped back, and Sherry appeared.

"Peyton, how are you?"

"I was in Reeds, remembered you said you were staying here, and thought I'd take you for coffee."

Sherry didn't immediately let her in either. She wore a long, thin sweater and jeans. Peyton noticed she wore no shoes on her feet.

"Sure," Sherry said. "That sounds great."

From behind: "When will you be back?"

The Eastern bloc accent was unmistakable. Peyton wanted to get inside the suite. She wanted to confirm a suspicion, and she couldn't do it from the hallway.

"Sherry, can I use your bathroom before we go?"

"No," Kvido, with the Eastern bloc accent, said from behind Sherry.

"Um," Peyton said, "ah, okay, I'll walk the four flights down to the lobby, I guess."

"There's an elevator," Kvido said.

"No, no," Sherry said. "It's fine. Come in. I'll get my purse while you use the bathroom."

Sherry stepped aside, and Peyton entered the room. Kvido stood, his back to her, dressed in khaki pants and a pale-blue button-down shirt. He was also barefoot.

Unlike room 210, this was a suite. But there was another difference: this room looked lived in—and there were two suitcases on the floor near the closet but only one unmade bed.

In Chip's room, there had been only one suitcase.

————

"It was kind of you to think of me," Sherry said.

They had exited the Hampton Inn, crossed the parking lot and the four-lane Route 1, and now sat in Tim Hortons.

"How are the funeral arrangements coming?"

"I need a florist," Sherry said.

"I can recommend a good one."

Sherry took out her cell phone and typed in Peyton's suggestion.

"Will your children attend the funerals?" Peyton asked.

"I don't think so. They're with Chip's sister in Portland. Do you think they should be at the funerals?"

"Do *I* think they should be?" Peyton said. "Well, it might be hard on them, but they might want closure. I don't know your children. How old are they?"

"Sam, my son, is nine, and Marie is six."

"You named her after your mother," Peyton said.

Sherry looked down at the table. "I learned a lot from my mother."

"What did you learn?"

"You're genuinely interested. I can see it on your face."

"Yes. Personally, I think your mother tolerated your father for too long." Peyton thought about her own mother, a farm wife, yes, but a fighter nonetheless. No one would push Lois Cote around.

"I don't see it that way. Sometimes you get into situations you have no control over, and you have to deal with the consequences."

"You always have control, Sherry. We all have choices."

"That's the difference between you and me. I don't believe that. I was never in a position to change anything. My strength was in dealing with the hand I was dealt."

"You're talking about high school, about us."

"I couldn't change anything then, so I made the best of it. I excelled, I went to Harvard, I did the best I could."

"Are you happy now?"

"Happy? What does that have to do with this conversation?"

"You seem to have it all: a career, two kids, and you married a doctor."

"You always have been like this, Peyton. It's what always drew me to you when we were kids. You have a way of making things seem clear, black and white."

"Is that a good thing?" Peyton asked.

"No. Because they never are black and white. People don't have the choices you think they do, and you need to be able to live with gray."

At the adjacent table, a young mother wearing designer jeans and a Maine Winter Sports T-shirt sat with a toddler in a highchair. She sipped a latte as her baby pushed Cheerios around.

"I shouldn't be having this donut," Sherry said. "It's the last thing I need."

"You look fine. How did you meet Chip?"

"I needed my teeth cleaned. He called afterwards."

"Really? When did you get married?"

"Seven years ago."

"But Sam's nine. Were you divorced?"

"No. Marie is Chip's. Sam is from a prior relationship."

"Hard being a single mom, isn't it?" Peyton said.

"Yes. You would know. That's partly why I married Chip."

For Peyton, it wasn't a reason to get married, but she didn't comment.

"Chip is fine, and I think he loves me, which is all that matters," Sherry said to her coffee.

"Not really."

Sherry looked up. "What do you mean?"

"Your happiness matters," Peyton said. "It's what I was trying to say about your mother."

"Sometimes it's hard to think like that," Sherry said. "I wish you lived in Portland, Peyton. You're easy to talk to you. You understand things."

"I know your past. We're all the results of our childhoods. You are, and I am. If I took time to analyze it, I'd probably realize I'm a Border Patrol agent because my mother did everything in her power to get me to be a farm wife."

"Sounds like you have analyzed it."

Peyton grinned. "God love my mother."

"We're not alike anymore, you know? I mean, look at us. I have a Ph.D., my teaching, my books, because my father made me do it. You have your life for the opposite reason, Peyton. I did what I was told. But you broke away." She turned back to her coffee cup. "Maybe I'm still doing what I'm told."

"Who was the man I met today? You never actually introduced us, Sherry."

"Just a friend, here to help me make funeral arrangements."

"And his name?"

"That's sort of a personal question, Peyton."

"Yeah, I guess it is since your suitcase was in his suite, or his in yours. But I guess that's just semantics. It's really up to you, Kvido, and Chip to decide which room Chip gets alone."

"Peyton, I don't like your tone."

"Why didn't Kvido join us the other morning when you and I met for coffee? He sat in the rental car, the one registered to you. We both saw him from the window. I met you that morning because I thought you needed a friend."

"I did. I *do*," she said. "Believe me."

"Who is he? Why was he watching us? Why did he need to do that?"

"That's none of your business, Peyton."

"And Chip is okay with whatever is going on between you and Kvido?"

"Chip's a sweet man, but he's naive."

"You're telling me he doesn't know?"

"He knows some things."

Peyton watched the young mother feed the baby Cheerios. Sherry's description of Chip didn't jive with the discovery session she'd witnessed—when Chip treated Sherry like a pet, repeatedly patting her on the thigh, telling her (and her attorney, no less) that he was in control.

"When Chip came in the diner," Peyton said, "he told you he'd seen Kvido. He knew Kvido drove away when he arrived."

"Listen," Sherry said, "let's talk about you. You dating anyone?"

"You act as if we're discussing a sweater Chip doesn't know you bought."

"Chip is pulling me in one direction. And Kvido is pulling me in another. Besides, Chip isn't very exciting."

"And Kvido is?"

"You have no idea. Don't you love the accent? I met him years ago in Prague. He attended a workshop I gave at a library. He's a big reader. He read both of my books, came to the workshop because he appreciates my scholarship. We had this wonderful intellectual connection immediately. Now he's come back into my life. He understands me in ways Chip doesn't. I've always had men push me around. You practically said that yourself. But Kvido is different. What we have is different."

They were quiet, Peyton thinking of Sherry's children, of where this left them.

"Are you leaving Chip?"

"Peyton, you ask a lot of questions. All of this is none of your business."

"It would be, if Nancy Lawrence was paid by you to be your brother's alibi."

Sherry looked down at the tabletop. She carefully pushed the donut aside, took a napkin from the dispenser, and wiped a coffee spot.

Finished thinking, she stood. "Thank you for the coffee and donut."

"Sherry, I'm trying to help you. I can't do that if you won't talk to me about Nancy Lawrence. What is going on?"

When Sherry turned to leave, Peyton pushed.

"Obstruction of a Criminal Investigation carries upwards of five years in prison, give or take, depending on how far this goes up the federal ladder."

Sherry turned back. "What?"

"You paid Nancy Lawrence—"

Sherry's head shook side to side, denying even before Peyton was finished.

"—to let Freddy sleep on her sofa the night Simon Pink was shot and the cabin was torched."

"No."

"Sherry, you need my help."

"No," Sherry said. "No. Mind your own business." She walked out.

Peyton called the station and asked for Mitch Cosgrove, the former CPA.

As they spoke, Peyton watched Sherry cross the four-lane highway alone, looking confused when a car honked at her and she had to step back—like a woman nearly blindsided by something she'd never seen approaching.

Then she set her jaw and continued on, moving forward almost blindly.

TWENTY-FOUR

MITCH COSGROVE, THE STATION's resident financial guru, was in Secret Service Agent Wallace Rowe's make-shift office—at the picnic table in what a week ago had been agents' breakroom. Each man had a laptop open, spreadsheets before them.

"Lunch party?" Peyton said.

Cosgrove smiled. Always clean-shaven, he was in his late forties and had a pale, fleshy face. He was not six feet but well over two hundred pounds. Originally from Seattle, he'd joined the Army after high school, attended the University of Washington after, and worked as a CPA on the West Coast before missing what he called "the life." He was one of those—Peyton had known many—who thrived in a rigid, militaristic atmosphere.

Small and wiry, wearing a navy-blue sports jacket, Wally Rowe looked like an accountant who ran 5Ks on the weekends, except his sports jacket gaped when he leaned over his computer, and Peyton saw the Glock 9mm in his shoulder holster.

"This is Agent Peyton Cote," Cosgrove said.

"I recognize the name," Rowe said. "You're the BORSTAR agent."

The Border Patrol Search Trauma and Rescue team was created in 1998 in an effort to save stranded migrants (and others). The tactical unit was comprised of forty-five agents selected from a nationwide applicant pool. It had been Peyton's top professional achievement.

She nodded. "I was nominated and appointed, but you really need to be on the Southern border. I gave up my spot."

"Tough decision?" Rowe asked.

She sat across from him. "El Paso was a great place for an agent," she said, "not for a single mom."

"Never knew that was why you left," Cosgrove said.

"Are you two working on something?" she asked.

"Sort of," Cosgrove said. "Wally did a lot of white-collar investigations when he was with the FBI—"

"About a hundred years ago," Rowe interjected.

"—which is sort of what I'm doing here with Dr. Chip Duvall."

"Perfect," Peyton said. "That's what I was hoping we could talk about."

"You're looking for a paper trail, I assume," Cosgrove said.

"I'm looking for twenty thousand dollars that Sherry St. Pierre-Duvall gave her brother."

"Not sure I have that," Cosgrove said, "but I can tell you what I do have: Fred St. Pierre was behind on his property taxes for five straight years until about thirteen months ago. Then he paid seventy-eight thousand dollars in back taxes. This payment, essentially, saved the farm."

She looked at him, waiting.

"That's what I have so far," he said.

"He had a good year?"

"An optimist," Wally Rowe said. "It's nice to meet one."

Cosgrove just smiled at her. "I'm sure that's it," he said. "Actually, Fred St. Pierre did have a better year. Except, given the price of potatoes that year, it's hard to see how he had seventy-eight grand left over."

"Hard to see, or impossible?" Peyton asked.

"Just telling you what I have," Cosgrove said. "You can devise your own theories. But Wally, who did this kind of work for the FBI, agrees with me."

She looked at Rowe, who shook his head.

"No friggin' way," Rowe said. "That's a big operation. A lot of overhead. He didn't have *that much* of a better year."

"So now we're trying to figure out," Peyton said, "where the seventy-eight grand came from?"

Both men nodded.

"The daughter is married to a dentist," Rowe said. "They live in Yarmouth, Maine, in a house valued at six hundred thousand."

"Think Chip and Sherry bailed out her father?"

"That's the trail I've been following," Cosgrove said. "And it's the one that confuses me most."

"Tell me all about it," she said.

TWENTY-FIVE

MONDAY EVENING, PEYTON WAS at the island in her kitchen, helping Tommy with multiplication.

"How was school?" she asked.

He shrugged, staring at his worksheet.

"Does that mean good, bad, or indifferent?"

Shrug.

On the stove, the lid bounced atop its pot, making a metal-on-
metal clicking sound. Her stool scraped on the tile floor when she
stood to add pasta to the boiling water. She splashed oil into the pot so
the pasta wouldn't stick and regained her stool across from Tommy.

"Look at me, Tommy."

"What, Mom?"

"Are you getting teased at school?"

"What? No. Why?"

"Tell me the truth."

He stared down at the worksheet, but she knew it had become
as inconsequential to her ten-year-old as the price of oil.

"No," he said again. "Nothing. I have lots of friends."

"Do they tease you because school doesn't come easily?"

He was staring at the worksheet. His shoulders started to shake. *Don't cry. Hit the table. Yell and scream. But don't cry.* She knew that if he cried, she would, too.

Her mind ran to a bright desert night several years before when she'd learned just how big the world could be for a child. His name was Pedro, and he'd been about Tommy's age when she found him a half-mile from the Rio Grande, near El Paso, sitting beside his mother, who had bled out following a gunshot wound to her thigh. Peyton never learned what had happened (A stray bullet? An intentional kill shot?) or how much the boy witnessed. But she'd never forgotten him—his wide-eyed stare, looking from one agent to the next, obviously terrified and undeniably alone in a world that was too vast and moving too quickly.

She watched Tommy white-knuckle his pencil and knew her son, whose father showed little interest in him, was also trying to navigate the world's swift-moving currents.

"They call me Lenny," Tommy said, looking straight at her now, tears tracing his cheek.

"Lenny?"

He nodded and sniffled. "Pierre said his brother read a book where the stupid guy is Lenny. So they call me that."

Of Mice and Men. She didn't speak.

"Mom, don't cry."

The water boiled over, and she went to the stove. "I'm not crying, sweetie. What do you say when they call you that?"

"I asked them not to, but they won't stop." He shrugged again, as if ambivalence was becoming his default emotion. "So I just let them."

She dished them each a plate of spaghetti. "Can you get the salads from the fridge?" she said.

He did, looking at her the whole time. "What are you going to do, Mom? It's okay. Don't make it worse."

She put his worksheet in his notebook and set it on an empty chair, brought the plates to the table, and poured two glasses of milk. "How would I make it worse?"

"Like you did with math," he said. "Now I have to leave class every day to work with Mrs. Robertson. I don't like being different."

"You're not different," she said, "and you're not like Lenny from that book. Let's eat, then I'm taking you somewhere special."

"Where?"

"Someplace where you'll learn what to do when people make fun of you."

"It sounds bad," he said.

"It might be," she agreed.

"That sounds fun."

———

"This is where you go in the afternoons?" Tommy said.

"Sometimes," Peyton said, as they crossed the parking lot in Caribou. "This is a dojo. I've spent a lot of time here. Started when I was in high school, but I think you're old enough."

The facility was the Leo Lafleur Gym. Lafleur had been a college wrestler, a Golden Gloves Champion, and was a third-degree black belt. Peyton had known him for more than twenty years. His gym offered fitness equipment, boxing, and karate lessons.

Peyton didn't stop at the front desk. She went right to the back, climbed the stairs, and knocked on the office door. She entered when a voice called, "What?"

"Oh, it's only you," Lafleur said.

"Only? This is Tommy," she said. "I want to enroll him in karate classes."

Lafleur had wrestled at 158 pounds in college. Peyton guessed he wasn't even 160 now, at age sixty-one.

"I'm not teaching the beginner classes. Actually I just hired a new guy to do a couple beginner classes every week. I've seen him with the kids. He's good." Leo Lafleur looked at Tommy and offered his hand. "Call me Leo."

Tommy grabbed Leo's fingers.

"Look me in the eye," Lafleur said, "and squeeze my palm when you introduce yourself." He extended his hand again.

This time Tommy looked at him. "I'm Tommy," he said.

"That's better. You want karate lessons?"

"Yes, sir," Tommy said.

"Why?"

"So I won't get teased."

"That's not a reason," LaFleur said. "Let's take a walk."

Tommy looked at Peyton.

She nodded. "You can go with him." She watched the slight grandfather lead Tommy out of the office. She knew LaFleur still sparred often, and he moved with the grace of an athlete who was still a practitioner.

She went to Lafleur's office fridge and took out a VitaminWater, then turned her chair to see out the picture window and watched Lafleur give Tommy a tour of the facility, talking intently all the while. Lafleur was two heads taller than the boy but repeatedly bent to look Tommy in the eye. Tommy listened and nodded.

Peyton couldn't help but smile. Lafleur had given her the same talk when she'd first entered this gym at age thirteen. There had been no mirrors and chrome then. Just free weights and two rings. But Leo had asked her a series of questions that day. She hadn't answered them, but Tommy was different. He'd already told Leo he was being teased, opening up to him. Again, she thought of her ex and of how badly Tommy wanted (and needed) a male adult role model in his life.

It had taken months for her to trust Leo. But eventually she told him about her father; about how the men from the bank appeared at their kitchen table with papers for her father to sign; about how the family had been left with one acre of land; about how it felt to hear others talk about her father's new job—as a janitor in her school— and about how it felt each time she and her father passed each other in the school hallway and he had to look away.

Eventually she realized why Leo wanted to learn so much about her: if she went the distance—and he saw something in her that told him she would—he was giving her lethal capabilities. He had to know she could handle the accompanying responsibility.

When Tommy and Leo Lafleur returned, he gave Tommy a bottle of chocolate milk from his fridge.

"Your instructor is getting changed, Tommy. He's in the men's locker room. Go down and introduce yourself."

Tommy looked at Peyton again.

She nodded. "I'll be right down."

When Tommy left, Leo got up and closed the door behind him.

"Ask him the standard questions?" she said.

He went to the window and stood watching Tommy, his back to Peyton. She got up and stood next to him.

199

"I don't have standard questions, Peyton. I like to get to know the students, especially the kids. This isn't like an aerobics class. Martial Arts is a way of life."

"I know that."

"He told me about his father."

"You were only with him ten minutes, Leo. What did he tell you?"

The crow's feet near his eyes tightened. "Said he doesn't think his father cares about him."

"Jesus Christ."

"Yeah," Leo said. "That's really shitty."

"He's having a hard time. That's why I'm here." She was staring at Tommy's back as he approached the men's locker room. "He's getting teased at school," she said.

"Pushed around physically?"

"Why do you ask?"

"We don't preach violence or revenge, Peyton. You've been with me too long not to know that."

"I'm talking about self-defense, Leo. I want him to be able to stand up for himself." She was still looking at Tommy, but felt Leo's eyes on her.

"I know you very well," he said.

She turned to face him. "This is my son. I want him to know how to defend himself."

"When he is physically assaulted? Or verbally picked on? There's a difference."

"It's a big world. A tough world, Leo. And Tommy has, essentially, one parent. And every day she leaves the house, there's no guarantee she's coming home. He has to be self-sufficient."

Leo was shaking his head. "Peyton, this isn't about you."

"Not me," she said, "my job."

200

"As a Border Patrol agent?"

"And as his mother. One influences the other."

"What are you saying?"

"I'm making damn sure he'll be able to handle life if I'm ever not here for him. Not just physically. Emotionally, too."

Leo looked at her for a long time.

"I'll have Stone work with him—I'll work with him, too—but let's be honest with each other, Peyton. This is about self-discipline and self-protection—not revenge."

"I wouldn't have it any other way," she said.

Stone Gibson, the state police detective she'd met at her mother's house, walked out of the men's locker room wearing a *gi*. She could tell he obviously remembered Tommy. When Tommy pointed to his mother in the window, Stone waved.

Peyton waved back.

"Know him?" Leo asked.

"We're working the same case," she said.

"Looks like you're working on two cases with him now," Leo said and pointed to Tommy, who was smiling at Stone Gibson.

———

The digital clock on the nightstand read 11:52 p.m.

Peyton sat up in bed at the periphery of her own consciousness, emerging from a deep sleep.

Someone was banging hard on her front door.

She stood, wearing panties and a Red Sox T-shirt, and pulled on sweatpants. Then she pulled her cotton bathrobe on and tied the belt across her waist. She opened the drawer of her nightstand and removed the .40.

She descended the stairs and approached the front door as the pounding grew louder.

When she pulled the door open, Dr. Chip Duvall stood before her, eyes wide open. Peyton thought his eyes also looked a little red.

"Can I, ah, come in?"

"You're drunk, Chip. And my son has school tomorrow. I hope you didn't wake him."

"May I come in?" he said again, eyes on the .40.

"What do you want?"

The rental Ford Escape was in the driveway behind her Wrangler. Beneath the spotlight, Chip Duvall didn't look like he'd rolled out of bed to come here—pressed khaki pants, starched white button-down, navy-blue blazer.

"It's about Sherry, Peyton. She's made some, ah, mistakes. We need to help her."

"She doesn't want my help," Peyton said, "and you need to sleep it off."

"I'm not drunk. Just tired. Please let me in." Before she could answer, he added, "She told me you know about the Nancy Lawrence alibi."

"I see you know about it, too."

"Just found out," he said, sounding as confident now as the man Peyton witnessed patting Sherry's thigh like she were a show dog during the meeting with DA Stephanie DuBois.

"Sherry didn't do anything wrong," he continued. "You need to believe me. Let me come in and talk."

She dropped the pistol in the pocket of her bathrobe and held the door. He followed her to the living room. She hit the wall switch and two lamps snapped on.

"I haven't slept in three days." He took a seat near her on the sofa.

She moved to the far end. "Tell me about the alibi, Chip."

"You're right. Sherry paid Nancy to say Freddy was with her."

"Chip, I need to make you aware of your rights."

He waved that off. The desperation she witnessed at the front door was gone. Now he was a man accustomed to being in charge.

"I don't think you're hearing me," he said. "I'm not here in an official capacity, Peyton. Sherry is a wonderful mother, a loyal friend." He leaned back on the sofa, legs crossed, looking at her.

"How is she as a wife?" Peyton asked.

"What do you mean?"

"The last time I saw that rental Ford, it was driven by Kvido."

"Kvido who?"

"I was hoping you could answer that."

"Are you trying to cause a rift in my marriage?"

"You have separate hotel rooms, Chip. Why are you still protecting your wife?"

He yawned. Five minutes earlier, wide-eyed, he'd pounded on her front door. Now he seemed relaxed, even tired. Coming down from a high? If so, it would go with what Mitch Cosgrove told her about what happened to Chip Duvall's dental practice.

"I really resent what you're saying about Sherry," he said. "And to think she considers you a close friend."

The statement struck her as odd. "We haven't seen each other in years," she said. "Does Sherry have girlfriends in southern Maine?"

"No, not really. Why do you ask?"

She didn't answer. But the desperation she'd seen in Sherry's pleading eyes—longing for someone to understand her situation (whatever that situation was)—made more sense now. If Sherry felt alone, it was because she truly was.

Chip was staring at a blackened living room window. "You're making a judgement of my marriage based on two, three days. My wife is a writer. She needs to be alone. She's working on a very important book. Whoever you saw driving our car was probably her research assistant."

When he entered the diner during Peyton's breakfast with Sherry on Friday, Chip made a point of commenting on the Ford rental leaving upon his arrival. Why was he denying knowledge of the driver now?

There were several questions Peyton still wanted to ask, but couldn't. This wasn't an official interview. And if she asked now, he—and his attorney—would know what was coming the next time they met.

"It's midnight," she said. "Go home to your wife, Chip."

"She's in her hotel room, writing. I have some free time."

She followed his eyes—and immediately pulled her bathrobe tight across her chest.

"What the hell do you think you're doing?" she said.

"Nothing. Just sitting next to an attractive woman."

"I think you're staring at my chest and incriminating you and your wife."

"You're a beautiful woman," he said and slid closer to her on the sofa.

"Stay where you are."

He offered a patronizing smile and leaned toward her, hands first.

She made a short, quick movement.

Then he was on the floor, clutching his windpipe, gasping for breath.

"It'll pass," she said and stood. "When it does, show yourself out."

It did.

And he did.

TWENTY-SIX

SHE MADE NOTES WHEN she was confused.

So Tuesday at 9 a.m., Peyton was at her desk, stylus in hand, a bowl of blueberries near her iPad. Scrawled notes and annotations covered the small screen—names, questions, and words: *cabin, money, bankruptcy, .22.* Lines and arrows connected people to questions and words. She was breaking the clutter into separate groups, seeing what connections she could make. And she was considering holes found in peoples' stories.

There were many holes, even more questions, and a few connections.

A week earlier, Marie St. Pierre saw two men cross her farmland at midnight. Who were they?

Hours later, Peyton had gone to the scene and found a torched cabin and (eventually) a corpse (Simon Pink) in it.

Peyton still didn't know if Pink was one of the two men Marie had seen.

What had Matt Kingston heard? Although she knew the state police had interviewed him, she still hadn't spoken with him since their parking-lot conversation. She underlined his name, needing to talk to him ASAP.

Fred St. Pierre had shot and killed his wife, then himself, after asking forgiveness and saying he hoped someone would understand. From whom did he need understanding?

A search of the farmhouse turned up passports for Marie St. Pierre and Simon Pink, and cash. The amount of cash—$900 for Marie and $500 for Fred Jr.—was too much to have on hand, given that the Duvalls had supposedly bailed out Fred St. Pierre, but not so much that it raised red flags. But it did make Peyton wonder where the disposable income came from.

Marie and Simon had been planning a trip to Prague. Why? And did anyone else know about the trip?

Could she prove Sherry St. Pierre-Duvall paid Nancy Lawrence to let Freddy sleep on Nancy's sofa? Or would Nancy testify that Sherry had paid her to do so, if it came to that?

"What are you doing?"

She looked up to see Miguel Jimenez eating an egg sandwich.

"Every time I see you," she said, "you're eating."

He shrugged. "What is that? Looks like the messy outlines I made for high-school papers."

"It's messy alright. I'm thinking."

"You looked pretty focused," he said. "I called your name twice."

"Sorry. How can you eat that? I can smell the Tabasco from here."

It was dripping off his sandwich onto his paper plate.

He smiled. "I like hot sauce. And Tabasco is for wimps. This is *mi madre*'s recipe."

"If I need to take the paint off my car, I'll call you," she said, then: "Who has the detonators that were found at the St. Pierre farm?"

"State police turned them over to the FBI."

"Really?"

"Yeah," he said. "Why? That mean something?"

Peyton looked past Jimenez at the breakroom. Wally Rowe was talking on the phone.

———

When Rowe hung up, Peyton crossed the bullpen and knocked on the breakroom door.

"Hi," Rowe said. "What's up?"

"Got a sec?"

"For a BORSTAR agent? You bet."

"*Former* BORSTAR agent," she said and smiled.

He wasn't wearing a sports jacket this day. He wore jeans and a dark windbreaker.

"Hey," she said, "what are you working on?"

He leaned back in his seat and frowned. "I'm Secret Service. I'm working on the president's security details."

"Any idea what the FBI is doing in regards to the cabin fire?"

"Why don't you call them?"

"That's not answering my question," she said.

He spread his hands as if to say, *You know I can't talk. Give me a break.*

She wasn't buying it.

"I'll tell you what I think: I think you're collaborating with the FBI. And that you could answer my question, if you wanted to."

"I'm Secret Service," he said again. "By definition my job requires discretion and secrecy."

"And self-importance. Maybe I was expecting too much to think we could share information like two professionals."

"Spare me."

She sat down across from him. He didn't seem pleased, his welcoming smile now long gone.

"Who told the county fire marshal to desist?"

"Just a Secret Service agent. That's me."

"Look, those detonators bother all of us. The FBI isn't here yet, and I know why."

"Why?" he asked.

"You were an FBI agent. You still have contacts there."

"Naturally," he admitted.

"And ties."

"I don't follow you."

"Yes, you do."

"I oversee the president's travel into this state, Peyton."

"I know that. Those detonators would raise red flags at the FBI. And when the FBI looked at the president's travel itinerary, someone at Secret Service got a phone call. You came up here early because of Simon Pink and what was found in that cabin."

Rowe looked at her. His blue eyes steady, his expression stoic, his hands folded calmly in his lap.

"You play poker?" she asked.

"Why?"

"You should," she said.

Finally, a smile. "Thank you. Look, Peyton, I don't want to waste your time. So let me say this: The cabin has moved up the federal foodchain. FBI isn't directly involved in it anymore."

She leaned back in her chair and offered a momentary smile.

"So the CIA has entered the picture?"

He said nothing, which was a confirmation.

"Time for a squeeze-play," she said and went out.

TWENTY-SEVEN

Tuesday, just after lunch, they were in an interview room in Garrett Station. The stationhouse had begun life as a ranch-style home. The room's north-facing window frame had been painted and repainted, but Peyton could see MAGGIE carved into it in jagged letters. She figured this had once been a child's room.

"Thanks for coming in, Dr. Duvall," Stone Gibson said. "I've asked Agents Cote and Cosgrove to join us."

"My attorney says I don't have much choice," Chip Duvall said.

Peyton sat between Stone and Mitch Cosgrove, across the table from attorney Len Landmark and Chip. Chip had a plum-colored bruise near his windpipe and dark rings beneath his eyes. He wore the same khaki pants and creased shirt he'd worn the night before. If he'd showered, his matted hair gave no indication. But Linda Cyr was right—Peyton smelled good cologne.

"Dr. Duvall, you were close to your wife's parents, is that correct?" Stone Gibson smiled warmly at Chip.

"Not particularly. We didn't have a lot in common, aside from my wife and daughter."

"You have a son, too. Is that correct?"

"I meant to say my wife, *my son,* and my daughter."

"You've spent a lot of time here recently, though. Isn't that true?"

"That depends on what you mean by 'a lot.'"

"It seems like you or your wife has come here almost every month for the past year."

"No, not that often."

Gibson looked at Cosgrove.

"You bought gas locally almost every month for the past year," Cosgrove said. "We have your American Express records."

"Didn't seem like we were here that often," Chip said.

Gibson continued, "Your father-in-law ran into some financial difficulty in recent years."

Chip looked at Landmark, who shrugged. Peyton remembered the last time she watched the two of them in a legal proceeding—during Stephanie DuBois and Landmark's discovery session. Chip hadn't let his rattled wife participate, even chastising Landmark publicly. Now, no longer sure of himself, he was looking to the lawyer for advice. He'd come to Peyton twice attempting to somehow skirt the legal system and help his wife—and to seduce Peyton. Those attempts had failed. Was he now running scared?

"Are you asking if Fred had money problems or telling me that he did?" Chip said.

Stone Gibson looked at Mitch Cosgrove. Cosgrove slid a spreadsheet to Chip.

"What's this?"

"Tax records," Cosgrove said. "Anything stand out to you?"

"No."

"What are we doing?" Landmark said. "Why is my client here?"

"Fred Jr. tells us your client helped his father-in-law pay off nearly a hundred thousand dollars in back taxes."

"Freddy told you that?" Landmark said.

"Yes," Cosgrove said.

"Is that illegal?" Chip asked.

"No, but it appears to be impossible. You filed for bankruptcy and closed your practice six months before you gave Fred St. Pierre the money."

"This is embarrassing," Chip said, "and unnecessary."

"Care to elaborate?" Gibson asked.

"That was my wife's money."

"Not possible," Cosgrove said. "She didn't have an extra hundred thousand dollars. We've seen her tax records."

"I don't do her taxes. But I'm telling you what I know. She makes damn good money on her books."

"How do you know that?" Cosgrove said.

"She told me."

"You haven't seen bank statements," Cosgrove said, "royalty checks, tax records, any of that?"

"Do *you* ask your wife for that stuff? No, I didn't ask for verification. I think her books sell well overseas. She's there often."

"How did you lose your practice?" Peyton asked.

Chip's eyes moved instinctively to the questioner. Then he looked away. "My goddamn throat still hurts," he muttered.

"What was that?" Landmark said.

"Nothing," Chip said and faced Peyton. "I lost my practice the way a lot of people lose businesses. I grew too fast. I needed more space. Instead of building one larger office, I got some bad advice and followed it."

"Can you explain that?" she said.

"Yeah, I built a small shopping plaza. I was going to put my practice in one of the store spaces. But then my goddamned anchor store backed out. This isn't easy for me to talk about."

"Please describe your brother-in-law's relationship with Nancy Lawrence," Stone Gibson said.

Chip looked at Landmark, who nodded as if to say, *This is what we prepared for.* Chip cleared his throat. "I guess he knows her."

"Are they intimate?"

"I don't know details of Freddy's love life."

"That isn't quite what you told me last night," Peyton said.

She knew Chip was smart enough to have told Landmark what he said to Peyton the night before. And Landmark would have counseled Chip to offer vagaries to avoid outright lies.

"I'm *not aware* of a relationship between them," Chip said.

"So they weren't dating," Gibson said, "when Fred Jr. spent the night on her sofa last week?"

"I'm not aware of a relationship between them."

"Do your children like to see their grandparents?" Peyton asked.

Chip looked at her. "Sure."

"When you visit, you typically go the St. Pierre farm?"

"Of course."

"And Freddy lives there with his parents?"

"Until they were killed, yes."

"And you or your wife has been here monthly for the past year?" Peyton said.

This time, Chip didn't answer. He sat staring at her.

"You see where I'm going, Chip. A single man, living at home? Do you think for a second that if there was a chance he'd met someone and might now have a life apart from his parents, that his sister, who is professionally successful and married to a doctor and has two kids of her own—his sister, who he has probably been compared to for years—would not know about it?"

"That is entirely speculative, agent," Landmark said. But there was very little bite in his words.

"That's correct," she said. "But here's what is not: all of us know damned well that the alibi won't stand up in court, so the question now becomes, Why did Nancy Lawrence agree to be Freddy's alibi and become complicit in a felony murder?"

Chip looked at Landmark again, and Landmark nodded. Chip shifted in his seat.

"Go ahead," Landmark said.

"All right, Peyton. I thought you were different. You're from here. I thought you would understand. Yes, Nancy Lawrence was paid by my wife." Chip leaned back in his chair, as if the statement took great effort.

"You know that?" Gibson said.

"Yes."

Stone Gibson wrote something on his legal pad. Then he said, "How much money?"

"I'm not sure."

"You have no idea?"

"I heard the figure twenty thousand dollars once."

"Where did you hear it?"

"Sherry was on the phone. She wouldn't say anything to me. That's her. Protecting everyone." Chip sniffled, and Peyton watched his eyes water. "Look," he said, "my wife is a good human being. Freddy didn't shoot anyone. We all know that. And Sherry was just trying to protect—"

"That's enough," Landmark said. Then to Gibson: "I think we're done here. My client has cooperated. He has answered your questions to the fullest of his ability."

"Are you still representing Sherry?" Peyton asked.

"Obviously not," Landmark said.

Stone Gibson looked at Cosgrove to see if he had additional questions. Cosgrove shook his head.

"Thanks for coming in," Gibson said.

When Chip reached the door, Peyton called his name. He turned back.

"When you lost your business, did you lose your home?"

"No," he said.

"That's enough," Landmark said again, and they walked out.

Cosgrove followed them out.

"I'm going to town for lunch," Stone Gibson said to Peyton. "Want to join me?"

———

Stone Gibson's invitation gave her lots to think about as she made the short drive to Gary's Diner.

Pete Dye hadn't called since the last time she'd seen him—a dinner date that ended early and silently. She took the prolonged and uncomfortable silence as an admission by both parties that their lives were not going to mesh. Pete wanted everything, and he wanted it now. But she was forever trying to balance single-motherhood with her commitment to her career, a commitment that her ex-husband and now Pete failed to understand.

She pulled the Ford Expedition onto Route 1, passing over the stretch of Crystal View River that wound through Reeds. Below, a man and woman stopped paddling their kayaks and simply drifted. The river weaved its way between Canada and the US, offering spots in both countries where one could dock with ease—a thought that gave her professional fits most days. This day, though, she considered the couple below with envy: drifting, not worrying about the complexities of life as a professional and a single mom, seemed pretty damned good.

She pulled into the lot at Gary's Diner but didn't get out of the Expedition immediately.

The realization that Pete Dye's inability to understand her commitment to her work meant that he likewise failed to comprehend her *need* for that commitment, a need which comprised so much of who she was, told her it was over between them.

———

It was 2:15 p.m., and Gary's Diner was nearly empty when Peyton walked in. Sitting at the white Formica counter, his back to the front door, was a dark-haired man in a navy-blue sports jacket and jeans, whom she recognized. He sat alone, reading the newspaper. Peyton glanced at him. He didn't turn around.

At the opposite end of the counter was Tom Dickinson, who made eye contact with her and immediately looked down. It took her a moment to place him in her memory because, although he still had the eighties-rocker haircut, he now wore a blue suit and a red tie with blue sailboats.

Stone Gibson sat at the north end of the diner, at a window booth. She turned away from the man at the counter and quickly went to the booth.

Stone smiled. She had to give her mother credit—Stone was nice-looking. No doubt about it. With dark hair and dark eyes, he had a smart, serious look. The kind of guy who would appear at home both hiking Mount Katahdin and toting a briefcase.

He said, "Thanks for coming," and stood when she approached.

"You don't have to get up."

He looked embarrassed and sat quickly, and she realized her comment was a mistake—he stood because this was a first date of sorts to him.

"Thanks for inviting me," she said.

The man at the counter was facing them now. She made eye contact, and he offered a smirk and raised his coffee cup as if to say, *Here's to you.*

"Who's that?" Stone said. "And what the hell happened to his hand? He's missing fingers, and that's quite a scar."

"I don't really know who that is," Peyton said. "Sherry St. Pierre-Duvall says he's her research assistant. But I think she's sleeping with him."

"That would explain why the family attorney, Len Landmark, told you he wasn't representing Sherry anymore."

"Yes, it would."

Tina Smythe came to the booth. When Stone dropped his eyes to look at the menu, Tina glanced at Peyton with a raised brow.

Peyton refocused on her menu.

"Tommy enjoyed his first karate class with you," Peyton said, after ordering a chef's salad. Stone had ordered a roast-beef sandwich.

"He's a nice kid. Strong, too, for his age."

Tina set two iced teas and some sugar packets before them. Then a bell chimed behind the counter—an order was up—and she hurried back to put a turkey-platter lunch special before the man Peyton knew only as Kvido.

Stone sipped his iced-tea. "You grew up with Freddy St. Pierre, right?"

"Sort of. He was younger than me."

"Think he did it?"

"Murdered Pink?" she asked. "It doesn't look good for him. We have the gun, and he's got a bad alibi. But we can't place him at the scene. And I know he knows more than he's saying. I'm trying to get him to realize he can help himself by talking to me."

"You've got the cabin. I've got the murder that apparently happened in it."

"A lot of overlap," she said.

"I think so. It would be nice if we could cooperate."

"Isn't that what we're doing?"

He smiled.

"Hear anything from our three-letter friends about the cabin?" she asked.

"Last I heard FBI was looking into it."

"They handed it off to the CIA," she said.

"That mean something to you?"

"CIA is usually interested in what we do only if there's an intelligence angle."

He looked at her. "So what's the CIA involvement mean?"

"Not sure," she said, "but they're interested in the detonators found in the cabin."

"You think Simon Pink was making bombs?"

"He had a chemistry background."

"And idiosyncratic crimes are on the rise," he said.

"I love that term," she said and shook her head. "To most people, it's shorthand for *disgruntled nut job who gets angry at the world and goes it alone.*"

"Alone or not," he said, "anybody can be dangerous."

"The shootings at the Colorado movie theatre, Sandy Hook, and poor Gabby Giffords showed us that," she said, and looked around. Only Kvido and Tom Dickinson were in the diner, but she still whispered it: "I cried each of those days," she said.

"We got the shooter—or they killed themselves—in each case."

"But someone lost a child—more than one mother did, actually—each of those days."

"And you're a mom."

She nodded. "Never told anyone I work with about crying on those days."

"Why tell me?" he asked.

She smiled. "You're a statey, not an agent. I don't technically work with you."

"Just a lowly state trooper," he said.

"Lowly," she repeated and smiled.

Stone Gibson was easy to talk to. She didn't know him well, but he seemed entirely relaxed—truth be told, more relaxed than she was. He sat deep on his bench seat, one arm on the back of the booth, the other on the table; he stirred extra sugar into his iced tea and glanced occasionally out the window at passing cars.

"The problem with idiosyncratic crimes," she continued, "is motive. It's hard to find the motive for a lot of these crimes."

"Because most of the time you have to be crazy to understand what they're thinking," he said. "Or the cowards kill themselves before we can interrogate them. Almost makes you miss the good old days of straight-forward terrorism."

220

"I wouldn't go that far," she said. "Don't forget it took two different presidential administrations and nine-eleven for us to *understand* bin Laden and take the bastard seriously."

Peyton drank some iced tea.

"If the president cancels his trip up here," Stone said, "then we'll know whatever the hell this is all about is serious."

"If he's going to cancel," she said, "I hope he does so today. Tomorrow a game warden and I are scheduled to spend the afternoon showing Secret Service agents a trail to a stream that the president wants to fish for brook trout."

"Heard he didn't catch a thing last year."

"He didn't," she said. "And I sat in a tree-stand with binoculars, like it was bow season, and swatted black flies for three hours."

Crows hovered near a garbage can in the parking lot. Two young moms pushed strollers on the sidewalk, talking. A green Ford Escape pulled in and parked near the window.

Kvido swiveled on his stool, saw the Escape, looked at Peyton and Stone, and said, "Be right back" to Tina in his thick Eastern bloc accent. Then he headed for the door, leaving his turkey platter on the counter.

Peyton watched Kvido hustle to the Escape. The driver's-side window was down. Kvido leaned forward and said something. There was a brief exchange loud enough to make the mothers pushing strollers pause and look. Then the Escape reversed and drove out of the parking lot. Kvido returned to the diner, took $10 from his wallet, and set it next to his untouched turkey platter.

"Your friend didn't want to join you?" Peyton called to him.

That comment stopped Kvido at the door, but only momentarily. He raised his burned hand as if to point a finger at her—he was missing his index and middle fingers. His mouth parted, but he said nothing. He turned and walked out.

Tom Dickinson stood, left some bills near his plate, and walked out, too. He'd barely touched his lunch.

"What was that about?" Stone asked.

Peyton was watching Kvido cross the parking lot and turn in the same direction the Escape had gone.

"I don't know," she said.

"Sherry St. Pierre-Duvall probably didn't want to eat near the cop investigating her brother," Stone said.

"That's the thing," Peyton said. "Sherry wasn't the one in the Escape. Her husband Chip was."

TWENTY-EIGHT

"I REMEMBER BEING HERE twenty years ago," Peyton said to Thomas Simpson, Garrett High School principal. "I was waiting for my father to arrive and bracing to be grounded."

"Matt will be down in a minute," Simpson said.

Peyton thanked him for his cooperation.

Simpson looked far too young to intimidate teenagers. Thin and blond, he looked more like a volunteer Little League coach than a disciplinarian.

"Ever meet Michael Garnett?" she asked.

"He was something of a mentor to me. He was principal here more than thirty years. Scared the hell out of everyone."

"Including me."

"That's not my style. I have an assistant principal who's as intimidating as Hulk Hogan."

She grinned. They were in Simpson's office. There was a photo cube on his desk. It held pictures of a blond woman and three little girls.

"Yours?" she asked.

"Rosey is eight, Mary is six, and Emily is four."

"My son, Tommy, is in fifth grade."

"He having a good experience in the school district?"

"Actually, he isn't. But I'm not here to talk about my son."

"I know that, but as a district administrator, I would like to hear about it."

"Tommy has struggled this year, was just tested, and it turns out he's dyslexic."

"We have excellent resource rooms."

"He's also being bullied," she said.

Simpson's eyes narrowed. He leaned forward. "That's unacceptable. Have you mentioned it to his teachers?"

"Not yet. Didn't want to make it worse."

Simpson wrote something on a sticky note just as there was a faint knock on the door. He stood, rounded his desk, and let Matt Kingston in.

"I'll give you a few minutes alone," Simpson said and left.

———

Matt Kingston, according to his birth certificate, had been born in Reeds and was eighteen. If she didn't have that information in a manila folder in front of her, she wouldn't have believed it. He looked all of twelve. His acne hadn't improved since she'd seen him Friday, and his shoulder-length hair hung in greasy clumps. His eyes made him look older than he was. They reminded her of her late-father's eyes at the end of the potato harvest—the dark rings, the drooping lids, the dullness from exhaustion. It was hard to remember he was a high schooler.

He again wore his light-blue work shirt, MATT stitched into the breast pocket.

"Do you remember me?" she asked.

He nodded and looked at the closed door.

"I bet this office gives you the creeps," she said. "It sure gave me the creeps in high school. I landed here too often. Once, we put Alka Seltzer in the fish tank during a science lab."

"No way," he said. "That's awesome."

"Don't try it," she said and smiled. "I got suspended for a day—and that was just for being in the room. The guy who dropped them in there was out for a week." She thought about how ironic it was that the culprit, Pete Dye, was now a teacher himself.

"Wow."

His reaction made her smile. He might have old man's eyes, but he was still a kid.

"Matt, do you work at Mann's Garage?" She pointed to his shirt.

"Yeah. I change oil for Tom Mann after school."

"Then you go to Tip of the Hat?"

"After dinner for a few hours, four nights a week."

"You're a busy guy," she said.

He shrugged.

"What do your folks do?"

"Dad farmed."

"But not anymore?" she asked.

He shrugged again. And that was all she needed: she could predict the rest of the story.

"I grew up here," she said. "My dad lost the farm when I was in seventh grade."

"So you know what it's like?"

"Oh, yeah. We lost everything. But to a twelve-year-old girl, I didn't care about the house, the land, the tractors. For me, it meant going to school in Kmart clothes and hand-me-downs. Half-used school notebooks. Buying inserts instead of getting new basketball sneakers."

He was staring at the worn toe of his boot and nodded.

"But you know what?"

He looked up.

"It's all bullshit," she said. "Doesn't mean a thing. I studied hard, went off on my own, and my family made it. My sister's studying to become a teacher. My mother is doing fine."

"And you became an agent."

She smiled.

"I got a letter from the University of Maine saying I would get a merit scholarship."

"So you're hard-working *and* smart."

"I don't want to blow the U-Maine offer," he said. "I need that scholarship. It's my way out. I can't blow it."

"You won't blow it."

"If they know I jack deer, they might rescind the offer."

"*Rescind* the offer?"

"SAT word. I study a lot."

She smiled. "I don't know one Border Patrol agent who can use that word in a sentence."

"That's *hyperbole*," he said.

"Now you're just showing off."

He smiled.

"You won't blow the offer, Matt. I can get you an attorney, if you want."

"Do I need one? Am I in trouble?"

"No," she said. "I'm not interested in deer-jacking, although you may want to give that up for a while."

"I only do it once a year. I usually try to take a two-hundred-pound buck. Get enough meat off that to feed my dad and me for a year."

"I want to know what you saw and heard last Monday night."

He moved his palms over the arms of his chair, wiping perspiration.

"It's okay, Matt. Take your time."

"It was dark," he said. "But I know I heard three voices."

"You are sure you heard three?"

"Yes."

"You could clearly differentiate three voices?"

"I heard three. I was along the tree line at the north end of the property. Johnny"—he stopped suddenly—"I mean, a kid at school, told me there were a lot of deer in that forest. He said they eat Fred St. Pierre's garden broccoli. Ever smell that stuff?"

She smiled and nodded.

"Well, you can smell it a mile away. No wonder no one wants to eat the stuff. Smells terrible."

She waited.

"Anyway," he continued, "I heard three people."

"Men?"

"I think so."

"Are you certain?"

"I think so," he said again. "One person was really quiet, hard to hear."

That wasn't good enough, but she had other things to cover, and he was scared. They could come back to that.

"Can you tell me what they sounded like? Do you remember an accent?"

"One had an accent. He was doing most of the talking."

"What did he sound like?"

"Kind of like the bad guy in *Rocky IV*."

"Can you remember anything that was said?"

"This is what I told the other officer. I don't think they were friends."

"You've spoken to another Border Patrol agent?"

"Well, yeah. She said she needed to speak to me about that night. It was the day after I talked to you in the parking lot at school. I figured you sent her."

Peyton immediately thought of State Police Detective Karen Smythe. But she hadn't told Karen about the young witness a day after Peyton had spoken to him. Had Hewitt notified her? Which trooper was leading the murder investigation, Stone or Karen?

"Was she in uniform? A state trooper?"

"No uniform."

"What did you tell her?"

"That one guy sounded Russian. And the other two didn't. That they were talking about money. And steps. I remember that word, *steps*."

"Can you walk me through the conversation you heard that night?"

"I got out of there pretty quick, didn't hear too much. I figured one of them was Mr. St. Pierre since it was his land, and I know he's a real hard-ass. But as I was walking out, I heard a gunshot—not a loud boom like a deer rifle; smaller, like a firecracker—but I saw a flash in the cabin."

"The shot came from inside the cabin?"

"Yes."

"Could you make out what each of the men looked like?"

"No."

"Clothes they wore?"

He shook his head. "I was behind a tree, staying out of sight. I saw the flash in the cabin window. Then I left."

"And you told all of this to someone already?"

"Actually, not the part about *steps*. I just remembered that."

"Did the officer leave a business card, say you could call if you remembered anything else?"

"No. Is there something wrong?"

"Just trying to see if I know her. What did the officer wear?"

"Sunglasses, a hat, and a windbreaker zipped up to her chin. It seemed too warm for the jacket, but I figured she was cold. We only talked for a couple minutes. She was in a hurry."

"Did she pull you out of class?" To do so, Peyton knew, required one to sign in at the desk in the main office—there would be a name in the log.

"No. Stopped me in the parking lot before school. Just wanted to know if I saw the men. When I said I didn't, she nodded and left."

———

"I'll start the grill," Peyton said.

It was 6:15 p.m., Tuesday, "sacred sister night." And Peyton and Tommy were at Elise's. Peyton had brought chicken.

"Have to love Aroostook County summers," Elise said, following Peyton out the sliding-glass door off the kitchen onto the deck. She carried a bottle of red wine and two glasses.

"That's what I told myself when we got three inches of snow the first week in April," Peyton said. "I'm cooking lemon-pepper chicken and asparagus on the grill. I brought a salad; it's in the fridge."

"Keep doing this and I'll ask you to move in." Elise poured two glasses of red, left one on the glass table for Peyton, then sprawled on a deck chair. Autumn was in a playpen nearby.

"I knew you had a late class."

"A senior seminar in pedagogy," Elise said. "I don't think the professor ever taught high school. I can't see him controlling a group of teenagers. He can't even engage us, and we're paying to be there. I volunteer at the high school—student teaching is still a year away, but it looks good on the resume—and the seniors I tutor would eat him alive."

"That's how practice-versus-theory goes," Peyton said. "How is tutoring?"

"Not profitable, but I love it. My advisor set it up. A woman a little younger than me has me come to her American Literature class one day a week and help students with their papers. I have thirty papers to read and comment on tonight."

"You don't happen to have Matt Kingston, do you?"

"Peyton, there are only a hundred and thirteen seniors in the Garrett High School graduating class. I helped him with an essay once. He was applying for a scholarship to U-Maine. Why?"

———

The table had been cleared. Max had his plastic John Deere tractor in the kitchen; Tommy was working on a math worksheet in the living room; and Peyton and Elise had just spent ten minutes loading the dishwasher.

"Everything I just told you is confidential," Peyton said. She settled Autumn on her lap, a book before the toddler, preparing to read to her. "Never leaves this kitchen."

"Of course," Elise said. "I'm glad Matt didn't actually see the shooting. From reading his essay and talking to him about it, I can tell he's a sensitive kid. Who do you think went to see him?"

"I have an email into Karen Smythe, and Mike Hewitt has contacted the Secret Service and the FBI to see if either of them sent someone."

"Could it be the CIA?" Elise asked. "You said they were involved now."

"If it was a CIA agent," Peyton said, "I may never know it."

TWENTY-NINE

"THE FBI DIDN'T SPEAK to Matt Kingston," Mike Hewitt said Wednesday at 8:15 a.m. at his debriefing with Peyton. "Neither did the Secret Service. And the kid doesn't know enough to make me think what he does know is worth lying about."

"CIA?" Peyton asked.

Her iPad was on her lap; she was typing. Behind her, yellow sunlight splashed through the window onto the thin gray carpet.

"If it was CIA," Hewitt said, "we'll never know it."

"That's what I figured. It wasn't Karen Smythe. I called her. If the CIA talked to Matt Kingston, there's much more to all of this than meets the eye."

"In that case, Simon Pink is a hell of a lot more important than either of us thinks he is."

"Matt Kingston says one man's voice sounded like Drago from *Rocky IV*. And others have said Simon Pink had a Russian accent."

"So if Pink was one of the two men Marie St. Pierre saw crossing her land at midnight," Hewitt said, "who's the second man?"

"Probably the person who shot him," Peyton said. "But Matt Kingston says three men were there, not two."

"Three?" Hewitt said. "So someone was waiting for the other two?"

"I don't know. But Matt was close enough to be reliable."

They were quiet, and Peyton added to her notes, typing furiously on the iPad's virtual keyboard.

"CIA involvement doesn't feel right," she said. "You know that, don't you?"

"I do," he said.

"A CIA agent would walk in here and demand to know everything I learned from Matt Kingston. They wouldn't sneak around behind my back."

"I wouldn't give them that much credit. They might tap your phone."

She thought about that. "Even so, if we assume it's the CIA, it gives us nowhere to go."

"Okay," he said, "so if it wasn't the state police, it wasn't the FBI, and it wasn't the CIA, who the hell went to see Matt Kingston?"

"Whoever it was wanted to know what Matt saw in the woods that night. Matt said it was a female, wearing a windbreaker zipped up to her chin, sunglasses, and a hat."

"In June?"

"Yup."

"Someone is fucking with this investigation," Hewitt said.

"That's what I think," she said and typed two names on her iPad.

Hewitt stood and went to the file cabinet near the door. A Mr. Coffee machine was atop the cabinet.

"You finally broke down and bought a coffee maker?" she said.

"I figured, Who am I kidding? I drink six cups a day. Why keep walking to the breakroom? Want a cup?"

She shook her head. He'd been military for a decade. And she'd heard all about military coffee. If she thought Tim Hortons was mediocre, she could only imagine how Hewitt made the stuff.

"We need an espresso bar in this town," she said.

"Go to a town council meeting and ask for one," he said. "I'm sure they'll get right on it."

He poured himself a cup and brought it back to his desk.

"I do have one update," he said. "Stephanie DuBois cut a deal with Nancy Lawrence's attorney for Nancy's statement and potential testimony admitting she was paid for Freddy's alibi the night Simon Pink was murdered."

"Really?"

"You surprised?"

"Stunned," Peyton said, using her stylus to circle one of the two names she'd typed. "She was at the top of my list of those who might have talked to Matt Kingston."

"Still could be," Hewitt said. "She has a lot to lose if she's in any way tied to Pink's murder. You're biting your lip and staring at the floor. What is it?"

"What's Nancy's agreement?" she asked.

"Probation—for her admission that Sherry paid her to let Freddy sleep on her sofa and to lie about dating him."

"Probation? For what might end up being accessory to a murder?"

He shrugged. "Don't blame me for the lawyer bullshit."

"When I first mentioned Nancy to Sherry," Peyton said, "she told me Nancy—she called her a 'little slut'—was somehow behind all of Freddy's problems."

"Maybe Sherry St. Pierre-Duvall, Ph.D. and all, is a little nutty," Hewitt said.

Peyton blew out a long breath. "Nancy's statement won't look very good for Freddy or Sherry. Do they know Nancy turned on them?"

"If they don't, they will soon." He narrowed his eyes. "You do realize this is a positive development, right? The noose is tightening on Freddy St. Pierre."

"If he did it, it's positive. If he didn't do it, we got Nancy Lawrence to give us the wrong guy. We still can't place Freddy at the crime scene, Mike."

"Maybe he's the third guy Matt Kingston heard," Hewitt said.

"Maybe." She wrote something on her iPad.

"Sherry paid someone to be her brother's alibi," Hewitt said. "That's an admission that he was guilty of something in my book."

"An admission of guilt for something, yes. But not necessarily of murder, Mike. And Len Landmark says he's not representing Sherry St. Pierre-Duvall now, only Chip."

"They splitting up?" Hewitt said.

"Sherry is sleeping with her research assistant."

"Not usually conducive for marital bliss," Hewitt said. "Where are their kids?"

"In Portland with Chip's sister. The son is Chip's adopted child. Sherry had him with someone else."

"So this will be her second divorce?"

"I don't think she was married. I was at the diner yesterday, and Sherry's research assistant, a guy from Prague, was at the counter when Chip pulled up. The research assistant stopped him in the parking lot. They had an exchange, and Chip drove off without coming in."

"I'd have met him in the parking lot, too," Hewitt said, "and I'd have kicked his ass for him, if I was trying to eat lunch and the bastard who was screwing my wife showed up."

"That's the thing," she said. "I can see why they wouldn't like each other. But it was the other way around—Kvido was eating and Chip showed up. Why didn't he walk in and punch Kvido's lights out?"

There was a faint knock on the door. Hewitt told whoever it was to come in.

"Peyton"—it was Linda Cyr—"Freddy St. Pierre has requested a meeting with you."

THIRTY

"I'm sitting here shaking my goddamned head, eh," Freddy said at 9:25 a.m. in an interview room in Garrett Station.

"I hear this is your last day in Garrett," Peyton said.

She'd just sat down across from him. The window was wire mesh, but the glass was bright, as if sunlight outside reflected off it.

Len Landmark—who said he no longer represented Sherry St. Pierre-Duvall (only husband Chip)—had apparently deserted both sister and brother because now it was young Steve St. Louis, a local attorney, who sat next to Freddy. St. Louis was all of twenty-eight and wore a Polo shirt and khaki pants. Peyton knew this was his first murder trial. His golf shoes were wet and full of grass.

"Come from the course?" Peyton asked St. Louis.

"Especially for this." He smiled eagerly—the same smile the salesman had offered her when listing all the accessories on her new Jeep Wrangler.

She said, "I hear they're taking you to Houlton tonight or tomorrow, Freddy."

She knew Freddy wouldn't like that, remembered well his comments about the farm outside Garrett being the last place he'd seen his mother happy. But she didn't care. Now that he wanted to see her, she could play hardball.

"They really moving me?" Freddy looked at St. Louis, who only shrugged.

"I just got here," St. Louis said, "but I'll be sure to look into it."

Freddy turned back to Peyton. "You bullshitting me?"

Peyton ignored him. "I also heard that Nancy Lawrence is kicking your ass to the curb. No alibi."

Freddy looked down at the tabletop between his forearms. "She's a bitch," he said.

"I'll ask that you treat my client with the respect and dignity that he deserves," St. Louis said.

"If I was treating him with the respect he deserves," she said, "I'd taser his ass. How come, when I asked you to talk to me last week, Freddy, you wanted no part of it?"

"I couldn't then."

"But you can now?"

Freddy looked up at her. "I have to now, eh."

"You're a real sweet-talker, Freddy. I can see why Nancy turned on you."

"She told them because a cop lied and said she could go to jail."

"It's no lie. It's called Obstruction of a Criminal Investigation."

St. Louis was taking notes on a yellow legal pad, and his first murder case had him looking like a freshman trying to keep up in a linear-algebra class.

"It's only true if I was guilty of something," Freddy said.

"Okay, Freddy," Peyton said. "Then can you please explain to me why you appear to be the first man in the history of the criminal-justice system to need an alibi when you are not guilty of anything?"

"We need to speak seriously," Freddy said.

She took her iPhone out, hit Record.

St. Louis reached over, tugged Freddy's shirt sleeve. "I think we should discuss whatever you have to say privately, Fred, before you speak to Agent Cote."

"I can't get myself in trouble, eh, because I didn't do it all."

Peyton sat up straight, made sure the iPhone was recording, and said, "I need you to explain that, Freddy." No longer exhausted and frustrated, she knew if she could get Freddy to start talking the spool might come unwound.

"Please be quiet now," St. Louis said.

"No," Freddy said. "I want you to separate the fire from the shooting. They ain't connected. I didn't shoot nobody."

"Fred, that's enough," St. Louis said.

Peyton leaned forward. "What are you telling me, Freddy?"

"I didn't know anyone was in there, Peyton. That's the truth."

"None of this is on the record," St. Louis said. "You hear me, Peyton? None of it."

"He's been given his Miranda warning, Steve," Peyton said. "You know that. Everything is admissible."

But she wasn't looking at St. Louis as she spoke. She was staring at Freddy St. Pierre. And processing what he'd just said.

"Did you set that fire, Freddy?"

He looked at her. She waited. Stranger things had happened on farms in Aroostook County. The year before, a farmer couldn't make payments on his loans. Mysteriously, his barn burned to the foundation. Three months later an insurance check arrived. It took the fire marshal six months to prove arson.

Beads of perspiration popped on Freddy's forehead.

"You don't have to say anything, Fred," St. Louis said.

"Can you separate the fire from the shooting?" Freddy asked.

"You need to tell me the whole truth, Freddy," Peyton said, "before we can discuss that. I need to know what really happened."

"I don't know nothing."

"You know something," she said.

"I didn't know that was part of the plan."

"Tell me what the plan was," she said.

"I don't know," he said. "I did what I was paid to do."

"Burn down your cabin?"

"Uh-huh."

"What did your father think of that?" she said.

"He didn't know."

"Who paid you?"

Freddy looked at St. Louis.

"Again, Freddy," St. Louis said, "I urge you to stop talking."

And he did.

She turned off the iPhone recorder, pocketed it, and drove directly to Garrett High School.

———

A half-hour later, Peyton was back in her service vehicle, driving toward a fishing spot called Black Water Creek, where she was to meet game warden Pete McPherson.

Traveling north on Route 1 toward Caribou, she glanced at the Crystal View River. At this time of day, she knew you had to fish the edges, casting toward the riverbanks, hoping to pick off trout or bass moving slowly in the mid-day sun.

She'd learned a lot in the past twenty-four hours from Matt Kingston and Freddy St. Pierre.

According to Freddy, he had built the cabin with his father, and then been paid—as part of someone's master plan—to burn it.

Freddy wanted to separate the arson from the shooting. Seeing as he was facing a murder charges and they had the weapon, and it was his, that was smart. He would say, she assumed, that, sure, he'd gone to the cabin—probably early in the morning—discovered no one around, and lit the fire.

What he didn't know was that Peyton's stop at Garrett High School had been highly productive: Matt Kingston recognized Freddy's voice instantly as one of the three people he'd heard when Peyton played her iPhone recording. In court, the recognition might be merely circumstantial. But if Kingston took the stand, his reaction—the quick nod, the knee-jerk "No question that's one person I heard"—could be damning for Freddy because it placed him at the scene of the murder when the murder took place. He may have met Nancy Lawrence at the Tip and slept on her couch, but he was definitely at the cabin earlier that night.

So Freddy had been there and the late Simon Pink had been there. Who was the third person?

She pulled to the side of the road, took out her cell phone, and dialed. When Stone Gibson answered, she said, "Remember when we said since you're heading the murder investigation and I'm looking into what was taking place in the cabin, there would be overlap? Well, I have some news for you," she said. "I can place Freddy St. Pierre at the crime scene when Pink was shot. Freddy doesn't know it yet."

And she told him what Matt Kingston had said.

THIRTY-ONE

"Thanks for volunteering to help out," Pete McPherson said, climbing out of his green pickup, the Maine Warden Service insignia on the door.

She liked McPherson, had known him a long time. He was in his sixties and had been a mainstay in the local law-enforcement community for as long as she could remember. He'd also been Tommy's Little League coach the previous spring.

"*Volunteering?*" she said. "Do people *volunteer* to pound their thumbs with hammers?"

"Are you saying you don't want to wander through six miles of trail," he grinned, "making sure the boogie man isn't out there preparing to bite the president? You're as cynical as your father was."

She smiled. "That's why you and I get along." She pulled her backpack from the pickup's bed and put a Nalgene bottle in the pack's side pocket. "You knew him well," she said.

"Old Charlie Cote. Cynical but generous. Word around town was if you needed a team sponsored, even when the economy was down and everyone—even the bank and grocery store—said no, just go ask Charlie Cote. Cote Farm will sponsor your Little League team."

"Or Pee Wee basketball team," she said, "or whatever team it was. Old softy. Until he lost the farm."

"And he'd probably have gone hungry to do so, even then," McPherson said. "I was at my grandson's soccer game, week before last and saw you there with your son. It made me think of Charlie."

"I wish he were here for Tommy, especially since I'm divorced."

She wore her backpack and her hiking boots were laced. In her pack were spare maps, PowerBars, an extra clip for her .40, a Maglite, and a first-aid kit with several Ace bandages. On her service belt were hair ties, her revolver, her handcuffs, a baton, and pepper spray. It might be a pointless, two-hour hike, but she followed protocol. As a BORSTAR agent, she'd seen what could go wrong when agents and hikers entered the wilderness unprepared.

"Are Wally Rowe and his guys already in there?" She pointed toward the mouth of the trail.

"The Secret Service isn't coming," McPherson said, "which, by the way, is a plus."

"I thought we were leading them through the trails," she said.

McPherson held his forest-green Maine Warden Service cap out and sprayed it with Ben's 100. He had a full head of white hair and thick, liver-spotted hands.

"Rowe cancelled," he said. "You and I are supposed to go through the trail along the brook today, find some nice fishing spots—which is to say easy-to-access spots—and then we'll lead them through when the president arrives."

"I think the president is going to cancel," she said.

"Why?"

"Last summer, when we did this, there were fifteen Secret Service agents with us, and we examined every knot on every tree."

"I don't think he's canceling. I think the Secret Service knows what a waste of time that was last year."

"And the Secret Service doesn't mind you and I wasting our time," she said, "as long as they don't waste theirs."

"Again, your old man's cynicism," McPherson said and smiled.

He took the lead, moving swiftly on the trail, with Peyton several steps behind. A bed of pine needles covered the path.

"The president and his grandson might actually catch some fish this year," McPherson said. "Judging from the pine-needle covering, no one's been out here in a while."

"So the brook won't be fished out," Peyton said, "if they actually come here." She swatted a fly. "Of course, you have to fight the black flies in order to stand along the water's edge to cast."

"That's why they make Ben's 100."

"Ever hear of DEET?" she said. She was maybe ten yards behind him, scanning the edges of the trail.

"Screw it," he said. "We'll all die of cancer anyhow."

The trail was narrow, its sides lined with pines and balsam firs. Through the canopied tree cover, she could see a red-tailed hawk circling.

"There are a few big, flat rocks to stand on," Peyton said. "Should we mark the trees near them? I've got some tape."

"Not our job," McPherson said. "They can hire a guide for that."

"I was also thinking we could flag rocks we thought would give Rowe and his colleagues vantage points to cover the president."

"Good idea," McPherson said.

"Wally Rowe didn't ask you to do that?"

"Nope," he called over his shoulder.

"Did he give any directions?" she asked. "Did he mention what we should be looking for?"

McPherson turned to see her. "He said just to do a walk-through. See if anything looks out of the ordinary."

"I don't see even one footprint," she said.

They walked for twenty minutes more, McPherson stopping at one point to throw a line in the brook.

"Wish I'd have brought waders," he said. "This is a good time of year to fish this brook. Ever come out here with Tommy?"

"Not yet. Came here with my father, though. The brook looks deep in the middle."

"No more than four feet," he said. "I've crossed it in waders."

"Fast moving," she said. "Shouldn't be crossing in waders. You ever slip, the current will pull you away. You'll drown for sure."

"Okay, mom. I don't cross it when it's four feet, Peyton. I do that in late summer. In the spring, I use a fly, toss it to the middle, and let the current carry it downstream. Caught an eighteen-inch trout last year."

"My father and I used worms here."

After several casts, McPherson reeled his line in, and they moved on. They were maybe a mile into the trail when McPherson slowed.

"What is it?" Peyton said from thirty feet behind.

"Just a couple footprints." He stepped closer and knelt.

"Border Patrol agents call that sign-cutting," she said.

"Yeah," he said, "I've heard Hewitt use that term before."

Sign-cutting meant reading a landscape's characteristics and deducing what might have taken place there. It could mean noticing a broken tree branch and deciding the corresponding footprints were traveling west. Or it could mean noting the difference between a wind-swept desert or snow-covered trail and one that had been swept with a broom.

"Tough to spot a footprint in pine needles," she said, moving closer, standing at his side, genuinely interested.

"See how these are turned over and crushed?" he said.

"Animal?"

"Boot," he said.

"You can distinguish a footprint from an animal track?"

"I do this all day, every day. And when I'm not working, I'm moonlighting as a guide."

She didn't dispute it. No one knew the Maine woods like game wardens who traipsed these trails for hours, year after year, checking licenses and looking for poachers. And no one would know these parts better than a warden who also served as a guide.

"What do you see?"

"Someone's been through here recently," he said, "maybe within the past twenty-four hours. But it looks like they tried to sweep over their tracks."

She knelt closer. "I dealt with this in Texas. People would tie a broom to their waist to sweep their tracks as they walked."

The pine-needle bed didn't much resemble a desert floor, but she saw similar brush lines.

McPherson continued on. It was eighty-five in the mid-day sun and humid. Peyton paused, took her pack off, unscrewed the top of the Nalgene bottle, and drank. The water was no longer cold, but it was refreshing, nonetheless.

She leaned forward to return the bottle to her bag when the overwhelming, startling rush of hot air hit her. The physical sensation was the same as she'd once had standing near a jet engine on the tarmac in El Paso. The sound, though, was like a shotgun's guttural rumble, but louder—it engulfed her.

She was on her back before she realized the explosion had knocked her off her feet.

THIRTY-TWO

In the aftermath of the blast, she sat up, disoriented but certain what she'd heard wasn't a gunshot.

"Mr. McPherson," she said, shaking her head and struggling to her feet. Off balance, she stumbled and fell. The blood and her torn pant leg—indicators of why she couldn't stand—served as ice water to her face: there had been an explosion.

No longer dazed, she yelled, "Mr. McPherson!"

On hands and knees, she swiveled to see him. Pete McPherson lay maybe thirty feet ahead of her. In her periphery, she saw something leathery that was streaked with red, the way paint beads when applied too thickly, and what looked like elastic cords draped over the object's side.

She recognized it as a boot. Tendons and ligaments, from a severed foot, were dangling.

She vomited once, then collected herself. Turning, she saw the corpse.

In three bloodied sections.

Mike Hewitt's face was the color of dead ashes; Wally Rowe, crest-fallen, leaned forward, forearms on his thighs, staring at his paper coffee cup; and Col. Mary Steuben, head of the Maine Warden Service, looked pissed off Wednesday at 3:45 p.m. in the Aroostook County Sheriff's Office in Reeds.

The four of them sat around a glass coffee table as if this were a social hour. Except the expressions on their faces made it clear there was nothing social about this gathering: they were there to talk about death and bombs.

"How's your leg?" Steuben said.

"Fine." Peyton made a small flutter with her hand. "It's nothing." And she meant it—eight stitches below her knee, compared to McPherson's fatal injuries, were nothing.

"Booby-trapped?" Steuben said.

The Maine Warden Service shared space with the Aroostook County Sheriff's Office. Steuben had a second-floor corner office overlooking Main Street. Her desk was twice the size of Hewitt's and looked like it was real cherry wood. There was a red leather sofa, two matching high-backed chairs, and glass end tables. A framed photo of Steuben with United States President Stu MacMillan hung on the wall.

"That's what we think," Rowe said. He didn't turn to face her. He sat staring at the floor.

"We have state troopers out there right now," Hewitt said, "to set up a half-mile perimeter to be sure no one gets near the area. There could be more explosives hidden."

"It wasn't a gas line?" Rowe said.

"No." Hewitt shook his head. "And the nuts and screws they pulled from Peyton's leg make everyone think this was a homemade job."

"Are we tying this to the cabin?" Peyton asked.

"We'll have to see."

"Bomb techs will be at the explosion site within an hour," Rowe said. "They'll work until sundown and then start again at daybreak."

Steuben folded her hands in front of her. "He was a good man."

Hewitt drank his coffee.

Peyton stretched her leg out before her. "Do you think that bomb was meant for the president?" she asked.

"We swept that area seventy-two hours ago," Rowe said. "We used dogs."

"It's a big area," Hewitt explained. "You couldn't have covered the whole thing."

"I wasn't there, personally. But this is what the Secret Service does. My guys wouldn't have missed it."

"Maybe someone planted an explosive after your guys went through," Hewitt said.

Rowe shook his head. "No one even knows where the president is fishing."

"The president told a bunch of townspeople he liked that stream last year," Peyton said. "I heard about it at the diner."

"And people here know when the president is supposed to arrive," Steuben said. "His daughter is already here."

"Is the daughter fishing?" Peyton asked.

Rowe shook his head. "Just visiting."

"Don't get defensive, Wally," Hewitt sipped his coffee. "This isn't on you."

Rowe said, "That poor sonofabitch."

"I just want to make sure Pete McPherson gets the credit he deserves," Steuben said. "I think a Congressional Medal of Honor is in order."

"So you're declaring this an assassination attempt?" Peyton said.

Steuben looked at Peyton. "Agent Cote, that decision will be made far from my office."

"In Washington," Rowe said. "And we can't be sure who that bomb was intended for."

Hewitt nodded. "Off the record, I think it was meant for the president, and I think this raises the stakes of what Customs and Border Protection does. I'd be willing to call it an act of terrorism."

"I don't think it's that well organized," Rowe said.

"I think we're looking at something we haven't seen before," Mike Hewitt said.

"And what is that?" Steuben asked.

"I don't know exactly. It doesn't feel well organized. But it feels like an assassination attempt."

"'Feels like' isn't definitive enough, Mike," Rowe said.

Peyton was nodding. "I know what you mean, Mike. It feels like someone took a shot in the dark. Plant a mine and see if the president hits it."

"That's a hairbrained scheme," Steuben said.

"Let's see what they find out there," Hewitt said. "If that's it, then that's it, and you're right."

"But I agree with Mike," Peyton said. "There's something here. And it feels more like a Gabby Giffords, Newtown, Colorado movie theatre situation than al Qaeda."

"Idiosyncratic crimes," Hewitt said. "A lone wolf goes after a target himself, does as much damage as he can before going down in flames."

"Except no one went down in flames," Steuben said.

"Just what I need," Rowe said, "something else to worry about."

"Idiosyncratic terrorism," Peyton said.

She lifted her paper cup to her lips. The ER doctor had pulled two screws and one nut from her leg. *Fate and seconds and inches,* she thought. If she hadn't paused to drink water, she'd have been closer to Pete McPherson, closer to the explosive. And she wouldn't be sitting here.

She wrapped both hands around her cup to prevent a spill— her hands were still shaking. *Stop thinking about what could have been, about yourself. Focus on the job.*

Bomb-making materials had been found in the cabin. How far did Simon Pink's murder and Freddy St. Pierre's arson reach?

"I know you want McPherson to get his due," Rowe said, "and I'm all for that, but we need discretion right now. You realize that, right? We can't be talking to the media about his heroism."

Steuben set her pen down, took off her glasses, and glared. "Are you questioning my intelligence?"

Peyton liked Steuben's no-bullshit attitude.

"And, the Secret Service, of all agencies, is telling me about discretion? Come on, Wally. Everyone within a hundred miles of this town knows the president is on his way as soon as the first blue government license plate arrives."

"Not so," Rowe said.

"You don't understand this place. This is a tight-knit community, an area where people talk and some haven't had a lot to feel good about."

"Until last summer," Peyton said.

Steuben looked at her. "That's right. You get it." She turned back to Rowe. "Wally, a lot of these people are farmers. They have to compete with Canadian farmers who get subsidized by the Canadian government. When they can't compete, they lose more than their farms—they lose their way of life, they lose their culture even."

Peyton nodded. "And they know that only five hours away, southern Maine is thriving. They feel forgotten."

"So having the president come here is a kind of approval?" Rowe said.

"Yes." Steuben smiled for the first time. "Last year, the president raved about the trout streams and how much fun he had with his grandson here. People can't wait for him to come back. And they know he's on his way."

"It's nice for me to find all this goddamned information out right now." Rowe's jaw clenched.

"Let's focus on some tangibles," Hewitt said. "We want to get the detonator from the bomb that killed McPherson—if there's anything left of it—and compare it to the one the fire marshal pulled from the burned-out cabin and the ones from the barn."

Peyton said, "Simon Pink is looking less and less like a truck driver."

"You said he had a chemistry background," Hewitt said, "and we found bomb-making shit out there."

She nodded. "Yeah, but, Mike, Pink's been dead more than a week. And Freddy St. Pierre is locked up. Who put the explosives out there?"

THIRTY-THREE

PEYTON WAS AT HER desk at 5:15 typing when a door at the back of the stationhouse opened and Stone Gibson walked out. She could see Freddy St. Pierre sitting at the table.

Stone closed the door to the interrogation room and walked to her desk.

"Peyton, thanks for doing the legwork and getting Kingston's information. Freddy, of course, denies it. He says he set the fire at three a.m. and that he was alone and never entered the cabin."

"Is that plausible enough to hold up in court?"

"The fire marshal says there's no way to say exactly when the fire began, since the explosion would have accelerated it."

"Shit," she said.

"Exactly," Stone said and went to the coffee maker.

Stan Jackman came out of Hewitt's office and said, "Peyton, I have something you'll want to know about."

Jackman, Garrett Station's senior statesman, pulled a chair to her desk, sat, and handed her a black-and-white photo.

"I know this guy."

"That's what I hear. How's your leg?"

"It's fine," she said.

"CNN has already reported the explosion and McPherson's name."

Peyton thought about Steuben's warning regarding discretion. She hoped Steuben didn't think she was the leak.

"They're calling it an assassination attempt," Jackman said. "And they've got a former CIA agent, who's now a correspondent, offering theories."

"Just what Washington wants."

"Hewitt asked me to look into the members of Sherry St. Pierre-Duvall's entourage." He looked away and shook his head. "Research is what you do when you get to be my age, I guess."

Jackman was creeping closer to fifty-seven, the mandatory retirement age for Border Patrol agents, and he'd suffered a heart attack a few years ago. Everyone at Garrett Station knew Hewitt was assigning him more and more desk duties.

"I think Hewitt's trying to bore me into retiring," Jackman said.

"He knows you're an excellent researcher. Not all of us can do that."

"You know that's bullshit, Peyton. You, of all people, would hate being chained to the desk as much as I do."

It *was* bullshit, but she could see the frustration on his face. And, after all, he and late wife Karen had invited Tommy and her to dinner soon after Peyton's return to the area. Peyton could still remember trying to explain to Tommy why Karen's hair was gone. Peyton attended Karen's funeral three months later. Even at his most trying time—nearing the end of Karen's life—Jackman had made time to welcome her to Garrett Station. She would never forget it, so she was trying to cheer him up now.

"I know his first name is Kvido," she said. "He works for Sherry."

"Sort of." Jackman took out a cigarette and put it, unlit, into his mouth.

"If I see you light that thing, I'll shoot you, Stan. I don't want you to have another heart attack. You're Tommy's surrogate grandfather."

"I'm not going to light the thing. Helps me think. Kvido was on the CIA's watch list years ago, but he's been under the radar for going on twenty years. And he and Dr. Sherry St. Pierre-Duvall are both academics, so maybe he is really working for her. It's not exactly easy to gather a lot of concrete facts right now."

She figured as much. The intelligence agencies would be moving a hundred miles an hour following the explosion that killed McPherson—and each going in a different direction. It meant that every piece of data was part of a fluid investigation. Therefore, everyone, everywhere would be hesitant to share it.

"What I do know is that Kvido's last name is Bezdek. He seems to have done a little of everything. Made some big, quick money in real estate in the Czech Republic and studied political science, earning a Ph.D. And before that, he was part of the Andela Group."

She pushed her chair away from her desk and looked up at him. "I've heard of that group," she said. "This just got really interesting. Simon Pink is also from the Czech Republic."

"You're connecting some dots," he said. "What do you know about Andela?"

She shook her head. "Not much. Nothing intel-based."

"So just what CNN tells you?" he said.

She grinned and nodded.

"Could be worse," he said. "You could be getting your information from Fox News."

"Tell me what you know," she said.

"The Andela Group was big about twenty years ago. It was a militia formed after a girl named Andela was killed when government-issued Czech military forces opened fire at a labor-union rally."

"The Andela group sounds liberal," she said. "I thought it was anti-West."

"It may have ended up that way," he said. "A lot of times these terrorist groups get in bed with each other in exchange for money, materials, and/or support."

"Politics makes strange bedfellows," she said.

"I've heard that somewhere. Bezdek is thirty-eight. Simon Pink was sixty-one. Pink came here ten years ago. As far as we can tell, Bezdek still lives in the Czech Republic, at least on paper. He teaches some classes and owns properties."

"And he knew Simon Pink?"

"That isn't confirmed," Jackman said. "Based on the Andela connection, I'm assuming they knew each other."

"How big was Andela twenty years ago?"

"Four thousand," he said. "I know. That's a lot of people, but the coincidence of them both being part of that group, and then being here together, is too large. I'm assuming they met there."

"Do we know how active either man was in Andela, or what either man did for the group?"

"No. I'm working on that."

"I'm willing to bet they were having a reunion party last Monday night at the cabin on Fred St. Pierre's property," she said, "and that Simon Pink didn't enjoy the reacquaintance. Have you told Hewitt any of this?"

"He's with Wally Rowe. They went to the Hampton Inn with two other agents and two troopers to get Kvido Bezdek for questioning."

She looked at the wall clock. "I'm leaving on time for the first time this week," she said. "I'll have my cell phone, if anyone needs me."

"You sound like a mother who's about to take her son somewhere."

She grinned. "And you sound like a surrogate grandfather who gets it," she said and patted his cheek lightly before walking out.

THIRTY-FOUR

DINNER CONSISTED OF A trip to Subway en route to the dojo in Caribou. Tommy's class began at 6:15 p.m.

Leo Lafleur, garbed in nylon athletic shorts and a Boston Celtics T-shirt, was in his office, leaning back in his leather chair, feet on his desk, a paperback copy of *Hamlet* in his hands, when Peyton entered and stood near the window, looking out at the mat below.

She pointed at the paperback. "Anyone ever tell you that you're a nerd?"

"Not without me kicking their ass." He looked at the gauze on her leg. "What happened?"

She was wearing shorts and a sleeveless blouse. "A few stitches. Nothing big. Anything in the fridge?"

"You know exactly what's in the fridge. You've been raiding it since you were a teenager."

"I bet there's a six-pack of Heineken, a gallon of chocolate milk, a couple bottles of some kind of sports drink, and some orange juice."

"Help yourself."

She took a Heineken from the fridge.

"You used to go for the chocolate milk," he said.

"A long time ago."

"You say that like it's been a hard day."

She didn't reply. But when she blinked, the backs of her eyelids were painted red—and the image of a leather boot with blood-stained tendons dangling from it flashed into her mind.

She squeezed her eyes shut.

"Peyton, you okay?" he asked.

"Yeah. Fine. Just a little tired."

He got up and stood beside her. "You ought to read this."

"I do read," she said.

"Not *Hamlet*. Here, listen." He flipped to a page. "*There's a special providence in the fall of a sparrow*. It's my favorite line in the play."

She sipped some beer. "Will you read that again?"

He re-read the passage.

"It reminds me of someone," she said. "I was thinking about her as I drove over here."

"It reminds me of a lot of people," he said, his eyes on her.

She looked away.

"That line reminds me of our talk," he said, "the last time you were here."

They were quiet for a time, each thinking.

Then he said, "Your career isn't easy, especially for a mom. It's a tough way to live."

"It's what I do. Who I am."

Leo motioned to the window, to Tommy below. "He complicates things, huh?"

"For sure," she said, "but I wouldn't have it any other way."

Speaking your feelings can crystallize your thoughts. And she smiled. She'd been striving for normalcy. Had come here because the lesson was on her to-do list: Tommy had an appointment. Work, no matter how traumatic, wouldn't get in the way of Tommy's life.

Stone Gibson looked up from the mat. She raised her bottle, saluting him. The gesture made him smile.

She was smiling back at him when her phone vibrated in her hip pocket. She looked at the number.

"Peyton," Hewitt said over the line, "have you heard from Matt Kingston today? He never went home last night. He went to work, but he never went home afterward."

"I haven't heard from him, no," she said. The phone felt heavy in her hand.

"Matt Kingston's father says he went to Tom Mann's garage after school. Mann confirmed that. He says Matt worked for him until six and then went to Tip of the Hat. We've confirmed that he got to the bar around six fifteen, ate dinner, and worked until ten."

On the mat below, Tommy was kicking Stone Gibson's padded hand.

"Some nights," Hewitt was saying, "Matt Kingston sleeps at a friend's house—a kid named Curt Paterson—and goes to school from there in the morning. The Paterson kid never saw Matt Kingston last night. The Tip of the Hat manager, Paul Kelley, says Matt left at ten. No one's seen him since he got his paycheck and walked out the front door."

"Did he cash the check?"

"It was late. We're checking ATM records."

Leo, sensing the importance of the call, pulled a chair to her, and she sat.

"He never went to school?" she said.

"No. The school called his home, but his father didn't pick up and didn't get the message until five tonight."

"Matt is a serious student. He wouldn't skip school."

"State police and two of our guys are interviewing people at Tip of the Hat," Hewitt said.

"Have the state police sent reinforcements?"

"Not for this. Augusta sent three troopers to help the four guys up here because the explosion and Pete McPherson's death were on CNN."

"Where does all that stand?"

"Got a call after we left the sheriff's. The bomb techs found other explosives in the area. I'm glad you're okay, Peyton."

"I might interview some people, Mike."

"Do what you think you need to do."

She was watching Tommy punch, moving slowly, emulating Stone's movements. What would have happened if she'd not stopped to drink from her Nalgene bottle? What if she'd have been a few feet closer to Pete McPherson? What if the boot she couldn't get out of her mind had been her own?

Where would that leave Tommy?

"They found another IED," Hewitt said. "The reports I'm getting say these weren't high-tech explosives."

"You're thinking they could've been made in the cabin?"

"I'll see what the bomb techs say, but it seems possible."

"Are the FBI and CIA letting you play?" she asked.

"I think so. Wally Rowe has his ties, and he says we're *useful*."

"How flattering. Did you talk to Kvido?"

"We haven't found him yet. He seems to have gone for cigarettes and not returned yet. Learn any more about who spoke to Matt Kingston at the school after you did?"

"No," she said; then: "Mike, Matt Kingston can place Freddy St. Pierre at the cabin with a guy with an Eastern bloc accent, who could be Simon Pink or Kvido Bezdek, at the time of the murder."

"I know. I read your report. His disappearance smells bad, Peyton."

She knew it did.

———

Wednesday at 9:20 p.m., Tommy was in bed, and State Police Detective Karen Smythe sat on Peyton's living room sofa, her bare feet tucked beneath her. In khaki short-shorts and a sleeveless blouse, she looked much more like the University of Maine cheerleader she'd been than a detective.

Peyton added more Pinot to Karen's glass and set the bottle between them. "Who does your hair?" she asked.

The bottle of Pinot was their second.

"Millie Davis in Houlton."

"She add the highlights?"

Karen nodded.

The windows were open, and a large moth tapped against the screen. Peyton looked up at the darkened window.

"Tommy's a sweet kid, Peyton. You're lucky."

"I know."

"You ever miss being married?"

"Not to Jeff."

"What, then?"

"I miss aspects of marriage."

Karen giggled and drank more wine. "I bet I know what those *aspects* are."

"Again, I don't miss Jeff."

263

Both women laughed.

"Get your mind out of the gutter," Peyton said.

"You, too. So these *aspects* you miss … is that where Stone Gibson comes in? I hear you had lunch with him."

"Your sister talks too much."

Karen grinned. "Stone is cute."

"He is."

"You seeing him?"

Peyton shrugged. "I was seeing Pete Dye for the past six months. I think that just ended."

"You *think* it ended?"

"It ended." Although, Peyton had to admit she hadn't given it much thought over the past few days. She looked at the white gauze on her leg. In fact, her relationship with Pete Dye seemed a long time ago.

"Everyone is looking for Kvido Bezdek," Karen said.

"He'll turn up. I'm more concerned with finding Matt Kingston."

"How well do you know Sherry St. Pierre-Duvall?"

"Not very. I knew her well when we were kids. We had coffee a couple times this week. I'm trying to figure her out."

"She seemed—I don't know what—during the discovery session."

"Neurotic? Desperate for something?" Peyton shrugged. "All of the above? Her father was terrible to her, verbally abusive."

"Not hard to believe, given what you and I witnessed."

Peyton poured herself another half-glass of wine. "Karen, she's not like we are."

"Drunk?"

"I'm not drunk. Sherry seems to be looking for something. *Searching* is probably a better word. And she's been that way, I would imagine, her whole life. She left here to attend Harvard, to show her father what she could do. But it wasn't enough."

"For him?" Karen asked.

"For her, I think. That's why she's still searching. I'm not sure exactly for what. But I know it goes back to her childhood, to her father."

"She seems to have it all—career, kids, and she's married to a doctor. Well, a dentist, technically, but still."

"That's a stereotype," Peyton said. "Defining women by their relationship to men."

"True. And her relationship to men is unstable. I hated the way her husband treated her during that meeting."

"If he patted me like that, I'd have broken his hand," Peyton said. "But Sherry was more concerned with what Stephanie Du-Bois thought of her. She was trying to prove something to Stephanie, trying to show her that they were equals."

Karen drank some wine. "Problem is, you need to believe it yourself, first, before you can prove it to someone else."

"Yes."

They were quiet. The refrigerator hummed in the kitchen. A window fan pulled cool night air into the room.

"What do you think she's searching for, Peyton?"

"I've thought about that a lot. And I don't know for sure. But it might be something you and I take for granted."

"What do you mean?" Karen asked.

"I'm not sure. Just thinking aloud."

Karen finished her glass of wine. "If I have another," she said, "I'll need to sleep here."

"That's what the guest room is for."

THIRTY-FIVE

THURSDAY, AT 7:35 A.M., traveling north on Route 1, Peyton saw KINGSTON spray painted in jagged letters on plywood and tacked to a white birch tree. She turned onto a dirt road four miles from the center of Garrett. Spring's "mud season" had come and gone, and it was clear that the Kingston's road hadn't been graded as her Ford Expedition traversed the six-inch ruts that had hardened following the spring thaw. Her work backpack, on the passenger's seat, contained her photo ID, her iPad, maps, water, a med kit, and Clif bars.

The rising sun cast shafts of light through the canopied tree cover as the SUV, its windshield dotted with dead flies, bounced along the rutted road.

She knew the state police and possibly other Border Patrol agents had interviewed Matt Kingston's parents already. But she was the first law-enforcement officer to interview Matt. There was a chance that she might piece information provided by Matt's parents with previous knowledge acquired during two conversations with their son to lead to his whereabouts.

The sides of the trailer were rust-streaked, the color of a faded blood stain. The screen door hung by one hinge. Peyton pulled next to a 1980s GMC Jimmy that, like a toothless smile, was missing its front grille. A man had the hood up and was pouring water into the radiator.

"Mr. Kingston?" she said, climbing out of the truck.

He straightened, holding a wrench. He was no taller than the door of the SUV, and he looked like he weighed less than she did. His face was pale, the skin around his eyes puffy, as if he'd been crying, and his nose and cheeks were mapped with red capillary lines. She knew what those were from.

"It's Dalton. Who are you?"

She told him.

Using a rag, he wiped his hands. "You gave Matthew your card. It's still on his dresser."

"I did. Does Matt's mother live here? If so, could we all talk?"

"She don't live here. She walked out when Matty was seven. She told him he was too much for her, that she couldn't handle him. Last thing she ever said to him. He remembers it, too. Talks about it once in a while."

She thought it might be tough to get him talking—he lived in near-seclusion, after all—but apparently he wanted to get some things off his chest, or to vent about his ex-wife.

Dalton Kingston put the wrench down on the rag, left the hood up, and led her inside the trailer. The gray walls had once been white, but a smoker's habit left them the color of an overcast sky. An SAT prep book lay the kitchen table.

"Do you have other children, Mr. Kingston?"

"No. Just Matthew. He's a good boy. Have a seat."

She did. There were crumbs on the table, the sink stacked high with dishes.

"I want to make sure Matthew doesn't get in trouble for poaching. He didn't shoot nothing. Never has. Not poaching, anyway. I sent him out a couple times. He always came back empty-handed. I don't think he has the stomach for it."

"Some people think it's cruel."

"I can tell you do."

She said nothing. There was a ketchup spot near the SAT prep book.

"It ain't easy making ends meet up here," he said. "I worked at the potato-processing plant. But not now. Matthew worked the harvest last year for Freddy St. Pierre. I was thinking maybe he could work for him again, since his father's gone."

A bottle of Wild Turkey stood on the counter. The coffee maker next to it offered no signs of life, just a half-filled pot with what looked like day-old coffee.

"What happened to your job at the potato-processing plant?"

He was leaning against the counter. He looked at his fingernails and shrugged. "Just didn't work out," he said.

"You like Wild Turkey?"

"It does the trick. Want a drink?"

She shook her head. "Matthew drink?"

"No. He studies."

And works to support you, she felt like saying, but didn't. "Any idea where he might be?" she asked.

He shook his head.

"He say anything strange recently? Act differently?"

"He told me he talked to you. I told him that was a mistake and to not get mixed up in anything. If Freddy shot some guy, stay the hell out of it."

"He knew he may have witnessed a murder, Mr. Kingston. Your son is very brave."

"This wasn't brave. It's looking like it was something else."

"What?"

"Dumb."

"Why do you say that?"

"Because he's gone. Either on the run, hiding, or worse. I ain't a fool." He wiped his nose on the back of his hand. He reached into the sink, dishes clattering, and came up with a water glass. "You want a drink?" he asked again, hand shaking as he doled out a shot of Wild Turkey.

She declined.

He drank quickly and wiped a tear from his cheek.

"Mr. Kingston, what have you told the other officers who came here?"

"Nothing. I ain't saying nothing."

"What does that mean?"

"It means I told my son to keep quiet, and he didn't, and what did it get him?"

"Mr. Kingston, we can't find Matthew unless you help us."

"I don't know where he is."

"Do you think he's hiding, or something happened to him?"

"I got no idea."

She believed him. "Do you think he knows who shot Simon Pink?"

"Who's that?"

"The man Freddy St. Pierre is accused of killing."

He looked at her. "I already told the cops."

"Would you tell me?"

"He saw them. It was dark, but he saw a gunshot. And he heard them talking before."

"Do you think he knows who shot Simon Pink?"

"It's what I told the others: he don't think Freddy did it."

"Who then?"

"Couldn't see. Too dark."

"Who did you tell this to?"

"The state cop, Miller, and that female cop that was here after him."

"Was she a state trooper?"

He shrugged, and something moved in the pit of her stomach.

"Was she in uniform?"

"No," he said. "Just wearing a windbreaker. She showed up last night at nine thirty."

"And a hat and dark glasses?" Peyton said.

"Yeah. How did you know that?"

———

Mike Hewitt wasn't in the office when Peyton arrived.

"Where's Mike?" Peyton asked.

"You know I can't disclose an agent's location," the silver-haired receptionist Linda Cyr said.

"I bet he's in Houlton, meeting with the FBI," Peyton said.

Linda winked at her, and Peyton smiled.

Agent Stan Jackman was at his desk, reading a document that was several pages long. He'd underlined some words and had written notes in the margins.

"Peyton, you're going to want to see this."

She pulled a chair close to Jackman's desk in the bullpen. The fabric of her uniform pants rubbed against the gauze covering her stitches.

Jackman slid his reading glasses to the edge of his nose and looked over them at her. He handed her his printout.

As she looked at it, he said, "I hear five hundred CBP agents from all over the country are coming to Pete McPherson's funeral, not to mention the game wardens and cops."

"He died trying to protect the president," she said, "and if he didn't step on that bomb, I would have."

And, she thought, *Tommy would be motherless in a rapid-fire world.*

"I hear he's up for a Congressional Medal of Honor."

"He'll get something," she said. "He earned it."

"They found six more bombs in all."

"What?"

"Six more. They were all near the first one. You were lucky."

She sat staring at him.

"Peyton, you okay?"

"Fine."

"You sure? I didn't mean to upset you."

"Fine," she said again. "So we know Simon Pink was from Prague."

"And that he studied chemistry there."

She looked at page two. "And he was part of Andela when Kvido Bezdek was in the group."

"Yeah. And the group evolved significantly after nine-eleven, but then fell off the radar."

"The material coming out of Washington has nothing new on Simon Pink," Jackman said, "nothing you don't know. Bezdek, though, is becoming a person of interest. He was arrested in Moscow once and failed a psychological evaluation."

"Clinicians don't say anyone *failed* an examination, Stan. What did it say?"

"He wanted to represent himself after being arrested during a protest. He was deemed unstable and to have anger issues."

"By Russian authorities?" she said. "That makes him a person of interest in the US?"

"He arranged anti-US protests as a teen, then eventually started visiting Moscow, and then the Khost Province in Afghanistan."

"That's quite a jump," she said. "How did he go from being pro-union to anti-US and then to hanging out in the Taliban's back yard?"

"Not much on that," Jackman said. "As information rolls in, I'll keep you posted."

"Sherry St. Pierre-Duvall said she met him at a workshop she gave related to her books. He loved her work."

"What's the focus of her work?" he asked.

"She told me it was the political landscape of the Czech Republic. She says what they have between them is 'special.' The way she talks, he's her intellectual soul mate."

"He might just be another asshole."

"You really are a clinician when it comes to psychoanalysis," she said.

Her cell phone vibrated against her leg. She took it from her cargo-pant pocket.

It was Hewitt. "You're looking for me?"

Peyton glanced at Linda Cyr. "I want to do something that might be a little, ah, unorthodox, Mike."

"Uh oh. That sounds bad."

"Not bad, just unorthodox. And I thought I should run it by you first."

And she did.

"That's your plan?" he said. "You think any lawyer would let you do that?"

"I was going to try to get around the lawyer."

"You march to the beat of your own drum. I'll give you that. Go for it."

She smiled. Mike Hewitt, for all his regulations, had a wild side after all.

THIRTY-SIX

"OH, HELLO, PEYTON," SHERRY St. Pierre-Duvall said when Peyton knocked on the door of suite 418 at the Hampton Inn in Reeds.

Sherry wore a navy-blue pant suit and open-toed heels. Her nails were bright pink, a contrast to her purple academic glasses. She looked ready to lecture at Harvard or meet an exec for drinks at the Ritz Carlton.

"I was wondering if you'd like to have lunch," Peyton said.

"That's a kind offer, but right now I'm in the middle of an important meeting." Sherry motioned over her shoulder.

Peyton assumed the meeting was taking place in the suite's back room.

"It really is a kind offer, though, Peyton."

The formal note in Sherry's voice hadn't been there when they met for breakfast, or the second time they had coffee. Now Sherry sounded like the alpha female she'd attempted to be during the discovery session between attorney Len Landmark and DA Stephanie DuBois.

However it had taken Stephanie all of five minutes to crush Sherry, and even today—despite the confidence her tone and outfit suggested—Sherry's eyes belied her outward appearance: they were bloodshot and their pinpoint focus hinted at desperation.

It made Peyton wonder just how much anyone really changed. Sherry—for all her academic accolades and accomplishments, and despite the image she worked so hard to cultivate and project—was still the same person who allowed her father to choose her friends.

"Are you appearing in court today?" Peyton asked.

The door was open four inches, the safety chain still attached.

"Can't a woman dress like a professional? Looking nice makes me feel good, Peyton. So I try to look nice often."

"What else makes you feel good?"

"What do you mean?"

"I'm curious," Peyton said. "You dress nice to feel good. What else do you do?"

Sherry looked at her. Unconsciously, her palm came away from the door, and she wiped it on her pant leg. "I don't follow you," she said.

"Does being accepted make you feel good?"

"You're making me uncomfortable, Peyton. What are you doing here?"

"May I come in?"

"I don't think it's appropriate for you to be here. A meeting is taking place now, and I need to be part of it."

"You can't break for lunch?"

"I don't think that would be appropriate either."

Whatever was being discussed in the back room led to raised voices. Peyton could hear bits and pieces of an argument. One voice, in particular, was familiar.

"Steve St. Louis is in there. Is he representing your brother *and* you now?"

Sherry didn't reply.

"Well, if you're meeting about your brother's case, I need to ask you some things about that, too."

"I'd rather keep our relationship personal, not professional."

"You don't get to choose, Sherry. And, after all, you called me, sobbing, at seven a.m. last week."

"I have Steve now."

"I'm out, he's in. It's that simple?"

"What do you mean?" Sherry said.

"Forget it. Where's Chip?"

Sherry took her purple glasses off and pinched the bridge of her nose.

"He left you, didn't he?"

Sherry nodded, looking at the floor.

"Because of Kvido Bezdek?"

"You won't understand. No one will. I'm not even sure I do."

"You're not sure?"

Sherry didn't speak.

"You'd better be sure, Sherry. You have two kids."

"Don't patronize me, Peyton."

"Where's Kvido now?"

"Not here."

"Do you know where he is?"

"He went out for cigarettes," Sherry said.

"Two people are dead. One was a wonderful man, a grandfather. I have questions to ask you. Cooperating is the best thing you can do right now."

"I'll have to ask Steve first."

"Steve's never defended a murder case, Sherry. You haven't lived in Maine for a long time, so I'll explain something to you: Conspiracy to Commit Murder is a class-A felony, punishable by ten to thirty years in state prison. If you want Steve with us, I'm fine with that, but whether he's with us or not, cooperation is your best bet."

"Sherry," Steve St. Louis called.

Sherry's eyes fell to the floor. "I need to go, Peyton."

"You're going to need to talk to me, Sherry."

"I don't need help."

"I think Nancy Lawrence would disagree."

"I didn't pay her to be my brother's alibi."

"Sherry, don't insult me by lying. The last time you pulled this, we were thirteen. You ran me out of your life."

Steve St. Louis was calling, "Sherry, where are you? We really need to talk."

"Even back then you always reached out. Called me, sat beside me in study hall..."

"That was a long time ago, Sherry. And this isn't a middle-school issue. Two people are dead. You can talk to me willingly, or I can have the state police bring you in. I'm giving you five seconds to think about it. Then I'm walking away once and for all."

"It's so risky," Sherry whispered, more to herself than to Peyton.

"St. Louis can be present, Sherry."

"It's not him I'm worried about," Sherry said.

Peyton looked at her.

Sherry didn't speak.

"Goodbye, Sherry." Peyton turned and walked away.

THIRTY-SEVEN

THURSDAY, AT 3:30 P.M., Peyton entered Garrett Middle School. She was led to the meeting room and took the only empty chair at the round table. Introductions were made all around: Kelli Link, the Garrett Central Schools director of special education; Dr. Tom Martin, principal; and Nancy Lawrence, Tommy's fifth-grade teacher.

"Hello, Peyton," Nancy said, and extended her hand. "I love your blouse."

"Thank you," Peyton said, trying to read Nancy's expression. Was the compliment sincere?

Peyton had returned to the station to change into jeans and a checkered blouse before the meeting. She didn't want to be in uniform for this sit-down with Nancy Lawrence. This encounter wasn't work-related. It was about Tommy, about the recommended accommodations for his diagnosis.

When they shook, Nancy's hand felt damp.

"Thanks for coming in," Kelli Link said. "I'm sure you're anxious to discuss the findings of Tommy's testing."

"I've read the materials several times." Peyton could feel Nancy looking at her.

"Let me begin by saying what a sweet boy Tommy is," Link said. "We all really enjoy working with him."

"Yes," Nancy said. "We certainly do."

Peyton watched Nancy closely. Her face was warm, welcoming—the face Peyton had seen at Nancy's front door, the face she'd seen when Nancy confided in her about her dinner date with the doctor. Since Nancy Lawrence first entered the Simon Pink murder investigation, Peyton had worried: would Nancy take her frustration out on Tommy?

Tommy had said, in so many words, that he was being bullied, but he'd never complained about Nancy. The initial parent-teacher conference had given Peyton a poor impression of Nancy, but perhaps the fifth-grade teacher with a Carrie Underwood poster on her classroom wall had a level of professional integrity Peyton had misjudged. Yes, Nancy had insulted her during an interview. But Peyton didn't put too much stock in that. She'd been insulted far worse during other interviews, and an interview rarely brought out the interviewee's best self.

"Tommy has worked very hard, especially this past week," Nancy said. "I spoke to him privately on the playground one afternoon. I was very impressed by how you've handled his diagnosis, Peyton."

Peyton looked at her. All of twenty-six, yet speaking to Peyton as if much older. Either she was ice-cool or highly professional.

"I told him this is the best thing that could've happened," Peyton said. "I told him that now he'll get help and school will be fun."

"That's wonderful," Link said. "As you know, it was determined that he has dyslexia."

"That confuses me," Peyton said. "He reads well, I think."

Link nodded. "Yes. He's certainly at grade level. Dyslexia is an information-processing affliction. Tommy's reading rate is slow, but his comprehension is strong. Math, though, is challenging."

Link explained Tommy's test scores and the consultant's findings. Then she said, "I'd like to begin working with Tommy next week and carry it into next year."

Peyton nodded. Her face felt flushed. What did it all mean for his future?

"Can he be cured?" she asked.

"He can overcome it," Link said. "Many people have learning differences, and some estimates are as high as twenty percent of the population. Albert Einstein had dyslexia. But, no, we can't 'cure' the way one learns or processes. However, we can help him to utilize his strengths and to be more efficient."

Link sounded like a recording. Peyton didn't want data; she wanted information as a mom.

"How will you do that?"

"He will leave the classroom for math and work with me one-on-one."

"So he'll be singled out? That'll be embarrassing for him."

"Receiving this diagnosis," Principal Tom Martin said, "is the best thing that could happen to Tommy, as you said. It will allow us to assist him in ways that we could not if he wasn't diagnosed. He'll get extra time on tests and even the SATs."

Nancy was smiling warmly and nodding.

"Sounds like a lot of extra work," Peyton said, remembering their conversation during the parent-teacher conference.

Nancy looked at Tom Martin and smiled. "That's my job. And it's not much really, an extra lesson plan here and there. No big deal."

Tom Martin smiled approvingly at Nancy.

An IEP, or an independent education plan, had been what Nancy had called it when Peyton had originally met with her. And then, Nancy had made it sound far from being "no big deal." If she was playing to the crowd, she was hitting all the high notes. After all, Martin was her boss.

"So tell me how this is all executed," Peyton said. "Will Tommy be doing different work? Extra work?"

"Nancy and I will work together to create some alternate activities for Tommy. Some might be more hands-on. Sometimes, I will simply work with him to be sure he is grasping concepts and is at grade level."

"Will he be doing many different assignments?"

"It will depend on the topic of the lesson," Martin said. "He does, after all, have a learning difference."

"Will the other kids know?"

"He'll leave the classroom and come to the resource room," Link said.

Her little boy was heading to the resource room.

"Are you okay with all of this, Ms. Cote?" Martin said.

"My son is being teased at school already."

"Teased?" Martin said.

"*Bullied* is probably a more accurate word."

"There's quite a big difference," Martin said. "A student was dismissed for bullying last year."

"I ask that you watch Tommy's interactions," Peyton said.

The room fell quiet, the educators looking at one another.

"What do you need from me at home?" Peyton asked.

Link offered her a folder containing literature on dyslexia, including some articles featuring methods to try when Tommy worked at home.

"And I certainly want you to feel welcome to visit and volunteer," Link said, "to take part in Tommy's education anytime you'd like."

"I might be able to come in for an hour or two a week," Peyton said.

Nancy had been writing something down but looked up then.

"Thank you for supporting my son," Peyton said to the room, as the meeting came to a close.

When Link stood, the others followed suit. At the door, Nancy touched Peyton's elbow. "May I talk to you?" she said quietly.

Peyton followed her into the hallway. Nancy waited until Link and Martin had moved out of earshot.

"Will you be coming to school every week, Peyton?"

"I'll try. It seems like that might help."

"I'm not sure about that. But, regardless, I just want you to know that I'm going to be cleared of having anything to do with Freddy's problems."

"Okay," Peyton said.

"Do you believe me?"

"Sure."

"Then there's no reason for Dr. Martin to find out that somehow Freddy implicated me."

"He won't hear it from me," Peyton said.

Nancy looked at her for several seconds.

"Nancy, that's my work; this is my life. When I'm here, I'm here as a mother."

Nancy's eyes continued to scrutinize Peyton's face. Finally, she nodded and moved away, her two-inch heels clicking quietly as she walked.

In her Jeep, Peyton took out her phone and called Stone Gibson.

"I need a favor," she said.

He listened.

"That's a big one," he said. "What do I do if he doesn't want to come with me?"

"Tell him he can pass on dinner and that I'll take him to a liquor store," she said and hung up.

THIRTY-EIGHT

PEYTON ARRIVED AT THE Tim Hortons on Main Street in Reeds, Thursday at 5:10 p.m. After ordering a black coffee, she took a window booth near the spot where she'd recently sat with Sherry St. Pierre-Duvall.

She took her phone from her purse and called Lois. "I'll be home by seven," she said.

"I'll have dinner waiting for you, sweetie."

"Anyone ever say you run the best daycare program in the world?"

"No, but I know I do," Lois said and chuckled. "Take your time, I'll bake something for Tommy. Maybe he can help me. Where are you?"

"Tim Hortons in Reeds. I need to meet Stone Gibson."

"I hope it's a date. He'd make an adorable son-in-law."

"Mom, please."

"I'm serious. Think of the children you'd have. They'd be beautiful."

"Oh my god, Mother. This is business."

"You spend too much time on business, Peyton."

Peyton said nothing.

"Tommy brought home a calculator and three math sheets he has to do tonight," Lois told her. "He says the teacher told him to use the calculator."

"It's part of his new math program," Peyton said.

She saw the dark Ford Interceptor pull in.

"I need to go, Mother."

"Did he just arrive?"

"Yes."

Stone Gibson got out, wearing a blue sports jacket, and carrying an iPad. He moved to the driver-side door and helped Dalton Kingston to his feet.

"What's he wearing?"

"Good God," Peyton said.

"Hey, I'm not too old to dream."

"Goodbye, Mother." She hung up.

As they crossed the parking lot, Stone Gibson moved fluidly, like an athlete; Dalton Kingston, though, was clearly drunk.

Stone held the door and said something to Dalton, who nodded. Both men entered. Stone Gibson led Dalton by the elbow to Peyton's booth.

He smiled. "Sorry."

"Wild Turkey?" she said to Dalton.

"I'm all alone," he said. "You know what that feels like?"

"I see you're off duty," Stone said to her.

"I had a meeting with Tommy's teachers, so I changed."

He nodded, understanding.

"Dinner is on me," she said, "if you're interested."

"I am," Stone said, "and Mr. Kingston will have coffee."

"Do you remember the female cop who came to see you?" Peyton said.

Dalton Kingston looked at her the way a confused dog does when tilting its head trying to grasp a command.

"Make that a large black coffee," she said, "and a sandwich—or anything with bread."

"I'll get on this," Stone said.

He went to place their orders. Given his detective rank, he didn't wear a uniform, but it didn't matter. Everything about him said *cop*, and two guys at the counter stepped several feet away when he approached.

Peyton went to the counter as well, leaving Dalton Kingston at the booth.

"That's how I found him," Stone said. "You were right about the liquor store. Not much he wouldn't do for a bottle of Wild Turkey."

"He say anything about Matt?"

"He's been mumbling about Matt since I got him."

"But nothing helpful?" she said.

"No. Do you think Matt got scared and took off?"

"He doesn't have a car. We'd know if he borrowed one."

"Maybe," Stone said, "but not necessarily. Teenagers keep secrets well. We have someone monitoring his Facebook page. Nothing was posted since Tuesday afternoon."

"I'm glad you're monitoring it. I feel terrible about this."

"Don't blame yourself."

"I do," she said. "I interviewed him."

"He came to you."

She gave Stone Gibson $20 to pay with and then went back to the booth.

"What are we doing?" Dalton asked.

"We're going to see if you recognize someone."

"Who?"

Peyton didn't answer; she didn't want to offer any information that might sway Dalton or lend bias to the experiment. Stone returned with two large coffees and one hot roast-beef sandwich. Dalton didn't press for an answer. He seemed content with his sandwich.

"Tommy's doing a nice job in my class," Stone said.

"He enjoys it. He mentioned you recently. I went in his room last night and found him doing push-ups. He said you told him they would be good for him."

"Sorry," he said. "I did tell him that. Was that okay?"

"Sure. I'm thrilled to see him motivated and taking his fitness seriously."

"I miss my boy," Dalton said. He no longer sounded like he was speaking with two fat lips.

"We're going to try to get him back, Mr. Kingston," she said. "You're going to help us do it."

———

They didn't cross the four-lane highway on foot—not with a not-quite-perfectly-sober witness in tow. Instead, they all piled into the Interceptor and drove to the Hampton Inn.

"We're going to the fourth floor," Peyton told Dalton.

"What are we doing there?" Dalton asked.

"You'll see," she said. "You won't have to do much."

Stone pushed the elevator button. They listened to the elevator hum and clang. Finally, the door opened, and they got in.

Dalton Kingston smelled like sweat, but at least the whiskey smell had given way to coffee breath, following two large black coffees.

"Just relax," Stone told him. "I told you. This has very little to do with you."

"Is Matty here?"

The elevator stopped and they got out on the fourth floor, walked the hallway, and stood before room 418.

Peyton knocked on the door.

"A woman is going to answer," she said. "I want you to tell me if you've seen her before."

"I can do that," he said.

Except he couldn't. Because a man answered the door.

Apparently, he'd returned from getting cigarettes.

"Can I help you?" Kvido Bezdek said to Peyton. Then he saw Stone, in uniform. "Oh, God. Is this about Sherry? Has something happened to her?"

THIRTY-NINE

"I'M A RESEARCH ASSISTANT to Dr. Sherry St. Pierre-Duvall," Kvido Bezdek said.

He had welcomed them into his hotel suite—a change from Peyton's recent visit, when upon learning she had to pee, he'd suggested she descend four flights to a ladies' room. This time, in fact, he'd held the door for her.

And now they were in the sitting area of his suite.

"You're the Border Patrol agent," Kvido said. "Sherry's friend."

"Yes. I'm not in uniform."

"And you?" he said to Stone.

"Maine State Police Detective Stone Gibson."

"When we arrived," Peyton said, "you asked if something had happened to Sherry. Do you think something might have happened to her?"

"I have no idea," he said. "We are very close. I certainly hope nothing is wrong. She should have been back long ago."

"Where did she go?"

"She said she had something to take care of. She never came back."

Peyton looked at Stone. He knew it had been nearly the same story Sherry offered when authorities arrived to see Kvido.

"Have you reported her missing?" Stone asked.

"It hasn't been twenty-four hours. I tried to call her repeatedly. Her phone goes right to voicemail."

"Do you have her number?" Stone said.

"I have it," Peyton said. She dialed the number—and got voicemail. She left a message.

"I enjoy working with Sherry a great deal," he said, "and I care about her. That's why I'm getting concerned. Who is this?" He motioned to Dalton Kingston.

"A friend," Peyton said. She stood and started walking to the bedroom.

"What are you doing?" Kvido said.

She didn't answer. The main room was a sitting area, where up to five could watch TV. The adjacent room was the master bedroom with a king-sized bed and two closets.

Behind her, a knock came on the hallway door.

"That's for me," she heard Stone Gibson say; then: "Come with me, Dalton. This is your ride home."

She heard Leo Miller's voice, then the door close.

"What are you doing?" Kvido asked again. He was behind her.

"I always wondered what these suites were like. How much a night?" She opened the closet door.

"That's enough," Kvido said. "I don't appreciate you going through my things."

There was no suitcase, no computer, no books or notes—nothing to indicate Sherry had been writing and researching for a book in this room. Peyton wondered if room 210 was still occupied by Chip Duvall.

She turned and went back to her seat in the main room. Stone Gibson was sitting on the love seat. Dalton Kingston was gone now. He'd gotten a decent meal in him, but otherwise his trip to Reeds from Garrett had been wasted.

"What exactly are you doing here?" Kvido asked.

"I came to see my friend Sherry."

Peyton sat next to Stone; Kvido stood in the doorway.

"How long have you been in the country?" Stone said.

"A week."

"Do you come here often?"

"I come to help Sherry, when she asks me to."

"You should know that Sherry has told me about your relationship," Peyton said, "so we can drop the pretense. I know Chip left her."

"I'm worried about her," Kvido said and slumped onto a chair across from them. "She must've told you about Chip, and how he treats her."

"How does he treat her?" she said.

"He doesn't understand her. He reminds me of her father. Domineering."

Had Sherry traded one domineering man for another? That wasn't atypical.

"What brings you to Aroostook County?" she said.

"Sherry's parents died. She needed support."

"Do you know how they died?"

"Yes. She told me. How terrible for her."

"You're from Prague?"

"I am."

"Sherry spends time there."

"Researching," he said, "and seeing me."

"How long has that been going on?"

"Which?" He spread his legs out before him, completely relaxed.

"Seeing you."

"For ten years," he said, "with a break for about three there in the middle."

"Why the break?"

He shrugged. "We just went our separate ways for a time. Then we came back to each other. You know the saying, *If you love something set it free, and if it comes back it was meant to be.*"

"Lovely," Stone said.

"I think so."

"So that's what happened?" Peyton said. "You set Sherry free?"

"It was mutual."

"Tell me about it."

"Not much to tell. She was getting tenure at her college, and I was building my business. The timing just wasn't right." He spread his hands.

Peyton looked at his missing fingers, the discolored skin.

"What business is that?" Stone said.

"Real estate. I own properties in Prague and the surrounding areas and now some throughout Europe."

"You are part of Andela," Peyton said.

He laughed. "I was. That was a long time ago. Back when I was young and naive. You know how that goes. Everyone's a political activist when they're young, right?"

His English was impeccable, save for the thick accent; his control of nuances and diction were clearly impressive.

"How did you injure your hand?" she asked.

"It's when I left Andela. It's when I knew the group was doing things I didn't agree with."

"Like what?"

"We began protesting for labor unions. Then the group got big, turned violent. This"—he held up his hand—"is the result of a Molotov cocktail. It was my final day as a member of Andela. That was almost twenty years ago."

"And you know Simon Pink," Stone Gibson said.

"Is that a question or a statement, officer?"

"A statement."

"Simon was much older than me. He was something of a father figure to me, after my own father died."

Peyton sat stock-still, riveted. She had expected Kvido to request an attorney the moment he opened the door. He hadn't. And now she was hearing things—from the suspect himself—that hadn't appeared in the federal file on this man. How much of the story was true?

"How did your father die?" Peyton asked.

"I thought you were here to talk about Sherry. Will you search for her? She left this afternoon and has not returned."

"Did she say where she was going?" Stone said.

"No. Just that she had to take care of something. I had a bad feeling about it. I feel like she's hiding something from me."

"Like what?"

"I don't know."

"Do you recognize the name Matt Kingston?"

"Who is that?"

"Could you speculate on what she might be hiding?"

"She hasn't set a date for the funerals of her parents. It's been a week. That seemed … odd? Maybe not. She has a lot on her mind with her brother. But I just feel like she's not telling me everything, which hurts because I care about her."

"And, of course," Peyton said, "her husband, who she has a family with, left her, which would add to her stress."

"You mean to say, who she has *a daughter* with."

"Yes," she said. "You know Chip, of course. How do you get along with him?"

"Well, actually, although I never thought he treated Sherry with the respect that she deserves."

"And you do?"

"I take offense to that."

"What's the difference?"

"Chip lost his business. He embarrassed her. I can support her."

"I see," Peyton said. "Tell me more about your relationship with Simon Pink."

"I did. I'm getting tired. What will you do to find Sherry?"

"Have you called her attorney or Chip? Have you texted her?"

"I called and texted her." He looked at the floor for a moment, then said, "What happened to Simon is terrible. And I can't believe someone related to Sherry could murder Simon. Simon was always anti-establishment."

"And he was your 'father figure'?"

"That was a poor choice of words. You know English is not my native language."

"You're doing fine," Stone said.

"He took me into Andela, made it sound like a club."

"You founded the group."

"No. The group was alive and well when I joined. I brought it to the media. I arranged the protests. Then, when I was told to throw the Molotov cocktail at the church, and I saw people inside

294

and hesitated, well"—he held up his hand again—"I knew it wasn't the right group for me."

"What did you learn from Simon Pink?"

"That's an interesting question. I learned to stand up for what you believe, I guess."

"And what do you believe?" she asked.

"Oh, in many things."

"Tell us about your father," she said.

"He was a great man. He died too young." He looked at his watch. "I really need for you to go. I'm going to make some more phone calls, try to find Sherry. You don't seem to be doing much to help." Kvido walked them to the door and shook hands before closing the door behind them.

In the elevator, Peyton shook her head. "That was unbelievable. The whole time we were in there, I felt like I was in a cage being circled by a Great White."

"He is good. Even shook hands. He knows he doesn't have to talk to us, so he can tell us what he wants and ask us to leave whenever he wants to. He even let you search his room."

"But," she said, "he doesn't want to talk about his father."

"We need to find Sherry St. Pierre-Duvall," Stone said.

Peyton took out her cell phone and dialed Sherry's number again. The ring went straight to voicemail.

In the parking lot, as they were getting into Stone's car, her phone vibrated.

"Cote here."

"Peyton." It was Hewitt.

"I was just about to call you." She told him about Kvido Bezdek.

"He's sitting in the hotel?"

"That's right. Why were you calling?"

"I know you're not on nights now, but any chance you can come in?"

The last time Hewitt had approved overtime there had been a $6.5-million drug bust at the border.

"What's up?"

"Chip Duvall is here with his attorney," Hewitt said. "He says he needs to talk to you."

FORTY

MIKE HEWITT WAS WAITING for Peyton and Stone Gibson at the front door of Garrett Station Thursday at 6:35 p.m.

"He came to us," Hewitt said. "We have started looking for him shortly, of course, since Sherry St. Pierre-Duvall is missing."

"Start with the husband," Stone said.

"Yeah, and he walked in the door with his attorney."

"He didn't go to the state police headquarters?"

"No. He came here." Hewitt looked at Stone.

"For Peyton?"

"Probably. He asked for her."

"Want me to put on my uniform?" she said.

"Do you think it matters?" Hewitt asked.

"No. I know him. This is the third time he's asked to speak to me about Sherry."

Hewitt nodded. "State police are getting Bezdek for questioning. FBI is coming for that. You'll want to be in uniform for that. But, first things first." He pointed to an office in the back.

Chip was seated beside a gray-haired man in a dark-blue suit, with a briefcase open before him. The attorney stood, rounded the table, and shook hands with Peyton.

"Jim Talon. My client wants to speak to you."

So Chip had upgraded lawyers. So much for Len Landmark.

"I'm all ears." She sat across from Chip; Hewitt sat next to her, a yellow legal pad before him, pen at the ready. Stone took a chair near the door.

"Peyton, I went home, to Portland, for a day to check on my kids. They were staying with my sister. I came back when I couldn't reach Sherry. I'm worried about her. This isn't like her. She may have a fling, but she wouldn't just disappear."

"You tried to call her?"

"Repeatedly."

"May I see your phone?" Hewitt said.

Chip looked at Talon, who took off his metal-framed reading glasses and held them before him.

"May I ask why?" Talon looked at him.

"I'd like to have your client's phone records checked."

"My client is here of his own volition. Now you're naming him as a suspect?"

"We have no suspects," Hewitt said. "We have no crime, unless you know something different."

"This is about Sherry," Chip demanded. "She doesn't handle stress well. You know her." He pointed at Peyton, urging her to agree with him.

His gaze was intense. He wasn't going to offer her a glass of wine now. She saw fear in his eyes, and he spoke directly to her, as if no one else was in the room.

It made her think of something. She took Hewitt's pen and wrote on his pad: *Search hotel room 210 for her suitcase. Windbreaker?* He nodded.

"I think she's overwhelmed," Chip said. "This isn't how she normally acts. Her parents are dead—in a horrific scene; her brother is accused of murder, and is linked to the murder weapon; and she thinks she loves a man from Prague. It's all coming at her so fast. I think she panicked and ran."

"Where to?" Peyton said.

"I don't know."

"Does the name Matt Kingston mean anything to you?"

"No. Should it?"

"Do you own any properties we aren't aware of?" Hewitt asked.

"No. Just our home outside Portland."

"Tell me about Simon Pink," Peyton said.

"The man Freddy shot?"

"The man Freddy's accused of shooting, yes."

"Didn't they match Freddy's gun to the scene?"

"Tell me about him."

"I've never met him. I don't think Sherry ever did either."

"How many times a year does Sherry go to Prague?"

"Two, three."

"Describe your relationship with your wife," Hewitt interjected.

The question came out of the blue, as Hewitt intended, and it set Chip on his heels.

"What do you mean? We have a fine—but sometimes confused—relationship."

"Can you describe it?" Hewitt said.

"I love my wife."

"And it's mutual?"

"Is this relevant?" Talon said.

"His wife is missing. She recently left him for another man," Hewitt said. "Isn't that right, Chip?"

"It's complicated."

"But she left you. How'd that make you feel?"

"It hurt."

"I bet it made you angry, too."

"I object to that statement, agent," Talon said. "It's leading, and you know it."

"Then how's this: Are you angry at your wife, Chip?"

"I'm worried about her."

"Do you know where your wife is, Chip?"

"No. I do not. I came here to help you find her. I have nothing to do with her disappearance."

"What did you tell your kids about their mother?" Peyton said.

Chip's hands were clasped before him. He was squeezing them together. "That was the hardest conversation I've ever had, Peyton. I had to tell them that Mommy and I might not be living together when we come back."

"So the marriage is over?"

"She left me, all right? We all know it. It hurts. I'm not angry, just sad."

"Do you know Kvido Bezdek?" Hewitt said.

"Of course, he works for Sherry. She dated him years ago. Have you interviewed him?"

"Why? Should we?"

"Sherry was staying with him, not me, when she went missing."

"Chip," Peyton said, "if you have any theories or thoughts regarding where Sherry is or what might have happened, now is the time to share them."

"I have no idea."

"Where are Sherry's things, Chip?"

"I don't follow you."

"She had a suitcase in room 418. She was staying there with Kvido. You had room 210. Where are her things—her clothes, her computer, her suitcase?"

He looked at her. "I have no idea. I assume they're at the Hampton Inn, still in Kvido's room."

Peyton took Hewitt's pen again, wrote: *I didn't see them. I walked through his room.*

Hewitt looked at Stone Gibson.

"I'll go over there," Stone said. "I'll put out a BOLO and call the airport, too." He left the room.

"Do you know where Sherry was last night at nine-thirty?" Peyton asked.

"I have no idea. I was in Portland."

"I assume you've been watching the news, Chip," Hewitt said.

He shrugged.

"You know about the IEDs found. One killed a game warden."

"Yes. I saw that on TV. It made CNN."

"Do you know anything about that?"

"What?"

"Do you know anything about that?"

"Of course not. Why are you asking me that?"

"We're here about his wife," Talon said. "The man is concerned about his wife."

"As we all are," Hewitt said.

"I think not, agent. I think you're looking to pin the IEDs on someone. And you should know that it won't be my client."

"We're just being diligent," Peyton said.

"What is your plan for finding my wife?"

"We will work with the state police, the FBI, and our agents. We will put out BOLOs and road blocks. Please describe the car she is driving."

"That's the thing," Chip said. "She has no car. I took the Mercedes back to Portland. Kvido has the rental, the Ford Escape."

"That changes things," Hewitt said.

"How?"

"It narrows our search. We'll comb the area around the hotel, maybe even go room to room, search the woods behind it."

"Oh my God," Chip said.

"Don't read anything into it," Hewitt said.

"You think she killed herself. I'm going to be sick." Chip was on his feet, sprinting to the door.

FORTY-ONE

THE NOON MEETING ON Friday was all-hands-on-deck, and all the agencies involved were represented, including a new player: FBI Agent Frank Hammond, who arrived from Boston.

Stone, Hewitt, Peyton, Wally Rowe, and Hammond were in the breakroom at Garrett Station.

"Are you the agent I spoke to on the phone last week about Tom Dickinson?"

"I don't know," Hammond said. "Who is Tom Dickinson?"

"He's in the federal witness protection program."

"Couldn't have been me," Hammond said. "We don't have anyone up here."

Peyton looked at Hewitt, who shrugged.

"I got Freddy and his attorney, Steve St. Louis, up early and spent two hours with them this morning," Hammond said. Standing in front of the whiteboard like a teacher, he faced the others who sat at the table and circled Freddy's picture.

Hammond was the FBI's executive assistant director of the Criminal Investigative Division and worked out of Boston. Peyton knew he was close to sixty, but small and wiry. He'd run three marathons and still ran 10Ks. She'd worked with him previously and had always been impressed. Where State Trooper Leo Miller spoke to hear himself speak during meetings, Hammond was a listener who could take in information, process it, and synthesize it in a manner that was useful to everyone involved.

Stone leaned and took an orange from his computer bag near his feet and began to peel it.

"Freddy freely admits that he burned down his cabin. He keeps saying that, 'My cabin,'" Hammond continued. "Smart guy. Can't be accused of arson unless he files a claim, which he won't do."

"But he was paid to burn it," Peyton said.

"You have the money trail that proves that?"

Peyton looked at Hewitt.

Hewitt shook his head. "Nope. And, if it's on his land, it's not a crime"—he pointed to Hammond and nodded—"unless he's going to commit insurance fraud."

"You see the problem here?" Hammond said.

"No one has ever called Freddy St. Pierre smart," Peyton said. "He's being advised well by someone."

"The lawyer, St. Louis?"

"I doubt that," she said. "Someone is pulling the strings to all of this. We need to find out who."

"His sister has a Ph.D., she might have given her brother twenty thousand dollars, and she's missing," Hewitt said.

Peyton nodded. "True, but she was as surprised as anyone when this all began. She was devastated by her parents' deaths."

"That assumes the murder-suicide is connected to Simon Pink's murder," Stone said. He took his cell phone off the table and checked to be sure the ringer was set to vibrate. "Maybe they aren't related. Maybe her father was just an abusive asshole who knew the cat was finally out of the bag."

The room fell quiet, each law-enforcement official processing.

Hammond folded his arms across his chest. "So Simon Pink and Freddy roof the cabin and work the harvest together." He started pacing. "The neighbors, who are Stone's sister and mother and therefore reliable, say they heard explosions in recent months. The kid, Kingston, goes to the farm to poach deer but hears three men talking about 'steps' and then hears a gunshot, but he can't provide visual confirmation of the murder. Peyton goes there the next day and finds the torched cabin, which Freddy now admits to."

"And his confession places him at the murder scene," Peyton said. "Matt Kingston recognized Freddy's voice that night. Freddy knows who shot Simon Pink."

"It's him," Hewitt said. "That's becoming clear. He tried to separate the arson from the murder because it was the lesser of the two."

"He appeared in court and entered a not-guilty plea," Stone said. "But he knows damned well Stephanie DuBois is moving forward with the murder charge."

"Three people were there that night." Peyton was shaking her head, frustrated. "Why isn't he trying to pin it on the third person? He's facing life in prison."

"We know one had an accent," Stone said. "We get Kvido in here, we can record him and play it for Matt Kingston."

Hewitt shook his head. "I disagree. It makes sense that the person with the accent was Simon Pink, who, we assume, didn't shoot himself."

Hammond nodded. "And even if that's not right, that's certainly how a defense attorney will spin it."

Peyton leaned forward and rubbed her forehead with her thumb and forefinger. "The third person, according to Matt, was quiet. He couldn't describe that voice. Why hasn't Freddy given us that person? That's what I'd do; we all would. We'd be throwing the third guy at the cops."

Stone ate part of his orange. "DuBois even said I could tell him we'd negotiate if he tells us who was there, what was going on."

"He knows the third person has more on him than he has on them," Hewitt said. "That's why he's not talking. He did it. He figures to take his chances at trial because the whole case is circumstantial."

"Makes sense," Hammond said.

"And without Matt Kingston," Peyton said, "there is no case against Freddy."

Matt Kingston had now been missing for two and a half days.

Hewitt blew out a long breath. "We need to find that kid."

"I'd like to get Freddy's sister in here, too," Stone said. "Kvido held up very well under questioning, but her brother would tell her things he wouldn't say to anyone else."

"Ask Kvido anything personal?" Peyton said.

Hammond moved to the table and took up his coffee cup. "We asked about his relationship with Sherry."

Peyton nodded. "He seemed to avoid talking about himself when Stone and I spoke to him."

Hammond pointed to his briefcase. "He let us record the conversation—it's on my phone, if you want to hear it—and he never asked for an attorney."

"So who set the IEDs in the woods?" Hewitt said. "Pink was dead by the time they were put in the earth, and Freddy was sitting down the hall."

"What do we know from the IEDs?" Stone asked.

Hammond went to his iPad. "I spoke to a bomb tech and read the report. The techs say the devices were grouped in a cluster. The first one was spring loaded, and it was designed to activate the others."

"They failed?" Hewitt said. He looked at Peyton.

She felt the blood drain from her face.

Hammond saw the two CBP agents looking at one another. "Thank God for that. All of this offers a picture of the suspect," he continued. "A profile is coming together. If this were an expert, he had a seriously off day. But this would mean enough to whoever did this that they wouldn't make a mistake."

"You're saying we got their best effort?" Stone had stopped writing. He set his pen down.

"Yes. We're not dealing with an expert."

"Some amateur asshole is trying to kill the president," Hewitt said.

"If this was al Qaeda or ISIS or Boko Haram," Stone agreed, "they'd have claimed responsibility."

Hammond shook his head. "Not always."

Peyton sat listening, but her head was spinning. She'd come even closer to death than she'd known.

"Have you searched Kvido's hotel room?" she asked.

"Yes," Stone said. "I served the warrant last night. We have his laptop. Our computer guys have gone through it. He's clean. Which is probably why he's staying around."

"I want to interview him again, Mike."

"Peyton, we talked about this." Hewitt pointed at Hammond. "He's taking that aspect of the investigation."

"I'll interview him again," Hammond said, "believe me. And you can be there when I do."

That surprised her. "Thanks." She stood.

Hewitt said, "Where are you going?"

"To do a reference check," she said.

"You hiring someone?" Stone said.

"Maybe a public policy professor," she said and walked out.

FORTY-TWO

It took three phone calls, starting with the University of Southern Maine's switchboard, but by 1:30 p.m. Friday, Peyton was in the bullpen on the phone with the associate dean of the Muskie School of Public Service, Dr. Suzanne Fontaine—Sherry St. Pierre-Duvall's supervisor.

Peyton quickly explained who she was. "I'm calling about Dr. Sherry St. Pierre-Duvall, a professor on your faculty."

"She's not a professor," Fontaine explained.

"Are you telling me she doesn't work at USM?" Peyton leaned back in her seat and crossed her ankles.

"She works here, but she is not a professor. I sincerely hope she's not giving people that impression. To call herself a *professor* would indicate that she is employed here full-time and on a tenure track. Sherry is neither of those things."

"What does she do?"

"She teaches an introductory social science course most semesters."

Peyton had her iPad and stylus and was scribbling furiously. "Bear with me, but I need to ask some rudimentary questions, Dr. Fontaine."

"Call me Suzanne. Is Sherry in trouble?"

"What makes you ask that?"

"I'm talking to a law-enforcement officer about her."

It made Peyton smile.

"No. She's not in trouble. I'm looking for some background information. That's all."

"Well, she was supposed to teach a summer-session course, but she hasn't taught the last two weeks."

"Her parents died suddenly," Peyton said.

"Oh, that's terrible. I wonder why she didn't simply tell us."

Peyton didn't speculate. "She has a Ph.D. from Harvard, correct?"

"Yes. And not just from Harvard. She was at the Kennedy School of International and Global Affairs."

"Prestigious?"

"Oh, very."

"And she's published books?"

"One."

"Suzanne, forgive my ignorance, but it seems that her credentials are excellent. Why isn't she working for you full-time?"

"Hiring decisions are confidential, Agent Cote."

"Call me Peyton. And, again, this is background only. This is part of an ongoing investigation."

"Involving Sherry?"

"I'll offer my confidential material," Peyton said, "if you share yours."

"I like you, agent. I've never heard of a criminal-justice officer bartering."

"I've never done it before."

Fontaine chuckled. "You first."

"Yes, this is part of an ongoing investigation."

"That's it?"

"That's it."

Fontaine chuckled again. She had a deep laugh. Peyton imagined her as one who liked to laugh and didn't take herself too seriously. "Well, I was hoping for more, but I understand your limitations, and I'll play along just the same. I guess all you need to know is this: most adjuncts teach to get a foot in the door."

"Teach a class to prove yourself?"

"Yes. She cried during her first class."

"Cried?"

"Yes. She broke down. She was lecturing, and a student challenged her. It's what we do. It's what most academics thrive on—intellectual debate. Sherry crumbled. I've worked with her since. She's gotten better, but not a lot."

"So she's a research specialist?"

"Well, she researches a lot."

"What do you mean?"

"She's written three books, but only one was published."

"The other two?"

"I guess no one wanted to publish them. It leaves her in an academic version of no-man's land. If you can't publish, you can't get a full-time position in this market. And usually if you can't get a full-time position, you have to turn to something else—working for the government or something like that where you can put your Ph.D. to work. In Sherry's case, she married a doctor."

A dentist, Peyton thought. *A broke one.* Aloud she said, "You said you're working with her. How is that going?"

"I said I *have* worked with her. She's applied three times for a tenure-track position—every time one has opened up the last few years. We can't tell her not to apply, but we don't even offer her a courtesy interview."

"She's that bad?"

"We need the intro classes taught, and the freshman won't intimidate her."

Peyton thought of Sherry's go-round with DA Stephanie DuBois. That intellectual sparring match hadn't ended well for Sherry either.

"What do you think is going on with her?" Peyton asked.

"She needs approval but lacks the confidence to gain it," Fontaine said. "I think it's fairly straightforward in the grand scheme of things. It's unfortunate. I wish I knew more about her past. There's something to it that holds her back. I fear that it always will."

"It's sad," Peyton said.

"I thought law-enforcement officers didn't get attached to people in their investigations."

"They don't," Peyton said. "I was merely making an objective observation. Thank you for your time."

———

That night Peyton was in her kitchen preparing dinner for Lois and Tommy.

"Thank you for having me," Lois said.

"It's the least I could do. You've held down the fort around here for the past week."

Lois went to the kitchen, rummaged through the vegetable drawer, and came out with salad fixings. Peyton washed a green pepper in the sink and looked out the window. The vast expanse of terrain between her and the Bigrock ski facility made her think of Matt Kingston. Where was he? He'd been gone three days now.

A mini van–sized bull moose wandered out from the tree line and into a field in the distance.

"Mother." She pointed.

Lois looked up from where she was chopping tomatoes and moved closer. "Ah, beautiful. I still don't think we should let people shoot them."

"You haven't hit one." Peyton had hit a moose in a Ford Expedition service vehicle one night three years earlier. "If I'd hit it head-on, I wouldn't be here. They need to be culled."

"But they're so dumb. It's like shooting a cow."

"Hey, Mom," Tommy said, running into the room, dragging his L.L.Bean backpack across the kitchen tiles. He hugged his mother.

"Is that a smile on your face?"

"What do you mean? I always smile," he said. "Look." He tore through the backpack and nearly ripped a folder as he removed it. He pulled out a paper.

Peyton saw a red B+ on it.

"It's my math test," he beamed. "I got it back today. Ms. Lawrence said I did a good job."

Peyton hugged him and kissed his cheek. "Yes, you did."

"That's enough, Mom. I'm too old for that stuff," the ten-year-old said and ran out of the kitchen.

"You'll never be too old for my hugs," she called after him. She turned to Lois. "Progress, huh?"

"It is. How's Stone Gibson?"

"Fine, Mother."

"Just fine?"

"How's that salad coming?"

313

The thing she loved more than anything was a long bath. She didn't get them often. On Mother's Day, she asked for forty-five minutes of uninterrupted time in the tub, and Tommy always obliged.

Other than that one day a year, there never seemed to be time. But this night, after Tommy was in bed, armed with a glass of red wine and a scented candle, which, according to its box, claimed to offer relaxing aroma, she climbed into the claw-footed tub on the first floor.

She hadn't opened her Lisa Scottoline novel since Hewitt had called a week ago, and she tried to find her place.

Peyton read, but she did so the way she had in college when she knew there was a party elsewhere in her dorm—with her mind adrift.

Where was Sherry St. Pierre-Duvall? She was as insecure and fractured as anyone Peyton had ever met. Peyton wondered about her life in Portland. What did she do when she wasn't teaching? She had no close friends; Sherry had told Peyton that directly. While trying to be formidable—whether it be attempting to face down Stephanie DuBois or flailing in her efforts to lecture at a university—Sherry was still a troubled and timid person, one who let her husband treat her like a show pony. She had never outgrown the silent and meek persona Peyton remembered from their teenage years.

It was this last thought that gave Peyton the idea.

She drained the tub and searched the Internet for Dr. Suzanne Fontaine's home number.

FORTY-THREE

"Let me begin by apologizing for calling," Peyton said. "I'm terribly sorry to bother you on a Friday night."

"I'm an academic, agent. I was reading."

"Actually, I was too."

"Want to trade secrets again? What were you reading?"

Peyton told her.

"You win," Fontaine said. "That's much more enjoyable than my book. What can I do for you?"

"Can you tell me when Sherry St. Pierre-Duvall's summer class meets?"

"You called on a Friday night at nine forty-five for that?"

"Again, I'm terribly sorry."

"No, it just seems so inconsequential. Now I'm curious. Her class meets Monday, Wednesday, and Thursday, from six to nine p.m. It's quite a grueling schedule, actually, but most of our students are non-traditional. They have jobs and families."

"And you said she hasn't taught the class in two weeks," Peyton said. "Is that correct?"

"Yes, that's right. I covered a couple nights this week myself. But last week, she just failed to show up one night, which I didn't anticipate, seeing as how badly she wants a full-time job here."

"Which night was that?"

Suzanne told her.

Peyton hung up and finished her glass of wine, then went to bed, thinking of what she'd just learned.

———

She slept with her cell phone on the bed stand and her .40 in the drawer, but neither allowed her a restful night's sleep.

She dreamt of a faceless boy wandering through a wooded path, trying to sidestep mines. When his foot touched one, she woke, breathing hard. The clock read 2:14 a.m.

She woke next at 3:33, but this time a dream had nothing to do with her stirring. Her cell phone was ringing. She fumbled with it.

"Peyton," Mike Hewitt said, "I'm sorry to bother you late at night."

"Don't worry about it."

"Listen, we found Matt Kingston."

She sat up in bed. "What? Where? Is he okay?"

"He's okay, if upset. There's something else. Something you need to get out of bed for."

"What's that?"

"He told us where Sherry St. Pierre-Duvall is. I need you to come with me to apprehend her."

"Apprehend her?" She was sitting on the edge of the bed now, trying to keep up with the conversation.

"Yes. Sherry kidnapped Matt Kingston at gunpoint, Peyton. She's armed. You negotiated a hostage situation in Texas, right?"

"Once. A long time ago."

"And you have a relationship with this suspect. If there's a standoff, I want you on the bullhorn."

"I can't leave Tommy home alone, Mike."

There was a long silence. Hewitt was thinking, and Peyton was wondering if she'd just shot her own chances at any promotion that might come her way.

"Miguel Jimenez is on the night shift. I'll bring him with us. He can stay with Tommy. We'll be there in fifteen minutes."

"I'll be waiting," she said.

———

"You have an overnight bag?" she said when Jimenez entered the kitchen.

"No, I didn't bring an overnight bag. I'm not a babysitter. I'm not happy about this. I should be going with you guys."

"I appreciate this. There's a case of beer in the garage. You can have it. Come by when you're off duty. The garage is always unlocked."

Jimenez went to her fridge and got a can of Diet Pepsi. He sat at the table, took the remote, and switched on the TV that hung beneath a cupboard.

"Miguel, you know this is my case, right? You know I have to be there."

He nodded. "Yeah, yeah. I know. But this still sucks. You get a soccer channel?"

"I get basic cable," she said. "Sorry. I owe you one." She closed the door behind her.

Mike Hewitt was waiting for her in the driveway.

"Stone Gibson got Matt Kingston's father and we all met Matt in the ER, where he was checked out. He's fine physically, a little shaken up, though."

"Understandable."

"Yeah. The kid is impressive. While the ER docs were checking him over, I asked him some preliminary questions. He walked into the Extra Mart across town, asked to use the phone, dialed nine-one-one, and told them he'd been kidnapped but escaped."

"How did he escape? Have you debriefed him?"

"Not thoroughly. Stone is with him and will get more. But he said she fell asleep and he somehow got loose and ran. This is time-sensitive. We need to go. She might be gone by now."

—————

"Where is she?" Peyton asked.

Hewitt drove the Expedition. FBI Agent Frank Hammond was in the passenger's seat. Hewitt wasn't using the siren, but the flashers were on, and they were pushing eighty miles per hour on a winding stretch of Route 1.

Peyton wore jeans, hiking boots, and a T-shirt. She opened her backpack and retrieved her Kevlar vest and service belt. As she checked the load in the .40, Suzanne Fontaine's remark—*I thought law-enforcement officers didn't get attached to people in their investigations*—came to her. She had fired her service revolver only three times in the line of duty. And Sherry St. Pierre-Duvall was about the last person she'd want to exchange gunfire with.

"She took him to her father's," Stan Jackman said. "They're on Fred St. Pierre's land." He was next to her on the back seat.

Hewitt glanced in the rear-view mirror. "I have someone from the Maine Warden Service meeting us. He knows where the second cabin is."

"There are two?" Hammond said.

Peyton vaguely recalled Fred telling her he'd built two cabins. She was surprised to see Jackman, especially since an agent had to stay with Tommy. Now she understood why Miguel Jimenez had been upset: Hewitt chose Jackman over Jimenez for this detail.

Peyton thought about that. What was Hewitt's motive? There was usually a reason for what he did. Was he trying to boost Jackman's confidence? She looked at Jackman. He was maybe thirty pounds overweight, his face bloated from beer and too much red meat. As he stared out the window with his .40 resting on his thigh, his right hand lay on the gun absently the way one sets his hand on a dog laying beside him while focusing on something else.

But this was the take-down of a kidnapper—no matter how unlikely a kidnapper Sherry appeared to be—and an armed one at that. Had Jackman been the better choice? Jimenez was young, fit, and had scored over 90 percent when qualifying with both his handgun and carbine. Jackman, as much as she loved the guy, had failed in his latest attempt to qualify, scoring 73 percent of the needed 80. But she stifled those thoughts. She respected Hewitt and would trust his decision.

Hewitt turned off Route 1. "Sherry St. Pierre-Duvall was waiting for Matt Kingston outside Tip of the Hat when he got out of work Wednesday night."

"We need to talk to her," Hammond said. "We need to find out the motive here."

"I think I know the answer to that," Peyton said.

Hewitt looked at her in the rear-view mirror. "Really? A theory?"

"Yeah."

Hewitt saw the warden's forest-green pickup and hit the brakes; the Expedition skidded to a stop. "Let's bring her in, and then tell me what you know. We're on foot from here," he said, killing the engine and flashers. "Stan, you're the point person."

Now Peyton knew why Hewitt had chosen him over Jimenez: he wanted a veteran quarterbacking this detail.

"We'll all have radios, but we'll split up. You'll coordinate, okay?"

"Got it," Jackman said.

"Obviously you know what to do if you see a car leave the property."

"I'll radio for backup and go in pursuit."

"Yes. And there's also a carbine in the back. If you hear gunshots, bring it."

"Will do, Mike."

"Sunrise is at four thirty-eight," Hewitt said. "That gives us about half an hour. We'll be in radio contact, Stan."

Hammond handed Peyton an earpiece, which she put in.

FORTY-FOUR

THE YOUNG WARDEN HAD a crew cut and introduced himself as Danny Bullier. Peyton didn't recognize him. Bullier explained that he'd recently been assigned to Aroostook County.

"I heard there was some poachers in the area," Bullier explained. "I walked back here around ten-thirty tonight and saw lights on in the cabin."

Hewitt checked his watch. "It's four-ten. Can you take us to the cabin?"

Bullier nodded and started walking. "Colonel Steuben herself called me and said that I was to give you my full cooperation. I'm all in. But may I ask a question?"

"Sure," Hewitt said. He was carrying an M4 carbine.

"Is this related to the dead guy they found out here?"

"Hard to know," Hewitt said. "We're dealing with an armed woman who kidnapped a teenager. The boy got out of there somehow when she had fallen asleep. She may have woken up and taken off in a green Ford Escape. I'm hoping she's in there and sleeping, and we can take her without incident."

They were moving in pairs, and Peyton was beside Hammond. Her .40 was drawn, the safety off, but her finger rested outside the trigger guard as she walked.

"Mike," she said, "Sherry might be more dangerous than we think."

Before Hewitt could reply, Bullier said, "The cabin is up here. It's in the middle of that field. How do you want to do this?"

Hewitt stopped walking. "Peyton, are you up for this?"

"Of course. Why do you ask?"

Hewitt, apparently catching himself, shook his head.

She waited, but he gave no answer. Had he asked because she was the only female present? Or because she had a relationship with the suspect? She wouldn't like his answer, regardless.

"What do you need, Mike?"

"I'm going to ask you to lead. You know her."

"Got it," she said. The cabin was a hundred yards away.

Hewitt motion to Bullier. "You circle around and take the back. Frank, you take one of the sides. I'll cover Peyton as she approaches the front door."

They moved out. The ink-colored sky had turned gray. In a few weeks, even with Fred gone and Freddy in jail, this land might still produce potato blossoms—tiny white flower buds, as far as the eye could see, that preceded the spuds themselves. The frosted fields would be a stark emotional contrast to all that had taken place here.

But the annual potato blossom was for later. Her eyes were on the cabin. The windows on each side of the front door were dark. There appeared to be no movement from within. She heard her own foot-falls scuffing the dirt; her breath, coming and going, like sandpaper on wood. Her pulse seemed to pound against the skin near her temples.

Three steps led up a small stoop to the front door. There were railings on each side.

Thirty yards from the cabin, she burst into a sprint, stopping under the window to the right of the door, her back against the building, her left hand clasping her right wrist, the .40 at the ready. She listened and heard nothing.

She looked at Hewitt. He was on his stomach; the M4 lay before him on a bi-pod stand. He was sweeping the rifle back and forth across the cabin, using the scope to look for any movement.

Peyton looked at Hewitt and nodded.

He returned the gesture.

Then she took a deep breath, pushed out the air, and moved swiftly and silently up the three steps and crouched below the window in the center of the front door.

She looked at Hewitt again.

He shook his head: still no movement from within.

Peyton stood slowly, forcing herself to the right of the door, in the small space between the door frame and the window. She glanced at Hewitt. Still nothing.

She leaned to look in the window. The cabin was dark. No movement.

Then she heard something that immediately reminded her of Suzanne Fontaine's story.

Peyton leaned away from the window and said into the mic pinned to her shirt collar, "She's in there. I can hear her."

"Copy that," Jackman said. "Can you get a visual?"

"No. It's dark inside."

"But you know it's her?" Hewitt said.

"I'm positive."

"With no visual?"

"Yes. She's crying. I can hear her. I'm going to try to talk her out."

"She's got a handgun," Hewitt said. "Matt didn't know what kind. It sounded small from his description."

"I'm sure it's big enough," Peyton said. "Is the back door covered?"

"Copy that," Bullier said.

Peyton crouched down and pressed herself against the wall to the right of the door. As if beyond her control, her mind did the last thing she wanted it to do: it ran to Tommy. She'd had one near-death experience already this week. Now here she was, asked by Hewitt to lead the extraction of an armed woman with very little to lose.

Holding the semi-automatic pistol with her right hand, she reached across her body with her left and knocked gently on the center of the door—several feet from where she crouched in case Sherry fired at the sound. Then she leaned back and exhaled, awaiting Sherry's reaction.

"*Go away!*" Sherry rasped from inside. Her voice sounded hoarse and thick.

"Sherry, it's Peyton. Leave your gun where you are and come out."

"It's not that simple, Peyton!"

"It's over, Sherry. You need to come out."

"I've really done it this time. I've really—" She burst into sobs.

"Sherry, it's going to be okay. It's time to come out."

"Are there police out there?"

"There are officers, yes. They want to help you. Please come out now, Sherry."

"No. I need to talk to *you*. Only you, Peyton."

"I'm listening, Sherry."

"No. Come inside."

"Out of the question!" It was Hewitt's voice in the earpiece. "Not going to happen, Peyton. Keep her on the hook until you get her outside."

"Peyton, I need to talk. I'm not thinking straight. My mother is my hero. She did the right thing."

"What did she do?" Peyton had to keep her talking.

"You know about it. About her and Simon. She was going to make a break. She did the right thing. She wanted to live in Prague."

"And your father found out?"

"I guess. I think I've really done it this time. Maybe my father did the right thing, too, in the end. Maybe that's the only choice sometimes."

"No. Sherry, you have two beautiful children. They love you. And they need you. Think about them. Nothing else right now. Put the gun down and come on out."

"He's not Chip's son."

"I know that. It doesn't matter. It never will."

"You don't understand. It *will* matter. He'll take Sam from me."

"Sherry, it's time for you to come out."

"Come inside. Please. I need help."

"Out of the question," Hewitt said over her earpiece again.

"Do you have a gun, Peyton? I know you do. Leave it there on the steps and come in. I really think my father made the right choice."

Peyton looked at Hewitt.

He shook his head vehemently.

"I can't let her kill herself, Mike." She set her gun down on the steps and reached for the doorknob.

———

325

"Close the door behind you," Sherry said.

There were no lights on in the cabin's interior, but the sun was rising now, and gray light shone in the windows. Peyton could see Sherry, garbed in a light-blue blouse, standing across the main room. The knees of her designer jeans were covered in dirt.

Sherry held what looked like a semi-automatic handgun, pointing at Peyton. Her hand trembled, and the weapon waved. Peyton wished Sherry's index finger wasn't on the trigger.

"Please sit down, Peyton," Sherry said.

Then it was Hewitt's voice: "I can't hear her. Can anyone hear them?"

There was a short burst of static, and then nothing. She'd lost radio contact.

"Sit down on the chair," Sherry said again.

Peyton walked very slowly to a wooden chair, the only piece of furniture in the room. The walls were bare. There was a single lightbulb hanging from the ceiling.

"He ran. I fell asleep. Can you fucking believe that? I can't even keep a teenager. I don't know how he got the duct tape off his wrists. But he was gone when I opened my eyes. I almost shot myself right then because, it's like, I mean, even that ... I can't even keep him here without screwing that up. Now everything he wanted is gone. He came back to me. Part of me always thought he would. But the other part thought he never would, you know?"

"Are you talking about Kvido?"

"I tried to move on." Sherry's voice quivered. "I really did."

Sherry was pacing slowly now. Her hair was unkempt and clearly hadn't been washed in days. Her eyes were red and puffy, and the faint traces of mascara streaked the corners of her eyes.

"I mean, I even married Chip. But then he came back to me. Said he needed *me*, needed *my* help. And there was Sam. There had always been Sam." She looked at Peyton. "Didn't having Sam mean it was meant to be?"

"Sherry. Set the gun down. Let's just talk."

Sherry looked at her, head tilted.

"Just talk. I'm not leaving. I want to hear it all. I want to help."

"You mean it. I can hear it in your voice."

Peyton's mind ran to Fontaine's words again. This was still a case she was working, but was it also something more personal?

Sherry sat down on the floor across from Peyton. She hadn't let go of the pistol, which did not look small—it looked like a Glock 9mm in the new light. If Hewitt had been looking for a window shot, Sherry had just taken it away from him. She was out of view from any windows. In fact, it was Peyton who was now in line with the cabin's rear window. She hoped the day's breaking light was enough for the men outside to be able to tell the difference between the women.

"Why did you take Matt?"

Sherry wasn't looking at her. One knee was up and bent in front of her. Her other leg lay flat on the floor. She draped the 9mm over her knee.

Peyton wondered if she'd fired the 9mm before. How accurate was she? She also thought about Simon Pink, about a hypothesis she had developed.

"I had to take the boy. I had to protect us all, Peyton."

"Who?"

"Kvido, Freddy, and me, too."

"Because Matt knows who was in the cabin the night Simon Pink was shot, doesn't he?"

Sherry looked up at her then. "That's enough, Peyton."

Peyton saw something in Sherry's eyes that made her theory even more believable. And it made her want to circle away from the subject of the shooting and come back to it.

"Was your father abusive when you were a girl, Sherry?"

"You know the answer to that."

"Physically?"

"If you're asking me if I was surprised to hear he hit my mother, the answer is no, I was not surprised."

"He hit you?"

"Yes."

"I'm sorry, I never knew," Peyton said. "Maybe I could—"

"What? Have helped me? Be real, Peyton. We were kids. I got over it."

"Was there more?"

Sherry's eyes narrowed then. "What exactly are you asking me? My father was a lot of things"—she looked away, as if gathering herself, and in a move Peyton knew was unconscious, Sherry's head bobbed once up and down as she spoke—"but he wasn't a pedophile, Peyton."

Peyton had learned it long ago; it was a staple of any interrogation: the unconscious head movement—whether a nod or a shake—that contradicts a suspect's statement always offers the truth. And Sherry had nodded before she'd spoken.

Peyton knew the reaction had been involuntary. She also knew what the contradiction meant: the bastard Fred St. Pierre Sr. had molested Sherry.

"I mean, really, Peyton. My father is dead."

"Your mother was preparing to leave him?"

"She came to see me in Prague, fell in love with the city. Then she met Simon. It's a small world—Simon knew Kvido."

328

There was a crackle in her earpiece.

"Peyton, what the hell is going on? Can you hear me, Peyton? We lost sight of her, and we can't hear anything."

"What is that?" Sherry said. "I heard something." She was on her feet, coming toward Peyton. She stopped six feet away, standing now in the center of the room.

"Everything is fine," Peyton said to both Mike Hewitt and Sherry. "Everything is *fine*."

"Take out the ear bud and unclip the wire on your shirt collar," Sherry said.

Peyton did so.

"Toss them over to me."

Again, she did as she was told.

Sherry stepped on both devices, crushing them.

"No one needs to know what we're talking about, Peyton."

"What your father did, Sherry, that's not your fault."

It was a mistake, and Peyton knew it the moment Sherry's face went from pale to red. Sherry's eyes grew wide. Her shiny forehead creased.

"How dare you even suggest that I would blame myself for that! How dare you! He grounded me for trying to be normal. Remember? I kissed Jimmy Fry, and he found out and ... You remember?"

"Yes. I remember. How could I forget? It was the beginning of the end for our friendship."

"Yes, it was."

"Sherry, we really need to go. They're going to come in here and get you if we don't. And if you don't put the gun down, they'll shoot you."

"I can't."

She was still standing six feet away.

"Sherry, you need to put the gun down."

"I can't. I won't."

Peyton knew she wasn't going to turn her weapon over. "You took Matt Kingston to protect yourself," Peyton said, "didn't you?"

"I did it for all of us."

"But only one person shot Simon Pink, Sherry."

"What are you saying? Why would I do that? He loved my mother. He was going to make her happy."

"Sherry, what does Kvido have on you?"

As she asked the question, she looked out the windows. Would the men outside be preparing for a shot? Was it light enough to take one? She hoped the assurance she tried to give Hewitt bought her some time with Sherry. If a shot was fired, it would come from Hewitt. No way he'd let anyone else take it, not with one of his agents inside. And she was glad for that; Hewitt would be careful.

"Sam," Sherry said. "Sam is Kvido's son. Chip knows Sam is from a prior relationship, but he doesn't know I was ever with Kvido before now. Sometimes Kvido says I'm not raising him right, that Sam's life is too easy. I think he wants to take Sam with him."

"Take him where? Does Kvido threaten you with that?"

"But I took care of all that. I left Chip. Now I don't have to worry about it. We can all be together."

"What about your daughter, Marie?"

"She'll be with us, too."

"Chip will agree to this?"

Sherry took a step back, away from Peyton, as if the force of Peyton's question had driven her back.

"You don't understand, Peyton. Whatever I've been through pales in comparison to his life. It's one of the reasons why he's so good for me." A faint smile crossed her lips. "I can't feel bad for myself around him."

"What makes you say that?"

"He was homeless as a boy. His mother raised him alone. He saw what she went through, what she had to do …" She shook her head.

Peyton knew that Sherry had more information about Kvido to share, much more than Washington had on him. And nothing in the conversation had made her think Kvido wasn't the one pulling the strings.

She had to keep her talking and hope like hell they wouldn't take a shot.

"I doubt his mother endured anything worse than you, Sherry."

"She had to prostitute herself after her husband was killed. It's why he turned to Andela. It's because of the CIA."

"The CIA?"

"They killed his father."

"Sherry, the CIA? In the Czech Republic? When?"

"It was Czechoslovakia then. Look it up. His father had the same name. He was organizing a union, and it would've cost the US export revenue."

"So the CIA killed him?"

"I looked it up." Sherry offered a patronizing smile then. "We've had this talk before, Peyton. You think the criminal-justice system in this country isn't flawed. Are you telling me you don't think the CIA ever assassinated someone?"

The more animated Sherry got, the more the 9mm waved back and forth. And Sherry hadn't been trained to keep her index finger over the trigger guard. It rested firmly on the trigger.

"After his father was killed, they lived in alleys and shelters. His mother became a whore, Peyton. He blames the United States for that."

Peyton was looking at Sherry when she heard the window on the front door shatter. But she wouldn't remember that until later. What she would remember, what would replace the memory of Pete McPherson's bloody boot when she closed her eyes, was the image of Sherry St. Pierre-Duvall's skull caving in and tearing apart. And the look on Sherry's face—eyes bursting wide, not in pain, but shock—for a split-second before her body fell to the cabin floor in a lifeless heap.

FORTY-FIVE

HEWITT HAD SENT HER home for a few hours of rest while he and Hammond and Stone Gibson debriefed Matt Kingston.

Now it was 10:30 Saturday morning, and it was her turn. There were chairs set in a semi-circle at the perimeter of Hewitt's desk.

Peyton told them everything she could remember from the conversation inside the cabin.

"Nothing's on tape?" Hammond said.

Peyton shook her head.

"And we heard absolutely nothing," Hewitt said, "because we lost radio contact. So, in effect, you disobeyed a direct order and risked your life and forced me to kill someone for no good reason."

"I realize you're right," she said, "but no one in this room would have sat by while someone killed herself."

No one denied it.

"So, yes, I was wrong to disobey an order. But I thought you were just worrying about my safety, Mike."

"This isn't a woman thing, Peyton. I put you in harm's way by having you lead."

"I know that. And I really thought I could talk her out of the cabin."

"It was taking too long, and we lost contact with you. I had to take the shot."

"I know. And I understand why you took the shot. But while I was in there I learned a lot of information no one had on Kvido Bezdek, information that can go in his file."

"You're a gutsy broad," Hammond said.

Peyton looked at him. "You mean I'm a gutsy *agent*?"

Hammond was pushing sixty, and if he understood her meaning, he gave no indication. "The piece about Bezdek's father is important, Mike," Hammond said.

Hewitt was still glaring at her. "I killed a woman this morning. That situation might have been avoidable."

"She wasn't putting the gun down," Hammond said. "I'd go easy on her, not that it's my business. But we now have a motive for the IEDs."

When Hewitt looked out the window, she smiled at Hammond. He nodded.

"And I think I know who shot Simon Pink," she said. "It makes sense, and it explains why Freddy isn't talking."

Stone Gibson had been following the conversation. "I'm all ears. I'm trying to see if this impacts my case, the Simon Pink murder. I don't think it does."

"Sherry shot Simon Pink," Peyton said. "Matt said there were three people at the cabin. One sounded like Drago from *Rocky IV*; that would be Simon. And one was quiet; that was Sherry."

"Can you prove that, Peyton?" Hewitt said.

"I think so."

"How?" Hammond was writing on a legal pad. "Even if she confessed, you have no recording, do you?"

"No. I've got something better. I think her brother was the third person. He said he was at the scene, but insists he was there hours later. I don't think so. I think he was the third person that night. Matt even ID'd his voice."

Hewitt held up his index finger, asking her to pause. "What are you saying, Peyton?"

"It explains why Freddy hasn't turned on the third person. He's just denied shooting anyone. Even when Stephanie DuBois offered a deal, he wouldn't talk."

"Because the shooter was his sister?" Hewitt asked.

"Yes," Peyton said.

Hammond shook his head. "You can't prove that."

"No, but Freddy has no reason to sit in the cell now, not if she did it. Why should he face a murder charge and life in prison when he can downgrade to Conspiracy to Commit? She's dead. He doesn't have to take the life sentence for her."

"Wait a minute." It was Stone Gibson. "I think we're getting ahead of ourselves. The murder investigation is mine. And Freddy only needs half a brain to know that he can walk if he throws his sister under the bus. I'm not sure I want Peyton planting that idea in his dull head. I've been working this day and night for two weeks."

"You're saying you want *someone* to go down for the murder?" Hammond said.

"Not *any* someone. I want the *right person* to go down. And I have a suspect in custody who admits he was at the crime scene. And ballistics proves the suspect's gun was used to commit the crime. That's a pretty good case. And nothing anyone has said in here makes me think Freddy isn't just as likely as his sister to have shot Simon Pink."

"You do understand my reasoning, right?" Peyton said. "That's why he didn't give anyone up. It absolutely makes sense."

"Yes, Peyton. It makes sense, but you can't prove it."

"No, probably not. But we can build a case. Kvido wanted to avenge his father's death."

"By blowing up the president?" Hammond said.

Peyton shrugged. "Everyone in this room has heard crazier plans. Last year, we had a drug smuggler tell us his priest told him to swim bags of pot across the river."

Hewitt chuckled at the memory. "He said the priest told him to do it when he was across from him in the confessional. I thought the priest was going to have a stroke when we brought him in. Poor old guy."

"A repentant pot dealer," Hammond said. "I'll have to remember that one."

Stone leaned back in his chair. "So we're saying that none of this has anything to do with Andela? Nothing to do with any group? This is just a kid with a screwed-up childhood who was looking for a way to get over it. That's what you think this whole thing is about?"

Peyton looked at Stone, then at Hewitt and Hammond.

"Yes, that's what I think," she said. "And Sherry had been abused—verbally, physically, and, I'm fairly certain, sexually—by her father. She was a broken individual. It made her needy. Kvido saw that and manipulated her. She told me it was a coincidence that Kvido knew Simon Pink. That was no coincidence."

"You think Simon was planted here by Kvido?" Hammond asked.

"Probably. I think he built the IEDs, and I think they paid Fred St. Pierre for the use of his cabin."

"So why was Simon Pink shot?" Stone asked. "Regardless of whether Freddy did it or Sherry did it. What's the motive to that killing?"

"Could be a lot of things," Peyton said. "Maybe Fred Sr. never knew what they were using his cabin for and found out. Maybe Simon told Marie, and when the truth came out, they all had to go."

"Or maybe," Stone said, "Fred Sr. knew all along, and when Marie found out, she had to go, along with Simon Pink. And Fred couldn't live with himself if he killed his wife, so he took his own life, too."

"This is all hypothetical," Hammond said. "Won't do a thing for you."

"We need to get Kvido in the box again," Hewitt said.

Hammond shook his head discouragingly, "He's very good. If we can't tie the IEDs to him, he can walk all the way back to the Czech Republic and let Freddy take the rap."

"*Someone* put the IEDs in the ground," Hewitt said. "Pink was dead and Freddy was in custody when they were buried."

Hammond nodded. "We'll ask him. We should be able to keep him here for a while. He's a suspect in a presidential assassination attempt."

"When Stone and I interviewed Kvido," Peyton said, "he called Simon Pink a 'father figure,' said Simon brought him into Andela. I'd love to hear how he injured his hand."

"I bet Simon Pink taught him about IEDs," Hammond said. "This all makes sense. Too bad it's all circumstantial."

Peyton was staring out the window, thinking. It was a sun-drenched Saturday. Tommy's last day of school was in two days.

Stone said, "Can you get a warrant to search his room?"

"We did that already," Hewitt said. "Found nothing."

"Mike," Peyton said, "I need a warrant to take a DNA swab from Kvido."

"DNA? Are you trying to link him to the murder scene? There's nothing left out there. Everything burned."

"No," she said. "I have an idea."

———

Sunday night, the house was quiet. Tommy was in bed after a day spent with Peyton. They'd gone to a karate lesson then fished a brook in the afternoon.

Now Peyton was alone on the living room sofa with a glass of wine and her thoughts, which ran continually to Dr. Sherry St. Pierre-Duvall.

Stone Gibson had walked her through the Matt Kingston debriefing: Matt had been in the cabin for several days. He'd been taken by Sherry Wednesday night and escaped Friday. Matt had spent the bulk of his hours in captivity in a small bedroom at the back of the cabin. The window had been boarded up, and the door had been locked. Friday night, he found a box cutter in his room, used it to cut the duct tape binding his wrists, and escaped.

Peyton was drinking a glass of Casamatta. She leaned back on her living room sofa and thought about that: Matt Kingston had gone missing Wednesday night, but Peyton had seen Sherry Thursday at the Hampton Inn.

Had Matt been bound and left in that cabin while Sherry was in her hotel room? Why didn't he see the box cutter before Friday night?

It didn't feel right. Something wasn't adding up. She picked up her cell phone.

When Stone Gibson answered, she said, "Sorry to bother you at home. I didn't think of this when we were at the dojo."

"You're apologizing as if I lead an exciting life and you might be interrupting me."

"I assumed you do and I was."

"The Red Sox are down four in the bottom of the seventh, Peyton. I've been on my couch for two hours listening to them on the radio and reading."

"Matt was abducted Wednesday night and taken immediately to the cabin, correct?"

"Yes, by Sherry."

"And he never left the cabin, right?"

"Yes. What's wrong? You sound skeptical."

"I went to the Hampton Inn and spoke to Sherry on Thursday."

"You did?"

"Yes. Who was with Matt Kingston while Sherry was at the Hampton Inn?"

Stone said, "He said he didn't hear anyone else in the cabin."

"You think they left him there alone?"

The line was quiet for a time; Stone was thinking.

"I wouldn't do it that way," he said.

"Why not kill him?"

"Because he's a kid?"

"I doubt it."

"Why then?"

"This whole thing feels wrong."

"Peyton, what are you getting at?"

"I think someone relieved her at the cabin. How else would she be out there without a car?"

"Bezdek?"

"He went missing for a time. Hewitt and Hammond went to bring him in for questioning and he couldn't be found. Then when I wanted to talk to him, he was happy to do it. It smells bad."

Stone was quiet.

"And why not kill Matt Kingston?" she asked again. "He's a liability, right?"

"Of course."

"For what?"

"To point a finger," Stone said.

"At whom?"

"The shooter in the Simon Pink murder."

"Yeah, and who's left? Freddy is locked up on First-Degree Murder charges, Simon Pink is dead, and then there's Sherry."

"You think she's a fall guy?"

"It looks that way. If Kvido Bezdek was the one behind all this—paying Simon Pink to make bombs, convincing Sherry to shoot Simon, and paying Freddy, through Sherry, to burn the crime scene—Kvido would have lots of reasons to want Sherry out of the picture."

"You're saying Bezdek used Sherry."

"If Sherry had come out of that cabin with me, and Matt Kingston is still alive, he could help us place her at the crime scene. Then she'd eventually be facing either murder or conspiracy charges. You see? Bezdek would *want* Matt Kingston alive—to testify against Sherry and Freddy because one would be going to jail for life and the other to jail for conspiracy, and Pink would be dead."

"And Bezdek would be in the clear."

"That's the thing, Stone," Peyton said. "As things stand, he still is."

FORTY-SIX

"When we get inside," Stone Gibson said, "I'd like the lead. The homicide is mine, after all."

"I'm just here in an advisory role," DA Stephanie DuBois said.

"And I have no problem with you leading," Peyton said.

It was Monday morning at 9:15, and they were outside a conference room in the Aroostook County Jail in Houlton.

"Does he know his sister is dead?" Peyton asked.

Stone nodded. "They told him yesterday, and they say he didn't take it well."

When they entered, Freddy, seated next to his attorney at a rectangular metal table, looked up. There were no coffee cups on the table this time, just Stone's iPhone, the voice-recording app activated.

"I don't got much to say to you fucking people." Freddy looked at Peyton. "You were there, eh? And you let it happen."

"Freddy," Stone said, "we are all terribly sorry for your loss. And you should know that Agent Cote talked your sister out of killing herself. She also tried to get her to leave the cabin. She attempted to help her, and risked her life to do so."

Freddy looked at Peyton, head tilted. "You did that?"

"Yeah."

Shelley Wong, Freddy's court-appointed attorney, had a legal pad out. She wasn't even thirty, but had gone to Columbia. There were two other changes Peyton noted: Freddy no longer wore his soiled jeans and shirt—he wore an orange jumpsuit—and he was sporting a first-class shiner.

"Where's Steve St. Louis?" Stephanie asked.

"Can't afford him now. Sherry was paying for him." He motioned toward Shelley Wong. "She's smarter than him anyway."

Karen Smythe had mentioned Shelley Wong to Peyton. Karen had told Peyton that Wong had an "adorable" baby and was married to a teacher. But this was neither the time nor place to mention their connection via a mutual friend.

"I wanted to stay in Garrett, eh?" Freddy said. "But they moved me here. You like my black eye?"

"Tough place?" Stone said.

"These guys are a bunch of assholes. Real criminals."

"And you're not?" Stone said.

Freddy looked at him. "I pled not guilty, didn't I? I got sucker-punched in the face yesterday."

"Well, county jail is better than state prison, believe me."

"I'm working on having you moved back to Garrett," Wong said, "until your trial."

Freddy listened then turned to the threesome seated across from him. "See? She's smart, eh?"

"Freddy," Stone said, "I'd like to talk some more about the night Simon Pink was killed."

"We been over that a hundred times."

"I'd like you to tell me who was in the cabin."

"I don't know. I told you already. I set the fire early that morning. All that shit happened before I got there."

"I think you're a really good brother, Freddy," Stone said.

"I don't see the relevance," Wong said. "Where are you going with that, detective?"

"It's a tragedy, but Sherry is dead now, Freddy."

"Again," Wong said, "relevance?"

Stone stared at Freddy. Freddy wasn't confused now. Peyton saw it in his steady eyes. Freddy St. Pierre Jr. was thinking.

He turned to Peyton. "My sister's gone now, too? First my parents, now her. And you were there, eh?"

Peyton nodded. "Freddy, there wasn't anything I could do. I talked her out of killing herself."

"She wouldn't do that, Peyton."

"What makes you so sure?"

"I know my sister. I thought you did, too, eh."

"She thought she had reason to do it, Freddy."

Freddy shook his head, growing frustrated. "What are you talking about?"

"I told her I knew the truth, Freddy."

"What's going on here?" Freddy said to Wong.

"Detective Gibson said he had something important to discuss. I'm certain these people will get to it soon." Wong looked at Stone. "Won't you?"

"I know the truth about what happened that night, Freddy," Peyton said again.

They locked eyes, and Freddy turned away.

"You're a good brother," Stone said. "I have a lot of respect for you."

Freddy cleared his throat. "I don't know what these people are talking about," he said to Wong.

Peyton said, "You're a good brother, Freddy. But it's over now."

"My sister didn't do nothing."

"And you pled not guilty," Stone said. "It's time for you to look at the big picture. Simon Pink was there. Your sister was there. And you were, too, Freddy. Not later, as you keep saying, but in the cabin when Simon was shot. All four of us know that's true."

"This is speculation, detective," Wong said.

"I'm trying to spare your client from serving life in prison, Shelley."

"He set a fire. That doesn't get anyone life."

Stephanie cleared her throat, and all eyes turned to her.

"Ms. Wong, we're here to offer your client a chance to cooperate with us and tell us the truth. He doesn't have to. I'm very confident that I can and will prove that your client admitted he was at the crime scene to set a fire to cover his tracks—to convince people that he wasn't there when the shot was fired. But let's look at the facts of the case that I have to work with: The fatal shot came from his gun. It happened on his land. In the cabin he built. And he knew the suspect had seduced his mother and was cheating on his father, a man he spent every day of his adult life with, which, as we both know, is a strong motive. We can play that game and probably get a conviction and send Mr. St. Pierre to Warren for life, if he would like. But the three of us on this side of the table want the truth not just a conviction."

"What is she saying?" Freddy asked Wong, who said nothing for several moments.

Then, finally: "I think I need a few minutes with Mr. St. Pierre."

FBI Agent Frank Hammond kept his word, allowing Peyton in on the interview with Kvido Bezdek. In fact, it seemed to Peyton, he'd allowed half the criminal-justice officials in Aroostook County in on it.

Peyton was beside Hammond and Mike Hewitt at the interview table in Garrett Station Monday at 2 p.m. State Trooper Stone Gibson, DA Stephanie DuBois, Agent Mitch Cosgrove, and Secret Service Agent Wally Rowe were in the back of the room.

"I appreciate you coming in," Hammond said.

"I am happy to help," Bezdek said in his thick Eastern bloc accent. He was all smiles, but he also had Len Landmark, the Portland-based attorney, with him.

"Welcome back to the area, counselor," Hammond said to Landmark.

Landmark didn't smile. "Let's get to it, gentleman. My client misses his homeland. He'd like to get this resolved in an expedient manner."

"We all would. I can assure you of that," Hammond said. "Could you tell me about your relationship with Sherry St. Pierre-Duvall?"

"I worked for her as a researcher. But I must admit that our relationship changed over the years. I loved her. Her death will be something I can never get over. It's why I am still here. I must attend her funeral."

Peyton had her hands on her lap. Had they been on the table, she'd have been tempted to slap him.

"Tell us about your hand."

"I injured it many years ago."

Hammond waited.

Bezdek glanced at Landmark.

"What would you like to know, Frank?" Landmark said.

"What happened to his hand?"

"May I ask why you wish to know that?"

"Sure. I'm curious to see if it had any influence on this case."

"If anything," Landmark said, "seeing as it's his right hand and he's right-handed, it proves that he could not have shot Simon Pink."

Hammond nodded. "I see. How were you injured?"

"My hand was burned in a fire."

Hewitt opened a manila folder that lay before him on the table, took out a sheet of typescript, and pushed it toward Bezdek.

"What's this?"

"It's a classified report," Hammond said. "Check out the second paragraph."

Peyton looked at Landmark. It was clear by his expression that he now knew why he was there—they were going after his client. He leaned close to the paper and read it.

"You can't prove it," Landmark said.

"Not sure I want to." Hammond pulled the paper back. "But it's interesting that the CIA has known your client and Mr. Pink were together many years ago in Andela and that Mr. Pink introduced Mr. Bezdek to bomb-making." Hammond looked at the sheet again. "A 'training accident,' huh? Jesus, what must have been going through your head when you first looked at your hand?"

"Want me to tell you?"

Bezdek's voice had a different quality now. Still the thick accent. But the polished, polite tone was gone, replaced by anger.

Landmark caught the tone and said, "That won't be necessary, Kvido. I'm still waiting for some degree of relevance, Agent Hammond. My client, after all, is grief-stricken but still managed to come here to cooperate in full because he wants to help."

"Here's the thing: revenge can come in many forms. But you need to be right-handed for most of them. Is that what you're saying, Kvido?"

"I don't follow you, agent." Bezdek's mouth was a tight slit now, his eyes narrowed. "And I'm tired of wasting my time."

"I know what happened to your father. I'd like to think our government agencies have gotten better in the years since. But, like Mr. Landmark says, that's not relevant. Your father was assassinated. I know that. And, hell, I might have even tried what you tried, had I been in your position."

"Speculation, agent," Landmark said. "My client hasn't been charged, so I would appreciate you not speculating on what he 'tried.'"

"I'm saying, given what happened to your father, given what became of your mother ... You have my sympathy."

"You know nothing about me or my mother." Bezdek's voice was a low, guttural growl. "Not one thing, agent."

"I know she was a prostitute."

Bezdek slammed his open palm on the metal table top. The sound reverberated throughout the room.

"That's enough! You're wasting my client's time. You can charge my client or we can walk."

Peyton knew Landmark was right. Everyone in the room did. She waited to see if Hammond had another card up his sleeve.

"I have several more questions," Hammond said.

Landmark shook his head. "You've burned this bridge, Agent Hammond. My client came when you called him. You have insulted him and done nothing more than fish for suspicious answers. Let's go, Kvido." Landmark stood.

"Okay. You want me to be direct, Len. How's this?" Hammond turned to face Kvido. "Tell me what you know about making bombs.

Where you learned it. And from whom. Period. That's what I want to know." He turned back to Landmark. "That fucking clear enough, counselor?"

"I know nothing."

Hammond leaned back in his seat. "So here we are, Kvido. I just had you read a classified document about yourself. The CIA knows you worked with Simon Pink. We know Pink made bombs for Andela. And you have admitted you were close to him ... "

Bezdek's eyes ran to Peyton. She held his stare. "'Father figure,'" she said.

" ... but you're going to tell me you know nothing about bombs? I can guess you flunked the exam by looking at your hand. But you must have learned *something*."

"Fuck you. All of you," Bezdek said, but the rage had left his voice. His words were quiet now, controlled.

"Come on, Kvido," Landmark said.

"I can ask State Trooper Stone Gibson back there to bring him in for questioning," Hammond said.

Landmark sat down again.

"Why don't you explain what Simon Pink was doing in Aroostook County?"

"I understand he was working," Bezdek said.

"Coincidentally? For your girlfriend's parents?"

Bedzek shrugged. And he smiled at Hammond, whose face colored. "Any more questions, agent?" Bedzek said.

"Sure. How come you gave Sherry St. Pierre-Duvall over two hundred thousand dollars? You see we have her bank statements. There were a couple accounts that took some finding, but you know how the government is in this country—too big. A lot of government employees have lots of time on their hands, like Agent Cosgrove back there."

Cosgrove smiled.

"My finances are my business," Bezdek said.

"Kvido," Landmark said, "that's enough."

"Agent Cote, here, raised an interesting question when we first spoke to Chip Duvall. She asked him if he lost his house when he lost his business. He said no. That was interesting to us. You see sometimes, no matter how well *you* plan, no matter how smart *you* are, the people you surround yourself with fail you, even if they try hard not to."

"Agent Hammond, you are way, way out of line here," Landmark said. "And you know it. This is insulting. You called us in simply to fish. There is no other reason."

"No. I'd like to know just why your client gave Sherry St. Pierre-Duvall two hundred grand. That genuinely interests me. I'd also love to hear where he got the money."

Landmark leaned close to Bezdek to whisper something.

Bezdek pulled back. "I need no help." Then to Hammond: "I gave her the money. It was a gift."

"Where did you get the money? I thought *she* paid *you*. You said you did research for her."

"As a hobby. I am passionate about her research. It is not my"—he searched for the right word—"*primary* job. I invest in real estate."

"What did Sherry do with the money?"

"Oh, that, I cannot tell you. You see, I do not know, Mr. Hammond. The money was a gift. She was free to do whatever she wanted with it."

"Did you know her father?"

"No. I never met him. Based on her, I'm certain he was a fine man."

"Actually he abused her, verbally and sexually."

"That is terrible to hear."

"Funny," Hammond said, "that she never mentioned it to you, seeing as you were close to her."

"Is there anything else?" Landmark asked.

"One other thing," Peyton said, "but I'm hoping we can avoid it." She slid the warrant to Landmark.

"You want to swab his mouth?"

"I don't want to. I'd rather be able to ask your client a question and get an honest answer."

"And what's that?"

"Sam Duvall, Sherry's nine-year-old son, is yours, correct?"

"Why do you ask?" Bezdek said.

"Sherry told me as much. I just want confirmation. I can do it with a DNA test, or you can provide the answer. Either way."

"Yes, he's my son. Sherry and I were together years ago. I told you I loved the woman."

"And she was raising your son?" Peyton said.

"Yes."

"And Chip? He adopted Sam?"

"No. Sam is *my* son."

"But Sam goes by Chip's last name. I'm told he legally adopted Sam."

"Sam is my son."

"Does Chip know you're the father?" she asked.

Bezdek didn't immediately reply. And he was too self-assured to look to Landmark for help. He simply sat staring at Peyton, his wheels clearly turning.

"We haven't discussed it. As you can imagine, with Sherry leaving Chip for me, Chip and I do not have a relationship."

"That's funny," Peyton said, "because I could've sworn he was meeting you for lunch when I saw you at the diner the other day."

"I have never met Chip for lunch."

"No," Peyton said. "He pulled in, but you went out to stop him before he came inside."

Bezdek shook his head.

Hammond was about to speak, but Peyton played a hunch, saying, "Yeah, Chip denied it, too."

Bezdek looked at her for a moment, then nodded, and leaned back in his seat: an unconscious gesture, one that told her Bezdek had just been reassured.

Of what?

"Can you tell us where you were Wednesday afternoon?" Hewitt asked. He and Hammond had gone to find Bezdek then but hadn't been able to do so.

"I don't recall."

"No? A smart guy like you? You can't remember?"

"Perhaps I was taking a walk. I cannot recall. Maybe in the gym."

Hammond said, "Do you know where Sherry took Matt Kingston?"

"No. I would have no idea and no way of knowing. And, honestly, I do not like to think about that, about how it turned out."

"Where were you the night Simon Pink was murdered?"

Bezdek smiled broadly. "Why I was in the air, flying here, Mr. Hammond."

"I hope the flight was smooth."

"Extraordinarily so. Thank you."

"I'm glad you'll be in the area for a few days, Mr. Bezdek. We may need to ask you some additional questions."

"Like I said, I will be at Sherry's funeral. She's being buried here."

"How does Chip Duvall feel about that?" Peyton asked.

Bezdek looked at her, thinking.

"I mean, surely he won't want you there, seeing as you were stealing his wife."

"*Stealing* is not the correct word."

"What is?"

"I was making her happy. If he cared about her, he should have wanted that for her."

"Is that what you wanted?" Peyton asked. "For her to be happy?" She felt Hewitt's eyes on her, and she knew why: her tone had changed. She reeled her emotions back in. "That's nice to hear," she said. "What happens to Sam and Marie now?"

"We are working that out."

"Who?"

"The people involved."

"And who is that? They're either going to you or Chip or you're splitting them up. What's the plan?"

"It's not finalized yet."

"Does Sam know you are his father?"

"Really, agent," Bezdek said, "what are we talking about?"

"It's time for us to go," Landmark said.

"Thank you for your time today, Mr. Bezdek," Hammond said and stood. The others followed him out.

———

Twenty minutes later, Hewitt and Peyton were in the breakroom. Peyton was eating a salad; Hewitt was having five cookies.

"Quite a lunch," she said.

"I ran six miles this morning. This is my reward."

"Healthy."

"Healthy enough," he said. "You were getting pretty upset in there."

"Not much to like about that guy."

"You were close to Sherry when you were kids, huh?"

She looked at him. He was staring at her.

"What are you saying, Mike?"

"I'm saying this isn't only about Sherry St. Pierre-Duvall, Peyton. This is also about Simon Pink, Pete McPherson, and, of course, what was probably an assassination attempt on the president of the United States, which comes above all else. Don't lose sight of that."

"I won't. But Sherry was used and tossed away by this asshole—and that led to all of the other deaths, Mike."

"She was paid, Peyton. Two hundred grand, in fact." Then he nodded. "But, yeah, she never expected things to end as they did."

Through the window in the breakroom, she could see the rolling farmland across the street. A large crop sprayer bounced across a field, its metal arms jutting out like mechanical wings.

"Freddy changed his plea after we left," Hewitt said. "Stephanie is in talks with Shelley Wong. In exchange for talking, Freddy's being released on his own recognizance. It was part of the deal. He really wants to get out of there and back to the farm."

"He's not cut out for prison life."

The tractor's huge tires moved carefully between the rows. Peyton was amazed at the speed at which the tractor traversed the land.

"He better get used to prison," Hewitt said. "Conspiracy to Commit Murder carries ten to thirty years. I doubt he's getting off without serving something."

"Might depend on how much he talks."

"He doesn't know all that much."

"Or he's playing dumb."

"He's not smart enough to pull that off. You saw him today. We were offering him a pass, and he didn't know it."

"You think no one knew what the cabin was being used for, except Sherry?" Peyton shook her head. "Farmers are some of the most observant people you'll ever meet, Mike. Hard for me to believe Freddy knew so little. I think he was scared when we interviewed him and didn't want to say anything to incriminate himself."

"Maybe."

"I'm certain Fred knew something was going on in that cabin, too. He was upset Marie called me to start all of this."

"Think she knew?"

"That's a good question. I don't think so. Simon Pink could've given her the money I found in her dresser—that would explain why she was so upset to learn of his death: he was helping her escape her abusive husband."

"So she called us, as any good citizen living near the border would?" Hewitt said.

"That's what I believe," Peyton said. "She called to report two men on her property. That's all."

"So what did Fred Sr. get out of this?"

"His back taxes were paid by his daughter. It's quite a gift, Mike. It let her parents keep the farm, avoid being disgraced. It's a bigger deal, maybe, than anyone not from here might realize."

Hewitt sat looking at her. "That Conspiracy to Commit charge is looking contagious."

"I wish Hammond would've pressed Kvido Bezdek on the IEDs, Mike."

"I've worked with him before. He's good. He got a warrant and tapped both hotel rooms this morning. He did it himself."

"Really?"

"He knows what he's doing, Peyton. You know, not everyone goes at things a hundred miles an hour."

"You saying I do that?"

"You started off convinced we had a crystal meth problem, if I recall correctly."

She smiled. "You recall correctly. Still, I want to know who planted and set the IEDs. Pink, we assume, made them, and he was dead. Sherry couldn't plant them; she wouldn't know how. And Freddy was in jail. That only leaves Bezdek. He might not be able to make them with that hand, but he could have set them out there."

Hewitt was nodding.

She took a bite of her salad and chewed quickly. "Well, Bezdek isn't staying here forever. Everything hinges on him—the money, the IEDs, the kidnapping, everything."

"We think."

"I know it."

"No," he said. "You think you do."

"I know it. Listen," she said, "we all want to nail this guy. I have an idea, but we'll need one more warrant."

"We tapped both hotel rooms this morning." Hewitt blew out a long breath. "If it's a decent idea, we might try it. What do you have in mind?"

"It won't be easy, but it's all there is left to do," she said.

FORTY-SEVEN

PEYTON WAS OUTSIDE THE Hampton Inn at 5:45 p.m. Monday night when Stone Gibson, wearing Oakley wrap-around sunglasses, jeans, and a dark T-shirt, slid onto the passenger's seat and closed the door.

"It's nice to work with a federal employee," he said. "A Toyota? You guys get undercover vehicles?"

"This is my mother's Camry. And I'm not getting overtime pay for this."

"Well, state police would never have gotten the warrant for the wire taps."

"Woe is me," she said. "You know that's not true."

"Well, we wouldn't have gotten it same day."

She didn't deny that.

"Our situations aren't so different," she said. "A team of Homeland Security Investigations agents are on the way. Once they get here, I'm probably back on border patrols. Field agents are a dime a dozen."

"Ever read the play *Death of a Salesman*?"

"I think so."

"This guy Willy Loman says he's not a dime a dozen."

"No one is," she said. "It's kind of why I'm here."

"For Sherry St. Pierre-Duvall?"

"And all of them. But, yeah, because, if I'm being honest, I do think she got a raw deal—not just on this, but in life in general. Her father sexually abused her. She spent her youth trying to prove to him she was good. Then she spent her adulthood trying to excel. But she couldn't because she was broken from the start."

"I respect your compassion," he said, "but it's dangerous."

"I thought you never went to college. How do you know who Willy Loman is?"

"Changing the subject? Okay. I read a lot. So you say Sherry tried to prove stuff. Maybe I do, too."

"Like what?"

"Like I'm not illiterate. You don't need a school to be educated."

"How much do you read?"

"Eighty books last year."

"Jesus Christ," she said.

"So what's the plan?"

"There's the green Ford Escape," she said. "Both of the hotel rooms face the other side of the building. So why don't you move the car near the door, and if Chip or Kvido come out, let me know."

"Got it," he said.

Peyton got out, and Stone did the same and moved to the driver's side. As the car pulled away, she did her best Sherry St. Pierre-Duvall impression—wearing sunglasses, pulling a Red Sox cap low, and raising the hood on her University of Maine Black Bears sweatshirt over her head. She went to the Escape and removed the Slim Jim she had pressed to her side inside her sweatshirt. She jimmied the bar back and forth inside the driver's-side window and unlocked the door. Once the door was open, she planted the tap. Finished, she walked back to the Camry.

"I'm going inside to make sure both rooms are still being used and to see if both men are home."

"I'll watch the lobby," Stone said.

———

"I'm surprised to see you," Chip Duvall said, when he answered the door of room 210 at the Hampton Inn.

"I was in the neighborhood," she said, "and I thought I'd drop by." She knew she'd used that line the last time she'd been at this hotel room.

Apparently, Chip didn't know it had been rehearsed previously.

"I'm not doing very well. I came here to help Sherry bury her parents. Now I'm"—his voice cracked, and he looked down, shoulders trembling—"burying her beside them."

The weight of his statement hit Peyton. She knew what he said was true, of course; but at the same time, she'd not thought of it. She'd been working the case and thinking of Sherry's plight. The irony of Chip Duvall's situation was evident by the pain on his face.

"May I come in, Chip?"

"Gee, I don't know if that's a good idea."

She looked at him. Could this be the same idiot who'd made several passes at her? Why the change? A show of respect for his late wife? If so, she wanted to hit him in the throat again—make him consider where that respect for Sherry had been a week ago.

"I have a few questions I need to ask you."

"You sound formal."

"The investigation is still ongoing."

"What investigation?"

"The murder of Simon Pink."

"Oh, that," he said and held the door. "Yeah, come in."

His suitcase was open, clothing strewn on the floor around it. "Excuse the mess."

"How are you holding up?"

"Not well."

"Do you have family?"

"My parents and my sister and her husband are coming tomorrow to help me."

"And your kids are coming here?"

He nodded.

"How are they?"

"My sister is very good with them. She has two teenagers. She told them about Sherry. They are, of course, devastated."

"They'll live with you?"

"Yes. Why do you ask?" He looked genuinely confused.

"Both children?"

"Of course. Why?"

"What if Kvido wants Sam? Doesn't he have a legal right to take him to the Czech Republic, if he wants?"

"I adopted Sam. What are you talking about, Peyton?"

"How did you keep your home when you filed for bankruptcy?"

"Why would Kvido want Sam?"

"How did you keep your home when you filed for bankruptcy?" she said again.

"It's common. That's one of the reasons to file."

"But you and Sherry paid off her parents' back taxes, which allowed them to keep the farm. How could you afford to give them a hundred grand if you lost your business?"

"What are you talking about?"

"Sherry received two hundred thousand dollars from Kvido, Chip."

"I know nothing about that."

"How old was Sam when you adopted him?"

"Two. I've raised him as I have Marie—like he's my flesh and blood."

"And that's why Sherry hired Kvido? So he could see his son?"

"His son?"

"What is your relationship with Kvido like?"

"Relationship? With him? My wife left me for him, Peyton."

"But you drove to the diner to meet him."

"No."

"Yes. He ran outside and stopped you before you came inside. What did you two need to talk about?"

He didn't speak. She saw perspiration on his forehead.

"And why couldn't you just meet here, Chip? What reason would you have for meeting somewhere else?"

"I think it's time for you to leave, Peyton."

"Me, too," she said.

———

Peyton took the elevator to the lobby. She didn't return to the Camry. Instead, she sat in an overstuffed chair near a glass end table.

In a chair near the elevator, a man wearing Oakley shades, a dark T-shirt, jeans, and running shoes sat reading *Crime and Punishment*. On the other side of the lobby, at the bar, a man drank coffee and sat with his back to the far wall. He wore glasses frames and a Bass Pro Shops hat. She expected to see those two men.

The man she didn't expect to see walked by her without recognizing her. Once again, he had traded the leather New York Yankees jacket and snake-skin cowboy boots for a suit—this time it was a conservative gray with a navy-blue tie—and he had a neck tattoo she'd seen only on inmates in federal prison.

It was Tom Dickinson—the man in witness protection who had worried that his chat with Sara Gibson in Tip of the Hat might lead to his anonymity being lost.

He was carrying a briefcase and walked to the elevator. He didn't press either arrow. Just stood, waiting.

Finally, the elevator doors opened, and Kvido nodded to him. Dickinson joined Kvido on the elevator, and it went up again.

Peyton moved quickly across the lobby and hit the arrow pointing up.

The man seated next to the elevator set down his copy of *Crime and Punishment* and ran toward the stairs. The man at the bar wearing glasses frames followed him.

FORTY-EIGHT

When the elevator opened, no one was in sight.

Peyton stepped out and moved toward room 418. She walked past the room and rounded the hallway corner, where she met Stone Gibson, who had removed his Oakley sunglasses, and Mike Hewitt, who had tossed the glasses frames and Bass Pro Shop cap.

"*Crime and Punishment*?" she said to Stone, shaking her head. "Not exactly inconspicuous."

"Who was the guy meeting Kvido?" Hewitt asked.

"That's Tom Dickinson, Mike. Remember him?"

"No."

"The guy who met Stone's sister, Sara, at Tip of the Hat. The guy in witness protection. He was at the diner when Kvido was the only other person there besides me and Stone. It was the day Chip showed up. Before Chip could enter, Kvido went outside to stop him. I thought it was because I was there, but maybe it had something to do with Dickinson."

"What's he doing here? And how the hell does he know Kvido?"

"I have no idea. You heard my conversation with Chip?"

Hewitt nodded. "Yeah. Hammond tapped both rooms."

"You stirred the pot pretty good," Stone said.

"Chip had no idea Sam is Kvido's son."

Stone shrugged. "He does now, and he's upset. We can use that to get him to turn on Kvido."

They heard the elevator stop. Peyton leaned out and saw Chip walking down the hallway with both hands thrust in the front pocket of a gray sweatshirt.

Peyton leaned back out of sight. "It's Chip."

The footfalls stopped at room 418. Chip took a deep breath. Then he knocked hard on the door.

"Who is it?"

"Open up!"

The door opened, then closed. Peyton looked around the corner. Chip was out of sight.

Hewitt reached into the breast pocket of his fishing shirt and retrieved a small speaker. Peyton and Stone huddled around it.

"*Who are you?*" It was Chip speaking.

Tom Dickinson's voice: "*Nobody, man. I was just leaving.*"

"*No.*"

"*Chip, this is my accountant. Let him go.*"

"*Kvido, tell me about Sam.*"

"*What do you want to know? Please put the gun down, Chip.*"

Without a word, Hewitt was sprinting, his .40 out. He nearly knocked Peyton over in the process. She grabbed her .40 and followed, Stone right behind her.

Hewitt kicked the door on the knob and it burst in, banging against the wall. Then he was inside, crouched in a shooter's stance to the right of the door.

Across the room, Kvido and Tom Dickinson stood facing Hewitt. Kvido had lost the swagger he'd possessed in their meeting earlier that day. He was sweating, his eyes pleading.

Chip was facing them, his back to Hewitt. He never turned around, as if he'd not heard the door frame splinter and the doorknob hit the inner wall.

Peyton moved in to cover Hewitt, crouching to the left of the door frame, her .40 drawn. She peered into the room.

Chip had a pistol pointed at Kvido.

"Drop the weapon," Hewitt said.

Tom Dickinson had both hands in the air.

"Don't shoot him," Dickinson said.

Kvido was saying, "I'm not a bad man, Chip. I've helped you."

"*You* helped *me*? Explain that."

"I paid off your home." Kvido's hair was matted against his forehead; sweat beads crawled down his cheeks.

"You took my wife. Now you've humiliated me. Sam is *your* son?"

"I was going to tell you."

"No you weren't. Neither was Sherry."

Peyton was looking at Hewitt. The shot was there. Chip had his back to him, and he had two hostages.

Hewitt looked at her, and she realized what he was doing: He was waiting to hear the conversation, trying to learn as much as he could, risking Kvido's safety to gain information needed to build a case against him. He had taken Sherry out when the opportunity presented itself, but not here. Situational ethics could make even routine decisions difficult. And when those decisions could be life-or-death, they became gut-wrenching. She had seen it when Hewitt spoke about having to kill Sherry.

"Put the gun down," Dickinson said with an air of authority that made Peyton take her eyes off Chip momentarily.

"We were going to tell you," Kvido said.

"You turned Sherry into a killer. Freddy told me this afternoon. He said you paid for bombs. You put them in the woods. *You* killed that game warden. You're insane. Do you know that? A minefield? It's crazy. I don't know what Sherry was thinking to go along with it."

"You didn't think it was so crazy when your wife bailed you out with her 'book money.'" Kvido's navy blue shirt was black with sweat now.

"Drop the weapon," Hewitt said.

Chip never turned around.

In the confined space of the suite's main room, the pistol shot reverberated for what seemed an hour. There was no second shot. Chip fell to his knees, his hand going limp at his side, the pistol falling to the floor. He stared at the hand that had held the pistol as if it were foreign to him.

Tom Dickinson leapt on him and pushed his face into the carpet. "You stupid shit." He pulled Chip's arms behind him. "Give me some cuffs."

Stone Gibson ran to him and cuffed Chip.

"You have the right to remain silent," Dickinson said. "Anything you say can—"

"What are you doing?" Hewitt said.

"I'm Greg Harris," Dickinson said, "CIA. I've been following Kvido Bezdek for two years. And it ends like this?"

Peyton had gone to Kvido. Chip hadn't been a skilled marksman, but he had pointed at the center of the mass, and from ten feet, that was good enough.

Kvido lay on his back, legs splayed before him, his eyes open and blinking. Peyton felt his wrist. The pulse was weak.

"Look at me," she said. His eyes rolled toward her. "Stay with me, Kvido." His eyes blinked once more, then remained open.

The slow pulse beating against her index finger stopped.

FORTY-NINE

A FEW HOURS LATER, Garrett Station was quiet. It was nearly 11 p.m., and Peyton, Hewitt, Stone Gibson, Frank Hammond, Wally Rowe, and Greg Harris were in the stationhouse working on final reports and debriefing.

The group had taken over the bullpen. Several worked on computers; others ate, and Harris even drank a beer.

"Greg Harris?" Peyton said. "Not Tom Dickinson?"

"My mother named me Greg." Harris nodded. He had his feet up on a desk. "I'm sorry for lying to you when we first met. But I was trying to help."

"Why didn't you tell me what you were doing?"

"Kvido Bezdek is a sociopath, and he's particularly violent. I was trying to keep as many innocent people away from him as I could."

"Like my sister?" Stone Gibson said.

"Yes. You should tell her she talks too much."

Stone didn't say anything.

"How did a woman with a Harvard Ph.D. end up with Kvido?" Hewitt said.

"It's like asking why Sherry paid the back taxes on her father's farm," Peyton said. "Maybe it doesn't make sense. Or maybe it makes perfect sense. It's who she was. Or who she became. She was pushed around and treated poorly by men her whole life. Her father started the cycle, and she never broke free of it. She wasted so much time trying to prove herself to her father and to everyone else."

"Sad," Rowe said.

"Remember the scene during the discovery session with Stephanie? Sherry was trying to prove she was more than her father and Chip and Kvido thought she was. It breaks my heart a little bit because I knew her when she was young, before all of this."

Peyton was looking at the floor, thinking not of Dr. Sherry St. Pierre-Duvall but of Sherry St. Pierre, back when they were kids, back when there had still been a chance for Sherry.

"Peyton, she also killed a guy," Hewitt said. "Don't forget that."

"I know that, Mike. I'm not excusing it. And I assume she told Freddy to get rid of the gun. And she tried to buy him an alibi. But, of course, he screwed up and we found the gun anyway."

Harris finished his beer, stood, and put the can in the recycling bin. "The bottom line is that she ended up with a guy who wanted to kill the president."

"Using a Goddamned minefield," Hewitt said.

"She was so much more intelligent than any of them, than any of this," Peyton said, and she thought of the line from *Hamlet* that Leo Lafleur had read to her.

No one spoke for a while. Peyton finished a bottle of water. Frank Hammond, who hadn't spoken, sat watching CNN on his laptop. The afternoon's events had not yet been broadcast.

Harris said, "I knew there'd be some collateral damage when Kvido got here. I wanted to limit it. I didn't do a very good job."

"This whole thing was fluid from day one." Hewitt looked at Harris. "Second-guessing yourself will just give you ulcers. It does no good. Christ, I didn't think Chip would shoot him. I could've taken him out before he killed Kvido, but I thought we'd learn something, and we'd talk him down. I was wrong."

"We did learn a lot," Stone said. "And what we learned may help Freddy St. Pierre when it comes to his sentencing."

"Freddy knows a lot more than I gave him credit for," Hewitt said. "But the primary is now dead"—Hewitt looked at Harris—"which doesn't help you very much."

"You were in a tough spot," Harris said. "Whether or not to take out Chip Duvall was your call. You did what you thought was right, given the situation. I've been there myself. So I know never to second-guess someone else's decision in a similar situation."

Hewitt looked at Harris for several seconds. "Thanks," he said.

"Kvido was bankrolling this whole operation," Harris went on. "I haven't gotten through with everything yet, but I'm pretty sure we're going to find out Simon Pink could afford two plane tickets to Prague courtesy of Kvido."

"And Kvido paid Fred's taxes, via Sherry, in exchange for giving Simon Pink use of the cabin," Peyton summarized. "When Marie innocently called us, Fred knew they were all about to get in some serious trouble. He was hoping *Sherry* would forgive them, for bringing attention to her illicit activities."

"Think he knew someone was paying Simon to make bombs out there?" Hewitt asked.

Peyton shrugged. "He knew enough to prefer the easy way out rather than face the consequences."

"So how much did Chip Duvall know?" Stone Gibson asked.

"Considering that everyone else involved, except Freddy, is dead," Greg Harris said, "I bet he doesn't know much."

Peyton leaned back in her chair and stretched. "I'm heading home, gentleman," she said. And she did.

———

Peyton drove home and entered the dark house just after midnight. Lois was sleeping in the guest room. She went to Tommy's room and watched him sleep for a few minutes. Then she went downstairs to the kitchen and poured a glass of red wine, which she took to the living room sofa. She enjoyed the silence of the house, the occasional creak, the low rumble of the ice-maker.

She reached for her cell phone and hit a number on her list of contacts.

"Peyton?" Leo Lafleur said.

"I was thinking about that line from *Hamlet* you read to me the other day. Could you read it again?"

"Seriously? It's almost one a.m."

"You don't go to sleep until much later. You've told me that yourself. And, besides, I'd really appreciate it."

"I don't need to read it," he said. "I know it: *There's a special providence in the fall of a sparrow.*"

"Thank you, Leo."

"That's it?"

"That's all I needed," she said.

She hung up and sipped her wine and thought about Sherry St. Pierre-Duvall as she stared at her own reflection in the blackened window, until the wine was drunk and sleep would finally come.

ABOUT THE AUTHOR

D.A. Keeley (United States) has published widely in the crime-fiction genre and is the author of seven other novels, as well as short stories and essays. In addition to being a teacher and department chair at a boarding school and a member of the Mystery Writers of America, Keeley writes a biweekly post for the blog *Type M for Murder*. You can learn more about the author and the series via Twitter @DAKelleyAuthor or at www.amazon.com/author/dakeeley.

WWW.MIDNIGHTINKBOOKS.COM

From the gritty streets of New York City to sacred tombs in the Middle East, it's always midnight somewhere. Join us online at any hour for fresh new voices in mystery fiction.

At midnightinkbooks.com you'll also find our author blog, new and upcoming books, events, book club questions, excerpts, mystery resources, and more.

MIDNIGHT INK ORDERING INFORMATION

Order Online:
- Visit our website www.midnightinkbooks.com, select your books, and order them on our secure server.

Order by Phone:
- Call toll-free within the U.S. and Canada at
  1-888-NITE-INK (1-888-648-3465)
- We accept VISA, MasterCard, and American Express

Order by Mail:
Send the full price of your order (MN residents add 6.5% sales tax) in U.S. funds, plus postage & handling to:

> Midnight Ink
> 2143 Wooddale Drive
> Woodbury, MN 55125-2989

Postage & Handling:
Standard (U.S. & Canada). If your order is:
> $24.99 and under, add $4.00
> $25.00 and over, FREE STANDARD SHIPPING

AK, HI, PR: $16.00 for one book plus $2.00 for each additional book.

International Orders (airmail only):
> $16.00 for one book plus $3.00 for each additional book